COVENANT HALL

Also by Kathryn R. Wall

In for a Penny

And Not a Penny More

Perdition House

Judas Island

Resurrection Road

Bishop's Reach

Sanctuary Hill

The Mercy Oak

COVENANT HALL

KATHRYN R. WALL

MINOTAUR BOOKS ☆ NEW YORK

This is a work of fiction. All of the characters, organizations, and events portrayed in this novel are either products of the author's imagination or are used fictitiously.

www.minotaurbooks.com

Library of Congress Cataloging-in-Publication Data

Wall, Kathryn R.
    Covenant Hall : a Bay Tanner mystery / Kathryn R. Wall.—1st ed.
        p.   cm.
    ISBN-13: 978-0-312-37535-5
    ISBN-10: 0-312-37535-2
    1. Tanner, Bay (Fictitious character)—Fiction. 2. Women private investigators—Fiction. 3. Hilton Head Island (S.C.)—Fiction. I. Title.

PS3623.A4424 C68 2009
813'.6—dc22

2009003624

First Edition: May 2009

10 9 8 7 6 5 4 3 2 1

For Norman—husband and best friend

ACKNOWLEDGMENTS

Covenant Hall does not exist, at least not where I placed it in this novel. In a way, it represents many old houses, scattered across the Lowcountry, where secessionist plans were hatched. Jacksonboro, Walterboro, and Edisto Island are real places with which I've taken some liberties for the purposes of the story. I hope the fine folks who live there won't be too put out with me.

No book is created in a vacuum, and this one is no exception. My thanks to my friends and sister writers Jo Williams and Vicky Hunnings, who continue to offer encouragement and support. I appreciate the efforts of all the good people at St. Martin's Minotaur, especially my editor, Jen Crawford, and publicist, Jessica Rotondi. Amy Rennert is both an agent and a friend, and her guidance over the years has been invaluable.

I also wish to acknowledge the readers who have taken the time to share with me their thoughts and comments on the books, as well as the many enthusiastic bookstore people and librarians who have recommended the series to their customers and patrons.

And special thanks to Elise Simon and Dr. Elizabeth Shelly for their generous donations to our island charities. I hope they're happy with the places I found for Brooke Garrett and Miss Lizzie.

COVENANT HALL

CHAPTER ONE

IT BEGAN, AS SO MANY OF LIFE'S CRITICAL EVENTS DO, with a phone call. One moment you're working or reading or sleeping or shopping, blissfully unaware that your whole existence is about to be altered; the next, some disembodied voice plunges your ordered world into chaos.

Wednesday afternoons are generally quiet at the office of Simpson & Tanner, Inquiry Agents. We occupy a small space in a one-story building just outside the gates of Indigo Run Plantation, about halfway down Hilton Head Island. It was unusually warm, even for March. In the Lowcountry of South Carolina, winter is generally confined to a few cold days at the beginning of the year, and spring bursts through with the azaleas, often in late February.

My partner, Erik Whiteside, worked on his laptop at the reception desk just outside my door. We'd been busy for the past couple of months steadily processing job applications and volunteer statements for the island's recreation board and several other county agencies. Background and criminal checks had become routine, even for me. Computers and I coexist, but there's no love lost on either side. Except for the fact that he's tall and blond and handsome, Erik could rightly be classified as a geek, and he'd taught me well.

I'd just finished running the final name on my list through the series of databases we'd subscribed to. I clicked on the icon to print out the report and leaned back in my chair. I stretched and tried to work the kinks out of my neck. Absently, I massaged the ache that had settled in my right thigh. The damage caused by the attack had healed well, with only a minor scar, and physical therapy had me nearly back to normal. I'd even begun jogging on the beach again, taking it easy until I built the muscle back to full strength. But when I sat too long in one position, it still tended to cramp up on me.

I stood and stretched again, and the tightness eased. The phone rang. I reached for the receiver, but Erik beat me to it. I paused, left hand extended, and studied my mangled ring finger.

This other remnant of that horrifying night had not fared so well. The jagged scar still throbbed when I let my hands dangle at my sides, and the nail had grown back in crookedly. Still, it could have been worse. The tenderness would fade, or so the doctor assured me. The swelling had taken a long time to go down, and it now resembled my other fingers more than it did a Vienna sausage.

In a few more days, I'd have no viable excuse for not putting on Red's engagement ring.

"Bay?"

"Yes?" I stepped around the desk and into the doorway of my office.

"It's Lavinia," he said. "She sounds kind of strange."

I whirled back and snatched up the receiver. Lavinia Smalls has been the principal caregiver in the old antebellum mansion on St. Helena Island since before I was born. Through the chaos of my childhood, her steady hand and loving heart had been the rocks to which I'd clung. In the past years, her care of my aging and crippled father had enabled me to live my life free of this burden and responsibility. I owed her a great deal.

"What's the matter?" I snapped into the phone.

"Nothing to get excited about," she said calmly. "Your father's been feelin' poorly today, and I'm taking him in to see Dr. Coffin."

I frowned. "Why isn't Harley coming to the house?"

Her pause set off tiny alarm bells in the back of my head. "He wants to run a couple of tests." Again she hesitated. "At the hospital."

"Tell me the truth, Lavinia. Are they admitting him?"

"Bay Tanner, I swear you just have to see the worst in everything. If it was somethin' more, I'd tell you, wouldn't I?"

I wasn't so sure about that. Lavinia had been protecting me—and my family—for as long as I could remember.

"Maybe," I said. "Should I meet you there?"

"No need, child. We'll be back in a couple of hours. I just didn't want you to worry if you called and we weren't here."

I glanced up as the outer door opened, and a striking black woman in a sharply tailored gray suit stepped tentatively through the door. Erik rose to greet her, and I snapped my attention back to the phone.

"You'll call me? As soon as you get home?"

"Of course. Now I have to go." I could almost see the softening of the stern expression on her wrinkled brown face. "Don't worry, child. I'll take care of things."

"Yes, ma'am," I said automatically before I realized she'd already hung up.

I replaced the receiver gently in the cradle. My stomach felt as if I'd been plunged suddenly to earth from a great height, like one of those drop-of-terror rides at Six Flags.

Retired judge Talbot Simpson had celebrated his eightieth birthday in January. Lavinia and I had thrown him a massive party, inviting all his former courthouse cronies, the remnants of his Thursday night poker gang, and his old hunting buddies. Truth to tell, there weren't all that many of them left, but those who were physically able showed up. There was a lot of talk of the old days—trials won and lost, doves and ducks blasted out of the sky, scandals and rumors of scandals, and whatever-happened-to-so-and-so reminiscing. For once, Lavinia let the bourbon flow unchecked and didn't even force the cigar smokers out onto the verandah. It had been a bang-up party, and the Judge had enjoyed himself immensely.

"Good to see everybody," he'd said when the last guest had shuffled down the steps. "Better than having them all standin' around gawking at me in my coffin."

I remembered I'd laughed at that. "I promise I won't let anyone gawk," I'd said.

"Good," my father had replied, not sharing the joke. "Just see you stick to that when the time comes."

A chill like the bitterest winter wind off the ocean shook me, and I sank back into my chair. A moment later, Erik stepped in and pulled the door closed behind him.

"Is the Judge okay?" he asked.

"Just some tests," I said, trying to force circulation back into my face. I knew my attempt at a smile must have looked more like a grimace.

"Lavinia will take care of it," he said, and I cringed.

"He's *my* father," I snapped, then deliberately relaxed my shoulders. "Sorry. Who's the woman?"

"Potential client," he answered.

"Any idea what her problem is?"

"Nope. She wants to talk to you."

I ran a hand through the tangle of my reddish-brown hair and sucked in a long breath. "Give me a couple of minutes and send her in."

"Right," he said and closed the door after himself.

I stood again and pulled the black blazer off the back of my chair. I was plenty warm in the white silk turtleneck, but I felt more professional with the jacket on. I straightened my desk, retrieved a clean legal pad from the right-hand drawer, and made certain the small recorder had a fresh tape. I smiled a little, remembering Erik's disdain for the antiquated technology, but it worked for me. Maybe if I lived another forty-one years I'd figure out how to use a BlackBerry.

My hands were folded demurely in front of me on the desk when the door opened.

"Bay, this is Joline Eastman. Please have a seat, ma'am."

"Thank you."

The slim black woman perched on the edge of the client chair and smiled briefly over her shoulder as Erik retreated. She didn't offer her hand, so I kept mine to myself.

"I'm pleased to meet you, Ms. Eastman."

"It's Mrs." Her thin smile didn't reach her deep brown eyes.

"How can we help you, Mrs. Eastman?"

She pulled a manila folder from a black leather briefcase and extracted a single paper and what looked to be an old photograph. She hesitated a few seconds, appearing reluctant to relinquish possession of the documents, then laid them faceup in front of me.

It looked like a genealogy, one of those charts you can print out from a computer program designed to keep track of the family tree. Lines and boxes spread out across the page. Without studying it too closely, I could see some prominent blank spaces.

The picture was indeed old, mounted on stiff cardboard and with that grainy, blurred finish so prevalent in early-twentieth-century photographs. It was a black family—parents and three children—and what were probably one set of grandparents as well, dressed in their best. The women's frilly, high-necked blouses and jaunty hats perched on upswept hair made me guess 1920s. The photo had been taken outdoors, and the backdrop looked to be some kind of store or business.

"Your family?" I asked and looked up to see Mrs. Eastman with another picture clutched tightly in her slim fingers. Unconsciously, she rubbed her thumb back and forth across its surface.

"Yes. Mine. My grandfather is the young man. I think." She paused a moment to clear her throat, and I saw pain flicker in her nearly black eyes. "I can't say for certain."

"They look like nice people."

Her expression changed again, and anger replaced the misery I thought I'd detected just a few seconds before. "I wouldn't know. That photo and these old letters are all I have to go on." She laid a bundle of envelopes on the desk beside the genealogical chart.

I had no idea where this was going, but I could sense some deep emotion barely held in check. I gave her time to gather herself by flipping the picture over to study the faded photographer's imprint. Hard to read, but I thought it might have said *Charleston*. Someone had written the date, 1919, in the upper right-hand corner, in pencil.

"I'm sorry." It sounded lame, even to me, but I couldn't think of what else to say.

"I want you to find them," Joline Eastman said. "My family. Or what's left of it." Suddenly she rose and laid the second photo on my desk. In color, it showed a gangly teenaged girl with light brown skin and braided black hair dressed in tennis whites, the racket held in front of her as if she were preparing to return serve. "If you can't," she said in a quavering voice, "my daughter is going to die."

CHAPTER TWO

I SPENT THE NEXT HALF HOUR TAKING NOTES AND recording the heartbreaking story of Kimmie Eastman.

She'd been diagnosed with a rare form of leukemia right before Christmas. The disease had advanced rapidly, and a bone marrow transplant had become her only hope.

"We've exhausted all the other possibilities," Joline Eastman said. "It's much more complicated for us than it is for . . . Caucasians." Her chin rose fractionally as if she expected me to argue with her.

"Why?"

"The survival rate for any kind of transplant is nearly forty percent less for African-Americans. The specialist said it's because of our heritage. Our race is older, and we have more complex tissue types."

"I assume you've had immediate family tested."

"Of course," she said. "Her brother came closest, but not enough to take the risk. At this stage of the disease, rejection would almost certainly be . . . would lead to a bad outcome."

I hated the medical doubletalk. Tiptoeing around the words seemed so pointless. What Joline Eastman meant was that her daughter's rejection of noncompatible bone marrow would be fatal. There would be no second chance to get it right.

"And your husband's family?" I asked. "May I have his name, by the way?"

"It's Jerry. Jerrold." She spelled it for me. "He's a doctor, an OB-GYN. But it's irrelevant. He's not Kimmie's father." She paused. "And you need to deal directly with me, Mrs. Tanner. Only me. I expect you to protect my privacy. I don't want my husband to be . . . bothered with this."

Bothered? It seemed a strange choice of words.

"Are you in touch with her biological father?"

"No." Joline tugged down the hem of her skirt and studied the floor.

"Have you made an effort to contact him?"

"There's no point. Leave him out of it."

The intensity of her reply seemed a little over the top, but I let it go. "Isn't there a registry for bone marrow donors? Like with other organs?"

Her head snapped up, and her eyes again flashed with anger. "Of course! Don't you think I've explored every possible avenue to save my child?"

It was a rhetorical question to which I had no answer, and I scribbled a few notes to give Joline time to get herself under control.

"So you need to find your own family." I picked up the old graying photograph and studied the smiling faces. "The photographer was from Charleston, but I can't make out his name. Do you know where this was taken?"

She shook her head. "My great-great-grandfather owned a grocery store. At least that's what I remember hearing. He and his brothers started it after the Civil War, I think. That could be where the picture was taken, but I'm not sure."

"It's a place to start. May I?"

When she nodded, I pulled the bundle of letters toward me and studied the tattered envelopes. They'd gotten damp at some point, and much of the ink had smeared and run. Most of the postmarks were indecipherable.

"They're from my grandmother, Esther Mitchell. Grandpa served in World War Two. He saved some of her letters."

"Are they still living?" I asked.

"Oh, no. Grandpa passed before I was born."

I looked up when she hesitated. The anger was back.

"Grandmother Mitchell and my mother were killed in a car crash. Drunk driver."

"I'm sorry. How awful to lose them both so senselessly."

Joline Eastman's eyes were dry. "Yes. Tragic. Especially since my mother was the drunk who was driving."

She wrote a check for our retainer, not flinching when I named the amount. Judging by her outfit and the Kate Spade bag she'd retrieved the checkbook from, I didn't think it would prove a burden. I tried not to give her too much hope, but she seemed to walk a little straighter when Erik opened the door for her on her way out. She'd left all the documents with me, and I'd given her a receipt for them.

Erik took the vacated chair in front of my desk, and I filled him in. He'd listen to the tape later and transcribe it for our files.

"Poor woman," he said softly.

"She's desperate," I said. "Without the bone marrow transplant, they've given her daughter only a couple of months."

He picked up the genealogical chart and studied it. "Lots of missing information—missing people—here. Does it have to be a direct ancestor?"

"I'm assuming the closer the blood relationship, the better the chances for a match."

"And you say Joline's mother and one grandmother are both dead, right?"

"And the Mitchell grandfather." I took the family tree from his hands and traced the lines with my fingers. "Joline's father skipped out when she was a teenager, but he's a viable candidate. If he's still alive. Maybe he has parents or living siblings. But the best bets are her two sisters, neither of whom she knows how to locate."

"That's strange. Did she say why?"

I shook my head. "Nothing helpful. The mother drank, so maybe it has something to do with that. At any rate, she hasn't spoken to"— I looked again at the chart—"Maeline and Tessa since before their mother was killed."

"It's always a problem trying to track down women when you don't have their married names."

"I know. But at least the given names are unusual. Betty and Sally would be a lot more difficult. I think they might be the best place to start."

"What about Kimmie's father?" Erik asked.

"She seriously didn't want to talk about him. Judging by her age when the girl was born, I'm guessing high school hormones gone wrong—a one-night stand or something like that. Joline didn't really tell me anything useful except that he's a dead end. The same with her mother's side of the family. Apparently they've all been ruled out."

Erik looked at the photo of the pretty teenager. "It's a damn shame."

I reached in the drawer for an oversized envelope and began placing the documents inside. "I know. But all we can do is work with the information she's willing to give us. And protect her privacy. She was pretty adamant about that, too." I paused and again studied the grainy photograph before handing it across to Erik.

"Do we know anyone who could work on this?" I pointed to the blurred printing visible on the building in the background. "Maybe bring this part into better focus? Most of these people are probably dead, but if we could pinpoint the location, it might give us a jumping-off point. Or maybe someone could raise that printing on the back, identify the photographer."

"I've got a couple of online buddies who do digital photo enhancement. I might even be able to find a program myself. Let me see what I can do." He rose and stretched. "Things have been kind of quiet, haven't they? I know all these background checks haven't been too exciting."

I rubbed the cramp in my thigh and smiled. "Boring is good," I said, then sobered. "I just wish the consequences of failure on this one weren't so damn final."

"I know. Let me get started on the photo," he said and turned back toward his desk.

I pulled the bundle of letters back out of the file and weighed them in my hand. Maybe a dozen, the lifeline between a wife and a husband separated by thousands of miles and a mountain of fear and uncertainty. *The Greatest Generation,* I thought. So few of them left now, but at least their grandchildren had come, if belatedly, to an appreciation of their courage and sacrifice on the beaches of the Pacific and among the hedgerows of Europe.

The Judge had missed his chance at war, a fact he often bemoaned when some of his older colleagues allowed bourbon and camaraderie to loosen their tongues and memories. My father had attended the Citadel, then gone on to law school at South Carolina. Educational deferments had kept him out of Korea, and age out of Vietnam.

I glanced at my watch. Lavinia had said they'd be gone a couple of hours. I wondered what kind of tests Harley Coffin had felt it necessary to order up on an octogenarian already confined to a wheelchair. My hand hovered over the phone, and I jumped when it rang.

"I've got it," I called and grabbed up the receiver. "Simpson and Tanner, Inquiry Agents. This is Bay Tanner."

"Hey, sweetheart. How's your day going?"

I felt my shoulders relax. Sergeant Red Tanner of the Beaufort County Sheriff's Office had been first my brother-in-law, then my friend and sometime antagonist, and finally, as of last Christmas, my unofficial fiancé. The ring he'd given me, with his two children watching quietly from the corner of my great room, still sat in its velvet box at the bottom of the floor safe in my bedroom closet.

"Not bad," I said. "We've got a new client."

"Interesting case?"

"Sad more than interesting. How about you? Out keeping the world safe from bad guys and speeding tourists?"

His laugh always reminded me of Rob's, and I flinched. I wondered what my murdered husband would think of my marrying his brother. In good moments, I liked to believe he'd be pleased for both of us. At other times, I wasn't so sure.

"Pretty quiet around here, too," Red answered. "I finished up testifying this morning on that drug case in Beaufort. Those two scumbags are going away for a long time."

"Good. So when will you be home?"

"I'm off at five. Want to go grab dinner somewhere?"

I hesitated. "I'm not sure. Lavinia called and said she had to take the Judge in to the hospital for some tests. I may want to run over there this afternoon."

"Want me to go with you?"

I smiled. Most of the time, Red defied the stereotype of the macho, gun-toting lawman. While he was perfectly capable of violence when the performance of his duties called for it, he could be as concerned and caring as his brother had been. I cursed myself for the comparison, a thing I'd promised myself not to do. It was unfair to the Tanner men, both the living and the dead.

"Thanks, but I'll be fine. Lavinia's supposed to call as soon as they get home."

"Well, keep me posted, honey. I'm sure it's nothing to worry about."

I gritted my teeth. Sometimes Red forgot I wasn't one of his children.

"I'll let you know."

After we hung up, I sat staring at the phone, willing it to ring, but the beast remained stubbornly silent. I drew a long breath and turned back to the letters Joline Eastman had left behind.

I switched on the desk lamp and rummaged in the bottom drawer for the magnifying glass I kept there. Erik had hooted when I brought it in, making Sherlock Holmes wisecracks for the rest of the day. I focused the lens on the first of the smeared postmarks, but there was nothing decipherable, and the ink on the return address, written with a fountain pen, was simply a blue blotch. They'd been addressed to Private First Class Chauncey Mitchell, which Joline had confirmed was her grandfather's name, but the rest was again a blur. He'd served in France, according to his granddaughter, but she had no other information about his time in the Army.

It had amazed me how little our client knew about her own background and history. Perhaps because aristocratic Southern families—my own included—were intensely fixated on the past, I found it hard to fathom how someone could grow to adulthood so completely oblivious to all those who had come before her.

I moved on through the nearly dozen letters, inspecting the envelopes. I knew I'd eventually have to extract the letters themselves, but I found myself postponing that invasion of the Mitchells' privacy, even though both husband and wife were long dead. Lavinia's disdain for those who pried and gossiped had been drummed into my head from an early age. My choice of a second profession still didn't sit well with her.

I found the first clue about halfway down the stack. The round circle enclosing the postmark had escaped the water damage to some extent, and I thought I could make out the letter *E* at the beginning. Joline said she had been born near Pritchardville, just up the road from Hilton Head on the mainland, but had no idea where her family was prior to that. The photographer's imprint on the old photo had looked to me as if it read CHARLESTON, even though that was primarily a guess. And just south of that antebellum jewel of the Confederacy lay Edisto Island.

I opened my mouth to call Erik when the phone forestalled me. I snatched it up.

"Bay Tanner."

"Honey, it's me." Lavinia's voice sounded strained.

"What's wrong? Is the Judge okay?"

"It's his heart. You'd better come."

CHAPTER THREE

BY THE TIME I DASHED THROUGH THE FRONT DOOR OF Beaufort Memorial Hospital, I'd worked myself into such a state of near hysteria that I could barely force my father's name through lips dry and tight with fear. The placid older woman at the main desk, no doubt used to dealing with frantic relatives, smiled kindly and directed me to cardiac intensive care.

When the elevator doors slid open, I nearly ran headlong into Lavinia, who had been pacing in the hallway.

"Thank God!" she said and gripped my arm. "I told them they can't do anything without your permission."

I stopped dead and jerked out of her grasp. "What do they want to do? Where's Daddy?"

"Hush, child. Over here."

Lavinia led me to a small waiting area. A television, tuned to Fox News, flashed pictures of devastation, probably from a bombing, probably in the Middle East, but without sound it was hard to tell. She pulled me down onto a narrow sofa.

"Harley thinks your father's heart is weakening. The beat's irregular, and he's having trouble breathing. They have him hooked up to monitors and oxygen." I could feel her body trembling. "The specialist, the heart man, wants to operate. I told them they can't do that without your permission. That's right, isn't it?"

"I don't know. I told him it should be you. Does he even have a medical power of attorney?" Then it struck me. "Wait! Why can't he tell them himself? Those things are only necessary if the patient isn't able—"

"He's conscious some of the time, honey, but he's not makin' a whole lot of sense. Harley thinks maybe he's had another . . . incident."

"Another stroke?"

I half rose, but Lavinia's strong brown hand on my arm pulled me back down.

"Maybe." She swallowed hard and stared off into the distance. "He doesn't seem to know who I am."

I felt her pain like a physical blow.

"They weren't going to let me go in at first. Only family, they said. But Harley made them."

"Bastards!" I said between clenched teeth, and for once she didn't scold me for the profanity.

Family, I thought. This kind, prickly woman loved both of us, my father and me, like her own.

"I want to see him."

This time she didn't try to stop me as I jumped from the sofa and marched toward the nurses' station. I found it deserted, but a moment later Harley Coffin, nearly as old and white-haired as the Judge, stepped from the doorway of a glassed-in room.

"Bay, honey, I'm glad you're here." He gripped both my arms and stared directly into my face, his faded eyes warm with compassion. "You calm down now, hear me? It's not as bad as it looks."

He glanced over his shoulder, and I followed his gaze. The Judge lay surrounded by tubes and machines, his snowy hair nearly invisible against the stark white of the hospital linen. His eyes were closed, but even from a distance I could make out the rise and fall of his chest beneath the sheet. I felt some of the fear ease a bit.

We moved over to lean against the counter of the nurses' station.

"The heart specialist—that's Dr. Tom Utley—he thinks there's a blockage. He wants to go in and see if he can clear it."

I stared at this man who had taken care of our family for almost as long as I could remember. "For God's sake, Harley, he's eighty years old! And already frail. Isn't there something else to try first?"

"We're doin' what we can, Bay, but there's no guarantee it'll work. Remember, there's been a lot of strain on Tally's heart with all these strokes. And that business with the kidnapping a couple of years ago sure didn't help any."

I shook off the wave of guilt. "You think this is a good idea? This operation?"

He sighed and shrugged his stooped shoulders. "I'm not a heart man, honey. I'm just an old country M.D."

"But you've kept him alive all these years, even after the strokes and . . . everything. Tell me what to do."

My gaze flashed again to the glass wall, and I gasped. My father's piercing gray eyes were locked on mine.

"He's awake," I said and darted around Harley and into the room. "Daddy?"

I crouched next to the bed and reached for his hand. The firmness of his grip sent hope surging through me.

"Can you hear me?"

He nodded, just slightly. I heard Harley Coffin step in behind me.

"Tally?" he said. "You back with us then?"

Again my father nodded.

"Do you know where you are?" Harley asked.

"Hospital."

"Good. And who am I?"

"Old fool," my father mumbled, and his lifelong friend laughed.

"He's coming around. I'll tell Mrs. Smalls and see if I can round up Tom Utley." The doctor turned and shuffled from the room.

I stood and pulled up a straight chair set next to the machinery, which beeped and hummed beside the bed. "Don't try to talk," I said, the cold knot of fear slowly dissolving from my chest. "They say you probably have an artery blocked. They want to go in and clean it out."

My father frowned, and the shake of his head was as emphatic as his weakness and the paraphernalia strapped to him would allow. "Thirsty," he said, trying to wet his lips.

I poured water from a carafe and stuck one of the bendable straws into it. "Here."

I held it, and he sipped, that small effort seeming to exhaust him. He closed his eyes.

"Daddy, don't fall asleep. I need to know where the papers are. Do you have a medical power of attorney? If you don't want them to operate, I need some ammunition in case . . ." I stumbled over the words. "If you're not able to tell them, I have to be able to make them do what you want."

"Chest. My room." His voice sounded stronger after the water. "No operation. Hear? No operation."

"I hear you. If that's what you want."

His eyes fluttered closed once more, and I set the glass back on the rolling table. I felt again for his hand beneath the crisp sheets, and suddenly he was staring at me.

"Vinnie?" he whispered, and I squeezed his fingers.

"She's coming," I said.

"Good girl," he mumbled, "good girl."

A moment before he drifted off, I thought I heard him say something that sounded like "Get Julia," but of course that made no sense.

Red and I nearly collided at the front door of the hospital.

"Bay! What's happening? I was out on a call, but Erik tracked me down. How is he?"

Before I could answer, he engulfed me in an embrace that nearly took my breath away.

"Not here," I said, easing out of his arms. "Let's go outside."

The air had cooled a little in the late-afternoon breeze off the

Beaufort River, but the sun offered some residual warmth. Red, still in his crisp khaki uniform, held my hand as we seated ourselves on one of the benches beneath the portico.

"Lavinia's with him. The heart specialist just left. He still thinks they should operate, but the Judge is adamant. He'll be here overnight at least, but he's already demanding to go home."

Red smiled, and I joined him. "He may be a pain in the ass sometimes, but he's a tough old guy. You've got to give him that."

"I need to run over to Presqu'isle and pick up some things for him. Lavinia gave me a list."

"Leave your car here. I'll drive you."

We made our way to the cruiser pulled up in a No Parking zone. I cocked an eyebrow at Red, and he laughed.

"Perks of the job. Damned few of them these days," he added, sobering.

Red had been passed over for promotion, and it had rankled. I'd wondered aloud if his old nemesis, Detective Lisa Pedrovsky, had had any hand in it, but he'd told me not to be ridiculous. Red's anger had been riding pretty close to the surface of late, and he'd begun making noises about resigning from the sheriff's department. I didn't take it seriously.

He avoided the late-afternoon downtown traffic by taking the fixed bridge to Lady's Island, then turning right toward St. Helena. We pulled into the semicircular driveway of the antebellum mansion as the sun began its slow slide into evening. The waters of St. Helena Sound, just behind the peninsula that gave the massive house its name, were tinged with the pinks and oranges of sunset in the Lowcountry. Together we mounted the sixteen steps of the split staircase, crossed the wide verandah, and stepped into the cool hallway.

"Would you mind hunting up a bag of some kind?" I asked, tossing my purse onto the console table next to the grandfather clock that had been keeping time in the old mansion for generations. "Probably in the hall closet. It doesn't have to be anything big."

The Judge and Lavinia never traveled, especially after the strokes had confined my father to a wheelchair. I wouldn't know where to begin to look for a proper suitcase.

In the room that had been the Judge's study before his infirmities had forced us to convert it to a handicapped-accessible bedroom suite, I moved to the cherry highboy in the far corner. It felt strange rummaging through my father's personal belongings, although I had often lifted his pile of pajamas to retrieve one of his illegal Cuban cigars. But my father insisted that these and his nightly intake of Kentucky bourbon and lemon were the only things that made life worth living. Lavinia and I both fussed at him, but he was a stubborn, cantankerous old man.

I laid the few items on his bed and gathered toiletries from the adjacent bathroom.

"Any luck?" I called to Red, but the thickness of the old walls kept my voice from carrying down the hallway.

I moved to the low mahogany chest that sat next to the window seat where I had often sought refuge as a child when bad weather forced me to stay indoors. Sometimes the Judge would be working at his desk, and I'd sit quietly, watching him from my perch, glancing occasionally at the boats gliding by on the Sound and the constant parade of herons and pelicans swooping by on the wind.

Blinking back tears, I lifted the lid.

I found the medical power of attorney where Lavinia had guessed it would be, in the file marked LEGAL. As I had suspected, my father had named me. It made sense, I supposed. As his only living relative, I *should* be the one to make life-and-death decisions, but the idea of it filled me with dread. It was cowardly, and I knew it, but I couldn't help how I felt.

There were two more envelopes in the file, one clearly labeled LAST WILL AND TESTAMENT. It was sealed and felt surprisingly light in my hand. The return address was that of Lawton Merriweather, Attorney-at-Law. Though he'd been dead for several years, I could still remember Law's kind face as we'd sat around the poker table on Thursday nights right here in this room. So many of my father's friends had died recently. I wondered if he felt the weight of his own mortality, especially . . .

The second envelope was unsealed and had my name printed in a bold, but shaky hand beneath the word OBITUARY. My father was nothing if not meticulous. I shouldn't have been surprised that he'd already taken care of writing his own notice for the newspapers.

I glanced over my shoulder, but Red still hadn't appeared. My fingers trembled only a little as I slipped out the single typed sheet and sat back on my haunches. A few last orange rays of the sinking sun flickered through the glass above the window seat and cast a glow over the simple words:

Former attorney, criminal courts judge, and longtime Beaufort resident Edward Talbot Simpson died _____ at _____. He was _____. Born January 29, 1929, in Ridgeland, he was the son of the late Edward and Anna Hancock Simpson. He was preceded in death by his parents; his wife, Emmaline Baynard Simpson; and an infant brother, Hancock Tyler Simpson.

A graduate of the Citadel and the University of South Carolina School of Law, Simpson lived briefly on Edisto Island before moving his offices to Beaufort where he practiced for more than thirty years. In 1982 he was elected to the bench where he served until his retirement. He was active in local Republican politics and held several positions within the party, declining to run for higher office despite the urging of his colleagues.

He was a member of the Beaufort County Historical Society, the Beaufort Chamber of Commerce, the Beaufort County and SC Bar Associations, the American Society of Trial Lawyers, and St. Helena Episcopal Church.

Judge Simpson is survived by his daughters, Lydia "Bay" Tanner of Hilton Head Island and Julia Simpson.

Funeral services will be private. Memorial donations may be made to the American Heart Association, the American Red Cross, or the St. Helena Episcopal Church Building Restoration Fund.

Attached to the bottom was a yellow sticky note, again in that same careful printing: I'M SORRY, HONEY.

The grandfather clock in the hallway chimed six, but I barely reg-istered its deep bass notes. Faintly, I heard Red calling my name, but everything around me had faded into a mist. I felt suspended, unable to take in enough air to make my lungs function, my eyes fastened on one word: *daughters*. Plural. And the name: *Julia Simpson*.

"*Get Julia*"?

I had a sister.

CHAPTER FOUR

"*H*ONEY? WILL THIS DO?"

I felt Red's presence behind me and frantically shoved the obituary back into the file. I slammed down the lid of the chest and snatched up the power of attorney.

"Found it," I said, sliding back toward the bed without turning. I didn't want Red to see the shock on my face, but he knew me too well.

"You're shaking." He tossed the small bag onto the duvet and gripped my shoulders. "What's the matter?"

I tried to fight him, but my legs wouldn't hold me up. I sagged onto the bed and ordered my brain to function. "Nothing," I said, not meeting his eyes.

"Bullshit! You look like you're going to faint. Tell me, sweetheart. What is it?"

"Bullshit yourself! I've never fainted in my life." I jerked out of his grasp and picked up the small satchel—a carpetbag it would have been called in the days when the halls of Presqu'isle had rustled with the whisper of crinolines and the soft shuffle of slaves' bare feet. I began cramming in the underwear and pajamas I'd taken from the highboy.

Red stepped back, stung.

"I'm sorry," I said, still afraid to face him. I wondered at my own reluctance to share the shocking news with him. Maybe that said more about my feelings than the ring I'd found excuses not to wear. I shook my head. I couldn't deal with all that now. I picked up the sheaf of papers from the bed and lied without compunction. "The medical power of attorney. It's me. I get to decide if the Judge lives or dies."

I didn't have to feign the quaver in my voice. Again I felt Red's touch on my shoulders, softer now.

"I'm so sorry, sweetheart."

I rested my cheek against his hand and allowed myself a calming breath. I'd been blessed with the ability to compartmentalize, and I used it. I slid *Julia* into an empty slot and firmly slammed the door. *Tomorrow.* I'd think about her tomorrow.

"Have you eaten anything?" Red asked, and I shook my head. "No wonder you're feeling shaky. Let's stop and grab some burgers on the way back to the hospital."

I nodded, not quite trusting my voice. I piled the last of the things from Lavinia's list into the carpetbag and snapped it shut. On impulse, I turned toward the staircase that bisected the hall.

"I'll bet Lavinia's planning on staying the night if she can," I said. "Let me just get her a change of clothes."

Without waiting for a reply, I dropped the bag at the foot of the steps, climbed to the second floor, and turned right. Some years ago, at the Judge's insistence, Lavinia had taken over my mother's old room with its imported furniture and walls filled with art. A dressing room connected it to the space my father would have occupied if he'd been able to manage the stairs. As it was, this airy room with its view across the Sound provided Lavinia with a haven, a place to escape the demands of running an old plantation house and caring for its failing master.

I emptied Lavinia's knitting from the needlepoint bag sitting next to her rocker and folded in enough clothes and toiletries to get her through the night. As if drawn by an unseen force, my eyes wandered to the heavy oak box squatting in the center of the dresser, and I paused. When I was a child, I had seen it in the same place of prominence in Lavinia's old rooms, in the servants' quarters she and her son had occupied. My refuge in times of distress. I remembered lying curled up on the colorful quilt spread across the iron four-poster while Lavinia hushed and soothed me. Sometimes she'd open the box, with a key she wore on a slim chain around her neck, but I could never see exactly what was inside. Papers, I could tell, and the glint of gold, probably from a piece of jewelry, although our housekeeper never wore anything but the chain and key.

I stepped closer, examining the tarnished hasp, and *Julia* popped back into my head. Did Lavinia know? Would she be the keeper of things my father wanted hidden from me? My hand reached out of its own volition, hovering over the worn and polished oak.

"Bay? Do you need any help?" Red's voice drifted up the stairs.

I snatched back my hand, scooped up the knitting bag, and nearly ran from the room. But the image stayed in my mind, even as I followed Red back out into the cool, clear night: The catch on Lavinia's box of secrets had not been fastened. I glanced back over my shoulder as we pulled away from Presqu'isle onto the rutted Avenue of Oaks.

We hit the Sonic on Lady's Island and wolfed down cheeseburgers as we drove through the deepening night back to the hospital. Stepping out of the elevator, I delivered both bags to Lavinia, who waited quietly on the sofa in the waiting room.

"Wish you'd brought my knitting instead," she murmured when I handed hers over. "I'm sorry, honey," she added almost immediately. "It was thoughtful of you to worry about me at all."

"How is he?" I asked, glancing down the hall toward the ICU.

"'Bout the same. He comes and goes. They say he's losing consciousness, but I think he's just napping." She smiled. "Like he does at home."

It wasn't like Lavinia to sugarcoat things, to try to fool herself—or me—but I liked her version of things a lot better than the doctors'.

"You go on home now, you hear? I'll let you know how things are going." Her voice soothed and comforted as it always had in times of trouble.

"He's my responsibility. If you're staying, I'm staying."

Beside me, Red laid a hand on my shoulder. "Why don't you come home with me now? Get a good night's sleep. I'll have you back here first thing in the morning, and Lavinia can call if she needs you."

I whirled, ready to tell him to mind his own damn business, but the look of tenderness and concern on his face brought tears rushing to my eyes. I gulped them down.

Behind me, Lavinia said softly, "Redmond is right, honey. No sense both of us sittin' here all night." She smiled. "Go on now. Get some rest."

As usual, there was no point in arguing with Lavinia. "Okay. But we'll stay at Presqu'isle. I don't want to be an hour away in case— I just want to be close by." I pulled the power of attorney from my bag and handed it to Lavinia. "He's designated me for medical decisions, so will you make sure they take a copy of this?"

She nodded.

"And no matter what it says in there," I said, pointing to the papers, "you know I would never do anything without talking it over with you first."

Again she bobbed her head, her grip on the legal document creasing the edges. "Go on now," she said again.

"Yes, ma'am," I answered.

Our eyes met, the unspoken bond of trust we'd forged over four decades hovering between us. The words slipped out before I even registered the thought.

"Do you know about Julia?"

If the question startled her, she gave no visible sign. "Julia who?"

I could read the truthfulness in her steady gaze, and my heart dropped. If Lavinia didn't know about my sister—or would it be *half* sister?—where would I begin to find the answers?

I ignored her question. "Did the Judge give you any papers to keep for him? Something he didn't want . . . anyone else to stumble across accidentally?"

When her gaze slid away, I knew she would lie. And that it would trouble her deeply to do so. "No, he didn't. What's this all about?"

"It doesn't matter," I said, lying myself. "Call me the minute there's any change. I'll keep the cell by my bed."

I wanted to plant a kiss on her wrinkled forehead, but I knew she'd stiffen at the effort. Since I'd grown up, we'd stopped being a *touching* family at Presqu'isle.

"Goodnight," I said awkwardly, glancing down the hall before turning for the elevator.

Behind me, I heard Red say, "I'm sure it'll be all right, Mrs. Smalls."

"Thank you, Redmond," she murmured. "If the good Lord sees fit."

I stabbed the Down arrow and suppressed a shiver. When I looked back, Lavinia's head was bent in prayer.

I left Red to light a fire in the back parlor and retraced my steps up to the second floor. The creaks and groans of the old house welcomed me as I put fresh linen on the bed and laid out a clean set of towels in the bathroom that had been mine when I was a teenager. Nothing had been changed in the intervening twenty-five years, the same flowered wallpaper and crisp white beadboard still surrounding the claw-footed tub.

Back in the bedroom, I pulled a pair of sweats from the stash of clothes I kept at Presqu'isle and hung my work clothes in the closet. I retrieved my cell phone from my bag, ready to tuck it into one of the deep pockets, when I realized it was still turned off. I'd automatically shut it down the first time I'd entered the hospital. I flipped it open and powered it back up, and a flurry of missed messages lit the readout.

Almost all of them were from Erik.

I glanced at my watch. At a little after nine o'clock on a Wednesday evening, I thought I just might catch him at home, but the landline switched over to voice mail. He picked up his cell on the second ring.

"How's the Judge doing?" he asked. "I got worried when you didn't call. I almost came over there."

"I'm sorry. He's staying the night at the hospital, and I've been running back and forth to Presqu'isle. They think he's got a blockage in one of his arteries, but he won't let them go in and check it out."

"Why not? That's a pretty simple procedure these days, isn't it?"

"The Judge said no, and I have to abide by his wishes." I swallowed around the lump in my throat. "I have his medical power of attorney, but I'm not going to do something he's against. It's his life."

"Anything I can do? Stephanie and I are just finishing dinner. We could come over there and keep you company."

My late partner's daughter had become a big part of Erik's life since that horrible night at the marina just south of Amelia Island. Ben Wyler's death still lay heavily on my conscience, although I never figured out exactly what I could have done to prevent it. The irrational but nonetheless profound sense of guilt kept me from accepting Stephanie's overtures of friendship. I never said it made any sense, but I just couldn't feel comfortable in her presence.

"Red's here," I said. "We're staying the night at Presqu'isle. But thanks for the offer."

"No problem. We're here if you need us." He paused. "Hey, I did find something interesting after you left. About the Eastman case?"

I welcomed the change of subject, dropped onto the duvet, and pulled my legs into an approximation of the lotus position. "You have some luck with the photograph?"

"In a way. I contacted this guy I know, back in Charlotte. I sold him a lot of equipment when I ran the electronics store up there. I scanned the picture and sent it up to him. Got a pencil? Or I could send it to your phone."

I laughed, and the very act made me feel better. "Get serious. It would probably be this time next year before I figured out how to retrieve it. Hold on."

I unwound my legs and rummaged in my bag for a notebook and pen. I sat down at the desk where I'd done my homework, its surface still bearing some of the scratches and dings of my teenaged carelessness.

"Okay, shoot."

"Ron—that's my friend—said he couldn't do a lot with it, but he did manage to raise some of the letters on the sign in the background. He came up with *e-l-l*, then a capital *B* and a small *r*. There was more, but it was out of the frame."

I looked at what I'd printed on the pad in front of me. "Probably Mitchell," I said, almost to myself. That had been Joline's grandfather's last name. I tried to remember what else she'd said about her family. "And I'll bet the last is *Brothers*. Mrs. Eastman said she thought her something-great-grandfather and his brothers started a grocery store after the War Between the States. Any hint about where it might be located?"

"Nope. I sent him the back of the photo, too, but all he could make out was the same thing you came up with. It looks like *Charleston,* and there's definitely something else there, but he couldn't do anything with it. He's going to try his computer at work tomorrow. Apparently it's got better software."

"If you have time, see if you can find anything on the Net about Edisto Island in the forties. I think that's where the letters were mailed from. See if there was a Mitchell Brothers grocery store there. It also may be a good place to start looking for Joline's . . . missing sisters." I stumbled over the last two words, but Erik didn't seem to notice.

"I can get on that as soon as I get home. You want me to let you know if I find anything tonight?"

I let the pen drop from my fingers and roll across the scarred surface of the desk. It felt like a supreme effort just to keep my head upright on my neck.

"No, that's okay. I'm wiped out. Either send it to my computer at the office or at home if you come up with something. Or call me tomorrow."

"Will do." A pause. "Everything's going to be all right with the Judge, isn't it?"

"I hope so. I'll let you know if— I'll let you know. Goodnight."

I hung up without waiting for his reply and looked up to see Red standing in the doorway.

"Everything okay?" he asked.

"Just Erik. Work stuff." I rose and stretched. "The bathroom's all yours. No shower, but the water's hot if you want a bath." It suddenly occurred to me that Red didn't have a change of clothes. "You want me to see if something of the Judge's will fit you?"

"I'll be fine. It won't be the first time I haven't been able to get home to change," he added as he moved toward the bathroom.

"Take your time," I said. "I'll get things locked up downstairs and make some tea. I'll bring it into the parlor by the fire."

By the time I stepped into the hall, he'd already closed the bathroom door. I automatically turned for the stairs, but the door of my mother's old room drew my gaze. The image of Lavinia's eyes sliding away from mine when I'd asked if my father had given her any papers to keep led my feet away from the steps. I paused, glancing over my shoulder, and reached for the knob. A stab of conscience stayed my hand. Invading Lavinia's space was the worst kind of betrayal, snooping in other people's business one of the most grievous offenses in her eyes.

But there was that word: *daughters*. And the others: *Julia Simpson*.

With a silent apology and another guilty look at the closed bathroom door, I twisted the knob and stepped inside.

CHAPTER FIVE

I EASED THE DOOR CLOSED AND FUMBLED FOR THE light switch. The skeins of wool lay piled in Lavinia's rocking chair, just as I'd left them. The rest of the furniture had been my mother's, most of it dark and heavy, more appropriate to the ancestor who had occupied this room a century and a half before. I crossed to the dresser and turned on the lamp, its soft glow spilling over the yellow silk upholstery of the chaise pulled up beneath the window.

The dark oak box held not a trace of dust as I skimmed my fingers across it. The action left a streak of moisture on the old wood, and I realized my hands were perspiring. I wiped them on my sweatpants and darted another anxious glance behind me.

"Knock it off," I said out loud, but softly, as if the walls might record my unforgivable violation of Lavinia's privacy. I drew a long breath and let it out slowly. "In for a penny," I whispered and threw open the lid.

The flash of gold I remembered from my childhood revealed itself to be a locket. I lifted it out, and it twirled on its chain, glittering in the lamplight. I set it carefully on the top of the dresser and removed the handful of papers. Beneath them was a photograph, old and slightly creased, its black-and-white edges torn a little from repeated handling. It was a young Lavinia, her Afro standing out from her head like a dark nimbus, a baby settled comfortably on her left hip. She was laughing, her head partially thrown back, her eyes nearly closed. The child—it had to be Thaddeus—grinned, too, his toothless gums exposed. They looked happy, a mother and her son caught in a moment of delight. I had never seen Lavinia in such an unguarded, abandoned moment.

I dropped the photo back into the box and riffled through the papers. Thad's birth certificate brought back sad memories of Judas Island and the grisly find Erik and I had made. I shivered in the warm glow of the lamp. Insurance policies and a couple of Thad's report cards slid through my fingers, along with the order of service from my mother's funeral. I paused over that, then moved quickly on.

The envelope was plain, no printed matter or return address. Just the Judge's handwriting, bolder and less shaky, so that I assumed he'd tucked the contents inside before his strokes had affected even his one good hand: TO BE OPENED IN THE EVENT OF MY DEATH.

It was sealed.

I turned it over and over in my hands. No more than two sheets inside, or at least that's how it felt. I passed it under the lamp, but nothing of the contents revealed itself. I stroked the words, my mind racing with tales from old mysteries: trembling fingers clutching purloined letters over a whistling tea kettle. Did it actually work? I wondered. And did I have the nerve?

"Bay?" Red's voice drifted up the stairs. "Where are you?"

I jumped and clutched the envelope to my chest. This had to be it. Lavinia had been lying when she said the Judge had never given her any papers to keep. I knew it. Here, in my sweating hand, I was convinced I held the answer. My sister. Julia Simpson.

"Bay? Honey?"

I couldn't. There had to be another way. I thrust all the papers back in the box and dropped the gold locket on top, hopefully just the way I'd found it. As I lowered the lid, another slim piece of paper, tucked up against the side, caught my eye. It was a newspaper clipping, old and a little yellowed. I could see the word *drowned* in the part of the headline just after the fold, and a date: *July* 7. Without conscious intent, I lifted it out and tucked it into my pocket, then used the sleeve of my sweatshirt to remove any moisture I might have left behind on the lid. With a pounding heart, I switched off the lights and slipped into the hallway.

"Coming," I called, more loudly than necessary, and nearly ran down the steps.

"Where'd you get to?" Red asked when I carried the tea tray into the parlor.

Unlike the more formal rooms at the front of the house, this had been the place where we'd gathered as a family on the rare occasions we were all home at the same time. My mother had grudgingly allowed a television to be installed, and it was often here the Judge had taught me the finer points of baseball as we followed the Braves and the amazing Hank Aaron's demolition of Babe Ruth's home-run record.

"Just checking out some things," I said, not meeting his eyes as I set the tray on the low table in front of the sofa.

I poured, then curled up beside Red and tucked my feet up under me. Firelight danced off the polished pine floor, and I found myself staring at the flickering patterns. I smiled, remembering the times I'd snuggled like this against my father, babbling about the high and low points of my day at school, the smoke from his cigar wafting up toward the ceiling. Those evenings had been few—and precious to me in a way I hadn't thought about in too many years. Somehow we'd drifted apart, and I could only partially blame it on my mother's alcoholic mood swings and often bizarre behavior. Somewhere along the way, I'd learned to harden my heart, to guard myself against caring too much. Rob had scaled the walls, and now I'd allowed Red to do the same.

I hoped I wouldn't live to regret it.

"Relax," I heard Red whisper against my hair. "You're wound up like a spring."

He pulled away from me a little, and his strong fingers worked the muscles bunched below my neck, careful as always to be gentle with the scar tissue on my left shoulder, an ugly reminder of how close I had come to dying with my husband that terrifying day his small plane exploded on takeoff.

"*Mmm,*" I murmured, squirming around to give him a better angle, and the fold of newspaper crackled in my pocket. I slipped my hand in and smoothed it out.

He finished the massage, and I leaned back into the crook of his arm.

"Would you want to live here again?" he asked, and I pulled back to look into his face.

"Why?"

I'd spoken more sharply than I intended, and his brow crinkled in a frown.

"It's something you'll have to face, if not now, then in the not too distant future. Even if the Judge survives this, he might need more care than Lavinia can give him. And when he passes away, you're going to have to make a decision about the house. I know he deeded it over to you last year on your birthday, but what will you do with it after . . . after he's gone?"

I felt myself stiffen. *None of your damn business* was the phrase that sprang immediately to mind, but I knew that wasn't fair. Red had proposed. I had accepted—sort of. I'd been secretly relieved when the damage to my finger had postponed my wearing his ring. I'd get over that feeling of panic. It would be okay. In the meantime, he had a right to question me about my future. But no law said I had to like it.

I blew out the sharp retort on a puff of air and said, "I haven't thought about it."

"You need to," he replied softly.

"I know." I burrowed closer, and his other arm came around me. "Just not tonight, okay?"

"Okay," he said and kissed the top of my head.

I awoke to the deep chimes of the grandfather clock in the hallway and found the fire had nearly burned itself out. I was alone. At some point, Red had eased my head onto a throw pillow, tucked an afghan around me, and taken himself off to bed. I sat up, my left shoulder stiff and a throbbing pain in my thigh keeping time with my heartbeat. I shivered in the chill room.

I rubbed sleep from my eyes and reached for the cell phone I'd left on the table next to the tea tray. No missed messages. I switched on the lamp behind the sofa and squinted in the sudden glare. My reading glasses were in my bag in my old room, but I thought I could make do without them. With a quick glance behind me, I stood and slid the newspaper article out of my pocket, then dropped back onto the sofa and pulled the afghan over my bare feet.

It was short. The portion of the header that would have told me the name of the newspaper had been cut away, but the location of the story made me sit up straighter:

> *Charleston—The body of a local attorney was pulled from the Atlantic Ocean yesterday, a tragic end to the Fourth of July weekend celebrations.*
>
> *Brooke Garrett, 40, of Edisto apparently drowned while on a holiday outing. She was reported missing by a family friend, and a frantic search by local volunteers and the Coast Guard failed to locate her until her body washed ashore late last night.*
>
> *The coroner will make an official ruling next week but the death is being treated by local officials as an accidental drowning.*
>
> *See obituary, page 6*

I sat for a long time staring at the few words, my mind unable to grasp what significance this woman's death had or why Lavinia would have so carefully preserved the notice of it among her private papers. Maybe it had been a relative, although I'd never heard her mention anyone named Garrett.

I flung off the afghan and carried the flimsy paper into the Judge's room. I found pen and paper in his old desk, now used more as a serving table, and copied the article word for word. I turned off the light and stood for a moment looking out over the Sound. The moon was setting, and only a slim trickle of light played across the water. Out toward the ocean, a faint hint of approaching dawn touched the edge of the night sky with a shimmer of gold.

I let the tears come, not even bothering to wipe them away. Once before I'd been forced to think about a world without the powerful force of my father's personality in it. I'd fought then, risked everything to see him safely home. But how could I fight age and infirmity and the inevitability of death?

Some time later, I dried my eyes on the sleeve of my sweatshirt and climbed the stairs. I tiptoed into Lavinia's room and carefully replaced the stolen scrap of newspaper in the old wooden box. Back in my own bedroom, I felt my way around in the dark and slid the copy into my bag. I set my cell phone next to the bed, slipped in beside Red, and nestled into the curve of his back.

When the phone rang, it was full light, and Red was gone.

CHAPTER
SIX

"I'M SORRY, BAY, DID I WAKE YOU?"

Erik's voice penetrated the fog in my brain, and I sat up, pulling the duvet around me against the chill morning air.

"What time is it?"

"Seven thirty. I'm heading out for the store, and I wanted to fill you in before I go. I found some interesting stuff on the Net last night."

I knew he wanted to string it out, to weave the information into a story with a dramatic punch line, but I wasn't in the mood.

"Just tell me, okay? I have to get dressed and get to the hospital."

The unspoken reference to the Judge sobered him. "Sorry. There was a Mitchell Brothers grocery store on Edisto. It's mentioned in some memoir-type things people have written for the Charleston paper. It catered mostly to the black population, but they sold sweet-grass baskets and some homemade stuff, so there was a lot of crossover. It started going downhill in 1942 when the last of the brothers joined up. There was an antique store in there for a while after the war, but the whole thing got wiped out when Hurricane Gracie went through in 1959. I sent the articles to your computer at home and at work."

While Erik talked, I'd been dressing, the phone tucked between my cheek and shoulder. By the time he finished, I'd moved into the bathroom.

"Interesting. Was there any mention about the rest of the family?"

"No, except the other brother. There were two of them left before the war, but the older one was killed over there, in Europe. When Mrs. Eastman's grandfather came back, the place had already folded, taken by the county for back taxes. The Mitchells moved down here, by Bluffton."

I ran water in the sink and stared into the mirror at my bloodshot eyes. With the tiny red lines radiating out from the vivid green centers, I looked more like my mother than usual.

"Maybe we need to concentrate the search around here then. Edisto may be a dead end."

"I'm not done," Erik said, and again I caught that storyteller's exhilaration in his voice. "I did some checking on our database sites and came up with a Maeline Hatcher in Jacksonboro."

I caught some of his excitement. "I know that place. It's right on 17. Rob and I used to pass through it when we took the back way down to Hilton Head from Charleston."

I could picture the town, just a few businesses, a couple of gas stations, and a wide sweeping intersection where the road turned off toward Walterboro. Rob had always slowed down to exactly thirty-five, because the little burg had a reputation as a speed trap. There couldn't be many houses. I felt the pull of the chase, but experience had taught me to tread carefully. The word *caution* should have been tattooed on my forehead for any number of reasons.

"Were there any others? With that first name, I mean?"

"Not that I ran across on a cursory search. But don't you think this one sounds like a winner?"

I smiled at myself in the mirror. I loved Erik's enthusiasm. "Yes, I agree. Did you send that info to me as well?"

"You bet." He hesitated. "We need to get you a laptop or an iPhone. You could be working on this stuff while you're waiting around at the hospital."

I knew he didn't mean to sound callous. Erik loved his toys and gadgets and just couldn't seem to understand why the whole world wasn't as wired up as he was.

"I have other priorities right now," I said, sounding pompous even to my own ears. Then the picture of the young tennis player, Kimmie Eastman, popped into my head. "But I'll make sure to pull everything sometime today and follow up. This could be a great lead. Nice work."

"Thanks. I hope everything goes okay for the Judge. Tell him I'm . . . I'm rooting for him."

That brought a smile. "I will. I'll call you at the store if anything comes up."

I set the phone on the shelf below the mirror, brushed my teeth, and ran a comb through my unruly mop of hair. The overhead light glinted off the red tinge I'd always been secretly proud of, but it also revealed a new crop of silver threading its way through the tangle of curls.

"Bay? Are you up?" Red's voice drifted in from the bedroom doorway.

"Coming," I called and swiped on lip gloss before tucking the phone in my pocket.

Red turned, and I followed him out into the hallway. "I was gonna start breakfast, but—"

"Don't worry about it. Let's grab something on the run," I said, eyeing Lavinia's closed door as we passed. "I want to get to the hospital."

"Did I hear the phone earlier?" Red asked.

"Erik. Some information about the new client's business."

I made certain the fire was completely out in the parlor and the flue closed before I led the way out onto the verandah. Red held the door of the cruiser open for me, and I slid into the seat. Even riding up front, I still felt awkward in the big car with its radio squawking in the background and an alarming array of wires and switches covering the dashboard. *Intimidated* was the right word, I decided and wondered how much worse it must feel to be stuck in the back behind the mesh screen that protected the officers from their prisoners.

"You didn't say much about this new case yesterday." Red glanced briefly in my direction.

"It's confidential," I said. "You know that."

"Anything you should share? From a law enforcement standpoint?"

He stole another glance as he maneuvered down the Avenue of Oaks, the giant trees forming a lush canopy over our heads while we bounced and rocked along the narrow sandy lane.

"Nope," I said, and for once it was the truth.

The ICU waiting area was empty. I glanced in on the Judge, who appeared to be sleeping peacefully, his good hand resting on the pristine blanket pulled up to his chin. I asked how he'd passed the night, and the nurse on duty answered, "Comfortably," in that brisk tone the medical professionals so often adopted with outsiders.

I found Lavinia in the fresh clothes I'd left her, seated at a round table in the cafeteria with three other black women. She looked up as I approached.

"Oh, Bay, honey. Good morning. You remember Glory Merrick? Mr. Gadsden's daughter?"

"Of course. How are you?"

The woman nodded, and her smiling face belied the terror she'd endured just a few months before when her missing octogenarian father had been the focus of an island-wide search.

"And this is Sallie Grant and Letha Barnwell. From the church."

"I'm very pleased to meet you," I said.

They murmured greetings and slid around to make room for me. I pulled a chair over from an adjoining table and sat down.

"How's the Judge?" I asked. "Any change? I stopped upstairs, but he was sleeping."

Glory Merrick rose. "We'll leave you to discuss your business in private," she said, and the other ladies joined her. "We're prayin' for your daddy, Bay. He's a strong man, and the Lord admires strength. He'll see Judge Simpson through." She patted my shoulder. "You just call on us if there's anything we can do, anything at all."

"Thank you," I managed to mumble around an unexpected lump of tears caught in my chest. "You're very kind."

"We'll be around visitin' for another hour or two, Lavinia," Letha Barnwell said. "We'll stop back and check on you before we go."

The sausage-and-egg biscuit I'd wolfed down sat like a glutinous lump in the bottom of my stomach as I studied Lavinia's worn face. "It's not good, is it?" I asked, and she shook her head.

"That Dr. Utley was by real early this mornin'. He said again that he won't be responsible for your father's . . . *outcome* if he doesn't get that balloon thing done."

Outcome? I thought. That was another of those euphemisms they all loved. I thought Joline Eastman had used the same word to describe the consequences if her daughter didn't receive a bone marrow transplant. And quickly.

I jerked myself back to the cafeteria and Lavinia's somber face. "Angioplasty? Is that what they're suggesting?"

"That's it."

"Did you talk to the Judge about it?"

Again she shook her head. "He wasn't quite . . . up to it this morning. After he has a little rest, Dr. Coffin said he'd be by, and we can discuss it, the three of us."

Lavinia picked up her cup and studied the contents as if the answers might lie within the overly sweetened dregs of coffee.

"He said no operation," I reminded her, barely controlling the sob of fear threatening to escape from deep within me. "We have to go by his wishes. It's his life."

"That I've spent the better part of mine nursin' and carin' for! He doesn't have any right just to give up! No right!"

The outburst stunned me and caused more than a few heads to turn in our direction. For a moment I sat speechless, staring at Lavinia's mottled, angry face. I swallowed hard and spoke softly.

"Yes, he does, Lavinia. It's the last real decision any of us are allowed to make—if we're given the opportunity to choose."

"I won't let him die, not like this. I won't. Not without a fight."

Though she'd lowered her voice, the fierce determination in her tone carried far past our single table. Behind me, I heard a chair scrape, and a moment later I felt a presence behind me.

"Excuse me, ladies, but I couldn't help overhearing. I agree with you completely, Mrs. Smalls."

I half turned and looked up. The standard white coat and dangling stethoscope hung on a tall rangy body now leaning over my right shoulder. I had a glimpse of piercing green eyes, much like my own, beneath a shock of nearly white-blond hair and a pair of thin lips compressed into what I thought might have been an attempt at a smile.

"Tom Utley," the man said, moving around so that I could look him full in the face. "I'm your father's cardiologist, Mrs. Tanner."

The hand he held out looked huge, much too large for the delicate surgery his specialty must sometimes require.

"Bay Tanner," I said, returning his handshake firmly.

"I know. Your reputation precedes you." Again he spoke around something resembling a smile, but there was an edge to the words that I couldn't mistake. Apparently the surgeon didn't entirely approve of whatever he'd heard about me.

Tough, I thought. "My father is opposed to this operation," I said while Dr. Utley seated himself, uninvited, in one of the chairs vacated by Lavinia's church friends.

"I'm sure among us we can convince him otherwise," he said, a hint of smugness tingeing his voice. "It's the only viable option."

"It's his life," I said, feeling as if those three words had become some sort of mantra. "His decision."

The doctor and Lavinia exchanged a look. "Not necessarily," he said. "I understand you hold his medical power of attorney."

"Which is only valid if he's comatose or otherwise unable to make his wishes known. And that's not the case here. He's lucid, rational, and has expressed to me in no uncertain terms that he doesn't want an angioplasty. Case closed."

"Bay—," Lavinia began, but Dr. Utley cut her off.

"Lucid and rational are not qualities I would necessarily apply to

your father's state of mind at this time," he said. "He has extended pe-
riods of unconsciousness, and his speech has become somewhat slurred.
He also fails to recognize persons he's known for years, like Mrs. Smalls
here."

A fleeting moment of panic gripped me as I remembered the
words he'd uttered while I sat by his bed: *"Get Julia."* Had his mental
condition so deteriorated that he'd confused me with his *other* daughter,
the one whose existence I'd known nothing about less than twenty-four
hours before?

I shook my head and stared straight into the doctor's face. "That
may be, but he was perfectly clear in his instructions to me yesterday.
And I intend to abide by them."

Again Tom Utley and Lavinia glanced sideways at each other, and
suddenly I understood.

"You will not declare him incompetent," I said, my teeth clenched
so tightly I could barely speak. Lavinia dropped her head under my
blazing stare. "You wouldn't do that to him, Lavinia. You couldn't. If
he ever found out—"

"I don't want him to die," she whispered, and a single tear dropped
onto the table in front of her.

Without thinking, I grabbed for her hand. "I don't either. You
know that. But we have to let him control what's left of his life. We
owe him that, don't we?"

She sat mutely, her head still bowed when the doctor spoke.

"You're making a grave mistake, Mrs. Tanner. I can't advise you
strongly enough to reconsider."

I released Lavinia's hand and rose from the table. "I'm sorry, Doctor, but my father's wishes *will* be honored. Even if you find some way
to have him declared incompetent, you'll still have me to deal with.
And I'm not changing my mind."

CHAPTER
SEVEN

BEFORE I LEFT THE HOSPITAL, I TRACKED DOWN HARLEY Coffin and made certain he understood exactly where the Judge—and I—stood on the operation question. I'd also sat for a while in the straight-backed chair, holding my father's hand while he slept. He seemed peaceful, some of the deeply etched lines in his face smoothed out. He must have dreamed of something pleasant, because occasionally I watched his wrinkled lips twitch into a brief smile. I also made certain the nurses' station and Dr. Utley's office had all my contact numbers and that the medical power of attorney had been copied and placed in the Judge's chart.

As I crested the second of the two bridges leading onto Hilton Head, I glanced at my bag. The original of the Judge's instructions lay tucked inside, and I'd decided to carry the document with me at all times. If it came to a showdown with the overbearing Dr. Tom Utley, I wanted to make certain I had my ammunition close at hand.

I bypassed the turnoff to the Simpson & Tanner office and headed for home. When I pulled into my driveway, I smiled to see Dolores Santiago's banged-up blue Hyundai squatting on the pine straw beside the house. There had been times in the past few months when it seemed as if I might lose this woman who had cared for me after my husband's murder, had nursed both my body and my spirit back to life.

Her troubles weren't over, but the local immigration attorney I'd hired on behalf of Dolores and her family was optimistic. In the meantime, we tried to carry on as if the events of the days leading up to last Christmas were just a bad memory.

I stepped into the foyer to the whine of the vacuum cleaner, picked up the mail stacked neatly on the console table, and carried it with me up the three steps into the kitchen. I checked the answering machine, but only Erik had left messages. I filled the tea kettle and set it on the stove.

Into the sudden silence, I called, "Dolores, it's me. I'm in here."

I heard the brisk tread of her feet on the hardwood floor a moment before she appeared in the great room.

"Ah, *mi pobre Señora*! *El Juez,* he will be better?"

"How—?" I began, then realized it didn't matter. Despite the annual influx of tourists, all of Beaufort County was really like a small town. News—both good and bad—traveled fast. "I don't know," I said honestly. "It's his heart, but he doesn't want them to operate."

"*Sí,*" she said, nodding. "He is tired, no?"

I hadn't thought about it that way, but perhaps she was right. Life had been a battle for my father ever since the first of his strokes. Maybe he'd just grown weary of the fight. I blinked against the tears.

The kettle whistled, and Dolores climbed the steps to the stove. "You rest, *Señora*. I make the tea."

I let her fuss over me, mostly because it gave both of us solace, a familiar assignment of roles we'd first assumed the day I came home from the hospital, burned and scarred from the explosion of Rob's plane. Without thinking about it, my hand strayed to the ropy tissue that scored my left shoulder.

We sipped tea in companionable silence while I sorted through the mail, tossing most of it aside. I looked up to find my part-time housekeeper studying me over her cup.

"What?" I said, and she smiled sadly.

"The good God will protect *El Juez*. I will pray."

"Thank you."

It seemed to me there would be a lot of messages heading skyward, in both English and Spanish, on behalf of my father. I wished I could believe they would do any good. I shook off my sadness and rose.

"Are you finished in the office? I have some work to do on the computer."

"*Sí.* I go now for the shopping."

"Fine. I probably won't be around here much, so don't overdo it."

"*Sí, Señora,*" she said. "I leave for you some things to heat. Very fast. No trouble."

"Thank you, my friend."

In the bedroom Rob and I had converted to an office, I turned on the computer and logged in to my e-mail account. I'd been reluctant to leave the hospital, but Lavinia had insisted. There was nothing I could do but watch my father sleep, and I knew she'd be on the phone to me the moment there was any change. Maybe if I kept busy, I thought, I could push away the horrible, sinking feeling in my gut. At least for a while. Besides, I'd made a commitment to Joline Eastman. Her fear of loss had to be at least as crushing as my own. Maybe more.

Erik had sent the newspaper articles as attachments, and I downloaded and printed them out. There wasn't much more than what he'd told me the night before: the fact of the existence of the family grocery store on Edisto and that a Maeline Hatcher, possibly née Mitchell, still lived nearby. I dialed the phone number Erik had included, but a robotic voice informed me that it was not in service. Some temporary problem, I wondered, or had the phone actually been disconnected? Had we come this close only to lose our best lead so quickly? Maybe I would have to go up there and find out, although the idea of being that far away from the hospital scared me.

I glanced at the phone, but it sat mute. *I should have given Lavinia a cell,* I thought and made a mental note to remedy that situation. Erik could get one for me quickly. In the meantime, all I could do was wait.

On impulse I turned back to the computer and Googled "Julia Simpson." The first ten of several thousand results popped up on the screen, and I scrolled through a few pages of them. Unfortunately, I had no way of knowing which, if any, of them was pertinent. I tried the search again, this time adding "Edisto Island," but it didn't change the results. There was nothing in my father's obituary to indicate where this *other* daughter of his might live, but I'd fastened on the mention of his having had a law practice there early in his career, something I'd never known. And then there was the newspaper cutting I'd found in Lavinia's treasure box. It, too, had involved Edisto, although there didn't seem to be any connection between the two.

Still, I logged on to the archives of *The Charleston Post and Courier*, the paper in which Erik had located the story about the Mitchells' grocery store, but found nothing relevant. I wandered around the Internet for a while, hunting for some other newspaper from which Lavinia might have cut the clipping about the drowning accident, but again I struck out.

I redialed the number for Maeline Hatcher and got the same disembodied message. I could feel the tension of inaction bunching in my shoulders.

"You're driving yourself nuts," I said aloud to the empty house. I needed to be doing something. I'd badger someone at the ICU nurses' station into giving me an update on the Judge. I reached for the phone again just as it rang.

"Bay, honey, it's me," Lavinia said.

"How is he?"

Her snort of laughter lifted my heart. "Almost back to normal. Cursin' and carrying on, just making everyone's life miserable." She paused. "They'll be glad to get rid of him."

It took me a moment to decode her meaning. "They're sending him home? When?"

"As soon as we can get him packed up and loaded in the van." Lavinia sounded almost giddy with relief.

"What's the prognosis? About the blockage, I mean?"

The silence lengthened, and I knew the news wasn't all good. "They're going to try some medication, see if that helps. Dr. Utley wasn't too happy, but your father wasn't gonna be budged on it. So he has a pas-sel of prescriptions we have to get filled, and he's been ordered to stay in bed for at least a week. Harley Coffin will check on him every day."

"That's great news." I felt myself smiling. "I'll be right over and help you get him home."

"No need, child. The ladies from the church are here. They'll give me a hand. It'll take us a while to get all the paperwork done, and he'll probably sleep most of the rest of the day. Why don't you stop by for supper? I could probably use your help then."

"You're sure?"

"Positive. He was askin' about you earlier. I'll tell him you'll be there tonight."

"Okay. See you then."

I hung up and dropped my head into my hands. The sense of relief was almost as emotionally overpowering as the fear had been, and it was a few moments before I could breathe normally again. Maybe Lavinia's and Dolores's prayers hadn't been entirely in vain.

I glanced back at the computer screen and checked the clock in the lower right-hand corner: 10:43. I had several hours before I needed to be at Presqu'isle, plenty of time to check out why Maeline Hatcher's phone was out of order. I closed Google, and a sudden thought struck. Perhaps fate had given me a chance to kill the proverbial two birds with one stone: The road out to Edisto Island lay not far beyond the little town of Jacksonboro. Maybe, if I had time . . . Outside, I heard the familiar whine of Dolores's old car.

No! Somehow, I had to put aside the mystery of my sister and the strange newspaper article tucked into Lavinia's keepsake box. Kimmie Eastman deserved all my attention, I told myself firmly as I signed off and went to help my friend carry in the groceries. I kept the teenager's face firmly fixed in the front of my mind as I helped Dolores restock the pantry. Twenty minutes later, I'd changed into comfortable slacks and a sweater, pulled a bottle of water from the refrigerator, and tucked a couple of granola bars into my bag on my way out the door.

If the gods smiled, I might have a compatible bone marrow donor for Kimmie nailed down by sunset.

Traffic on Route 17 came to a complete standstill as a massive front-end loader lumbered across the highway several cars ahead of me. The widening project had been going on forever, it seemed, and I'd forgotten how snarled things could get. I drummed my fingers on the steering wheel, my mind floating to my father and the doctor's decision to let him go home. From there it was a short mental leap to his obituary—the necessity for which was now indefinitely postponed, thank God—and then a quick jump to Julia Simpson.

I'd never had even the slightest clue such a person existed. It still didn't seem real to me. How could he have kept such a secret all these years? *Who* was she? *Where* was she? Maybe I should just ask him. The envelope holding the obituary hadn't been sealed. Maybe he *wanted* me to find it. I thought about that for a few moments. He hadn't given a residence for Julia in the almost terse summation of his life he'd prepared for the newspaper. Had that been intentional? Or maybe he didn't know. What if all this had been orchestrated? What if he'd sent me to find the power of attorney knowing full well my curiosity would get the better of me?

I jerked back to reality when a horn sounded behind me, and I realized traffic had begun to move again.

What if he didn't know where she was, and this had been his way of sending me off to find her? *"Get Julia,"* he'd mumbled from his hospital bed. *Don't be ridiculous,* I told myself. He'd been in and out of consciousness, the flow of oxygen to his brain interrupted, or so the doctors claimed. He wouldn't have been able to formulate something so devious in his condition.

Would he?

CHAPTER EIGHT

IT WAS ALMOST ONE O'CLOCK WHEN I SLOWED FOR the wide curve and drifted into Jacksonboro. I scanned the small businesses on both sides of the road, finally coasting into the gravel parking lot of a small restaurant with a couple of pickup trucks parked out front. The Jaguar looked decidedly out of place as I cut the engine and worked out the cramp in my thigh.

Outside, the air felt considerably cooler than it had when I'd left Hilton Head, a hint of rain in the dark bank of clouds gathering out across the ocean. Bells jangled when I pulled open the door, and two men in almost identical jeans and sweatshirts turned to register my entrance before turning back to their interrupted conversation.

"Sit anywhere you like," a disembodied woman's voice called from the direction of the kitchen. "Be with you in a sec."

I sat down at one of several empty tables and dropped my bag onto an adjacent chair. The waitress appeared, plastic-coated menu in hand, and set a glass of water down on the Formica tabletop.

"Here you go, hon," she said. "Somethin' else to drink?"

"The water's fine." I accepted the single sheet of the diner's offerings and glanced over it quickly. "I'll have the chicken salad on white."

"Good choice. Just made it myself this mornin'. You want that bread toasted?"

I looked up into her lined face and smiled. "No thanks."

"Comin' right up."

I scanned the small room and located the restroom sign. The eyes of both my fellow customers followed my progress across the shiny linoleum.

Back at the table, I checked my cell phone for messages and pulled out the paper on which I'd jotted down Maeline Hatcher's particulars. I tried her number again with the same lack of success. I closed the phone and let my mind wander. The Judge should be home by now if the endless paperwork involved in breaking out of the hospital had been successfully negotiated. I pictured the smug face of the self-righteous Dr. Tom Utley, creased in anger or frustration that his patient had managed to escape his clutches. The mental image made me smile, and I decided to cut the good doctor some slack. The man was just doing his job. It had to be an occupational hazard of surgeons to believe that cutting open the human body was always the best solution to every medical problem. In fairness, the angioplasty wouldn't have been surgery in the true sense of the word. I even thought they might do it without general anesthesia, although—

"Here you go."

I looked up to find the tired eyes of the waitress and a heavy white china plate clutched in fingers curled a little with arthritis. I moved my elbows off the table.

"Thanks. It looks great."

"You need extra mayo or anything, just holler," she said, turning as the two men rose from their table. "See you boys tomorrow," she called and watched them climb into their respective trucks.

I swallowed a bite of the creamy chicken salad. "I wonder if you could help me," I said and saw a hint of wariness replace the fatigue on her face. "I'm looking for someone in this area. I have a general address, but I'm not from around here."

Her light snort of laughter sounded almost ladylike, and her gaze shot to my Jaguar S, now sitting alone in her parking lot. "I kinda guessed that," she said. "Charleston?"

I smiled. "No. Hilton Head. I'm trying to locate a Maeline Hatcher." I pulled the paper from the pocket of my slacks. "She lives on Holly Hill Road. I tried MapQuest, but it wasn't any help because I don't have a house number."

"Lots of Hatchers in this neck of the woods," she said and moved away toward the table the *boys* had vacated. Absently she began gathering up their dirty plates and silverware. "She black or white?"

I felt my shoulders stiffen, but I couldn't detect anything in the question except a request for information. "Black," I said. I munched a couple of potato chips and took another bite of my sandwich while I waited for a reaction.

"Holly Hill Road runs out toward Walterboro," she said. "Houses are pretty scattered. Bunch of Hatchers out there, both colors. I don't know any . . . what did you say the other name was? Marlene?"

"Maeline," I said and spelled it for her.

"Nope, sorry. Doesn't ring any bells."

I finished off the chicken salad and wiped my fingers on a paper napkin. "Can you point me in the right direction?" I asked.

"Sure thing. Just go back to the intersection, the way you came, and head toward Walterboro, then go about two miles or so. Holly Hill crosses the highway. Could be right or left, though. I can't help you with that."

"That's fine. I appreciate it."

The waitress deposited the pile of dishes on a counter and pulled a handwritten check from her pocket. She dropped it on the table in front of me and disappeared into the kitchen. While I'm usually a stickler for using the company credit card for tax purposes, I pulled a twenty from my wallet and left it next to my plate. I slipped my bag onto my shoulder and rose just as she reappeared from the kitchen.

"Thanks," I said. "The salad was delicious. And again, I appreciate your help."

She glanced at the bill on the table. "Let me get your change."

"No, that's okay." I turned toward the door but pivoted back around a moment later. "Have you lived here a long time?" I asked, and the woman's eyes once again glinted with wariness.

"A bit. Born here, but I went away for a while. Came back when my daddy passed, about ten years ago. Why?"

"I'm trying to find someone else, too," I said, not sure how to approach the subject. "Do you know of any Simpsons? Or Garretts? I think they used to live on Edisto."

She shook her head at the last word. "That's a long ways from here, honey. Different world. You want to know anything about Edisto, you best take a run out there. Edisto folk has always kept themselves to themselves."

"Well, thanks anyway." I felt her curious gaze on me as I stepped out into a cold wind and slid into the Jaguar.

I backed around and sat for a moment facing the highway. Right toward Edisto? *"Get Julia."* The Judge's mumbled words echoed inside my head. And then there was Brooke Garrett, drowned at the state park on the same island. A steady trickle of traffic passed in front of me, everyone crawling along at the posted speed limit. With a sigh, I waited for a gap and turned left, back the way I'd come. A couple of minutes later, I took the turn toward Walterboro.

My own personal ghosts would have to wait. Kimmie Eastman couldn't.

I found Holly Hill Road just where the waitress said it would be. I took a right down the narrow macadam road and began scanning for mailboxes. They were few and far between, and many of those I managed to spot had no names or numbers. Overhead, the sky had darkened, the heavy bank of clouds I'd noted out over the ocean now rolling rapidly onshore.

I slowed for a sharp curve to the left and suddenly found myself bumping past a NO OUTLET sign onto a twisting, potholed lane. The undercarriage of the Jaguar scraped against the uneven dirt, tufted here and there with wild grasses and weeds. A moment later I jerked to a stop at a huge piece of board nailed to the trunk of a beautiful live oak. Its message had been rendered in a shaky hand with a can of red spray paint. Some of the letters had run, but the sentiment came through loud and clear: KEEP OUT! PRIVATE PROPERTY! NO TRESPASSING! BEWARE DOGS!!!

All that was missing was barbed wire fence and a guard tower, I thought with a smile, but the mention of dogs sobered me. *Once bitten, twice shy*. The old adage made me shiver.

I glanced ahead, seeking a break in the stretch of trees that lined both sides of the lane for a place wide enough to turn around in. I inched forward and finally found a spot I thought might work. As I maneuvered the big car back and forth, I caught a glimpse of a patch of gray roof, the worn brick of two chimneys poking up above a flash of dingy white clapboard, just visible through the tall tree branches now whipping in the rising wind. Bouncing back out toward the paved road, I wondered if this old path, like the Avenue of Oaks leading to Presqu'isle, had once been the allée of a plantation house. There was nothing to distinguish it—no historical marker or discreet placard with a name like *Tombee* or *Pond Bluff* to lure antebellum house hunters to further investigation. Good thing, too, I thought, since the owners obviously didn't encourage drop-in visitors.

I had no choice but to retrace my route back toward the highway. At the intersection, I waited for traffic and pulled across onto the opposite end of Holly Hill Road. I brightened at the first mailbox, shining silver against the fading light as the storm neared the mainland. Here the houses were more visible and better maintained, many with neat lawns and children's plastic toys scattered in their driveways. In less than ten minutes I located a box with the name HATCHER in faded black letters.

I let the Jag's speed drop to barely above an idle as I studied the house. A one-story bungalow, its yellow paint had faded over the years in the harsh Lowcountry sunlight, but its green shutters looked fresh. No bikes or Big Wheels littered the yard, and there were no cars visible, either. As I cruised by, it seemed to me that the place had a desolate look, as if it might have been abandoned.

I pulled farther down the road and into one of the few paved driveways I'd encountered on Holly Hill just as a school bus lumbered into view, stopping at the house next door to the Hatchers'. I watched two children climb down to look both ways before skipping across the blacktop toward a newer ranch sitting close to the street. The older of the two kids, a boy who looked to be about ten or eleven, paused at the mailbox. When the bus moved away, I stopped out front and rolled down my window.

"Excuse me," I called, and the boy looked up. His light brown hair flopped down across his eyes, and he flicked it away with a practiced gesture. "I wonder if you can help me."

His eyes darted toward the house then back to me. "Is that a Jaguar?" he asked, his still-high voice crackling with wonder.

"It sure is. Do you like cars?"

"I build models," he said, "but Dad only likes to do old things. You know, like stuff from the sixties and seventies. How many horses does it have?"

I smiled back at his earnest expression. "I have no idea, but it's pretty powerful."

"I bet it'll do a hundred and sixty easy."

"I probably won't ever find that out," I said. "At least I hope not."

The boy clutched the two pieces of mail he'd removed from the box, checked both ways again, and scooted across the road.

"Wow! Real leather," he said, resting his hands on the open window. "I bet this thing cost at least a million dollars!"

I laughed and glanced up at the sound of a screen door slamming. The woman's voice sounded shrill in the quiet of the darkening afternoon.

"John Michael! Get away from there!"

The boy started guiltily and jumped back from the car. I shoved the gearshift into Park and cut the engine. I had no intention of scaring this mother into thinking I was about to abduct her child. As the boy moved away, I opened the door and stepped out.

"He was just admiring the car," I called and lifted both hands to show she had nothing to fear from me. "I was going to ask him about your neighbors, and we got sidetracked."

The woman moved out onto the concrete stoop and down the two steps into the yard. "Get in the house and get started on your homework," she said, her stance conveying that she still didn't entirely trust the stranger in her neighborhood. "Go on, git!"

The boy smiled and shrugged before scampering into the house.

"What business you got with the Hatchers?" the woman asked, her arms still folded protectively across her chest.

I took the few steps to the other side of the road and stopped at the mailbox. "I'm trying to locate a woman named Maeline Hatcher. Does she live next door?"

"Why? She in some kind of trouble?"

"No, ma'am. I'm a private investigator from Hilton Head. My client is trying to find her sister. They've become estranged over the years, and it's a matter of some urgency that I locate her. I'm hoping your neighbor can help me."

John Michael's mother stood her ground. "Is your client a . . . a person of color?"

"Yes, ma'am. Is Mrs. Hatcher?"

She nodded. "Not that it matters a whit to us. They're good neighbors. We look out for each other. What's this woman's name?"

I hesitated, then decided parting with a little information couldn't hurt. "It's Joline."

"Never heard her mention anyone by that name."

"What about Tessa?"

The woman shook her head. "Sorry."

"Will she be home soon do you think?"

She was shaking her head again before I finished my question. "They're gone. Left a couple of weeks ago. Jessie—that's Mae's husband—he took a new job over in Georgia. They've been tryin' to rent out the place." Her sigh said a lot about the relationship the two women had obviously enjoyed. "Sure hated to see them go. Never know what kind of folks you'll get with renters."

"Do you know how to contact Mrs. Hatcher? It's very important that I get in touch with her."

"They were gonna be stayin' in a motel until they found something. She said she'd send me her address when they got settled, but I haven't heard anything. You might check with the post office. They must be gettin' their mail forwarded because Henry doesn't stop there anymore."

"Thanks, I'll do that. I appreciate your help."

As I turned back toward the car, she called, "I hope the boy didn't bother you. About the car, I mean. All he thinks about these days. I wish he spent as much time worrying about his times tables."

I waved. "No trouble at all. He was delightful. Thanks again." A thought struck, and I whirled around. "Ma'am? I wonder if I could ask you one more thing."

"Sure."

"When I was looking for the Hatchers', I ran into a dead end on the other side of Holly Hill. It looked like it might have been an old plantation house. Do you know anything about it?"

I had no idea what had prompted the question. I supposed the crude sign and that tantalizing glimpse of the chimneys had piqued my always lively curiosity.

"The old McDowell place?" It might have been my imagination that she shivered in the brisk wind rising ahead of the approaching storm. "Used to be a rice plantation back before the War. Nobody much goes out there except for Duke Brawley when he delivers their groceries. Two women live there. Lots of gossip, but I don't hold with that. Some folks say one of them's a nurse and the other's not quite right." She touched a finger to her forehead. "Anyway, not the sociable kind, if you catch my meaning."

I smiled. "I gathered that from the sign. Well, thanks again." I reached through the open window of the Jaguar and pulled a business card from my bag. "If you hear from Mrs. Hatcher, would you ask her to be in touch with me?"

I crossed back over and handed her the card.

"Sure."

I waved and climbed into the car. By the time I'd pulled away, the woman had retreated back into her tidy ranch. I checked my watch and figured I had enough time to make the post office before it closed. I turned back toward Jacksonboro, wondering about the old plantation house and its strange occupants. It almost sounded like something out of one of the gothic romances I'd devoured in my middle school years, the ones I'd had to hide from my mother, who believed the only writers worth reading were Eudora Welty and William Faulkner.

A crazy woman and her nurse who had barricaded themselves inside a decaying mansion on the edge of nowhere, protected by a pack of dogs.

I would have loved that book.

CHAPTER
NINE

IT DIDN'T SHOCK ME THAT THE POST OFFICE WOULDN'T give me Maeline and Jessie Hatcher's forwarding address, but it was extremely frustrating. At the suggestion of the lone postal employee behind the tiny counter, I ripped a page from my notebook, included my card with a brief explanation, and bought an envelope that I addressed to the house on Holly Hill Road. For an additional charge, I requested a change-of-address notification, which I wouldn't get back until an attempt had been made to deliver the letter. Crazy, I thought. God forbid the government should give me for free something they could charge an extra buck for. And force me to wait three or four days before I received it.

The storm broke just as I crossed the wide expanse of marsh that separated Beaufort County from its neighbor. The driving rain turned the wide swath of dirt, graded and smoothed into the roadbed for the two new lanes, into a river of mud that cascaded across the road, slowing the already bumper-to-bumper traffic to a tortoiselike crawl.

I violated one of my own unwritten rules and pulled my cell phone from my bag. I justified it by telling myself this creeping along at fifteen miles an hour couldn't actually be classified as driving. Lavinia picked up almost immediately.

"Hey, it's me. How's the Judge doing?"

"He's all settled in and about to drive me out of what little mind I've got left," she grumbled, but I could hear the suppressed delight in her voice. My father being ornery and demanding meant things were returning to normal.

Though we'd switched over to Daylight Savings Time in the middle of the month, the storm had brought on a heavy twilight, and all the cars had their lights turned on. The clock on the dash read 4:47.

"I'm heading your way, but the traffic's a bi—a bear," I amended quickly. "It may be going on six by the time I get there."

"Perfect," Lavinia said. "I've got a roasting chicken in the oven."

My meager lunch seemed like a distant memory. "Sounds great. I can help you feed Daddy."

"Not likely. He insists he's comin' to the table just like always. We may have to strap him into that bed."

I laughed. "Between the two of us we'll knock some sense into him. I'll see you when I get there."

As cars inched by me in the opposite lane, I found myself mesmerized by the passing headlights and the rhythmic sweep of my wipers across the windshield. In spite of my concern for Joline Eastman and her desperately ill daughter, I found my mind shifting again to my own mystery.

The minute I'd heard the Judge had been released from the hospital, I'd determined to confront him about Julia Simpson. How could he have allowed me to spend a lonely childhood, isolated in that old mansion with a ranting, alcoholic mother, when all the time I'd had a sister? Where was she? How could my father have kept something like that from us? Or did Emmaline Baynard Simpson—aristocratic Daughter of the Confederacy, leader of local society, and arbiter of all things Southern and genteel—

Had she known? The idea struck me with the force of a physical blow. There had always been secrets at Presqu'isle. Even as a child I'd been aware of a current running just below the surface. Later, I'd put it down to my mother's closet drinking. And perhaps the Judge's shame. In my twenties, I'd done some reading about children of alcoholics, about the personality traits so many of us carried into adulthood. I'd made a conscious effort to overcome them, determined not to let my mother's weakness influence the rest of my life.

I'd be damned if I'd become a syndrome.

A scene flashed into my head, a confrontation between my father and me on the back verandah of Presqu'isle the summer after Rob was murdered. I swallowed hard, remembering how I'd shouted at him that Emmaline's *secret* had been obvious to everyone, including all the kids at school, some of whom had taunted me unmercifully. If Lavinia hadn't interrupted, I would have asked him how he could have let her treat me as she did, why he didn't divorce her. It would have been the perfect time for him to come clean about his illegitimate daughter— my *sister,* for God's sake—but he'd stood mute.

The storm passed on and the long line of traffic began to break up just as I approached the turnoff for Beaufort. *Illegitimate.* The word had just materialized in my head. Did I know that for certain? Maybe my father had been married before. Was that possible? Why else would Julia have been given—or taken—his last name? No, it was more likely a fling, I told myself and tried to picture the kind of woman who might have attracted him. Someone soft and yielding, yet intelligent. A calm woman, so sure of herself and her worth that she could defer to the man she loved without losing her own identity. Attractive, but not flashy, who could run to the store without a full complement of makeup. Someone who laughed easily and often . . .

Enough speculating. I'd gauge the Judge's health and temperament when I got to the house. Maybe not tonight, but soon, I'd make him tell me the truth if I had to shake it out of him.

There'd been enough secrets in my life.

That plan fell apart the moment I pulled into the driveway in front of the massive antebellum mansion. A black Lincoln Town Car sat at the foot of the stairway, and the house blazed with light. I took the steps two at a time and raced down the hallway into the kitchen.

Dr. Harley Coffin sat in my place at the scarred oak table, a cup of coffee steaming in front of him.

"What's the matter?" I wheezed, my breath coming in labored gasps. My injured leg protested its abuse, and I dropped into the opposite chair. "Did he have a relapse?"

"Calm down, child." Lavinia turned from the stove. "He's fine."

"He's not fine, Lavinia, and you damn well know it." The doctor's gruff countenance dared her to contradict him.

"You know what I mean, Harley." She smiled. "Bay tends to dramatize things." She moved her head in my direction. "Dr. Coffin just stopped by to make sure your father was comfortable and had all his medications." She leaned over to pull open the oven door. "I'm trying to talk him into stayin' for dinner."

I drew a long calming breath and smiled at my father's old friend. "Sorry. I didn't expect you to be here. It scared me."

Harley Coffin patted my hand. "Tally's doin' all right, considering. But he's not the best patient. Damn fool thinks he knows better 'n I do about what's good for him. I'm counting on you and Lavinia to keep him calmed down. Rest and quiet is what he needs now." He paused to sip from his coffee cup. "I've already told him I'll have him sedated if he doesn't follow orders. Or drag him back to the hospital by the scruff of the neck if that's what it takes to make him behave himself."

I smiled and sank back into the chair. "We'll keep him on the straight and narrow. Can he get up for dinner?"

The doctor shook his head. "Prop him up in bed with a tray. At least for the next couple of days." His voice sobered, and the look he gave me knotted my stomach. "He's a very sick man, and he needs that angioplasty. I'm hopin' we'll be able to talk him into it now that he's back in the comfort of his own house. The two of you need to make him see reason."

I remembered Dolores's words and leaned forward. "But what if he's just tired? What if he doesn't want to be poked and prodded anymore?" I glanced at Lavinia's back. "What if he just wants to play out the hand?"

Harley smiled at my poker reference. "I know what you mean, Bay, and I'm not unsympathetic." He sighed. "I've felt that way myself, ever since Janie passed. Some days I don't know why I bother gettin' out of bed." He cleared his throat, and the pain of his wife's death more than ten years before deepened the lines in his wrinkled face. "But I figure God has His own plan, and medicine is part of it." He rose and reached for his bag. "And I believe that as long as He's still letting us draw breath, we need to do what we can to hold on to the life He's given us."

"Amen," Lavinia murmured from across the room.

It was a battle, but between the two of us we managed to keep my father in bed. We both knew he'd pitch a fit about eating off a tray, so I pushed the poker table up close enough for him to reach and set it with the everyday china and cutlery we used in the kitchen. He grumbled and spluttered, but it was hard to hold on to a bad mood with Lavinia's roast chicken, mashed potatoes, and creamed corn sending tantalizing aromas drifting through the house.

Over tea, I told him about the new case, Kimmie Eastman's battle with leukemia, and the slim leads we had toward finding a possible donor among her mother's scattered relatives. I kept close watch on him while I told the story, hoping for some glimmer of recognition, perhaps a start of guilt at the similarities to our own situation, but his face betrayed nothing. Perhaps he'd forgotten those mumbled words, "*Get Julia.*"

A few minutes later his eyes fluttered closed, and I tiptoed out with our cups and the teapot balanced precariously in my hands. I'd just made it safely to the kitchen and deposited my load on the counter when my cell phone jangled in my pocket. Lavinia looked up from the sink.

"Sorry," I said and stepped out into the hallway. I recognized my own home number on the readout, and my heart sank. *Red!*

"Hey," I said, forcing a brightness I didn't feel into my voice. "You're at the house."

"And you're not." Terse. Not quite angry, but working up to it.

"I know. I had to run up toward Charleston this afternoon, on the case, and I stopped at Presqu'isle on the way back. They've sprung the Judge."

"He's home?"

I welcomed the thaw in Red's voice. "He refused the angioplasty. Harley wants him to stay in bed, but you know Daddy. I thought Lavinia could use some help keeping him tied down."

I was babbling a little, mostly to cover my own chagrin. I'd been thoughtless in not keeping Red in the loop, and he had every right to be ticked off. Why my soon-to-be husband had completely slipped my mind was a question I'd leave for another day.

"Are you coming home anytime soon?" The edge hadn't entirely left his voice.

"I'm leaving in a few minutes. See you in about an hour."

"Drive safely," he said, as if I were a teenager who needed reminding. I hung up without replying.

Back in the kitchen, Lavinia had most of the dishes washed and stacked in the drainer. I picked up the towel and began drying.

"Just leave those, honey. Why don't you go in and keep your father occupied," she said. "I'll manage here."

I draped the towel over the edge of the counter and leaned against it. "Can I ask you something?"

Her gaze stayed fixed on the dwindling suds in the sink, but I could see her shoulders stiffen, almost as if she were anticipating the question.

"You really shouldn't leave the Judge alone too long. Harley says he shouldn't sleep so much, and he's got pills to take before he goes down for the night."

She spoke without looking at me, and her fear was almost a palpable presence in the gray light drifting in through the mullioned windows. The clouds had moved off, and it looked as if we'd have a sunset, but Lavinia's eyes seemed to be fixed on some point—or time—far distant from the warmth of Presqu'isle's kitchen.

I studied her, this deeply religious woman, one of the rare ones who actually lived her beliefs, and asked myself if I really wanted to force her to choose between telling me the truth and lying to protect the man she loved. Over the rattle of the dishes in the sink, I could almost hear the debate raging inside her head.

For a long moment, neither of us spoke, then I smiled and laid a hand gently on her shoulder.

"It'll keep," I said and slipped quietly from the room.

CHAPTER TEN

M Y PHONE RANG JUST AS I PULLED INTO THE driveway. I snugged the Jaguar in next to Red's Bronco and shut off the engine. I didn't recognize the caller ID. I glanced up to find Red standing in the doorway from the garage into the house, his face wrinkled in impatience. Out of nothing but sheer orneriness, I pushed the Talk button.

"Bay Tanner."

"Miz Tanner? This is Peggy Watts. We met this afternoon?"

My mind ran through the women I'd encountered: at the hospital, at the little diner in Jacksonboro, next door to the Hatchers' . . . That was it. I didn't think I'd gotten her name, but this had to be the boy's mother.

"Yes, ma'am. How are you?"

"Just fine. Listen, it's the strangest thing, but I heard from Mae tonight. Right after supper, and I said to Jimmy—that's my husband— I said how weird it was that you had just been here askin' about her, and there she was."

I sat up straighter and grabbed my bag off the seat. "That's terrific! Did you give her my message?"

"Yes, ma'am, I sure did, but she says she doesn't have a sister named Joline."

I dropped the pen and notepad I'd finally located back into my purse. "Oh." It was all I could manage to say around the crushing disappointment that stabbed my chest. I'd been so certain—

"But she did say that she knows of one other lady with her same first name."

I jerked upright. "Really?"

"Uh-huh. A person from her church had a cousin or somethin' like that. Said my Maeline was the only other one he'd ever heard tell of."

I jumped as Red suddenly appeared at the side of the car, his scowling face filling the driver's-side window. I held up a hand to keep him silent. "Do you have Mrs. Hatcher's contact information?"

I scrabbled once more for pen and paper and copied down the number Mrs. Watts rattled off.

"She and Jessie are in Pembroke. That's right by the big Army base. Jessie does somethin' with computers, and I guess his company sent him over there. Mae says they found a cute little place, and the kids'll be startin' school on Monday."

Red pulled open the door and leaned against it, his head ducked down so he could watch my face. I resented the hell out of his butting in on what was company business, which was definitely none of his, and I hoped my expression adequately conveyed my displeasure.

"Thank you so much, Mrs. Watts. This is very encouraging. I'm going to call Mrs. Hatcher as soon as we hang up."

"I'm glad I could be of help. By the way, my boy said to tell you he thinks your car is the coolest, and you should see how fast it'll really go some time."

I laughed. "I'll think about it. Give him my best. Thanks again, Mrs. Watts. You have no idea how important this information is."

"Happy to do it. You take care now."

"You, too," I said and disconnected.

Red stepped back as I swung my legs out, the notepad and my phone clutched in one hand.

"What was that all about?"

"Business." I climbed the steps and dropped my bag next to the console table in the foyer before continuing on into the great room. I kicked off my shoes and perched on the edge of the sofa.

"Bay, I need to talk to you."

"Later," I said, my fingers already punching in the numbers. "This is important."

"And I'm not?"

I held up my hand again, and this time he spun on his heel and stomped up into the kitchen.

She answered on the second ring.

"Mrs. Hatcher? This is Bay Tanner, calling from Hilton Head. I've just spoken with your old neighbor, Mrs. Watts."

"Of course. She said you're lookin' for someone with my first name. Sorry I can't be a lot of help. Peggy says it's important for you to find this person."

"I can't divulge the nature of my client's business, but I think it's fair to say that this is truly a matter of life and death. Can you give me some more information about this other Maeline?"

"No, ma'am, not directly. But you need to talk to Ellis Brawley in Jacksonboro. He's the one told me he had a second cousin or some such called Maeline."

The name rang a faint bell, but I couldn't pull it up from the back of my mind. I shook my head and glanced up at the sound of pots and pans being banged around in the kitchen. Red was definitely in a mood.

"And how can I get in touch with Mr. Brawley?"

"I don't have his number right off the top of my head, but he's in the book. He and his uncle run a little grocery store in town."

It hit me then, the reason the name had sounded familiar. Talking with Peggy Watts about the old mansion on the other end of Holly Hill Road. She'd said something about a Duke Brawley delivering groceries.

I hesitated before asking the next question, but it was a crucial one. "Is Mr. Brawley a man of color?"

Maeline Hatcher didn't miss a beat. "He sure is. He and his family have been around Jacksonboro for more 'n a hundred years, I'd guess."

"That's terrific. Thanks so much for your help."

"I don't suppose you can tell me any more about this client of yours. I have to admit you got my curiosity stirred up."

"No, ma'am, I'm afraid I can't. Maybe when it's all resolved I can let you know how important your information really was."

"I'd like that. Well, you have a good night."

"Thanks again," I said and hung up.

I itched to trot right in to my office and begin tracking down the Brawley family, but I knew I needed to smooth things over with Red. I slipped the phone into my pocket, let a long exhalation of breath calm me, and mounted the steps to the kitchen.

"What are you cooking?" I asked, and my voice sounded falsely cheerful even to my own ears.

"Eggs," he said without turning around. "I brought a couple of steaks home to grill, but I'm sure you've already eaten."

Uh-oh, I said to myself. I'd definitely screwed up this time. "I'm sorry I'm so late. I should have called."

"Yes, you should have."

I bit back the retort that sprang so easily into my mind and swallowed my aggravation at his tone. I'd gotten out of the habit of being answerable to someone—*anyone*—for where I went and what I did. I needed to work on that. I didn't want to fight, but I'd be damned if I'd grovel. I clamped my lips shut and pulled the toaster from the cupboard, then carried a plate and cutlery to the small table set in the bay window of the kitchen. We worked in silent unison until Red slid the eggs onto his plate. I placed the toast alongside them and sat down across from him.

"The Judge looks better," I said. "Harley wants him to stay in bed for a few days, but his color's improved, and he's cranky as ever. I stayed to help Lavinia get dinner into him." It was as close to an apology as I was prepared to offer.

The scowl on Red's face relaxed, although he couldn't yet bring himself to smile. "That's good. I bet he drove them crazy in the hospital."

"No doubt. You said you needed to talk to me. What's up?"

Red scraped up the last of his eggs and leaned back in the chair. "I'm going to quit the department." He said it softly, almost as if he were talking to himself. "I've made up my mind."

I knew he'd been turning the idea over for quite a while, but the finality of his decision surprised me. "Are you sure that's what you want to do?"

"Why? You think it's a bad move? I'm not going to live off you, Bay, if that's what's worrying you. I'll get another job."

The barely concealed venom in his voice shocked me. "Where the hell did *that* come from?"

"If we're getting married, I expect to support you. And my kids."

The *if* sent my stomach plummeting to my feet. "Red, let's both calm down a little, okay? I know you're angry that I didn't call, but you should be used to that by now. When I get embroiled in a case, I sometimes forget to eat."

My conciliatory tone eased some of the tension from his shoulders. "I wanted us to have a nice dinner and talk this over," he said. "I know it's a big step, and you should have some input."

I covered my confusion by carrying the used dishes to the sink. Over my shoulder, I said, "It's entirely up to you. I just want you to be happy."

I jumped as his arms encircled my waist, and I felt his warm breath against my hair. "I'm sorry. I worry when I don't know for sure that you're okay. So many bad things have happened lately."

I turned and leaned back so I could look into his eyes. "I know. I'll try to do better."

I finished loading the dishwasher, and we walked hand in hand down into the great room. Red flopped on the sofa and pulled me down beside him. Tucked into the curve of his arm, all my aggravation and indecision evaporated. We sat quietly, the open French doors letting the cool night air drift around us. An owl hooted somewhere off in the distance, and out on the ocean the deep horn of some passing vessel sounded its mournful note. I snuggled down closer and pulled the afghan over my legs.

"So what are you going to do?" I asked.

For a long moment, Red didn't reply. I glanced up to see if he had dozed off. His crazy hours, split shifts, and the constant exposure to crime and its miseries over the years had taken a toll. I suddenly found myself completely at peace with his decision.

"Want another partner in the inquiry agency? I have some pretty good experience in investigating."

My head snapped up, and I pulled away to look directly at him.

"Just kidding," he said, but the smile didn't reach his eyes. They held a wary, questioning look I couldn't quite interpret. "Actually, I have a line on a business venture I'm pretty excited about. An old buddy of mine from the Marines."

"What kind of business?"

"Charter boats. Fishing. He operates out of Broad Creek Marina. It's seasonal, mostly during the summer tourist months, but he makes enough to tide him over through the winter. He's looking to expand, and he needs someone he can trust to run the other boat he's buying."

I ordered myself to keep my voice neutral. "You know anything about running a charter service? I mean, you and Rob didn't grow up on the water. I don't remember either one of you being into fishing and all that."

I hadn't thought how mentioning my dead husband—Red's brother—would affect him, but I could tell from the stiffening of his arms around me that I'd put my foot in it again.

"I know it's not as glamorous as being a hot-shot lawyer for the attorney general's office, but I've never been cut out for the suit-and-tie routine."

I sighed audibly. "I know that, Red. I wasn't suggesting you work in an office. I'm just saying that I ran into a lot of clients back in my CPA days who got involved with business ventures they didn't know a whole lot about. Too often they ended up losing their shirts. I'm just asking."

I could feel him pulling away, emotionally as well as physically. "I have some money saved. I'm not asking you for a loan." Suddenly he stood and stared down at me. "And I'm not asking for permission. I just hoped you'd be a little more supportive."

"God damn it, Red! Why are you so determined to pick a fight? I said I didn't care what you did, and I meant it. I didn't agree to marry you so you could take care of me in my old age. I'm perfectly capable of looking out for myself."

I gazed up into his angry face, and we stared at each other for what seemed like an age.

"I know. And that's the trouble," he said softly and turned away.

A few moments later, I heard the roar of the Bronco's engine receding down the drive.

CHAPTER
ELEVEN

NEXT MORNING I SLIPPED MY KEY INTO THE LOCK of the office door a couple of minutes before nine and dragged myself inside. I hadn't slept for longer than a few minutes at a time, and I felt as if someone had taken a baseball bat to my head.

In my office, I draped my blazer over the back of the chair and popped the lid on my first Diet Coke of the day. The rush of caffeine made me dizzy, and I dropped into the chair. A moment later, Erik opened the door, stopping in mid-stride to stare in my direction.

"Jeez, Bay, what happened? Is the Judge worse?" He crossed the Berber carpet and stood hovering in front of my desk. "You don't look so hot."

I managed a smile. "Thanks, pal. No, the Judge is home and doing better. I didn't sleep well last night. In fact, I didn't sleep at all. No big deal."

If he was dissatisfied with my evasion, he let it go. "I hate when that happens. Makes you feel like you're in a fog for the rest of the day."

"Well, I need to get it together. I went up to Jacksonboro yesterday, but the Hatchers had moved. I recruited a neighbor who put me in touch. Unfortunately this isn't the right Maeline, but she knew someone who knows another woman with the same first name. I'm going to reach him this morning and see if he can put us on the trail again."

"Sorry that didn't pan out. I guess it was too much to hope for that we'd hit pay dirt on the first try." He turned then and retreated to his own desk. "I'll check messages."

I pulled the aspirin bottle from my bottom drawer and downed two with a long swallow of Coke. I'd either lose the pounding headache or end up facedown on my desk. At that point, either option would have been an improvement. I took my notebook from my bag and signed on to my computer.

After Red stormed out the night before, I hadn't had the heart to pursue the lead Maeline Hatcher had given me. I paced the great room for hours, alternately fuming and weeping, though whether from frustration, anger, or sadness I couldn't have said. As the clock on the mantel ticked off the long minutes, and midnight, then one o'clock came and went, my thoughts veered wildly, my always overactive imagination conjuring a dozen scenarios of where my life might be headed. At one point, I found myself kneeling on the floor of my bedroom closet, the door to the safe gaping open. The ring I had been so reluctant to retrieve slipped easily over my injured finger, the small square-cut diamond glittering in the overhead light. I sat there for a long time staring at my hand, the clothes hanging from the rods providing a comforting cocoon. I even dozed off for a couple of minutes, some noise outside jerking me awake, my heartbeat accelerating in anticipation of familiar footsteps that never came. . . .

I realized I had been staring unseeing at the computer screen and jerked myself back from the pointless remembering. I jabbed at the keys. Switchboard.com yielded up a home number in a matter of seconds. I also took down the one for the store, conveniently named for its owners. No one answered at Ellis's house, so I tried the listing for Brawley's Stop 'n Save.

"Brawley's. This is Duke." The voice was soft, with a slight hint of the native Gullah of the Sea Islands.

"Good morning, sir. My name is Bay Tanner. I'm a private investigator calling from Hilton Head. May I speak to Ellis Brawley?"

"He's out right at this moment. Private investigator, you say? The boy in some kind of trouble?"

"No, sir," I rushed to assure him. "Maeline Hatcher, who used to live in Jacksonboro, thought he might be able to help me. I'm trying to locate his cousin who I understand is also called Maeline. Do you know her as well?"

The silence lasted a couple of beats. "Heard the name, I believe. She the one in trouble?"

"No, sir." I gave him the same limited information I'd communicated to both Maeline Hatcher and Peggy Watts. "The unusual name is almost all we have to go on, and it's vital that we contact my client's sister as soon as possible."

Again I waited while Duke Brawley digested what I'd said.

"I don't know. I mean, I'm sure you're exactly who you say you are and all, and I guess it can't hurt nothin', but I'm a mite leery about it, I don't mind telling you."

"I perfectly understand, sir. What can I do to assure you that I mean your nephew no harm and that your cooperating with me will cause no trouble to your family?"

"Let me think on it. You got a office number?"

I gave it to him and reiterated how important it was that this be resolved quickly. He promised to get back to me before the day was out.

"Anything?" Erik called from the outer office.

"He's going to call us back. But he didn't react at all to Joline's name. You'd think if this other woman was family, he'd know if she had sisters."

"Maybe not. She could be related by marriage. I don't think it's totally out of the realm of possibility that he doesn't know any more."

"Well, there's nothing to do now but wait. Any messages?"

"Mrs. Eastman called and asked for a report."

"Let's hold off on that until Duke or Ellis Brawley calls back. Maybe we'll have some good news for her."

"I can't imagine what it must be like to know that your kid is going to die and there's not a damn thing you can do about it."

My mind flashed to the Judge—and Harley Coffin's warnings. I shook my head. "Anything else?"

"Red left kind of a strange message," he said, glancing down to the pad on his desk, completely oblivious to the effect of his words on my heart rate.

I bit down hard on my lower lip. "What did he say?"

"That he'd be by the house later to do some cleaning. Doesn't he trust Dolores to take care of that?"

I tried to match his mischievous grin and failed. I couldn't deal with explanations. "Private joke." I turned away to hide the tears that threatened to spill over. "I've got some personal calls to make. I'll just shut the door around."

In the emptiness of my office, I grabbed a handful of tissues and stuffed them against my mouth. My breath came in short, labored gasps, and my legs felt as if they wouldn't hold me. I slumped in the chair, Red's words echoing wildly through my head. He'd said just enough to convey his intent without embarrassing me in front of Erik. I supposed I had to thank him for that. But I perfectly understood his meaning: He'd be by the house later to do some cleaning . . . *out*.

It seemed as if another Tanner was about to abandon me, this one by choice.

CHAPTER TWELVE

I MANAGED TO KEEP HALF MY MIND OCCUPIED FOR most of the morning with the mundane routine of verifying the previous employment and educational credentials of applicants for county jobs. The turnover was incredible, much more frequent than I would ever have thought before Simpson & Tanner landed the government accounts. No wonder the bureaucracy worked so ponderously. The reason for many people's frustration in dealing with anyone official could be because half the folks they talked to were new on the job.

But the urgency of Kimmie Eastman's situation was never out of my thoughts, and I chafed at the wasted time. My eyes strayed continuously from the computer screen to the telephone, but Ellis Brawley didn't call.

By noon, the lack of sleep and Red's enigmatic but pointed message, plus my anxiety for my client's daughter, had my nerves stretched to breaking. I leaped from my rolling desk chair, sending it banging into the file cabinet on the back wall, and Erik's head snapped up. I whipped my blazer off the back of the chair and shoved my arms into the sleeves.

"What's the matter?" he asked in a calm voice.

"I've got the yips," I said, and his brow furrowed in confusion.

"What's the yips?"

I stuffed my notebook into my briefcase and snatched up my handbag. "You know, the willies, the heebie-jeebies. The fidgets," I added and surprised myself by smiling. "That's what Lavinia used to call it when I couldn't sit still. Which was most of the time, as I recall." I sobered. "I need to be moving. I think I'll run back up to Jacksonboro and talk to the Brawleys in person. Kimmie Eastman doesn't have time for us to sit on our butts and wait for things to happen."

"Okay. But before you head out, I just heard back from my buddy up in Charlotte. You know, the photography guy?"

It took a moment for my muddled mind to grasp it. "Right. About the old picture of Joline's family." I perched on the corner of Erik's desk. "He find something?"

"Not exactly. He's positive one of the words on the back is Charleston, so he checked with some of the old-timers he corresponds with. One of them's a retired professional photographer, lives here on the island, in fact. This man says he remembers hearing about a firm back in the twenties. The guy who owned it was old even then, but he was the only black photographer in the state, far as he knew. Ron thinks we might want to talk to his friend, especially since he's right in our backyard."

"It's worth a shot. Got an address?"

Erik handed me a slip of paper.

"Jonathon Morley," I read aloud. I lifted my head and stared at my partner. "He lives at The Cedars."

"I know. Maybe you could drop in on Miss Addie while you're over there."

Adelaide Boyce Hammond had been a bosom friend of my late mother. The families had been intertwined through proximity and social status for more than a century. We'd bonded a few years before when a shady land deal in which she'd invested the remainder of her family's considerable fortune had led me to my second confrontation with violent death. Maybe she would know something about the mysterious Julia Simpson. Why hadn't I thought of her before?

I whirled back around, dropped my briefcase and bag back on my desk, and picked up the phone. Mr. Morley answered on the second ring.

"Good morning, sir. My name is Bay Tanner, and I'm a private investigator here on the island. I'm trying to locate family members for one of our clients, and your name came up in the course of our inquiries. You used to be a photographer in Charleston, is that correct?"

His voice held the soft drawl of a native and lifelong South Carolinian. "Is this concerning the picture Ron Balczer e-mailed me about?"

"Yes, sir. I have the original, and I wondered if I might stop by and show it to you."

"Don't know how I can help, but I'd welcome the company. You know where I'm located?"

"I sure do. I have a friend who lives in the main building. Adelaide Hammond."

"Of course! We've met a couple of times at the socials and whatnot. Lovely woman."

His approval of Miss Addie raised him a few more points in my eyes. "Yes, she is. What's a good time for you?"

"Right now would be fine, if you're free. I'm just finishing up lunch."

"Give me ten minutes," I said and hung up.

I told Erik to forward any calls from the Brawleys to my cell phone and headed for the car.

I felt a small twinge of guilt as I accepted the pass from the security gate guard and rolled into the upscale retirement complex which boasted a skilled nursing facility as well as single-family homes tucked into stands of oaks and pines. The main building housed condominium units like Miss Addie's along with a restaurant and clubhouse for residents. It had been a long time since I'd been to visit. Way too long. Like my father, Adelaide Boyce Hammond didn't have that many years left.

I parked alongside the building and took the elevator. The door opened almost before my finger had left the bell.

"Mrs. Tanner? Hey! Come on in." Jonathon Morley held the door as I slipped by, then closed it quietly behind us. I turned to find his age-spotted hand extended. "Welcome."

He was short, almost wizened, his back bent a little with age, but I didn't think he'd been much above five-five or -six in his prime. Most of his hair was gone except for a thin band of white resting on his ears. His smile was wide and pixyish, his eyes a clear but faded blue, and I towered over him.

"Bay Tanner," I said, gripping his hand.

"Come in, come in. Have a seat. Can I get you anything? A sweet tea maybe?"

"Thank you. That would be great."

I set my briefcase and handbag next to the bright green sofa and looked around the sparsely decorated living area while my host disappeared into the kitchen. Unlike Miss Addie's place, which contained almost every heirloom piece of furniture, art, and bric-a-brac her family had ever owned, Jonathon Morley's taste obviously ran to the spare and modern. Instead of heavy oils in ponderous gilt frames, his photographs—mostly black-and-white landscapes, and mostly framed and matted in those same two stark colors—were artfully arranged in groupings on the larger walls.

In a moment he was back, bearing a small tray with two tall, frosted glasses. He handed one to me and settled into a low chair opposite. We chatted about the weather for a few moments before he said, "I'd like to get a look at that photograph Ron was telling me about, if you don't mind. I have to say it piqued my interest a bit."

"Of course." I pulled the yellowing picture from my briefcase and handed it over.

Jonathon Morley ran his arthritic fingers lightly over the surface and tilted it to several different angles, letting the sunlight wash over the faded image. I sipped on my tea and waited.

A few moments later, he said, "Silas Barnfeather. I'd bet anything on it."

"That was the photographer?"

He nodded. "Only colored fella takin' pictures back then, if this date in the corner is accurate. Sad to say there probably weren't any white ones who would have bothered with a Negro family, no matter how prominent they'd become. Ron said your partner told him you thought this store in the background might have belonged to them."

"Mitchell Brothers," I said. "Ron brought out the letters there on the building. Not all of them, but enough so I can be pretty certain that's what it says."

Jonathon turned toward me, his face grave. "He also said it was a matter of life and death. Was the boy exaggerating?"

"No, I'm afraid not. And I'm also afraid I can't give you any details. Client confidentiality. But someone's life definitely depends on tracking down what's left of the Mitchells. Do you think any of Mr. Barnfeather's family would still be around Charleston? Would anyone likely have his records from that far back?"

He was shaking his head before I finished my questions. "If I'm right about it being Silas's work, his place burned to the ground back in the late twenties." He shifted uncomfortably in his seat. "Story around Charleston is that it was the chemicals he kept stored there, but somethin' had to set them off. Sad to say there was a lot of that back in the day. Negro store owners getting burned out or beaten up. Silas moved away right after, or so I've heard tell."

So, a dead end, I thought. Kimmie Eastman couldn't afford too many of those.

"Well, thank you for your help. You've saved me from trying to track on a cold trail."

He looked at me strangely. " 'Track on a cold trail'? Don't tell me you're a hunter?"

I laughed. "No, but my father used to let me tag along on some of his expeditions. Out on the islands. St. Helena, Fripp, Hunting. Before they all got developed, of course."

"I used to scare up a quail or two myself," he said, rising with me. "Haven't been out in decades."

"Me, either." I turned at the door and held out my hand. "Thank you so much for the information. And for the tea."

His faded eyes looked somber. "Not much help, I'm afraid. I hope you have better luck."

I couldn't argue with that. I smiled and stepped out into the hallway as he closed the door behind me.

I rang Miss Addie's bell and knocked loudly a couple of times, but she was obviously out. I checked my watch. At a little after one, she might still be at lunch. I took the stairs and emerged into bright sunshine. By the time I'd walked a few steps, I was peeling off my jacket and tossing it over my arm. I had just reached for the handle of the door into the main part of the building when it suddenly swung open, forcing me to jump back.

"Lydia! You scared the life out of me, child! What are you doin' here?"

Adelaide Boyce Hammond, her eyes bright behind rimless spectacles, gazed up at me. Beside her, another elderly woman stood back a couple of paces.

"I had to be here on business, and I decided to track you down."

"Evelyn and I——" She turned and gently urged her companion up beside her. "Evelyn, this is Lydia Tanner. I mean, Bay. Child doesn't particularly like her given name, though I've never understood why. Lydia, this is Evelyn Kellerman. She's just moved in, and I've taken the liberty of makin' her feel to home."

The woman was taller than Miss Addie, and her hair was a bright red that God never intended, but her smile was sweet. "And just about saved my life, I don't mind telling you," she said. "I was about to die of boredom. Nice to meet you."

"You, too." I fumbled a little, unsure now that the moment was upon me whether or not to approach Miss Addie about my mystery sister. I certainly didn't want to broach the subject in the company of a stranger.

"Well, I've got a bridge game to get to," Evelyn said, unwittingly solving my problem. "Talk to you later, Adelaide. Nice to meet you," she said again.

She turned and walked off toward the parking lot, her gait stiff as if arthritis might have invaded her hips or knees.

"What kind of business brings you here?" Miss Addie said. "Or shouldn't I ask?"

I linked my arm with hers as we moved around to the side entrance. "It's a case. Someone in your building I needed to talk to. Jonathon Morley. He says you two have met a couple of times."

"Of course. He lost his wife, you know. Very sad."

I held the door for her and punched the elevator button. "Can I talk to you for a minute?"

"Of course, child," she said as we stepped into the tiny cubicle. "I'm always happy to see you, you know that."

Inside her apartment, I perched on the edge of an ancient wing chair. "It's about my family, something I found out about just a couple of days ago. You know the Judge has been in the hospital?"

"Cissy Ransome mentioned it. I was going to get someone to carry me over there, but then he's already gone home, isn't that right?"

"Yes."

"Is it serious?"

"They think they can correct it with medication. But I had to go through some of his papers, and I found his obituary. He'd written it out himself. For when . . ."

Miss Addie nodded. "I've done the same. I don't have much of anybody left who knows enough about me to write it."

Since she had never married—some disappointment in her youth, at least according to local legend—Miss Addie's family had been reduced to an ailing sister and some nieces and nephews widely scattered across the country. And of course, her brother Win, but we didn't talk about him.

I hesitated, and the look on my face must have forewarned her.

"I've never been a party to gossip, Lydia, and I won't start now. Not even for you."

The sharpness of her words stung. We stared at each other, this tiny, soft-spoken woman and I, and I was the first to look away.

"It's important to me," I said evenly. "Did you know about—?"

Her upraised hand, shaking a little, stopped me. "No. Please, Lydia." Miss Addie used the arms of her own chair to push herself to her feet. "Your mother was one of my dearest friends, in spite of her troubles. She trusted me. And so does Tally. If you have questions to be answered about the family, you should talk to him."

I rose and looked down on her soft white curls. Her slim shoulders were set, and her chin had risen as if in challenge. I smiled and admitted defeat.

"I understand, Miss Addie. Thanks anyway."

At the door, she reached for my hand. "You're not angry with me?"

"No, ma'am," I said, meaning it. "It'll be okay."

"Remember there are others who don't share my scruples," she called after me as I moved toward the elevator. "Don't you go believin' everything you hear. Your father and mother are honorable people. Don't you for a minute think otherwise."

As the doors slid closed, I could see her still standing in the open doorway, a look of sadness clouding her usually bright eyes.

And her strange words ringing in my ears.

CHAPTER THIRTEEN

I SAT FOR A WHILE IN THE CAR, THE WINDOWS DOWN to let in the soft breezes that drifted in over the marsh, and thought about what Miss Addie had said.

She knew. Or she had an inkling about what I'd intended to ask her. She was still sharp, and my reference to the Judge's obituary had given her the clue. Survivors were always listed; and, if she was privy to the existence of my sister, she would know that's what I'd found. I twisted in the seat, wildly craving a cigarette, settling finally for a fuzzy peppermint I managed to excavate from the bottom of my bag.

Her reference to my parents' *honor* had been another telling remark. Julia Simpson must be illegitimate, in spite of her having taken our last name. What else could be dishonorable about the situation? I wondered who she thought might be willing to spread malicious gossip about my family, those people she'd urged me not to believe.

An image popped into my head: Loretta Healey, daughter of one of my late mother's close friends. A former immigration attorney and current consultant to Homeland Security, she'd dropped suddenly back into my life just before Christmas. The memory sent my hand massaging my injured right thigh. "Aunt" Loretta had been scathing in her recollections of growing up in the Lowcountry, her Paris clothes,

French cigarettes, and cosmopolitan manners almost defiant of her upbringing. She'd barely concealed her contempt for all of us. If Loretta
knew something that would reflect badly on us, she'd be thrilled to be
able to share it.

I started the car and backed out onto the driveway. I had her card
at the office. I'd give Loretta Healey a chance to spill her guts.

I opened the door to the office and found Erik on the phone.

"One second, sir. She just walked in." He held the receiver against
his chest. "It's Duke Brawley. From Jacksonboro."

"Thanks." I crossed the room and picked up my own handset.
"Bay Tanner, Mr. Brawley. I appreciate your calling me back."

"Not a problem, ma'am. As I was tellin' your young man there, I
talked to Ellis when he came in. He said he doesn't want to get involved."

I bit my tongue and drew a calming breath. "I guess I can understand that, sir, but this really is a matter of life and death. All we want
to do is put our client in touch with her sister. If that's in fact who this
Maeline is. I can promise you that no one intends her any harm." I
forced myself to speak calmly. "Sir, all I need is a last name. I can't
stress enough how important this is."

The silence stretched out on his end. I waited. Sometimes that
worked better than filling a void with words. Gave the other person a
chance to think.

"I just don't feel right about it, especially if Ellis is dead set
against it. Don't see the problem myself, but it's on his mama's side,
and they're no real kin to me. Married my brother Carl, and Ellis is
their boy. I'm real sorry."

Before I could launch another plea, he hung up.

"Damn it!" I yelled, and Erik appeared in the doorway.

"No go?"

"I swear I don't know what's gotten into people these days. Used to

be everyone was willing to help each other out. Now it's 'I don't want
to get involved' everywhere you turn." *Even Miss Addie,* I thought as I
sat down hard in my desk chair.

"Did you get anything I can use? We've got all those databases at
our disposal."

I ran my hand through my hair and let my breath out slowly.
"Maybe. We've got Carl Brawley. It's his wife who's related to Maeline
number two. Ellis is their son. Maybe you could find a marriage license or something, get her maiden name."

"It's a start," Erik said, turning back toward his computer. "Let me
have a run at it." He paused. "How'd it go with the photographer?"

It took me a moment. "Jonathon Morley. No, that's another dead
end." I gave him the gist of my conversation with the charming older
man. "You could try checking out this Silas Barnfeather, but I don't
hold out much hope. How about the other sister, Tessa? Any luck with
her?"

He shook his head. "It's too common a name, and it could be short
for something else. I came up with about fifty hits just in South Carolina, and there's no guarantee either of the sisters is still in the state.
But if we have to, we can start working those."

If we have to, I thought. Even though we didn't have many choices
left, I reminded myself that Kimmie Eastman didn't have any.

I listened for a while to the sound of Erik's fingers flying over his keyboard, my thoughts a jumble of Red, Miss Addie, Julia Simpson, and
the Eastmans. I felt confused and frightened—by a lot of things, not
the least of which was being unable to find a donor for Kimmie before
it was too late. I pulled a legal pad from the drawer and popped the
tab on a Diet Coke. Time for a list.

I ended up creating three: one for Julia Simpson, another for the
mysterious Brooke Garrett, whose drowning had somehow affected
Lavinia, and most important for Kimmie Eastman. The "what we know"
column was distressingly short all the way around, the bulk of my notes

filling up the section for unanswered questions. I could feel the first bite of panic gnawing at the middle of my chest.

I pulled my Rolodex toward me and fished out Loretta Healey's card. Maybe I could resolve one of the mysteries quickly. Before I could think better of it, I picked up the phone and tapped in her cell number. I didn't expect her to answer, especially since she probably wouldn't recognize my number on her screen. I waited for voice mail and left a message for her to call me at her convenience. I had to force myself to sound nonchalant. I didn't want to give her any hint of how important the call was to me. I planned an ambush when I finally got her on the phone, and I didn't want her to have a chance to prepare for it.

I logged on to the Social Security Death Index, a free service on the Web, and typed in "Brooke Garrett." The combination of names gave me ninety-seven hits, and I scrolled down through about half of them, looking for South Carolina as the last place of residence, before I found a match. The date of death corresponded to the newspaper article, and her year of birth worked out right. I could apply for her SS-5 letter which, for twenty-nine dollars, would get me a copy of her Social Security application, but I wasn't sure how that would help.

Help what? I asked myself and failed to arrive at any satisfactory answer. Why was I wasting time barking up this particular tree? I smiled at the hunting metaphor, no doubt triggered by my conversation with Jonathon Morley. I forced myself to look at it dispassionately and realized the name itself had been the impetus. Brooke Garrett. It sounded like a white name, almost aristocratic, conjuring up images of a preppy woman in Bass Weejuns and perfectly pressed jeans. It didn't sound like someone Lavinia would have ties to, so why was the notice of Garrett's sudden death tucked away in her treasure box?

And why are you wasting Kimmie Eastman's precious, dwindling hours fussing about it?

I didn't have an answer for that, either.

Ellis Brawley was still the best lead we had toward finding Joline's sister. I checked my watch. A little after three. I could be in Jacksonboro before dark. I rose and once again stuffed the Eastman file back in my briefcase. Too damned bad if he didn't want to get involved.

I intended to take that option off the table.

I turned on my left blinker and waited for traffic to clear. The Stop 'n Save sat next to a small gas station with two pumps out front and a façade that looked as if it hadn't been updated since the Carter administration. The mini-mart, on the other hand, gleamed with fresh paint, brightly colored posters in the windows, and an overall air of being well cared for and profitable. I parked toward the end of the paved apron. The waning sun cast shadows across the glass as I pulled open the front door. Bells jangled as I stepped inside.

Unlike your typical convenience store, Brawley's wasn't stuffed with snack food, cigarettes, and fifteen different kinds of beer. They carried those things, of course, but there were also aisles of grocery items, more than just the basics of bread and milk. Walterboro was a good drive away, and Charleston would be another forty-five minutes or so north. Brawley's apparently tried to cater to the needs of the local population, more like a mini version of a supermarket than a grab-and-run kind of place.

I prowled a little, scoping things out, while keeping my eye on the young man behind the counter. I guessed his age at midtwenties. His face was a soft mocha brown, smooth and clean-shaven. He wore pressed khakis and a white polo shirt with some sort of logo on it. His voice was soft and educated.

"Help you with something, ma'am?" he asked, and I made my way toward the checkout counter.

"Are you Ellis?" I asked, pulling a business card from the pocket of my blazer when he nodded. "I'm Bay Tanner. I believe your uncle may have spoken to you about me."

"Cousin Maeline," he said without enthusiasm.

"Right. Did your uncle explain how important this is? I know it sounds melodramatic, but it's vital that I find out if this woman is the one I'm looking for. A life depends on it."

"Somebody need a donor for something?" he asked. "Kidney?"

Dealing with someone sharp was both a blessing and a curse. "Yes, it's medical." I chewed for a moment on the inside of my cheek, deciding. "I will tell you that it involves a child. And that's really all I can say. I hope you understand. My client is a very private . . . person."

"How do I know this isn't some sort of scam?" His deep brown eyes held mine, and I stared right back.

"Check me out. You'll find I'm not involved in anything shady— no shakedowns or questionable business practices." I managed a smile. "I even belong to the local chamber of commerce."

"So do we," he said, relaxing visibly. "Too bad there's not a secret handshake or something."

I let my stiff shoulders sag a little. "Or a password." I stepped a little closer to the counter. "Look, Mr. Brawley, it's a pretty simple thing. The woman I'm looking for grew up around Pritchardville, near Bluffton. She has two sisters, Joline and Tessa. Her mother and paternal grand-mother were killed in a traffic accident a number of years ago. She would be in her midforties. And black. If your cousin doesn't fit those parame-ters, I'll go away and leave you alone."

A tinkling of bells and giggly voices heralded the entry of two teenaged girls. One looked fairly normal, I noticed, as they slouched their way toward the back of the store. The other glittered with studs and gold hoops stuck haphazardly in ears, nose, lips, and probably a lot of other places I didn't want to know about. Ellis Brawley tracked their progress. I watched them pause in front of the beer cooler, both sets of eyes darting to the round metallic disc angled so the person at the cash register had a view of the far aisles. They moved to the next section, extracted identical cans of Coke, and sashayed to the front.

"Hey, Cinda. Brittany. That be all?"

"Yeah." The studded one handed over damp, tattered bills, and Ellis returned her change. "How's school going?"

"Fine," Miss Normal muttered.

"It sucks," the Metal Queen countered.

A moment later they slouched back through the door.

Ellis Brawley and I exchanged a smile.

"My mother would have slapped my sister silly and locked her in her room if she ever came home looking like that," he said.

"I probably wouldn't have lived to see my fifteenth birthday," I added.

Silence descended, not entirely uncomfortable, and I realized I liked this quiet young man. But business was business.

"So how about it?" I said, my professional face back in place. "Can you help me?"

"Maybe. I'm not sure."

I couldn't tell if the hesitation came from a genuine lack of knowledge or the vestiges of his unwillingness to involve himself in whatever tragedy might be playing out.

"Time is critical," I said, forcing myself to keep my voice level. "For the child."

I saw the shift in his eyes, and I knew he was going to cooperate. My years of bluffing my way through the Judge's weekly poker game kept my own gaze steady.

"The problem is—," he began when the door once again swung open.

The black man who entered filled the space, his shoulders almost brushing the sides of the opening. He didn't have to duck, but it was a near thing. An empty box dangled from a massive hand. His deep-set eyes darted from one to the other of us.

"You own that Jaguar out there?" he asked without preamble.

"Yes, sir, I do."

"Got a passel of kids hangin' around it. I shooed 'em off, but they'll be back."

I recognized the soft bass voice. "Duke Brawley, isn't it?" I advanced toward him and held out my hand. "Bay Tanner from Hilton Head. We spoke earlier."

His gaze darted to his nephew and back to me as we shook. "Didn't expect to see you up here after we talked."

I didn't intend to apologize. "I took the chance I might be able to convince Ellis to help me." I glanced at the younger man. "I think he understands now how important it is."

"Suit yourself," he said, and his unconcern seemed genuine. "You got the order ready for the Hall?" he asked his nephew.

"All set in the back. Except for the syrup. Only thing we had left was that low-fat kind, and you know Miss Lizzie hates that stuff. I'll tell her."

"Good luck," the older man said and lumbered toward a door in the rear marked EMPLOYEES ONLY. "Glad you'll be the one doin' the explainin'. Ma'am," he added over his shoulder, nodding in my direction.

"Nice to have met you," I said, but he didn't reply. I turned back to the nephew. "So. You were about to say something about a problem?"

Ellis's gaze dropped to the countertop. The spell had been broken by Duke Brawley's entrance. I felt my stomach tighten when he continued to avoid my eyes.

"Ellis?" I prompted. "If you can just give me Maeline's last name and address, I'll get out of your hair." Nothing. "Please. This poor kid really needs your help."

"They don't talk," he said softly, his face still hidden from me. "Something bad happened, a long time ago. I've never even met Maeline, just heard her name mentioned in a couple of phone conversations I eavesdropped on when I was a kid. If I hadn't gotten to know Mrs. Hatcher at church, I probably would have forgotten all about it."

"Do you think your mother would talk to me?"

"No, I honestly don't. It's like that side of the family just doesn't exist. She'd never tell you anything."

I fought hard to keep my temper under control, but my frustration level had redlined. "What kind of family feud could be more important than a child's life? For God's sake, Ellis, this kid is going to die!"

His face flushed, and I could see the genuine anguish in his soft eyes. "Let me see what I can find out, okay?" He picked up my card and studied it. "I'll get back to you as soon as I can." He shrugged. "It's the best I can do."

I surrendered. "Please don't wait too long. You're sure there's nothing at all you can tell me now? What was your mother's maiden name?"

"I don't really know. We don't talk much about the past. And never about Mama's family."

"Thank you," I said. "I really appreciate your sharing that with me."

"I have to make a delivery out at the Hall now, ma'am, if you'll excuse me. I'll get in touch as soon as I know anything."

"Thank you," I said again and held out my hand.

Ellis Brawley took it reluctantly, but his grip was firm and assured.

Outside, I chased away a couple of teenagers who'd decided to use the Jaguar's trunk as a bench and pointed myself south. Ellis hadn't told me much, but it was something. I'd get Erik on it as soon as I got home.

Home. The word stuck in my throat, and Red's angry face danced in front of me. A sudden chill made me shiver, and I flipped on the heater.

When the turn came up out of the deepening twilight, I took the coward's way out and headed for Presqu'isle.

CHAPTER
FOURTEEN

My TIMING COULDN'T HAVE BEEN BETTER. I COULD smell the pot roast from the front verandah even before I opened the door.

"We're back here," Lavinia replied in answer to my call. "I'll set a plate," she added as I moved down the hall and into the kitchen. My father's wheelchair was pulled up in its usual place.

"I thought you were supposed to stay in bed for a few days," I said, dropping a brief kiss on the top of his head.

"Harley's an old woman," he growled, dragging a hunk of potato through the rich gravy.

I slid out a chair and faced him across the scarred table, wincing at what all that fat must be doing to his already clogged arteries. His color was a lot better, and he'd lost that transparent look to his skin. He'd dropped a few pounds in the hospital, but judging by the heap of food on his plate, he'd have them back in no time.

Lavinia set a dish in front of me and resumed her seat. Steam rose from the chunks of beef. She'd left off the cooked carrots—never one of my favorites—as well as the peas. Meat and potatoes. And cornbread. It's a wonder I don't weigh two hundred pounds.

"I did my best," she said, nodding in the Judge's direction, "but you know how stubborn your father can be."

They exchanged a smile that made my heart turn over.

"Vinnie knows better than to try to win a battle of wills with me."

"Stubborn," she muttered again and bent her head to her plate.

We ate in silence for a while, the ticking of the grandfather clock down the hall punctuating the stillness of the old house. I wondered if Red had been and gone at my place. He didn't keep much there, even though he'd practically been in full-time residence since Christmas. It wouldn't take him long to—

My father's voice cut into my depressing thoughts, almost as if he'd been reading my mind. "Where's Redmond? Haven't seen the boy in a month of Sundays."

"Busy," I said and stuffed potatoes dripping with gravy into my mouth.

But the Judge knew me too well. "Somethin' the matter? You two have a falling-out?"

I sighed and laid my fork across my plate. "Not exactly. He's thinking of quitting the sheriff's department."

"I'm not surprised," the Judge replied. "It's a hard business. Too much misery for a body to deal with day after day, and he's been at it a long time. What's he gonna do?"

I really didn't want to get into it, but I couldn't exactly tell my father to mind his own business. Well, I could—and *had* on more than one occasion—but I didn't have the energy for the inevitable confrontation that would follow.

"He's thinking about going into a charter business with an old Marine buddy."

My hope that the Judge would leave it there was unrealistic and short-lived.

"He's not a fisherman as I recall. Or much into boats. What's he know about chartering?"

"His friend has been at it for a while. Red could learn from him."

"What do you think about it?"

"I told him I'd support him in any way I can, but—"

"But he's proud and doesn't want anything from you except your blessing. Am I right?"

I smiled. "Pretty much. He thinks he has to support me, financially I mean. I said I didn't—"

"Didn't need him to keep you, right?" My father shook his head. "No man likes to hear that, daughter. Haven't you learned anything from bein' alive for forty years?"

"Leave her alone, Tally," Lavinia said. She laid a hand on mine where it rested on the old oak table. "He'll get over it. Men and their pride are a fearsome thing. Give him some time."

The jangle of my cell phone saved the situation from turning maudlin. I excused myself and stepped out into the hall. The caller ID showed an 843 area code, but I didn't recognize the number.

"Bay Tanner," I said, turning my back on the kitchen.

"This is Ellis Brawley. From Jacksonboro?"

I felt at least 75 percent of the tension drain from my body. "Yes. Thanks so much for calling back. Do you have any information for me?"

"Sort of," he said, the hesitancy thick in his voice. "I talked it over with Miss Lizzie, out at the Hall. She's been like a grandmother to me, since . . . well, since I didn't really know either one of my own."

I couldn't let that slide. "Neither of your grandmothers is living?" I did a quick calculation, based on my assumption of Ellis's age. He would have been a teenager when Joline Eastman lost her mother and grandmother. Did that mean anything? Which generation should I be concerned about? I snapped back to the young man's voice.

"Uncle Duke's and my father's mama passed before I was born." He paused. "I don't know about the other one. On my mother's side. Or at least I didn't."

I held my breath and let it out slowly. "You've found something?"

"I don't know if it will help, but Miss Lizzie said I should do what I can. She said not wanting to get involved is what's the matter with the world these days."

I wanted to meet this wise woman, who apparently shared my feelings, but that was for another day. "So what did you find out?"

"My mom had to go out to a PTA meeting tonight, and Dad's in his workshop. Mom's a teacher, you know. So I looked in the old Bible she keeps by her bed. There's some names in there—births and deaths and so on."

I wanted to reach through the phone and shake him. "And is Maeline in there?"

"Yes, ma'am. Best I can make out, Patience—that's my mom—and Maeline's father Shadrack were first cousins."

I tried to work it out in my head, but I'd never been much for genealogy. "So that means one of Maeline's grandparents and one of yours were siblings. Is that right?"

"It's hard to tell from this, but I think that sounds right. Anyway, I thought I'd copy it out on a piece of paper. I can scan that and e-mail it to you."

"That would be great! Does it list Maeline's last name?"

"Just her birth name. Mitchell, same as Mama's. And Maeline has two sisters—Joline and Contessa. So does that help?"

I wanted to scream, both with joy and frustration. "Absolutely. It helps immensely. I can't tell you how much I appreciate this, Ellis. You've done a good thing."

"Don't know that my mom would agree with that, but I figure I'll just keep it to myself. I'm normally not a sneaky sort of person, but, like I told Miss Lizzie, this is for a good cause, right?"

"Absolutely," I said. "And thank Miss Lizzie for encouraging you. I'd like to meet her someday."

I could hear the smile in his voice.

"Not much chance of that. She almost never leaves the Hall, and they don't welcome visitors. Especially strangers. Whole place is full of signs and warnings."

Something clicked in my head. "Is this hall out at the end of Holly Hill Road?" I remembered that Peggy Watts, the wrong Maeline's neighbor, had called it the old McDowell place.

"Yes, ma'am. How did you know that?"

"I ran into it accidentally when I was looking for Mrs. Hatcher. I turned around in the drive, and I saw some of the signs. Miss Lizzie must like her privacy."

Ellis didn't take the bait. "Yes, ma'am," he said. "I should go and get this copied so I can send it to you before Mama gets home. Should I use this e-mail address on your card?"

"That would be great. Thanks again, Ellis. This information could make all the difference."

"You're welcome. I know you said it was confidential and all, but could you maybe let me know how things work out?"

"I'll sure try," I said.

"Okay," he said and hung up.

I hit the End button and immediately punched in Erik's cell. He was as thrilled as I was.

"Contessa, huh? There can't be more than one or two of those floating around in the databases. I'll give him about half an hour and then check the office e-mail account. Are you home?"

"No," I said, and the weight of Red's probable desertion crashed down around me. "I'm at Presqu'isle. I should be leaving here in an hour or so."

"I'll get going on this as soon as I get the e-mail and call you if I come up with anything."

"That'll be great."

I ended the call and stood for a moment staring through the door-way into the front parlor. With all the Christmas decorations gone, it had returned to its austere splendor, every piece of art and china back in its assigned place. I remembered my mother standing in this very spot, a satisfied smile curving her generous lips, as she gazed at her treasures. I'd never appreciated their beauty or their history and probably never would. *Things* didn't matter that much to me. Life was all about people—the ones you loved and the ones who loved you. And the ones you lost. Rob's image seemed to float in the still air of the elegant room, the warmth of his smile lighting the cold space. So much like Red. Were *both* of them gone? I could feel the tears threatening when Lavinia's voice from the kitchen offered me a welcome reprieve.

"Bay, honey? You about done out there? I'm puttin' an apple turnover out for you."

"Coming." I stood for a moment longer staring into the empty fireplace across the room. Cold and empty. Just like my house would be. I turned back toward the light, wondering if I had already played my last hand. And lost.

CHAPTER FIFTEEN

PROCRASTINATED AS LONG AS I COULD, TELLING MY-
self I was waiting for a call from Erik, but in truth just postponing the drive home. So it was after ten when I finally coasted
through the security gate at Port Royal Plantation, slowing so the
uniformed guard could recognize my resident's sticker. It used to be
that I knew most of the security people, could call them by name.
Lately, though, there'd been a lot of turnover, and most often now it
was a stranger who saluted the Jaguar and waved me through.

Change. Never one of my favorite facets of life, especially lately.

I took the first right and puttered down the narrow blacktop skirting the golf course. I put down my window, inhaling the heavy scent of
the azaleas and bougainvillea that provided a buffer between the rolling
fairway and the street. The breeze off the ocean, just a short distance
ahead, had lost its wintry bite, and the mixture of the sweet smells of the
flowering shrubs and the salty tang of the sea air washed over me in a
kind of benediction. Whatever awaited me at home, I'd get through it.

I pulled into my empty driveway, hit the garage door opener, and
sat idling while the heavy door rolled up. Even though I'd expected to
find it gone, the absence of Red's restored Bronco still stung. I eased into
the middle of the space and shut off the car. In the late-night stillness,

the ticking of the cooling engine sounded unnaturally loud. I waited for the door to rumble closed behind me before I got out and climbed the steps.

Inside, I dropped my bag on the floor in the foyer and tucked my cell into the pocket of my slacks. All the messages on my answering machine were junk, and I erased them. I tidied up the dishes I'd left in the sink that morning, straightening up and wiping surfaces that already gleamed from Dolores's twice-weekly visits.

I prowled the great room, stacking a few scattered magazines into a neat, perpendicular pile on the coffee table. My eyes were continually drawn to the hallway, toward the bedroom Red and I had shared nearly every night for the past few months. I whirled and flung open the French doors to the deck that ran around three sides of the house and stepped outside.

A pale half oval of moon rode the night sky out over the ocean, and the evening star glimmered in the distance. Rustlings in the palmettos off toward the dune that separated my house from the beach betrayed the foraging of the nocturnal creatures—raccoons and opossums, and other things I probably didn't want to know about. Before people changed the entire balance of the island, the land had been brimming with wildlife, from wild turkeys to herds of whitetail deer. One of the first modern developments had been a hunting camp, preserved now as the Coastal Discovery Museum at Honey Horn. Wealthy men from the North had plundered first the ducks and quail, and then the pristine beauty of the marshes and forests. In spite of Charles Fraser's good intentions—his dream of an island utopia amid the natural splendor—concrete had inevitably found its way to Hilton Head. Much had been preserved, but much more had been lost.

I propped my elbows on the railing and listened to the muted calls of the birds settling into the pines and live oaks surrounding the house. Peaceful times like these made me angry at myself, for my arrogance in building my home almost right on top of the dune. I was as much to blame for the despoiling of this beautiful place as any of those who came before me. I could feel the tears pooling behind my eyes, not for the loss of the land, but for myself. I loathe self-pity, the ultimate act of self-indulgence. I swallowed the lump in my throat, turned, and stomped back into the house.

In the bedroom, I flung open the closet door to the empty space of rod devoid of hangers, just as I'd expected to find it. Once before, I'd stood like this, staring into the mute evidence of a man's sudden desertion.

"Darnay." I jumped, realizing I'd said his name out loud for the first time in more than two years. "*Bâtard,*" I added almost immediately. The smile sneaked up on me. Bastard. I'd had to look the word up in a French-English dictionary at the library, but I had no trouble remembering it. Somehow his name and the profanity would be forever linked in my memory.

The brief smile faded as I moved to the dresser. The drawer I'd allotted to Red for his underwear and socks held nothing. Ditto the bathroom, where only a thin circle of moisture marked where his aftershave had rested on the glass shelf. I pulled a tissue from the box on the counter and obliterated that last remnant of Red Tanner—from my house if not from my mind.

I stripped the bed and stuffed the sheets and pillowcases into the washer. I pulled out fresh linen and tucked the clean sheets into place. I marched out into the kitchen and yanked open the refrigerator. There were three bottles of beer left. I opened them and poured their contents into the sink. I thought about trashing the coffee as well, but just in time I remembered that Dolores liked to make herself a cup when she took a break from cleaning.

I stood in the middle of the kitchen floor, my heart racing, scanning the room for any evidence I'd overlooked. I wanted nothing to be able to sneak up on me, to attack the new wall I was constructing around my feelings. I'd let too many people breach the old fortifications, allowed too many to wiggle and worm their way in, only to desert me almost from one breath to the next. *No more,* I told myself. *Never again.*

The sharp ringing of the phone sounded like a call to arms in the silence of the empty house. I made certain to check caller ID before I picked up.

"Erik, hey. Did you find something?" I marveled at how easily I could change gears. I was going to be okay.

"The mother lode, I think. I almost don't know where to start."

"Hang on a second. I need to get something to write on."

I carried the portable phone into the office and flipped on lights. A legal pad lay on the desk. I took a pen from the drawer and held it poised over the paper.

"Okay, shoot."

"First off, I found a woman named Contessa, last name Girard. She lives in the Upstate, near Greenville, or at least she did in 2000 when the census was taken. I couldn't find a current listing for her, though. Husband, Roland, died in 1995. I'm still hunting for their marriage license, so I don't know if she was a Mitchell, but I've got a good feeling about it. I'm going to keep checking, see if I can come up with a current address. I only had time to search South and North Carolina, but I'll keep at it."

"That's great. How old was she in the census records?"

"Twenty-nine."

I did the math. "That's sounds right, or close enough. Joline said both her sisters were older. And you said this woman's husband died in ninety-five? He had to be awfully young. Anything on what happened to him?"

"Not so far. I'll do more if it looks like it will help."

"Sorry. Didn't mean to get you off track. What else?"

"Okay. Patience Brawley was a lot easier. She was born in Walterboro and hasn't strayed too far from home. Her birth certificate and marriage license were a piece of cake, but I don't know if they help us much. I'm working on her parents now. Then we can backtrack to her grandparents and see what the connection is to Mrs. Eastman's family. It has to be that generation where they first cross paths, so to speak, if your guy Ellis and Maeline Mitchell are second cousins."

I stopped scribbling and chewed a moment on the end of the pen. "That's all great, Erik, but how does it help us? We need a close blood relative of Joline's. It has to be one of the sisters. I wonder if I could get Ellis's mother to talk to me."

"Worth a try. But what about Kimmie's biological father? I keep thinking that he's a lot closer genetically. Maybe you should try to get Mrs. Eastman to give us his name. Think she might?"

"I don't know. She was pretty adamant about keeping him out of it." I took a moment to wonder about that. It didn't really make a lot of sense.

"But why leave any possibility unexplored? The girl is running out of options. And time. Do you think there's another reason she doesn't want us to know who he is? Or to contact him?"

I shivered a little in the cooling air as night wrapped itself around the beach house. I could hear the wind rising outside, the leaves of the palmettos clacking in the freshening breeze.

"I don't know. Could be. I need to give her an update anyway. I'll call her tomorrow and give it a shot. Anything else?"

"That's all I had time for tonight. I'm working at the store tomorrow, but I'll bring my laptop along. If it's slow, I may have time to do some more searching."

"That's good. Maybe I'll drop by and let you know if I find out anything new from Joline."

"You know, one thing we haven't explored is asking Red to do a check and see if any of them have ever been arrested. Even a speeding ticket could give us a way to narrow down the search parameters. Think he'd do it?"

A lot of my newfound courage seeped away at the mention of Red's name. I'd have a lot of explaining to do, to a lot of people. No time like the present to get my story straight.

"That could be a little sticky right now. We've decided to take a break. For a while."

Ego? Wishful thinking? I wasn't really sure if either made me shade the truth, but it worked.

"I'm sorry, Bay. Anything I can do?" When I didn't answer right away, he added, "Too bad Ben—"

He stopped himself in mid-sentence. Ben. Our dead partner. I swallowed and took a deep breath.

"I know. He would have found a way to get the information for us." I waited a beat before adding, "And thanks, but I'm fine. You free tomorrow night? Maybe we can get together and compare notes. I'll buy."

His hesitation made me want to slap myself in the forehead. Of course. Stephanie.

"Never mind," I said before he had to start hemming and hawing. "I forgot I have to be somewhere. Let's talk Sunday, okay?"

His voice told me I hadn't fooled him for a second. "Sure. Sunday. I'll call you in the morning."

"Great. Thanks for all the hard work on this, Erik. Put in for overtime."

He laughed. "Right. Talk to you soon."

I heard him hang up, but still I clutched the phone to my ear. After a few moments, I flipped my cell closed.

Suddenly, I felt overwhelmingly tired. I turned out the lights and stood in the doorway of my bedroom across the hall, staring at the freshly made bed. I crossed to the dresser and pulled out a pair of my favorite ratty sweats, peeled off my clothes and stuffed them in the hamper. I glanced at the mystery novel I'd been reading for the past couple of days, abandoning it as I moved back into the hallway. In the great room, I scanned the shelves built into either side of the fireplace and took down my favorite comfort read, its cover worn thin over many years of handling. It had been a gift from my father on my thirteenth birthday, and he'd written an inscription on the flyleaf. I smiled, remembering my disappointment. I'd really wanted a horse.

I curled up on the wide sofa, pulled the afghan around me, and opened to the first page.

When he was nearly thirteen, my brother Jem got his arm badly broken at the elbow, Harper Lee had written.

I scrunched down, my eyes scanning the beloved words, and let my mind wander the streets of Maycomb with Scout and Atticus and Dill. And Boo Radley.

CHAPTER SIXTEEN

I SLEPT SURPRISINGLY WELL, WAKING A LITTLE AFTER seven with *To Kill a Mockingbird* spread open on my chest. I longed for a shower, but sunlight streaming through the panes of the French doors beckoned me toward the deserted beach.

By seven thirty I was jogging along the waterline, the placid ocean ebbing out toward low tide. A couple of locals walked their dogs, and we nodded to each other in passing. If there were early-spring tourists at the Westin Hotel, they'd decided to sleep in. I kept my pace slow and steady, trying not to favor my injured leg. After a few minutes, the muscles responded, and I slipped into the zone where the soft *thud* of my Nikes on the packed sand and the rhythmic beating of my heart took over my thoughts. My mind floated, worries and fears submerged in a flood of endorphins. It felt as if I could run forever.

Eventually, of course, my body intervened. The thigh began to tighten, and I executed a wide turn and slowed to a brisk walk, heading back toward the house. There was more activity as I neared the hotel. Some hardy Northern souls had even spread blankets, and I watched a young couple, maybe honeymooning, strip off T-shirts and tiptoe cautiously into the chilly water.

I crossed the dune and sprinted the last few yards to the deck just to prove I could still do it. The high had definitely worn off. My glance flicked of its own accord to the empty driveway before I jerked it viciously away.

The shower felt like heaven, and I stood under the steaming spray for a long time. By ten I sat at the glass-topped table in the kitchen alcove, finishing up an English muffin smothered in extra-crunchy peanut butter. *Protein,* I consoled myself as I scanned the *Island Packet.* More killing in the Middle East. The article about a couple of drug busts in Bluffton made Red's face flash briefly across my mind before I stamped it out. An accident at the intersection of 170 and 462 had killed a Beaufort teenager and sent three more to the hospital.

I searched in vain for some cheerful news, carried my single knife and plate to the dishwasher, and seated myself at the desk in my spare bedroom turned office. I checked e-mail and found the information from Patience Brawley's Bible her son had sent the night before and that Erik had forwarded on to me. I retrieved my briefcase from the car and emptied the Eastman file on my desk. I laid out my copy of the nearly empty genealogy chart Joline had given me alongside the scanned sheet from Ellis. I was able to fill in a few of the blank spaces, but not enough to give me a new direction.

I spent a few minutes organizing my thoughts on paper before tapping in Joline Eastman's home number.

"Good morning," she said after I identified myself. "You have news?"

"Nothing solid," I said, adding, "yet," when I heard her sharp intake of breath. "We do have some leads, and I have a few more questions for you."

"Of course. Anything."

I gave her an edited rundown of my conversation with Maeline Hatcher, the information she'd provided that led me to Ellis Brawley, and the fact that she and her sisters were listed in the family Bible.

"But this says that your other sister's full name is Contessa. Does that sound right to you?"

"I never heard that before. She was always just Tessa. Why wouldn't I know something like that about my own sister?"

Her voice rose with every word until, by the end of the sentence, she was nearly shouting. I heard muffled sounds in the background, as if someone else was speaking close to the phone. Joline said, "I'm all right, Jerry. Please, just close the door." A pause, and then I heard her say, "I'm entitled to some privacy in my own house!"

The husband, no doubt concerned about the panic I could hear floating just beneath the surface of Joline's voice. It was understandable, I supposed, given her daughter's tenuous hold on life. But she seemed to be even more tightly wound than when we'd spoken in my office, and I wondered how much more she could bear before she lost it completely. The fear and tension must be reaching intolerable limits.

"We found a Contessa who was living near Greenville in 2000. She'd been married to a man named Roland Girard who died in 1995. Does any of that ring a bell for you?"

"No. I'm sorry. As I told you at your office, I haven't been in touch with either of my sisters for years. Have you contacted this Contessa?"

"She's not at the same address as when the census was taken. And she may have remarried, but we're on it. I'm going to try to speak to Ellis's mother in person, see if she can help us with Maeline. You never heard of her marrying? Steady boyfriend or anything like that? Or other friends we might try? A last name would make things so much easier."

"I've been through all that," she said, obviously straining to keep herself under control. "I tried doing this on my own before I came to you. There were a couple of girls I remember from when Tessa and Maeline were in high school, but they were all a lot older than I. I found one of them still living outside Bluffton, but she said they all lost touch after graduation."

"Let me have her name and contact information," I said. "It can't hurt to have another run at her. Maybe now that she's had a chance to think about—"

"We're wasting time! You need to find Mae and Tessa. The doctors say they're the best hope of a match."

I gave her a moment to calm herself before I said, "Why isn't

Kimmie's biological father the closest match? She got half her genes from him."

The silence hung between us for a long time. For a moment I thought Joline Eastman might have quietly hung up the phone.

"It's not possible, don't you get that? Forget about D—" She cut herself off. "Forget about him," she said so softly I could barely hear her. "Find my sisters. Save my baby. I'll pay you anything you want."

"It's not about money, Joline. We're doing everything we can to find Tessa and Maeline. Give me the name of the woman you spoke to, the one from high school."

I waited while Joline found her address book. I wrote down the information on my legal pad: Keisha Spencer in Bluffton.

"Thank you. I'll get right on this. And we'll continue to follow the leads we have." I hesitated, fearful of pushing her too far, but the issue needed to be faced. Somehow I had to make her see it. "I strongly urge you to give us the name of Kimmie's father, too. You can't afford to leave any avenue unexplored."

"Don't tell me what I can and cannot afford to do, Mrs. Tanner. Kimmie's . . . father is off-limits. Period."

I waited to see if she had anything else to say. A long moment later, she cleared her throat, and the iciness left her voice.

"I know you're trying to do your best for us, and I appreciate it, believe me. Even if I gave you a name, it wouldn't do any good. He can't . . . he wouldn't help us. Please, just find my sisters." The sob took me completely by surprise. "My baby's so sick, so sick . . ."

"We'll do everything we possibly can," I said. "I'll call you the minute we have any news."

She hung up without saying goodbye.

I sat for a while, staring out the window at the live oak whose branches dipped toward the deck as if reaching for something to hold on to. Long gray strands of Spanish moss swayed on the light breeze off the ocean, and a red-bellied woodpecker hopped onto the railing. He strode back and forth, searching for some wayward seed or morsel. Maybe he had nestlings to feed. Families, whether avian or human, needed constant attention. Parents and children, the circle of life. The Judge refusing a surgery that could keep him alive; Kimmie Eastman desperate for one that could give her a chance.

I shook off the gloom that seemed to be settling over me like a dark cloud. Action was the best remedy. I pulled up switchboard.com and typed in "Keisha Spencer." Her address hadn't changed. I had to do a map search for the unfamiliar street name and finally found it in one of the dozens of developments that had sprung up on the mainland along Buckwalter Parkway in the past few years. I listened to the phone ring, doodling on the legal pad until I suddenly realized I'd been unconsciously working on Joline Eastman's little slip. *D . . .*

David? Daniel? Dale? Or it could be Desmond or Donald.

I waited through ten rings, but no one picked up. No answering machine or voice mail, either.

I turned back to the computer and searched for Patience Brawley. She and her husband and son lived on Holly Hill Road, the same one on which I'd spent time searching for Maeline Hatcher. Sometimes coincidences happen. Or maybe it was just that Jacksonboro is a small town. I wondered which side of the Walterboro highway they were on, maybe the same dead-end stretch that had led me to the unfriendly lane with all the warning signs.

On impulse, I moved to Google and typed in "McDowell Hall" plus "South Carolina." Mrs. Hatcher's neighbor had called it the old McDowell place, and Ellis Brawley and his uncle had made several references to "the Hall," the word spoken as if it should be capitalized. I found a few articles about a family of that name, rice planters who'd been prominent in antebellum society, but I couldn't nail down anything specific about their plantation or its location. There were dozens more references to check, but I logged off. I didn't have time to chase rabbits down nonproductive holes.

Patience Brawley picked up the phone almost the moment it rang. I'd been formulating the right approach in my head, and her voice took me by surprise. She had to say hello twice before I finally got myself together.

"Good morning, Mrs. Brawley. My name is Bay Tanner, and I'm calling from Hilton Head."

"We do all our giving at the church," she said politely. "Thank you—"

"I'm not soliciting, ma'am," I rushed in before she had a chance to hang up. "I was up in Jacksonboro yesterday, and I talked to your son and—" It took me a second to get the connection right. "To your brother-in-law. At the store."

"Yes?"

The single word and its inflection told me Ellis hadn't mentioned our meeting—or his snooping—to his mother.

"I'm trying to track down some folks, and your son was kind enough to help me a little. But I think you might be the person who could—"

"I don't want to be rude, young woman, but I got no time for this. It's my little granddaughter's birthday today, and I've got about fifty people expecting to be fed in a couple hours. Don't make me feel bad about havin' to hang up on you."

"I'll call again," I said. "Thank you."

"You have a real nice day." It was polite and final.

Ellis had children? I gazed once again out the window. No, probably not. He still lived at home, and I remembered then that he'd mentioned a sister. Maybe more than one. The woodpecker was back, and I watched him tapping and hopping along the top rail of the deck. *A family birthday party. Fifty people.* I picked up the phone and dialed the Stop 'n Save, but there my luck seemed to run out.

The girl sounded like a teenager.

"Good morning," I said, glancing at the clock. It was nearly noon, and I'd accomplished exactly zero so far. "May I speak to Ellis, please?"

"I'm sorry, he's not here. Can I help you?"

I heard the jangle of the bell over the door, and I knew I didn't have much time. "Will he be in at all today? I know his mother's throwing a party, so maybe he's helping her out?"

Let her think I was someone with close connections to the family. The deception didn't bother me in the slightest.

"Yeah, that's where he is. Miz Brawley has him hoppin', I'll bet."

"Listen, maybe you can help. I haven't picked up a gift yet, and I've completely forgotten how old little—" I stopped in a panic. I had no idea what the child's name was. I backtracked. "I can't remember how old that precious little girl is gonna be. I want to get just the right thing."

"Oh, I'm sorry. I'm not real sure. Four, maybe? Anyway, she ain't in school yet."

Okay, good. "And can you tell me how to spell her name? Don't want to mess that up, either."

It was a short silence, but I thought I might have blown it.

Finally, the girl said, "Well, *H-o-p-e*, I guess. Just like it sounds."

My acting like an idiot was in a good cause, and I shrugged it off. "That's what I thought. Just wanted to make sure. Thanks so much."

I hung up quickly before I could say anything else to make myself sound like a complete moron. A couple of hours, Mrs. Brawley had said. So around two. Not much time to get myself dressed, find a gift, and make it up to Jacksonboro, but I'd give it a shot.

In the bedroom, I selected a pair of tan slacks and a yellow cotton sweater, then slipped my bare feet into loafers. Hopefully, mine wouldn't be the only white face in the crowd, but that couldn't be helped. Unless I got tossed out on my ear, I might walk away from Hope's birthday party with some answers for Joline Eastman.

I gathered up my bag and made certain my cell phone was fully charged. I spared a thought to what my late mother would have said about my crashing a family gathering of total strangers without the slightest compunction. It definitely broke about twenty of Emmaline's rules of acceptable behavior for a young Southern woman born into wealth and family. Maybe it was a blessing she wasn't here to be humiliated by my behavior—this one and so many more.

As I backed the Jaguar out of the garage, the thoughts of my mother made me realize I'd never heard back from Loretta Healey. I hoped I'd have better luck at cracking the Mitchell family secrets than I was at unraveling my own.

CHAPTER
SEVENTEEN

I GUESSED RIGHT ABOUT WHICH END OF HOLLY HILL Road the Brawleys lived on, and from there it wasn't hard to pinpoint the location of the party. Almost at the end of the blacktop, I passed cars lining both sides of the street and others pulled up at odd angles in the front yard of a rambling bungalow that looked as if it had been added on to several times over the years. The white paint was fresh, though, and I wondered if Ellis had spent last summer crawling up and down ladders.

I had to drive all the way to the end of the blacktop and turn around before I found enough of a space to squeeze in the Jaguar. I glanced down the overgrown lane to the old plantation house, but I could detect no activity. The warning signs nailed to the beautiful old oaks trembled a little in the breeze. I hitched my bag over my shoulder and retrieved the gaily wrapped package from the passenger seat. Thank God for Barnes & Noble and a knowledgeable young woman in the children's section. The richly illustrated picture book about ballerinas had enchanted me. I was assured that any little girl would love it.

As I neared the house, I could hear the low rumble of a lot of voices coming from the backyard. There was a sudden shriek of feminine laughter, and the general volume rose. I walked up beside a gravel drive packed tightly with vehicles and followed the sounds of hilarity around the left side of the house. The scene spread out before me drew a smile.

Beneath a stately old oak, tables covered with a variety of colored cloths groaned under the weight of more food than I thought I'd ever seen in one place. A few yards away, an entire pig—minus the head and feet, thank God—sizzled over a smoking pit. The smell of fat crackling as it dropped onto the glowing embers made my knees weak. Barbecue, hot and spicy, was definitely on the day's menu. Other grills held quartered chickens turning brown over beds of charcoal. As I watched, a steady stream of women trekked from the back of the house to the tables, carrying who knew what other Lowcountry delights like dirty rice and maybe a banana pudding. I determined at that moment that I wouldn't let them throw me out before I had a chance to eat.

My resolution hit an immediate snag when a young woman with a child in tow approached. She would have been pretty if someone had gotten her braces at an early age. As it was, her front teeth stuck out so far she could barely close her lips over them. Still, her smile, puzzled but welcoming, made the first blush of shame wash over me.

"Hello," she said tentatively. "I'm Faith Godwin." Her face beamed as she smiled down at the child. "And this is the birthday girl."

I squatted and held out the package. "Happy birthday, Hope. This is for you."

The mother relaxed a little at my use of her daughter's name, but I could still sense her wariness in the way her hand never left the child's shoulder. I completely understood her caution.

"Say thank-you to the nice lady," Faith instructed, and Hope complied.

"You're quite welcome, honey."

"It's very kind of you, Miss . . . ?"

Showtime. I held out my now empty hand. "Bay Tanner, Mrs. Godwin. I'm a friend of Ellis's."

"Oh. He didn't—I'm very glad to meet you."

Her skin felt like velvet, although her grip was tentative.

"He's over there by the pit," she said. "He and Uncle Duke are arguing about whether it's time to start pickin' the pig." She looked down at her daughter, who was ripping the paper off her gift. "Oh, Hope, honey, you shoulda waited."

The child's squeal of delight when she finally revealed the book made the two of us smile at each other. In an instant, Hope abandoned the scattered bits of wrapping paper and dashed off on her fat little legs crowing, "Gwammy! Gwammy! Wook what I got!"

For a moment, Faith Godwin and I stood awkwardly together. I noticed more than a few dark eyes glance questioningly in our direction.

"I'll just speak to Ellis," I said. "Thanks for making me welcome."

Faith laughed. "I'll bet half of Holly Hill Road is here, and probably a lot more people that I've never laid eyes on. When Mama throws a party, she usually invites the whole town. I hope you enjoy yourself, and thanks for the book. Hope likes to pretend she knows how to read, and she really loves the pictures."

She moved away then with a quick wave, and I negotiated the maze of lawn chairs filled with older black men and women, most of whom nodded as I edged my way past. There were other white faces scattered around the huge backyard, and I felt less conspicuous than I'd feared.

Ellis wore a gray T-shirt saturated with sweat, the heat from the smoldering coals sending beads of perspiration coursing down his cheeks. He stood talking with his uncle, and I waited for an opening before edging closer. Duke Brawley's face clouded, and his nephew looked as if he'd stepped on a copperhead a moment before I spoke.

"Hey, Ellis. Mr. Brawley. I took a chance I'd find you." The word *brazen* floated into my head. I was certain it was the one my mother would have used.

"Mrs. Tanner? What are you doing here?"

Ellis looked genuinely shocked, and I wondered if he was afraid I'd come to blow the whistle on his snooping into his mother's Bible. Duke mumbled something about getting a beer and stomped away.

"I'm sorry. I know this is beyond the bounds of anything resembling good manners, but I desperately need to talk to your mother. I called her this morning, and she mentioned the party and pretty much blew me off. I just want to find Maeline Mitchell, and I'll be out of your lives. Believe me, this isn't something I normally do, crash private parties, I mean. But a young girl's life is at stake, and I just took the chance that you and your family would eventually forgive me. Or at least understand."

Ellis had been slowly moving away from the fire as I spoke, and at the end I found myself talking to his back. I followed quietly behind until he finally stopped and sank onto an old concrete bench, its once white finish now green with mold. A crape myrtle, left to run wild, dropped welcome shade, shielding us a little from the speculative eyes I could feel being cast in our direction.

"You shouldn't have come," he said softly. "Mama will know what I did."

"She doesn't have to," I said, matching his tone. "I called her, as I said, and gave her my name. I can stonewall on how I came up with the information." I tried for lightness. "In my business, skirting the truth is part of the game. Just get me ten minutes alone with her, and I'll do the rest. I promise I'll keep you out of it."

"Don't see how," he mumbled, but at least he didn't grab me by the arm and drag me off his property.

"Which one is your mother?" I asked, glancing around the flurry of activity in the yard.

Apparently those who were convinced the pig was ready had won the argument. Several men, including Duke Brawley, were hoisting the beast off the fire toward an old door, covered with newspaper and resting on two sawhorses. Depending on the custom of Ellis's family, either the women would use long-handled forks to pull the succulent meat away from the bones into huge pans, or each guest would be supplied with his own fork and do his own pickin'. However the process unfolded, I was sure there would be vats of homemade barbecue sauce to slather over the meat once it had been removed.

I flinched at the unladylike rumbling of my stomach and turned as Ellis's voice penetrated.

"She's over there in the yellow apron."

Patience Brawley had stopped to speak to one of her elderly guests seated in a lawn chair close to the pit, and I wondered that the poor thing wasn't dripping sweat. The daughter had inherited her protruding teeth from her mother, but Patience's skin matched Ellis's, a creamy mocha that told of Caucasian blood somewhere back in her heritage. And maybe in Joline's as well? I wondered. She was a tall woman, perhaps equal to my own five-ten, I thought, and her hair was a soft cloud of gray around her head.

"I'll introduce myself if you get her over here," I said. "Just tell her someone needs to speak to her, then you can disappear."

He seemed reluctant to move, and I restrained myself from giving him an encouraging shove.

"Please," I said, hoping it sounded more like a command than a request.

Finally, he shrugged and moved off. I watched him approach his mother and lead her away. When they began moving in my direction, I sat down on the bench and folded my hands demurely in my lap. I intended to present as nonthreatening a picture as I could manage.

"Yes?" she said, stopping in front of me. "Ellis said you wanted to talk to me about something?" Before I could reply, she added, "I don't believe I know you."

"No, ma'am," I said softly. "Do you have a moment to sit?"

"Young lady, I've got more 'n sixty mouths waterin' over there and a stack of presents so high it looks like there were ten little girls having a birthday. It could take 'til midnight just to get through 'em all. So I have no time to waste, you understand?"

Her tone was scolding, in the way of women who deal a lot with small children. I'd bet she taught elementary school. Sighing in resignation, she dusted off the bench with a dishtowel she pulled from the waistband of her apron and sat down beside me.

"Now, what do you want, if you'll forgive my bluntness?"

I determined to give it to her straight up, with no embellishment. "My name is Bay Tanner, and I'm a private investigator from Hilton Head. I called you this morning. I have a client who desperately needs to locate one or both of her sisters. There's a little girl dying, and only a blood relative can help save her. I need to find Maeline or Tessa Mitchell, born around Pritchardville, and I strongly believe you're the one person who can help me do that. I need last names, married names, for these women—and addresses, if you have them. I guarantee no harm will come to them, and whether or not they choose to help will be entirely up to them. My job is to give them the chance to do the right thing. The rest is on their shoulders."

I paused to draw a breath and to steal a glance at Patience Brawley. Her face had lost its wary but pleasant look. It felt as if she'd taken a giant step back, although in reality she still sat ramrod straight on the bench beside me. I couldn't read her expression, but her deep brown eyes had slid nearly shut as if she could make me disappear by shutting out my image.

"Will you help me? Help this poor child?" I asked softly.

Her shoulders slumped a little, and I sensed some of the resistance leave her. "I didn't ever want to have to think about them again," she said quietly. "I don't know where those girls are, nor do I care. Is it Joline's child that's sick then?"

"Yes," I said. "Kimmie. She has a blood cancer. She needs a bone marrow transplant, and no one in the rest of the family is a match. The doctors think her sisters might be their last hope. Can you help me?" I asked again.

She thought about it for a long time. "I believe I would, in spite of— It would be the Christian thing to do. But I can't. I haven't seen or heard of any of the Mitchell girls for years. I'm sorry."

On the other side of the yard, people had begun to stir, and I guessed the picking was about to begin. I had precious little time before I lost Patience Brawley for good. With a silent apology to Ellis, I said, "Are you certain you haven't spoken to anyone about Maeline? Maybe on the phone?" I felt her stiffen, and I hurried on. "I don't want to cause any trouble, Mrs. Brawley. I hope you can believe that."

A squeal drew our attention to the yard. Apparently, little Hope had been given the first stab at the steaming pig in honor of her birthday, and the task appeared to both delight and frighten her at the same time. I turned to find Patience smiling.

I spoke very softly. "If it were Hope who needed help, wouldn't you want anyone who had even the tiniest bit of information to share it? No matter how personally painful it might be for them?"

She sighed, her eyes never leaving her granddaughter. "You have no idea what you're asking," she said.

I waited, holding my breath for fear of interrupting the inner struggle I could see going on behind her gentle eyes.

"Jefferson," she said, and I had to strain to catch the next words. "Maeline married herself a no-account white man named Jonas Jefferson. I heard they lived a while in Macon, Georgia. He ran out on her. After that, I don't know. I have no idea about Tessa. Neither one of them could be bothered to even show up at their own mama's funeral. Left it to the rest of the family to take care of everything. I haven't spoken to any of them since . . ." Suddenly she rose and stared down at me. "I have to tend to my guests. You're welcome to stay and have a bite with us, but please don't come back. You tell Joline I'll hold her and her little girl in my prayers. That's the best I can do."

I watched her move resolutely through the throng of her family and friends to pick up a squealing Hope and crush the child to her chest.

I took out my cell phone and called Erik.

Back at the Jaguar, I leaned against the warmth of the rounded fender and turned my face up to the sun. After I'd relayed the information about Maeline to my partner, I'd found my appetite had entirely deserted me. I hadn't even bothered to seek out Ellis or Patience and take my leave of them. Another of my mother's strict rules of etiquette trampled in the dust. No one paid any attention to the interloper who slipped around the side of the house and hurried away.

A rustle in the bushes behind me made me turn, but it must have been a bird or a squirrel for I could see no one in the immediate vicinity. I rubbed my hand unconsciously over my chest, the longing for a calming hit of nicotine making my knees wobble. I settled for another of the peppermint candies that seemed to breed in the bottom of my bag. I had just pulled my key ring into my hand when again the muted noise of something moving in the untamed brush sent me spinning around. I caught a brief glimpse of a face, perhaps a child's, and the impression of wild dark hair standing out among the soft browns and tans of the withered foliage before the rustling turned to thrashing.

"Wait!" I called, though *why* I couldn't have said, and took a few tentative steps down the lane. "It's okay. I won't hurt you."

I followed the intruder's progress by the disturbance he —or she— made through the tall weeds before my watcher gained the path and sprinted away. Faded jeans, rolled up, and the bright splash of a red plaid shirt against the stark trunks of the oaks. Bare feet flashed in the sun, and long dark curls flew out behind the sprinting—woman. Too tall for a girl and without the grace and effortless gait of someone young and agile. In a few seconds, the vision disappeared around a bend in the lane, leaving me to wonder if I had imagined the whole thing, if it had been perhaps a trick of the sunlight dappling through the low-hanging branches of the live oaks. I waited, but the strange woman didn't reappear. With a shrug, I clicked the locks on the Jaguar and pulled open the driver's door.

"You're trespassing on private property."

The voice came out of nowhere, and the suddenness of it made me drop my keys in the dirt. I turned slowly to find a small woman standing at the rear of the car, her booted feet planted in the powdery dust of the driveway, her fists jammed against her hips. It took a long moment for my heart rate to return to normal.

I gazed into her cold eyes. "I'm sorry. I thought the shoulder of the road was public."

"You're not on the shoulder. This is McDowell land."

I stooped down and retrieved my keys. "Then I'll get going." I couldn't decide if her terse challenge had made me more angry or afraid.

She reached up to shield her eyes from the sun, and I noticed her hands were roughened, as if she did a lot of manual labor. Her dark hair was liberally streaked with gray and pulled back into a loose ponytail at her neck. She, too, wore jeans, faded from many washings, molded to her slender frame. The long tails of a man's pale blue shirt hung down over her narrow thighs.

"You're a friend of my neighbors?" she asked, moving around so that we stood closer. Her eyes narrowed as she studied my face. "Have we met before?"

Suddenly I didn't like being crowded by this woman who, though she came only to my shoulder, seemed fit and strong under her loose clothes.

"I'm sure I'd remember," I said. "I'll get my car off your property."

I slid into the seat and pulled the door closed. It took a little maneuvering to get the long body of the Jaguar out of the tight spot, and I wondered if the old woman intended to accost everyone parked around me as they left the party. When I finally gained the blacktop and looked up into the rearview mirror, the woman was still standing at the entrance to the lane, staring after me. I gunned the engine and quickly put distance between myself and the weird encounter. As I turned back toward Beaufort, I thought I had probably just made the acquaintance of Ellis Brawley's wise but very strange Miss Lizzie.

CHAPTER EIGHTEEN

 STOPPED FOR GAS AT A WIDE PLACE IN THE ROAD called Ashepoo. A while later, I took a left at Gardens Corner and wound my way through downtown Beaufort, across the bridge, and on to St. Helena. The pearly luminescence of approaching twilight glowed in the sky out over the Sound as I pulled up to Presqu'isle and shut off the engine.

"It's a friendly burglar," I called from the front of the long hallway, forcing a lightness into my voice that I certainly didn't feel. I pushed the heavy oak door closed and dropped my bag on the console table, but not before tucking my cell phone into the pocket of my slacks. I hoped Erik would have news before long about Maeline Mitchell Jefferson, onetime wife of the faithless Jonas, lately of Macon, Georgia.

The Judge's wheelchair was pulled up to the table while Lavinia stirred something on the stove. The whole place smelled like Thanksgiving.

"Are you cooking a turkey?" I asked and sat down in my assigned seat. "Hello, Your Honor," I added. "How are you feeling?"

"Like a chick in the middle of a bunch of old, meddling hens," he snapped.

Lavinia turned and smiled at me. "Don't mind him, honey.

Dr. Coffin just left. He read Tally the riot act about taking it easy. And you know how much your father loves folks tellin' him what to do."

"I'm sick to death of talkin' about pills and arteries and all the rest of that folderol. What's going on out in the world, daughter? Talk to me."

I hadn't wanted to burden him with my lack of progress on the Kimmie Eastman situation. It seemed especially inappropriate considering his own close brush with mortality. But I also knew how his mind worked. He'd be picking at the threads, worrying the case like his hounds Hootie and Beulah used to gnaw old soup bones. So while the house filled with the savory aromas of Lavinia's cooking, I brought him up to date on my efforts, most of them futile. When I finished, I watched him steeple his index fingers and rest his chin on them, his eyes half closed. It was such a familiar pose I had to smile. That towering intellect of his had mostly survived the strokes and arterial blockages and his eighty-plus years of living, and I knew he was formulating and discarding possible avenues of investigation.

I left him to it and rose to stand beside Lavinia as she pulled open the oven door to peek inside.

"What's the occasion?" I asked, eyeing the golden skin of a small turkey whose drippings sizzled and popped in the roasting pan.

Lavinia shut the door and turned her back on the table where the Judge still sat contemplating, his lips working in and out as if he carried on a silent conversation with himself.

"Your father asked for it," she said, and my breath caught in my throat at the expression on her face. "He said he might not make it to another holiday season, and he wanted to—" She broke off on a muffled sob and shook her head. "It's a small enough thing to ask. I couldn't say no."

I resisted the urge to put an arm around her trembling shoulders. I knew she wouldn't welcome my sympathy. We'd learned to handle our griefs and sorrows with stoicism, we women of Presqu'isle.

"We're so lucky to have you," I said softly. "Both of us."

That brought a watery smile, and I left her to compose herself. I removed three plates from the cupboard and carried them to the table. I had begun to pull the everyday cutlery from the drawer when the Judge spoke.

"You need to find the father," he said, nodding once as if agreeing with himself. "He'll be a much closer match than the sisters. Make her tell you his name. Or track it down yourself."

I laid the knives and forks on the folded linen napkins and avoided his gaze. "Erik checked out Kimmie's birth record right up front, but there's no father listed. I talked to Joline this morning, and she was adamant about it. Although, she did say something kind of odd that's been nagging at me."

"What?"

"She started to say he *couldn't* help and changed it to *wouldn't* in midstream. It made me wonder if he might be dead."

"That would certainly put him out of the picture. But there's something not right about this, daughter. If he's alive, that woman would be moving heaven and earth to find him and have him tested. And if he's dead, why doesn't she just say so? Unless there's something fishy going on."

"Like what?"

"How the hell should I know? You're the detective, aren't you?"

I didn't have a good answer for that, but my father's old familiar crustiness made me smile.

"You know, I think she almost said his name this morning. She got out a *D* before she stopped herself."

The Judge's head snapped up. "That's it? Just the one letter?"

I thought about it for a moment. "That's all I caught. I was doodling, and the first possibility I wrote down was David."

"That would be my first choice. Of course there are plenty of other possibilities." He listed a few of those I'd already considered.

"Or it could be something out of the ordinary, like a family name," I said. "That would make the choices pretty much infinite."

Behind me, I heard the *whir* of the electric mixer as Lavinia whipped potatoes.

"Bay, would you get the gravy boat out of the cupboard for me?" she asked over the noise. "The china one, not the silver."

"Sure." I set it on the counter next to the stove. "Anything else I can do?"

"No thanks. Just sit there and keep your father from driving me crazy askin' when we're gonna eat."

"Been fussin' around in here for the better part of the day," my father grumbled before turning his attention back to me. "Even if we could figure out the man's first name, you don't have a gnat's worth of information to go on, do you?"

"Nope. A teenager at the time, or so I'm assuming. Maybe white? Kimmie is light-skinned. So a young man, maybe named something that begins with a *D*, who lived somewhere around Pritchardville fifteen or sixteen years ago, and who might have had a one-night stand with a beautiful black teenager. It's not like we can put an ad in the personals."

"Track down this friend, the one who lives out in Bluffton. Girls know things like that about other girls." He paused to eye me quizzically. "Don't they?"

"Generally. But remember that the sisters and their friends were a lot older than Joline. They would already have been out on their own or in college when she got into trouble. It's too bad the mother and grandmother are gone. She'd have been more likely to confide in one of them, I'd think. Or maybe she really didn't tell anyone. Maybe she's just kept it to herself all these years."

"Secrets," my father mumbled, shaking his head. "No good usually comes of 'em."

It was a perfect opening. I drew in a breath a second before I felt Lavinia's hand on my shoulder. I turned to look up into her face.

"I need your help," she said, and I could plainly read the naked pleading in her deep brown eyes. "Please."

I exhaled and let my shoulders relax. "Yes, ma'am," I said and rose from the table.

I thought a lot about that look on the drive back to Hilton Head. Full night had fallen, and traffic was sparse. On many stretches of the road I felt like the last person left alive on the planet, like something out of one of the black-and-white horror movies from the fifties that Rob used to love watching.

At the hospital, a few days before, Lavinia had convinced me that the name *Julia* meant nothing to her. Over more than forty years, we'd come to read each other pretty well, and I would swear that she'd been telling the truth. But she'd interrupted what she'd rightly interpreted as my intention to call my father on the subject of secrets and had intervened to keep me silent. Was there something else she was trying to conceal? Was there another family secret she *did* know about? Maybe it had to do with that old newspaper clipping I'd found in her treasure box. Or the sealed letter. Could she somehow have figured out that I'd been snooping?

I worried at the problem all the way home, accomplishing absolutely nothing.

Pulling up to the house, with only the security lights glowing softly and the concrete pad in front of the garage achingly empty, drove everything else temporarily out of my head. It was Saturday. Normally Red picked up the kids from Sarah around noon. We'd gotten into the habit of doing something fun with them—a road trip to the zoo in Columbia or maybe a long walk on the beach—before returning to my house for dinner. Usually by this time the place would have been ablaze with lights and laughter and sometimes the smell of popcorn as we settled in for a G-rated movie on DVD or sat over a board game on the coffee table in the great room.

I trudged up the steps and reset the alarm. The echoing silence that greeted me spoke of my old life, before Red and Scotty and Elinor had become so much a part of . . . I let that thought trail away. During the years since Rob's murder—and Darnay's desertion—I'd learned to be alone. I'd get used to it again. I just had to give myself time.

I spared a moment to wonder how Red had explained my absence to the kids.

My heart beat a little faster while I played the messages on the answering machine, but the familiar voice was not among those eager for me to call them back. Nothing that couldn't wait. I nuked a cup of water in the microwave and dropped in a tea bag to steep while I changed into my flannel pajamas and wrapped my nearly threadbare chenille robe around me.

It was only a little after eight thirty. I fixed my tea and carried the cup into the office. I found my notes from my earlier conversation with Joline Eastman, including the number for Keisha Spencer, the friend of the elder Mitchell girls in high school. She answered on the second ring, taking me by surprise.

"Is this Keisha? Keisha Spencer?"

I could hear a television blaring in the background along with the piercing cry of a baby very unhappy about something.

"Yes?" Her tone was wary.

"My name is Bay Tanner. I'm a private investigator here on Hilton Head." The wail now sounded as if someone were sticking pins in the poor infant. "I'm calling about Maeline and Tessa Mitchell. Is this a bad time?"

She didn't bother to cover the receiver with her hand, simply shouted, "Galen! What's the matter, boy, you gone deaf? Go see what's wrong with your sister!" A little more quietly she said, "Sorry about that. He's supposed to be watchin' her, not playin' some damn fool video game. Who did you say you were?"

"I'm working for Joline Mitchell. Mrs. Eastman now. I believe she spoke to you about trying to locate her sisters."

"Oh, sure. Jo-Jo. Yeah, she called me. I told her I didn't know what happened to Mae and Tessa. You really a private eye? Like on TV?"

"Yes, I am. Mrs. Spencer, did Joline tell you how important it is to find her sisters?"

"She said it had to do with her little girl bein' sick."

Since Joline herself had already breached confidentiality, I felt free to abandon all pretense. Most people, especially those with children of their own, could more than relate to the anguish the Eastmans were facing with Kimmie's illness. All cards on the table seemed the best way to elicit the information we needed. Time was running out.

"Only a bone marrow transplant can save her," I continued. "Blood relatives are obviously the best candidates. That's why it's imperative that we find Joline's sisters. Can you help us?"

"Like I told Jo-Jo, I got no idea where they could be. Last time I talked to Mae was after her husband ran off. Told her he was a loser. White trash. No offense."

"None taken," I said, although I wondered about her assumption.

"Tessa and me was never that close. I heard she got married, but I don't remember anything about who it was or where she might be living. Like I told Jo-Jo, we just fell outta touch after high school."

"Is there anyone you can think of who might know how to locate either one of them?"

Keisha Spencer gave it some thought. The cries had quieted, and now only the crashes and blasts of the video game pierced the silence.

"No, I'm sorry. Everybody kinda just drifted away. I don't see none of them anymore."

"No old boyfriends?"

"No, ma'am. None that I can think of."

I could feel the knot tightening in my stomach as another promising lead evaporated. How could two women who had been born and raised not fifteen miles away from where I sat simply vanish? It made no sense, and yet it seemed to be exactly what had happened. It wasn't the way families were supposed to work. A fleeting image of what my own unacknowledged half sister might look like now floated through my mind, and I forcibly kicked it aside.

"You talked to her cousin about this?" Keisha's sudden words made me jump.

"Which cousin?"

"I don't rightly remember his name. Deshawn? Something like that. Or maybe he wasn't a real cousin. Anyway, he used to hang around the Mitchells a lot back in those days. Funny, I haven't thought about him in ages, not even when I talked to Jo-Jo. Don't know what made it pop into my head just now. Maybe it was you askin' about boyfriends. He used to be kind of sweet on Jo-Jo. He even stayed with them for a while one summer, if I remember rightly."

"And you don't remember his last name? Or anything else that might help me find him?"

"Sorry. But Jo-Jo should be able to say. I'm surprised she didn't already try him."

I only half heard the words. My brain raced as I thanked Keisha Spencer for her time and hung up the phone. Without conscious thought, I'd picked up a pen and printed Deshawn's name in capital letters on the desk pad, underlining the first letter so hard I ripped through the paper.

D . . . *for Deshawn?*

CHAPTER NINETEEN

I STARED AT THOSE FEW LETTERS FOR A LONG TIME, A whole movie's worth of possible scenarios running through my head, along with about a million questions: Why hadn't Joline Eastman told me about this Deshawn person? Could he be Kimmie's biological father? If so, then my assumption about a one-night stand had to be completely off base. But why would she risk her child's life to keep such a critical piece of information from me? Who was she protecting? And why?

I leaned back in my desk chair and ordered my mind to slow down. I pictured Joline Eastman as she'd sat in my office: a private woman, quite beautiful, perfectly dressed and groomed, but with a deep current of suppressed emotion running just below the surface. Proud? Embarrassed? Scared? Any of those words could have described my client and might also explain her insistence that I not divulge to strangers the dire need to find her family. And yet . . . Could her pride—or fear—be that important to her? More important than saving Kimmie's life? There had to be more to it than that.

Secrets. Hers. My father's—

The jangle of the phone startled me. My hand trembled a little as I leaned forward and picked up the handset.

"Good, you're home," Erik said when I answered. "I don't really have much news, but I thought I'd check in."

"Nothing at all?" I asked and the sinking feeling took hold of my stomach again.

"I found a Jonas Jefferson who's still in Macon. He says he used to live with a Maeline Mitchell, but they weren't married. Said her drinking got to him, and he threw her out after she totaled his pickup one night. He doesn't know what happened to her or where she went."

"Damn it! How can living, breathing human beings just drop completely off the radar like this?" I took a deep breath and let it out slowly. "Okay, so that's another dead end. And another wasted day. Although, I did have an interesting conversation this evening with a woman who knew Maeline back in high school."

I gave him a brief synopsis of my talk with Keisha Spencer as well as Joline's earlier slip about Kimmie's father.

"So you think this Deshawn who used to live with the Mitchells could be the guy?"

"You know how I feel about coincidences." A thought struck. "Keisha said he might be a cousin. Do you have those photocopies Ellis sent from the family Bible?"

"Hold on a sec." I could hear him rustling papers, but he was back in less than a minute. "Nope. No Deshawn listed. But it could be from the other side of the family. Do we know Joline's mother's maiden name?"

"No. But she said they'd already tested everybody on that side, so we should concentrate on the Mitchells."

"Maybe there's some reason she doesn't want us digging around in her mother's family."

"Like what?" I asked.

"I don't know. Skeletons in the closet she doesn't want us rattling?"

"It's possible, I suppose. I'm beginning to think she hasn't been completely up-front with us about much of anything. Trouble is, I'm not sure I can bring myself to call her on it. It seems like kicking someone when they're already down. Besides, I get the feeling that she's riding pretty close to the edge right now. Emotionally."

"I know what you mean. So we just have to do our best with what we have to work with." Again Erik hesitated. "And you have to stop feeling as if this kid's life or death is one hundred percent on your shoulders. We can only do what we can do, right?"

I sighed. "You're right. I'll try to keep that in mind. So now what?"

"Without a last name, there's nowhere for me to go on Deshawn."

"You know, we've never talked to her husband. Dr. Eastman. I wonder if he'd be more forthcoming. There might be things Joline has told him that she doesn't want to share with us for some reason."

He didn't answer for a long moment. "Do you think that's right? I mean asking a man to betray his wife's confidences? Besides, didn't Joline specifically say not to involve her husband?"

"Yes. But that makes no sense. He must have feelings for Kimmie. Surely he'd want to do anything he could to save her life, even if she isn't his natural daughter."

"Touchy. But you do what you think you have to. If you come up with anything I can check, let me know. I'm off tomorrow. Stephanie and I are going to run into Savannah and bum around a little, but you can get me on the cell if something pops."

"Have fun," I said and hung up.

My tea had gone completely cold, so I carried the cup into the kitchen. While it whirled around in the microwave, I pulled the phone book from under the built-in desk and flipped to the yellow pages. Dr. Jerrold Eastman, OB-GYN, had an office in the medical complex right behind the hospital. I jotted his business number on a notepad just as the bell dinged. Hot tea in hand, I wandered back into the office.

Instead of sitting down again at the desk, I curled up on the chaise I'd added a couple of years before. *When Darnay moved in,* I thought. I'd needed space in the bedroom for another dresser, so the chaise had ended up along one wall of the office. I'd had misgivings about letting someone as volatile and secretive as the former Interpol agent share my house, let alone my life, but I'd decided to take the risk, a leap of faith it had taken only weeks to regret. His desertion had been devastating, a blow from which I had just begun to recover when Red had renewed his assault on my emotional battlements. And once again I'd lowered the drawbridge. . . .

Geoff Anderson. Darnay. Red. *You never learn,* I told myself, and took a sip of the strong, sweet tea. I set the cup on the floor and stretched out, tucking both hands behind my head. I closed my eyes, and bits and pieces of quotations, long ago learned and mostly forgotten, flitted through my mind. When I was young, the Judge and I used to challenge each other, flinging out memorized passages and daring the other to name the citation, points awarded for correct title and author. I smiled, remembering how my best childhood friend, Bitsy Quintard, and I used to sit on the back verandah on rainy days, she with her *Anne of Green Gables* and I with my nose buried in Bartlett's *Familiar Quotations.*

There was something . . . I concentrated on bringing the elusive words into focus. *Madame de Staël, was it?* I asked myself. The original was in French, eighteenth century, if I remembered correctly. I couldn't come up with it exactly, but it was something about love being the entire history of a woman's life, but only an episode in a man's. Maybe that was the problem. Nature of the beasts, male and female. Yet, it hadn't been like that with Rob. We had connected immediately, had—

The shriek of the alarm sent me leaping from the chaise. I kicked over the cup, and a dark stain spread across the pristine white carpet. In less than a moment, the noise abruptly ceased. My eyes shot to the doorway across the hall, to the closet with its floor safe and my pistol. No time. I cast around for something else to use as a weapon when I heard the familiar voice.

"Bay? It's okay. It's me." A moment later, Red stuck his head slowly around the doorway.

"You're damn lucky the Seecamp's in the safe," I said, my heart thudding wildly in my chest for a number of reasons I didn't want to examine too closely.

"Sorry. I screwed up the code." His grin was a little forced, and I could hear a tentative quiver in his voice.

"I meant to change it." I reached down to pick up the overturned cup.

"I'm glad you didn't."

I stepped over the sticky puddle of tea and set the cup on the desk. "What do you want, Red?"

He moved all the way into the office then, his hands shoved into the pockets of his jeans as if he didn't quite know what to do with them.

"To apologize, beg forgiveness, grovel at your feet. Any or all of the above. Your choice."

Again he tried to smile, to joke his way past the awkwardness, but I could see the confusion in his eyes. And the hope, too.

I stalled by crossing in front of him and into the bathroom across the hall. I pulled a rag from the vanity under the sink and ran cold water over it. Back in the office, I again gave Red a wide berth and knelt to begin blotting at the spilled tea.

"Aren't you going to say anything?" he asked. "You can yell and scream if you want. I deserve it. I'm even prepared to take a punch or two."

I glanced up, unable to stop the stony glare from settling into my eyes. "I don't plan on getting arrested for assaulting a sheriff's deputy." I rose and carried the sopping cloth back into the bathroom. "And you can knock off the Mr. Charming act. It's not working."

I turned the faucets on full blast, drowning out his reply. Back in the office, I resumed my work on the stain.

"Did you hear what I said?" he asked softly.

"No."

"I said there's no chance of you being arrested for assault on a police officer. I quit." My head snapped up. "Effective immediately. No badge, no gun. I'm officially a civilian."

Some part of me had never been convinced he'd actually go through with it. I pushed my own righteous indignation aside and really looked at him. He seemed fine with his decision. In fact, there was an ease to his shoulders, a hint almost of relief in his eyes.

"If that's what you want, I'm happy for you," I said, applying myself to my cleaning duties once again.

"Stop screwing around with that rag and look at me." All the wheedling, make-nice tones had fled from his voice. "I'm trying to apologize, damn it. The least you can do is pay attention."

Wrong tack. I jumped to my feet and stared straight into his face. "I'm not interested in that kind of apology. You can't just take all your stuff and stomp out of here in a huff because something I said pricked your damn male pride. I did absolutely nothing to provoke that kind of reaction, and you know it."

I waited then for a word or a gesture that told me he got it, that he understood how deeply his actions had hurt me. He let the opportunity slip away.

"Fine," I said and stepped back.

"Bay—"

"No, Red. Too late. Leave the key on the foyer table. And don't try the alarm code again. I don't think you'd enjoy the view from the *back*seat of a sheriff's cruiser."

He reached for me then, and I turned away. Suddenly, his hand fastened around my wrist. I whirled and glared at him, and he loosened his grip, then let it drop.

"Listen, Bay. I know I acted like an ass, okay? But I was hurt. You treated me like some sort of gigolo, as if I planned on living off you and spending all day at the beach."

"I never said anything like that."

"Maybe not in so many words, but you weren't exactly jumping for joy, either."

"You never gave me a chance." I felt myself relaxing a little as we talked.

"I know," he said again. "That's what I'm saying. And I was scared.

I've got responsibilities—Sarah, and the kids' child support. And you. I want to be able to support you, Bay. And I will. It's just going to take a little time. Rick and I can make a go of this charter business, I know we can."

He stepped back. I wrapped my arms around myself and stared into his eyes.

"I love you, Bay. Please give me another chance."

There was no mistaking his sincerity this time, but somehow I couldn't bring myself to speak. It seemed as if my brain had shut down, as if all the turmoil of the past few days had rendered me mute.

We stood like that, inches apart, neither of us speaking for a long time.

"The kids miss you," he said softly.

"Low blow," I answered in an equally quiet voice.

He stepped around me, his fingers trailing a gentle caress down my arm as he passed, and I shuddered. I felt him pause in the doorway.

"You know where to find me," he said, and a moment later I heard the front door close.

The rain beating against the French doors woke me.

I'd fallen asleep on the sofa again, this time unintentionally. I couldn't tell if it was dark because of the storm or because the sun hadn't yet risen. The inside of my mouth felt as if I'd eaten sand. I flung off the afghan and stumbled up into the kitchen. As I ran the cold water tap, I checked the clock. Only a little after five. A huge clap of thunder rattled the windows, and I nearly dropped the glass in the sink. The reverberation was followed quickly by a zigzag of lightning.

In the brief flare, I saw myself sitting on the back verandah at Presqu'isle, my quivering body wrapped in the Judge's arms, his voice low and soothing as we rocked.

When you see the lightning, start counting like this: one one thousand, two one thousand, three one thousand.

In my head I could hear my childish *Why?* muffled by some soft

material, probably one of his old sweaters that always smelled of to-
bacco and aftershave.

*You keep doin' that until you hear the thunder. That way you can tell
how far away the storm is.*

Standing now in front of the sink ignoring the steadily running
water, I tried to recall how old I'd been. Five? Six? I remembered my
father had gone on to explain about the difference between the speed
of sound and the speed of light, but I didn't understand much of what
he said. I had been content just to snuggle in the safety of his arms,
certain that nothing could ever harm me as long as he was there.

Had he known even then that I wasn't his only daughter? Did he sit
on another porch, calming the fears of another little girl when he was
supposed to be at some conference or meeting? Did he sneak off and
leave me after I'd gone to sleep so he could cradle *Julia* in his strong
embrace? Did he love her, too? More?

The next crack of thunder jerked me back. I filled the glass and
drank greedily, and slowly the visions faded. I wiped my face on the dishtowel and trudged back to the great room. On the sofa I wrapped the
afghan around me and stared out into the blackness, sky and sea melded
into one dark mass broken only by the occasional fork of lightning.

I'd buried the anguish of my father's deception. And Red's desertion.
Two sources of pain I'd felt unable to deal with. *No, three,* I reminded myself. Kimmie Eastman's imminent death if no compatible family member was found. I'd elevated compartmentalization to an art form, but in
the cold gray hours before sunrise, I forced myself to open all those for-
bidding doors and stare inside.

After a while, I let the tears come, slow gentle drops that rolled
down my cheeks and soaked the soft wool of the afghan. Finally spent,
I snuggled back down onto the cushions. Red and I would work things
out. We'd find Joline's sisters. And my own.

Another streak of light split the sky. I fell asleep counting.

One one thousand, two one thousand . . .

CHAPTER TWENTY

BY THE TIME I SURFACED FROM A DEEP, UNTROUBLED sleep, the storm had wandered out to sea, and bright sunlight flooded the great room. I stretched, relieved to find the stiffness in my thigh only minimal. In a matter of minutes I'd pulled on running shorts and a long-sleeved T-shirt, laced up my battered Nikes, and was trotting down the wooden walkway across the dune.

I wove in and out of the early-morning strollers, pounding down the packed sand at the edge of the retreating tide, emptying my mind of the previous night's turmoil. I smiled at a trio of dolphins, arching rhythmically beside me in the surf, almost as if they were keeping pace with my run. The morning sun bathed them in a soft glow and caught the sprays of water they kicked up in an iridescent cascade.

When I bounded up the steps to the deck nearly an hour later, I felt centered again.

I showered and dressed, brewed a pot of tea, and scrambled two eggs. I laid my breakfast out on the table in the screened-in area of the deck and spread the Sunday *Island Packet* open beside it. Despite its bulk, when stripped of the dozens of inserts and advertisements, it took me very little time to skim through the paper. I had just checked the book review and folded open the page with the *New York Times* crossword puzzle when the doorbell rang.

I checked the clock above the kitchen sink as I hurried to the front door. I rarely had visitors and almost never at ten thirty on a Sunday morning. I glanced out the sidelight, my hand poised over the alarm keypad. A tall, distinguished-looking black man in a blue cotton sweater, his hands thrust into the pockets of his neatly pressed khakis, filled my small porch. I punched in the code and opened the door.

"Mrs. Tanner?"

His voice was deep and soft at the same time. A tentative smile briefly lighted his face and then disappeared.

"Yes?"

"I'm sorry to bother you at home, and on a Sunday morning like this, but . . . I'm Jerry Eastman. Joline's husband."

I'd guessed as much, although I couldn't have said why I'd been so certain of his identity. Maybe because he looked like a doctor, or at least like my image of one. It was the eyes, I thought, as I swung the door all the way open. Deep brown and gentle. Caring. Definitely nonthreatening.

"Good morning, Dr. Eastman. Won't you come in?"

"Thank you."

He stepped around me and into the foyer. His height matched my own, and he carried himself with the easy grace of a man certain of his place in the world.

"I'm just having tea out on the deck. Will you join me?"

He nodded, and I led the way through the great room. He took one of the rattan chairs with the brightly flowered cushions and crossed his long legs at the ankles.

"I'll just get another cup," I said and hurried back into the kitchen.

I took a moment to gather up the sugar bowl and pour milk into a small cut-glass pitcher. I didn't have any lemons. Back in the small outdoor room, I poured from the pot and offered a spoon.

"Help yourself. I don't know how you take it."

"Straight up," he said, and the gentle smile stayed this time. "Thanks."

I pushed the newspaper onto the floor and leaned back into my own padded chair.

"I know this is highly irregular," Jerrold Eastman said, "but I didn't know what else to do."

Behind his calm manner, I detected the strain his stepdaughter's illness must be putting on everyone in the family.

"Is it about Kimmie? I hope she's not—"

"No, nothing's changed. Nothing drastic, that is. We admitted her to the hospital again a few days ago, but that was planned. It's too much for Joline to try and care for her at home right now. She needs constant monitoring of her white count, and there are some new medications we're going to try. But . . ."

Again his voice trailed off, and I didn't have any trouble filling in the blank spaces he'd left dangling. It was the beginning of the end for Kimmie, the slow slide into her eventual death without a compatible bone marrow donor.

"I'm sorry," I said, knowing as the words hung between us how futile they were.

Jerrold Eastman set his barely touched cup back on the table and let his large clasped hands dangle between his knees. "I was somewhat surprised to find out Joline had hired you," he said. "Nothing personal, you understand. It's just I didn't . . . don't see the point. Of course, we'll continue to do everything in our power for our little girl, but sometimes you just have to face up to the facts."

I liked him for his choice of pronoun—*our*—but I cringed at the idea that he'd given up.

"I don't have children of my own, Dr. Eastman, so perhaps I don't fully comprehend what Joline is going through. But I can certainly understand how a mother would fight until there were no options left. Surely that's been your experience? I mean, you must have had patients who've tried everything to keep their newborns alive in spite of overwhelming medical odds against their surviving."

He sighed and leaned back in the chair. "Of course. I've counseled too many young parents to accept nature's decision and let a seriously damaged child go. Believe me, I know what a difficult choice it is."

"You have a son, you and Joline, is that right?"

He smiled. "Christopher. Yes. He's nearly seven."

I smiled back. "Could you just let him go?"

The doctor's face clouded. "If you're implying that I'm being heartless because Kimmie isn't my biological child, you're way off base, Mrs. Tanner. And I have to say I find the suggestion offensive. I couldn't love her any more—" He cut himself off. "I love her like my own. But I'm a physician. I know when it's time to give up the fight and prepare yourself for the inevitable. Joline is . . . convinced that she can save Kimmie. I just want her to accept that nothing more can be done and spend what time she has left with our daughter in peace and acceptance."

I felt myself bristle. I understood about not giving up, about holding on to every last shred of hope for as long as possible. I opened my mouth to call him on it when I saw the look of pain on his face, and I checked myself. When I spoke, it was with more compassion than I'd been feeling for the past few minutes.

"So you've come here to ask me to stop trying to find your wife's sisters? To stop contributing to her false hope of saving her daughter?"

Jerrold Eastman swiped at his eyes with the flick of a long, elegant finger. "Yes," he said softly.

"Let me ask you something, Doctor. If a compatible bone marrow donor could be found, is there still a chance it could save Kimmie?"

He swallowed and cleared his throat before replying. "There's always a chance. But it would have to be soon. There's a point in the progression of the disease when nothing more can be done."

"And is Kimmie there yet? At that stage?"

"No, not yet."

"How long?"

"It's hard to say, precisely."

"Guess."

"I can't give you a date. This isn't an exact science, Mrs. Tanner. We can only judge by past experience, and every patient is unique."

"Then there's still time. I'm sorry, Dr. Eastman, but I've been employed by your wife to find her sisters. Unless and until she calls me off, I'm going to keep on doing my damnedest to meet that obligation. I understand your concern, believe me. I'm dealing with something similar in my own life."

I thought of Lavinia's cry in the hospital cafeteria. She wasn't ready to give up on the Judge, even though he'd made his wishes perfectly clear. It was a terrible burden, hope.

"I'm sorry. But I would think then you'd understand my position."

"I do, sir, believe me. But I'm working for your wife. My commitment is to her and what she wants." I paused, and his face tightened into a mask of disappointment. "Have you discussed this with her? Does she know you're here?"

"No. I told her I had some patients to attend to. I thought perhaps you and I could come to some satisfactory conclusion. If it's a matter of your fee—"

"I know you don't intend to be offensive, any more than I did," I said curtly. "Rest assured that I don't need your money."

"I'm sorry. I'm usually not so clumsy. I only meant that I'd be happy to compensate you for your time and expenses so far."

"Your wife gave us a generous retainer which has not yet been exhausted. Naturally I'd return any unexpended funds to her in the event our search is unsuccessful."

The doctor leaned forward in his chair. "Then it seems we have nothing more to discuss. I'm sorry to have troubled you at home, Mrs. Tanner. You've been most gracious in allowing me to state my case."

"Wait!" I said as he made to rise. "May I ask you something?"

He sat back. "Go ahead."

I fumbled for a way to broach a subject that would be awkward at best, painful and embarrassing for the doctor at worst. I trusted that our candid exchange of the past few minutes would hold a while longer.

"Your stepdaughter's biological father. Your wife has told me very little about Kimmie's . . . conception." I heard his sharp intake of breath but ignored it and plunged ahead. "Do you know who this man is or where he could be located? Joline has been strangely reluctant to name—"

Jerrold Eastman fairly leaped from his chair. "How dare you!" His anger rippled in a wave between us. "This is absolutely none of your business, Mrs. Tanner."

He towered over me, and I stood to even the playing field. "My research tells me that the natural father is the best possible candidate for a match with Kimmie. If you're really committed to saving her life, one of you needs to tell me what you know about him."

The doctor's strong hands clenched and unclenched at his sides, and for a moment I thought he might strike me. I took a step back, my legs colliding with the edge of the chair. We glowered at each other for what seemed like a long time.

"I believe his name is Deshawn," I said, my voice even and controlled, "and that he once lived or stayed at the Mitchell house. If you know his whereabouts, I don't understand why you wouldn't tell me. If you love Kimmie as much as you claim."

Jerrold Eastman's anger ratcheted up a couple of notches. "What did she tell you?"

"Nothing, really. I assumed from her reluctance to discuss the matter that perhaps she'd had a fling with someone she barely knew and that he might even be unaware of Kimmie's existence."

The doctor's brief snort of laughter held no trace of humor. "At least you have part of it right. Leave it alone, Mrs. Tanner. If you care as much about my daughter and my wife as you claim, just drop it."

He made an effort to move around me back into the house, but I blocked his path. "You'll have to do better than that, Doctor," I said in an even tone. "I take my job very seriously. And don't forget, I'm working for your wife."

I held my breath, mesmerized by the emotion in his deep brown eyes. When he spoke, I had to strain to catch his whispered words.

"Leave it alone, Mrs. Tanner," he said again. "Please. For the love of God, just drop it."

When he pushed by me, I didn't try to stop him.

A moment later, I heard the front door slam.

CHAPTER
TWENTY-ONE

A WOODPECKER ATTACKED THE RAILING, ITS SHARP *rat-a-tat* against the weathered wood the only sound that broke the stunned silence on the deck. The naked pleading in Dr. Eastman's eyes the moment before he nearly ran out of my house had left me disoriented. I sank back into my chair and reached for my cup. I sipped the tepid tea and tried to organize the chaos of my thoughts.

Had Joline Eastman lied to me about how her daughter was conceived? I broke off that thought. Wait. She hadn't actually told me *anything*. I had assumed a scenario that might explain her strange reluctance, but I had not one shred of evidence to support it. So why had her husband been so determined to steer me away from the subject of Kimmie's biological father? The notion that the man who had contributed half the child's DNA wouldn't be a good candidate for a bone marrow transplant made absolutely no sense to me.

I tried to picture Joline as a young woman, fiercely proud, defying everyone to do what she thought was right and keep her baby. That must have cost her dearly. College would have been out of the picture as she embarked on a life of struggle and sacrifice as a single teenaged parent. Jerry Eastman must have seemed like a knight on a white horse, offering her and her child comfort, security, and stability.

And now, suddenly, all that was about to become meaningless as she faced even more pain, more than any woman should have to bear in one lifetime.

What if she'd been attacked, raped? The idea appeared out of nowhere. That could be the reason both she and her husband refused to discuss Kimmie's biological father. I chewed on the scenario, twisting it around in my mind from all angles. It fit all the known facts, of which, I had to admit, there were precious few. It would explain a lot. I had no idea what kind of emotional—or physical—trauma Joline might have suffered, how such an experience might still be affecting her even this many years later. But if the man who attacked her could be found, he might be the brightest hope for saving Kimmie's life. But how—and where—could I begin to look?

I dumped out my half-eaten scrambled eggs and tried to settle back in with the crossword puzzle, but it was no use. My mind kept flitting to all the dead ends we'd encountered in our search for Joline Eastman's sisters. And the near impossibility, it seemed, of locating Kimmie's biological father. I tossed the pencil angrily onto the folded newspaper and sprang from my chair. I grabbed my keys from the console table, tucked my cell into my pocket, and shoved on my sunglasses. A moment later I jogged down the steps and back over the wooden walkway across the dune.

The bright sun in a pristine blue sky had lured locals as well as the scattered tourists onto the sand. Couples strolled hand in hand while children and dogs dashed in and out of the gently rolling surf. Overhead, gulls wheeled and squawked. I turned away from the Westin Hotel and the condominiums farther down, wandering aimlessly in the direction of the sandbar that jutted out into Port Royal Sound, disappearing now beneath the incoming tide. The farther I walked the fewer people I encountered until I reached a stretch of nearly deserted beach. I flopped down in the soft sand above the tideline, gathered my knees in my arms, and stared out over the water.

The rhythmic shushing of the waves stilled some of the turmoil in my head, and the sun beating down felt like a soft blanket wrapping me in its warmth. I let my mind wander, refusing to allow it to settle on any one of the secrets and tragedies that had occupied me for the past few days. I thought about Red and his earnest apologies I'd so cavalierly swatted aside. I missed the kids. I never thought I'd hear myself say that, but it was true. Their ready acceptance of my change of status from distant but indulgent aunt to leading candidate for stepmother made me smile. I'd been so afraid of their rejection, of a situation arising in which Red would be forced to choose between me and his children. Instead, I'd somehow managed to alienate him all on my own with my stubborn refusal to forgive.

Pride, I thought, *just like Joline Eastman.* False pride, in my case. Red loved me. He'd proved it in a hundred different ways over the years since Rob's murder. And now I seemed willing to jeopardize all that because I was too proud to accept my role in our argument. *Stupid, stupid, stupid.*

I reached into my pocket and hit the speed-dial for his cell before I could stop and analyze what I was going to say. That was one of my biggest problems, I thought, as the phone buzzed in my ear. Sometimes I just had to think a problem to death. Sometimes it was better just to—

"Hey! It's you." His voice held a mixture of surprise and relief. "Where are you?"

"I'm sitting on the beach looking across at the islands wondering when I turned into such an idiot."

His laugh lifted my heart. "I'm not touching that line. Loaded with possibilities, none of them good." He paused when I didn't reply. "Want some company?"

"Where are you?"

"Sitting in your driveway trying to work up the nerve to knock on the door. I checked to make sure your car was in the garage."

"Head toward the sandbar. I'll meet you halfway."

"That's all I've ever wanted," he said, the double meaning of his words not lost on me. "See you in a few."

We decided on lunch at the outdoor patio by the Westin pool. We didn't talk about the fight or its aftermath. In fact, we said hardly anything at all as we strolled back down the beach. Red's hand had automatically reached for mine the moment we met, and I'd made no effort to break the contact. Our silence had the quality of contentment, of an understanding that needed no words. Besides, an idea had begun to form as I'd sat on the beach, and I needed time to think it through.

We ordered pulled pork sandwiches and fries, the pungent aroma of barbecue sauce carrying me back to Patience Brawley's backyard the day before. I shoved that image away. We had to break our handclasp to squeeze lemon into our sweet teas, and I used the opportunity.

"I want to talk to you about something."

I felt him pull back a little, but his smile held only a trace of apprehension. "Okay. Shoot."

"How committed are you to this charter thing? I mean, have you and your friend signed any papers or anything like that?"

I sensed his wariness level increase, but he kept his gaze locked on my face. "Nothing formal," he said. "The new boat won't be delivered for another few weeks, and business is still pretty slack right now. I thought it would give me time to learn the ropes before we make it official. Why?"

I ignored the knot in my stomach and plunged ahead. "How would you like to work for me? For the agency, I mean. For a while. Until you're ready to go full-tilt into chartering. I—" I realized I was babbling and forced myself to back off. "What do you think of the idea in general?"

"You're serious?"

I nodded. "Yup."

"You know I was only kidding about that before, right? I mean, I wasn't angling for a job."

"I know. This doesn't have anything to do with that. I need your help on this case, and we don't have a lot of time." I swallowed and shoved aside the picture in my head of a smiling Kimmie Eastman in her tennis whites. "The case is going to resolve itself, one way or another, probably in less than a month."

"What's it about?"

"I need to have you on the payroll before I can give you any specifics." I held up my hand when I saw the protest rise to his lips. "It's the way the license works. Once you're an employee, the confidentiality agreement in the contract binds you as well as Erik and me. And the Judge, since he's a partner."

"Got it."

The waiter slid plates in front of us at that point, and I took him up on his offer of extra sauce. We sat silently for a few moments, shaking salt on the fries and getting cutlery arranged to our satisfaction. When the boat of spicy red barbecue sauce sat between us, I risked a look across my dripping sandwich at Red. His face was creased in concentration. I wiped my chin and shoved a few fries in my mouth to cover what was becoming an awkward silence.

"If you aren't interested, just say so. No harm, no foul. I realize it's come out of the blue, and—"

Red reached a sticky hand out and covered mine. "Where do I sign?"

CHAPTER
TWENTY-TWO

WE LAY STRETCHED OUT SIDE BY SIDE ON THE CHAISES on my deck, the fading sun still carrying enough warmth to make us drowsy. After lunch, we'd meandered back up the beach, then driven the Jaguar to the office. I'd printed off a copy of the employment contract I'd had drawn up by our attorney in case I ever wanted to hire someone. In a matter of moments, Red had become an official employee, temporarily anyway, of Simpson & Tanner, Inquiry Agents.

Back at the house, I'd given him the file on Kimmie Eastman to read while I fixed a pitcher of iced tea. Thankfully, Red hadn't asked for a beer. I'd definitely need to add a six-pack to Dolores's shopping list since I'd dumped his last three bottles down the drain. I set the glasses on the round table between us and flopped back onto the chaise.

"So what do you think?" I asked.

Red's eyes had drifted closed, and he didn't answer right away. I glanced over at him and saw the troubled creases wrinkling his brow.

"That is almost too sad to think about," he said softly.

"I know." I brought him up to date with a verbal report on my efforts to find Joline's sisters and my conversation that morning with Dr. Eastman. "What else should I have done? What did I miss?"

"About the only thing would have been to ask me to check the sisters out for criminal records. If they've ever been in the system, we might have gotten a more current address."

Erik had suggested it, but I'd balked at the idea, primarily because Red and I hadn't been on the best of terms at the time. I hoped my stupid pride hadn't made things worse for Kimmie.

Red turned his head to face me. "Chances are it wouldn't have helped, but it would have eliminated one more avenue of investigation."

"Any chance of it now?"

"Doubtful. Although I do still have some friends at the office who might be willing to bend the rules a little. I'll make a couple of calls tomorrow."

I relaxed at his words. "Good. What else?"

"This guy Deshawn is intriguing. Do you seriously think he might be the girl's father? I could check to see if there was a rape reported around that time."

"I'm not even sure there was one. I could be way off base. But if Joline was attacked, I'm betting the family hushed it up. Otherwise everyone would know about it, don't you think? And the guy would be in jail."

"I suppose. I could check for convicted rapists named Deshawn, but that's the longest of long shots."

I shook my head. "I just don't understand why she didn't tell me the truth. I can't believe she's more interested in covering up her attack than saving her daughter."

"I know. But we can't judge how deeply it might have affected her emotionally. She might have blocked it out so well that she doesn't consciously remember exactly what happened. I've seen it before. Remember—if it happened—she was just a kid."

The sun had disappeared behind the house, and a cool wind off the ocean set the Spanish moss rustling in the live oaks. Without thinking, I reached for Red's hand. His warm fingers grasped mine and held on tightly.

"Well, whatever happened, there's nothing we can do about it tonight. What do you want for dinner?" I asked.

Without letting go of my hand, he rolled onto his side and gently kissed the soft skin on the inside of my elbow. "You," he said, and I smiled.

When I awoke, the sun had just begun to streak the darkness out over the ocean. I lay wrapped in Red's arms, my head nestled against his shoulder. Even before, when he'd all but officially moved in after Christmas, there hadn't been many mornings when he wasn't gone by the time I woke up. I sighed contentedly, savoring the warmth of his body.

I disentangled my left hand and squinted into the dark, turning my fingers in different directions in an effort to capture the sparkle of my engagement ring. After dinner the night before—delightfully postponed for a couple of hours—I'd retrieved it from the floor safe. In the great room, Red had dropped to one knee and ceremoniously slid it onto my damaged ring finger. I smiled into the lightening room. *"God's in his heaven—All's right with the world,"* I thought. Robert Browning. *Pippa Passes.* Two points.

I snuggled back down under the duvet. Red mumbled something unintelligible and gathered me closer.

I must have dropped back to sleep, because the sound of the shower across the hall roused me for the second time. That and Red's slightly off-key bellowing of "Yellow Submarine." A diehard Beatles fan, he knew the lyrics to every song they'd ever recorded. I smiled and kicked off the covers.

Half an hour later we faced each other across the breakfast table in the kitchen, downing eggs and shuffling sections of the *Island Packet* back and forth. I'd asked Red the night before if he wanted to go home and change, but he sheepishly admitted that he'd never taken his clothes out of the Bronco. In a matter of a few minutes, everything was back in place as if our brief breakup had never happened.

I checked my watch. "Time to get rolling."

I carried plates and cups to the sink, and Red stacked them in the dishwasher.

"How do you think Erik's going to react?" he asked without looking at me.

"He'll be fine. The biggest problem is where you're going to sit. We only have two desks. And no room for another one."

He waved off my concern. "I don't need a desk. If I'm going to be any help to you, it isn't going to happen staring at a computer. Let me do the legwork. I've built up a lot of connections over the years. Time to put them to good use."

I gathered up my bag and a light blazer. "We should take two cars, don't you think?"

"Absolutely. If I have to go chasing down leads, I don't want to leave you stranded."

I opened the door to the garage and paused. "You sure you're okay with this? Working for me, I mean? We don't always see eye to eye on things."

He gripped my shoulders and kissed me soundly. "That's what makes life with you so interesting, sweetheart." He stepped back and grinned. "Come on, let's get going. I hear the boss can be a real terror if you're late for work."

Erik's grin when I explained Red's presence—in civvies—told me all I needed to know about how he would deal with our having another employee. I started to explain that Red's salary would come out of my share of the profits, but he wasn't having any of that.

"He's on the payroll, just like I am. No different."

Erik had been gradually buying into the business over the years, insisting that he wouldn't accept a full partnership until he could pay his own way.

I resisted the urge to hug him. "All right, then, let's get cracking."

We rolled out my chair and the one for clients that usually sat in front of my desk and gathered in the reception area. I filled Erik in on Jerrold Eastman's visit on Sunday morning, and he typed while I talked.

"Red is going to see if someone at the sheriff's office will run a check on Maeline and Contessa Mitchell. Don't forget to try the married names as well. Erik will print you out the details."

"Done," Erik said, and a moment later the printer whirred to life.

"I want to find this Deshawn guy," I said, "whether he's Kimmie's father or not. He may know something that could help us find the rest of the family. Suggestions?"

The silence lasted for a solid minute. "I've been thinking about something," Erik said, his index finger working the scrolling wheel on his mouse. "Here it is. You said that when you talked to Patience Brawley on Saturday she hinted at some big blowup in the family, something that made them estranged. Let's look at that and see if it has any connection. Seems to me the timing is about right. Didn't she say she hadn't had any contact for ten or fifteen years?"

"It's a possibility. You're thinking maybe somehow the possible attack on Joline is related to the family rift?" I asked, and he nodded. "We need a time line. Can you work on that? Factor in the probable date the rape would have occurred based on Kimmie's birth date. I think Joline would have been around seventeen. Double-check that, too. And when her mother and grandmother were killed in that accident."

Erik's excitement had translated to his fingers, which were already dancing across his keyboard. "I'll lay everything out in a database and get it organized. Give me a couple of hours to do the research and get it all together."

"Great. Red, see what you can shake out of your former colleagues. We still need to find the sisters. And one of them may know how to track down Deshawn."

Red gave me a mock salute. "I'm on it, chief," he said and grinned. "Probably best to do it in person. I have some paperwork to fill out at the office about my pension and a few other things." He turned and retrieved the single sheet from the printer tray. "I'll call you."

I saw him hesitate, then decide kissing the boss goodbye probably wasn't good office etiquette. With a wave, he disappeared out the door.

"You sure you're okay with this?" I asked.

Erik nodded. "I think it's a great idea, especially on this case." His face sobered. "We're running out of time, and another pair of eyes and legs could make the difference for Kimmie Eastman."

"Okay. I'm going to go through those letters Joline gave us, the ones between her grandparents during the war. I didn't think they had any relevance at first—and it felt too much like prying into their private lives—but now I'm wondering if there might be some usable clues. And maybe I can fill in some more of the blanks on that genealogy."

"I could get you a program for that," Erik said. "There's a couple out there we can download."

"I'll let you know," I said. "Sometimes I think better with a pen in my hand."

I returned the chairs to their rightful places in my office and cleared off the top of my desk. I retrieved the envelope that held the letters Joline Eastman had left with me along with the sparsely filled-in family tree and spread them out. I pulled a Diet Coke from the mini-fridge, hung my jacket on the hook behind my door, and rolled up my sleeves.

I picked up the first envelope, the one on which the postmark hadn't been completely obliterated, and studied the smeared ink. What little I could still see of the water-damaged handwriting looked almost like a child's, like the kind of stilted, formal penmanship once taught in elementary school. It reminded me in a way of my father's ornate writing style, and the thought stopped me in my tracks. I swallowed the knot of guilt and picked up the phone.

"Lavinia, it's me."

"Why didn't you come to dinner yesterday, child? Your father wasn't happy, I can tell you that."

The unspoken tradition of my taking Sunday dinner at Presqu'isle had gone completely out of my mind the day before. What's more, I hadn't even called to check on the Judge's condition. Whatever misery Lavinia wanted to heap on my head would be well deserved.

"I'm sorry," I said, meaning it. "Red came back."

Her soft laugh absolved me. "I understand. And so will Tally. So everything's all right with you two?"

I smiled, remembering the hours we'd spent reconciling in the king-sized bed. "Yes, ma'am. I'm wearing the ring."

"I'm happy for you."

"So how is the Judge?"

"He's still a little weak, and shoveling that medicine down him takes up most of my time. I told him last night that all his fussin' and complaining is grating on my last nerve."

I laughed. "You're wonderful, do you know that?"

I could almost feel the heat of her blush through the telephone. "Why don't you and Redmond come to dinner tonight? I'll make something special. To celebrate."

"We'd love to," I said, for once not having to check with Red to see when he was scheduled to be on duty. "Seven?"

"Make it a little earlier. Your father tends to flag as the day wears on. He'll be better company around six."

"Six it is," I said, then a sobering thought struck. "We're working on this case of the sick little girl. Red's helping me. The only thing would be if we get held up chasing down a lead on that."

"Understood. You do what you have to. If you can't make it, we'll do it some other time. Nothing's more important than saving a child."

"Amen," I whispered and laid the phone gently back in its cradle.

CHAPTER
TWENTY-THREE

Y DEAR HUSBAND, THE FIRST LETTER BEGAN. *I hope this finds you safe.*

Joline's grandmother's handwriting was the same as on the envelope, each word carefully constructed. I pictured her hunched over the kitchen table, the pen clutched tightly in her fingers as she struggled to swallow her anxiety and speak of the everyday, mundane goings-on of the Mitchell family. A lot of the ink in the body of the letters had been smeared, too, so there were gaps in the narrative. But as I paged through the sparse information that had escaped the water damage, a picture of life in wartime South Carolina began to emerge. Mrs. Mitchell spoke of shortages and rationing, of her garden and how she shared its bounty with those less fortunate folks on Edisto Island. And of the blessings of being close to the sea where fishing and shrimping provided food they might otherwise not have been able to obtain.

Reading between the lines, I could tell that their store was in trouble. I checked the signature on the letter. Joline's paternal grandmother had been named Esther, and she obviously struggled daily to obtain goods with which to stock the almost barren shelves, although she made light of it when corresponding with her husband. She spoke rather of their friends and neighbors, of humorous incidents around the tiny island, the day-to-day minutia of small-town life in the forties. No mention of other husbands and sons off fighting, of wounds or injuries or of the dreaded telegrams from the War Office that devastated tens of thousands of families during World War II. Even if she'd been inclined to burden her husband with such sadness, it probably wouldn't have made it past the censors.

As I perused the next letter, and the next, more information began to emerge. I pulled the genealogical chart over in front of me and traced the lines back to Chauncey and Esther's generation. Joline's grandfather had five siblings, represented by four empty boxes and the one I had filled in from the information in Patience Brawley's Bible. Patience's father Joseph and Joline's grandfather had been brothers.

I turned back to the letters, scanning them for proper names and any clues to their relationship to the family. In a matter of a few minutes, I'd managed to extract the names of what I was pretty certain were the rest of Chauncey Mitchell's siblings: Ezra, Zachariah, Ruth, and Mary. Someone had been a student of the Bible. Mention of birthdays gave me a couple of their dates of birth as well. I penciled the information in on my copy of the chart.

I studied the many interconnected boxes and lines, trying to fix in my mind the relationships and how any of it might help us find a donor for Kimmie Eastman. I leaned back in my chair and rubbed my eyes behind the reading glasses perched on the end of my nose.

"Hey, Erik?" I called, and a moment later he stood in the doorway.
"Yes?"

"Take a look at this with me, will you? I think I've stared at it so long I'm losing perspective. Do you see anything there that we can use? I'm beginning to think this whole family tree thing will turn out to be a waste of time."

He sat in the client chair, and I swung the genealogy around so we could both look at it.

"The letters didn't help?" he asked while his fingers traced from the bottom to the top of the page.

"Too early. Joline's father wasn't born until after the war—1946— so most of his generation wasn't even alive when these were written. I managed to fill in a few empty boxes, but I can't see anything worth pursuing."

He continued to follow the convoluted connections from level to level. "This is interesting," he finally said, tapping a box on the far right of the paper.

"What?"

"Right here. See? Did you make this entry? For Patience's sister, Charity?"

"Yes. She was listed in the Bible. Why?"

"She has the line indicating a child, but no marriage. And there's no name in the box."

I pawed through the papers strewn across my desk and finally pulled out the list Ellis Brawley had e-mailed us.

"Here it is. Charity. It just says, 'child.'" I slid the chart back in front of me. "Okay, so Charity, Shadrack, and Patience are of the same generation. That means her child would be a contemporary of the Mitchell girls." I paused. "And that would make him or her Joline's second cousin or something like that, right?"

"Right," Erik said. "And if it was a boy, it could be the mysterious Deshawn."

I tried to suppress the rising excitement. "Can you check the notes you entered from my conversation with Keisha Spencer, the older Mitchell girls' high school friend out in Bluffton?"

He stepped out into the reception area and typed standing in front of his desk. "Got it. What do you want to know?"

"Didn't she say Deshawn was some sort of cousin?"

He scrolled. "Yes. Here it is. She used those exact words, according to your notes. 'Some sort of cousin.' And that he might have lived with them one summer."

"And Kimmie was born when?"

"September twentieth. I just entered it in the time line."

I did some quick math. "So Kimmie's conception had to occur around December the year before. That sure isn't summer."

"But Keisha also said he used to hang around the house. Even if he didn't live there doesn't mean he didn't have . . . access."

"True. So now what? Anything you can do with the information? If his mother wasn't married, he probably went by Deshawn Mitchell, don't you think? Can you work with that?"

"I can sure as hell try," he said, dropping down into his chair. "Let me take a run at it."

I thought back to my conversation with Joline on Saturday morning, and something clicked. "You know, when Joline said that he couldn't help, I assumed she meant Kimmie's father was dead. What if it's something else?"

Erik looked up. "Like what?"

"I'm not sure. Maybe he's in the military and deployed overseas. Or maybe he's a respectable married man with a family of his own now. Or he could be in prison. I guess there are lots of other possibilities that she might consider insurmountable reasons." I paused. "Or maybe she has no idea what became of him after the attack or whatever it was that happened."

"I'll get started," Erik said.

"Good."

I sat for a moment staring out across the reception area at the framed print of sunset over the marshes that hung on the far wall. Maybe we were completely off base with this Deshawn thing. Red was right—I did have a bad habit of latching on to an idea and trying to manipulate the known facts to fit my preconceived notion. We could be wasting Kimmie's dwindling time—

The phone jerked me back to reality.

"I've got it," I called and picked up the handset. "Simpson and Tanner."

"Hey, boss, it's me." Red's voice held a hint of laughter along with an exuberance that I suddenly realized had been missing for some time. His decision to leave the sheriff's office might have been long overdue.

"Did you find something?"

"Yes and no. We came up dry on the sisters. No record either of them was ever arrested for anything, at least not in South Carolina. Of course, if it was in some small jurisdiction and didn't result in jail time, it wouldn't be in the database. Or if they've remarried, and it happened under different names."

"So what's the 'yes' part?"

He sobered. "I ran across something completely by accident while I was checking out the names, and I think it might be relevant. In fact, more than relevant. But it isn't actually good news."

"Why am I not surprised?"

"Okay," he said. "There's an unsolved homicide, right here in Beaufort County, about fifteen years ago. Body, male, probably African-American, approximately midtwenties to early thirties, found by some kids playing in a swampy area out past Pritchardville near Rose Dhu Creek. Nothing much left but the skeleton, and even some of that was missing." He swallowed hard. "Gators must have been at it."

The buzzing in the back of my head almost drowned out his next words.

"But the skull was intact. Single gunshot wound. They also recovered a couple of ribs with nicks on them that could have been caused by bullets. The body was never positively identified, and it's been a cold case almost from day one."

I could feel the pieces tumbling around in my brain, trying to fall neatly into place. I forced myself not to jump to conclusions, but the temptation was almost overwhelming.

"Why do you think this is connected to Joline and Kimmie?"

"Because the only missing person's report that even came close at the time to matching the dead man was filed by a woman named Patience Brawley." He paused for effect. "On her nephew—Deshawn Mitchell."

"Jesus, Mary, and Joseph," I whispered, and Red added, "Amen."

CHAPTER
TWENTY-FOUR

§O WHAT DOES IT MEAN?" I ASKED AFTER I'D MANAGED to catch my breath. "Why couldn't they make a positive identification back then? What about DNA?"

"Early times for that," Red reminded me, "and it wasn't as readily accepted as it is now. Besides, Mrs. Brawley refused to give a sample."

"Why?"

"Well, according to the report, they contacted her. When this body was discovered. She told the sheriff in Colleton County that her nephew had come back home, so it couldn't possibly be him."

"Did anyone check it out? I mean, to see if he really had turned up alive?"

I could hear the hint of exasperation in Red's voice and the effort he was making to control it. "We—they didn't have the manpower to spend on it. We assumed the woman would know. They took a quick look at her—solid citizen, teacher, no record. Ditto for her husband and kids. Without an ID, there really wasn't anything they could do."

I hadn't meant it as a criticism of the sheriff's office in either county, but it seemed strange that they'd just taken Patience's word for it.

But what if she'd lied? What if Deshawn Mitchell *had* been the cousin who'd lived a while with Joline's family? What if he'd impregnated her—willingly or not—and revenge or punishment had been exacted? That could explain the rift between the two sides of the family, especially if they all knew what had happened to Deshawn. Patience and her sister might not have wanted one of their relatives to go to jail, but they certainly wouldn't have forgotten. Or forgiven.

It could also be why Joline's father had skipped out. And why Joline had been so evasive about so many things in her past. I had no trouble envisioning a scenario in which her father—maybe with help from others, maybe not—had murdered Deshawn Mitchell and dumped his body in the swamp.

"Bay? You still there?" I heard Red say.

"Sorry. Yes. I'm just trying to digest all this."

"I'm on my way in. We can talk about it then."

"Okay," I mumbled and hung up without saying goodbye.

Thoughts and images raced around in my head. The scenario fit all the known facts, but . . .

"Damn it!"

"What's wrong?" Erik called from his desk.

"It doesn't matter." I flung down the pen I'd been gripping and dropped my head in my hands.

He stood in the doorway and spoke softly. "What doesn't matter?"

I sighed and leaned back in my chair. "That was Red. He found a cold case. Unidentified body of an African-American male shot at least a couple of times." I filled him in on the rest of the details. "It might actually fit. Deshawn rapes or at least has sex with Joline. Her father shoots him and takes off. Patience figures it out and cuts off that branch of her family. And the timing is about right, too."

"So what's the problem?"

"Even if the murdered guy could genetically be Kimmie's father, it doesn't help us. He's dead. And our job is to find a live donor." I sighed, reluctant to let go of the mystery of Deshawn Mitchell's death. But our duty was to a sick teenager and—

"Mitchell," I said aloud and slapped my hand on the desk. "God, sometimes I'm such an idiot."

I looked up to find Erik staring at me. "What are you talking about?"

"The Shack. Haven't I ever taken you there?" He shook his head. "It's down on Skull Creek by the shrimp docks. Run by a family named Mitchell. Bubba used to play pro football, but he blew out his knee."

"You think there's a connection to our Mitchells? It's a fairly common name."

"I know, but I should have thought of them right off. They could be some kind of shirttail relations, and they've been around here for generations. They know everybody."

I looked up as Red opened the door.

"Wait right there," I said, snatching up my bag from the lower desk drawer.

"What's up?" Red asked.

"We're going to lunch at the Shack." I turned to Erik. "You want to join us?"

"I'm still working on the time line, and I've got a couple of other things I want to check out. I'll have a pizza delivered."

I crossed the floor, took Red's arm, and spun him ahead of me out the door.

"What's going on?" he asked, sliding into the car as I clicked my seat belt and spun out of our parking lot.

"Dwight and Bubba Mitchell," I said, coasting through the stop sign. "Ring a bell?"

Red gripped the door handle. "Take it easy, okay? They're not going anywhere. Besides, there's a ton of Mitchells around here. Family's one of the oldest on the island."

"I know, but it's a lead we can't afford to ignore."

I knew he wasn't convinced, but at least he had the good sense to keep his reservations to himself.

A few minutes later I turned into the dirt driveway and slowed over the ruts as we bounced our way to the back of the property. Smoke rose from the drums set out beside the tiny building that housed the restaurant. With its few tables and ramshackle appearance, it hardly qualified for the name, but the fresh seafood was among the best on the island. I pulled up under a canopy of drooping tree limbs and Spanish moss, sending up a cloud of dust before I cut the engine.

When we stepped out into the sunshine, a warm breeze carried the dank smell of decades of fish and shrimp hauled ashore from the nets of the Mitchell family's fleet of sturdy trawlers. It mingled with the smoke from the cooking fires creating a uniquely Lowcountry perfume. It always amazed me that the town fathers hadn't shut the place down years ago for any number of zoning violations, although it probably had something to do with the fact that most of our local officials were regular customers.

Bubba was hard to miss. His girth approached that of the live oak he stood beneath, his shaved head glistening with sweat as he added hunks of cut wood to one of the barrels. He turned at our approach, and a wide grin split his shiny black face.

"Hey, you two! I was beginnin' to think I'd done fed you some bad oysters or somethin'. Where the hell y'all been?"

The hand he extended to Red and then to me could have swallowed a basketball.

"Time just seems to get away from us, Bubba." Red paused, waiting for me to take the lead. "You know how it is."

If the giant of a man wondered why Red was out of uniform, he let it pass without comment. "Good to see you, Sergeant. You, too, Miz Tanner. Y'all come for lunch? It's a mite early, but you can grab you a table. I'll have some shrimp on the fire here in just a second. Won't take but a couple minutes."

He reached down into the white plastic bucket at his feet and lifted out a handful of the large Lowcountry delicacies. Thankfully, their heads had already been removed. I have a hard time eating something that's staring back at me.

"Sounds great," I said.

Bubba Mitchell slapped a blackened grate on top of the drum and began tossing on shrimp from the bucket.

"I wonder if I could ask you something," I said.

"Sure."

"Do you have any family up in Jacksonboro? Or around Pritchardville?"

Bubba slid a wooden paddle under half a dozen sizzling shrimp and expertly flipped them over. "Used to be lots of Mitchells in Bluffton," he said. "Some of Daddy's family come from there. But mostly here on the island. Not many left, though. Why'd you ask?"

"I have a client," I said, measuring my words. "From the inquiry agency. They're trying to track down some relatives named Mitchell. Father's name was Shadrack. I thought you might know them."

"Nope," he said without hesitation. "No one by that name on Daddy's side. I'd remember."

I knew he was right. It was an unusual name. I closed my eyes and conjured up a mental image of the genealogical chart. "How about Patience or Charity? They're sisters. Or Deshawn."

Again his massive head moved from side to side. "Sorry." He turned and lifted a battered metal tray from the stump of a long-dead tree. "You might ask Dwight, but I'm pretty sure they're no kin of ours." A look settled over his face, part sadness, part question. "Mama might've known more, but she passed, you know. Last year."

"I know. I was sorry to hear of it. She put up a good fight against the cancer."

Bubba nodded and used the paddle to slide a couple of dozen pink shrimp onto the platter. "This be enough for you?"

"That'll be great," Red answered and took the tray. "Thanks."

Inside, Bubba's equally towering brother, Dwight, greeted us with a wave. "Mornin'. Y'all want red sauce or butter?"

"Both," I said, climbing up onto a stool at one of the round wood tables, each of which had a hole cut in the middle with a dented metal bucket stuck down inside for shrimp and oyster shells.

Dwight lumbered over and slapped down two bowls.

"Thanks," I said. "I was asking Bubba outside if you had any relatives over in Jacksonboro. He said he didn't think so. They'd be Mitchells."

"None I heard of."

"Thanks anyway."

"Eat up," he said and turned away.

A few more customers wandered in while we peeled our shrimp. Dwight had brought us a basket of chips and a pile of napkins on one of his trips by, along with two icy cans of Coke. None of that diet stuff at the Shack. We ate and sipped in silence for a couple of minutes. I avoided the red sauce and opted for the warm butter with big slices of garlic floating on top. A few moments later I was groaning with pleasure and licking butter from my fingers.

"So what's our next step?" Red asked.

I looked up to see his eyes watering from the horseradish in the red sauce.

"I don't know. Back to the sisters, I guess. Even if the dead guy from the marsh is Kimmie's father, it isn't going to help her now." I sighed. "I wish Joline would just tell us the truth—all of it. I still don't understand why she would withhold information that could save her daughter's life."

Red drained his Coke. "It's frustrating, I know, but that's how it is sometimes. Maybe as a cop I just got used to people knowing stuff they don't want to share, no matter how good the reasons were for them to come clean. We ran across it all the time, and it had nothing to do with social or economic status, or race, creed, or national origin." His smile was rueful. "It's just human nature, I guess. People have secrets. No sense fighting it."

Secrets. I stared straight into his eyes, and the words popped out of my mouth without any conscious thought or intent.

"I have a sister," I said.

CHAPTER
TWENTY-FIVE

ED STARED BACK AT ME. HIS STUNNED LOOK WOULD have been comic if not for the subject matter. A dribble of shrimp sauce ran down his hand and over his wrist, but he ignored it.

"Say that again."

I concentrated on cleaning butter and garlic from my fingers with a fresh napkin. "Remember when I was looking for the Judge's medical papers that night he spent in the hospital?"

I looked up to find his eyes locked on my face. He nodded.

I told him then about the obituary, about "two daughters," and the name *Julia Simpson*. "And just before that, when I first went in to see him. He was dropping off to sleep, but I could have sworn he said, 'Get Julia.' It didn't make any sense until later, back at Presqu'isle, when I was going through his files."

"Did you ask him about it?"

I shook my head. "I've tried, a couple of times, but . . ." I let my head droop. "I just can't bring myself to open up something he obviously wants to keep from me." I swallowed hard, fighting tears.

Red's hand closed over mine where it rested on the table, a paper napkin clutched so tightly in my fingers it had begun to disintegrate. "Does Lavinia know?"

"I don't think so. At least she didn't react to the name."

I almost blurted out the other mystery that had been scratching at the back of my mind: the newspaper clipping about the drowning death of Brooke Garrett. But that would have meant admitting to my unforgivable snooping in Lavinia's private business, my violation of her treasure box, and I didn't yet know why I couldn't get that out of my head.

"You have to talk to him about it." Red squeezed my hand one last time and let it go. "These are the kinds of things that can tear a family apart, Bay. You and the Judge have been through some tough times lately, but this is something you need to get cleared up before—"

My head snapped up. "Before he dies?"

Red didn't flinch. "Yes."

"We need to get back to the office." I threw some cash on the table and headed for the car.

Red caught up to me just as I was about to pull open the driver's door. "Wait. Hang on a second."

He gripped both my shoulders, turned me around to face him, then gathered me into his arms. I fought him briefly, half-heartedly, finally relaxing into the reassurance of his embrace. We stood that way for a long minute before I leaned back to look into his eyes.

"I'm okay about it," I said, forcing a smile. "The sister thing. The idea just takes a little getting used to."

He kissed my forehead and let me go, and I slid into the warm leather seat. When he'd slammed his own door behind him, I pulled back onto Squire Pope Road.

"Have you tried to find her?" Red asked, and I could feel his gaze on the side of my face.

"Sort of. I've done some checking in our databases, but it's a common name."

"Like Mitchell," he said, and I smiled.

"Right."

He let a moment of silence go by. "When this other . . . thing is all over with, we'll make an effort to locate her. If you still don't want to ask your father straight out."

"We'll see," I said, forcing my mind back to the only problem that should be occupying it at the moment: saving Kimmie Eastman's life.

The office door was locked when I tried the knob, and I glanced around to find Erik's black Expedition missing from the parking lot. I dug in my bag for my key ring and let us in.

"Remind me to get you a key," I said over my shoulder to Red, my mind shooting back to all the arguments Ben Wyler and I had had on the subject. My late, supposedly silent, partner had been something of a bully, a charming know-it-all who knew exactly how to push all my worst buttons. Depriving him of easy access to the office had been petty, but it had given me at least a slim feeling of having control over my own business.

"Don't bother. I can't see any reason I'd need to be in here without you or Erik."

I smiled at the note propped up on my telephone. "Erik's on the trail of something," I told Red. "He says, 'Got an idea, but I need to track it down in person. Back as soon as I can.'"

"Is he always that mysterious?" Red sat down in the client chair.

"Sometimes. He loves to string out a story or drop some bombshell in my lap. Drives me crazy once in a while, but he's so good at what he does I can't complain."

I straightened out the Mitchell papers I'd left strewn across my desk, returning the letters to their envelopes.

"Anything there?" Red asked.

"Nope. I added a little data to the family tree, but nothing helpful. If your cold case guy turns out to be Kimmie's father . . ."

I didn't have to spell it out for him. "I know." He gestured at the blinking light on the telephone on the corner of my desk. "Have you heard from Dr. or Mrs. Eastman since yesterday?"

"Let's see." I checked the message queue and listened for a moment before hitting the Delete button. "Insurance," I mumbled. I wiped out the next one as well, a request for me to join a travel club. I was prepared to go three for three when Jerrold Eastman's voice stopped me.

"Mrs. Tanner. Please call me as soon as you get this message. It's very important that I speak with you."

I grabbed a pencil and scribbled down the two numbers he'd recited before disconnecting.

"The doctor," I said and punched in the first seven digits.

"Dr. Eastman's office," the pleasant voice answered. "How may I help you?"

I pulled the rolling chair under me and sat. "This is Bay Tanner. I'm returning the doctor's call."

"Oh, yes, ma'am. He's expecting you. One moment please."

The hold music was surprisingly upbeat, and I found myself tapping the eraser end of the pencil against the desk while I waited. In what was probably record time for any physician I've ever tried to get on the phone, Jerrold Eastman picked up.

"Mrs. Tanner? Thank you so much for returning my call so quickly."

"It sounded urgent."

"I want to apologize for my abrupt departure yesterday. As you can imagine, the subject is a painful one, and—" In the background, I heard the click of a door opening. "Yes, Margaret, what is it?" His voice was muffled but still understandable. "I asked you not to disturb me for the next few minutes."

I didn't catch the nurse's reply, but the doctor let out a long, slow sigh. "Tell her to get to the hospital. I'll meet her there." A pause. "I'm sorry, Mrs. Tanner. One of my patients is in hard labor. I have to go."

"I understand, Doctor. We'll talk another time."

"Wait! Apologizing isn't the only reason I called. I need your help."

That was certainly a complete about-face from his attitude the last time we'd spoken. Before I could ask what I could do for him, his voice came again, this time in a rush of words and emotion.

"Joline's gone."

"What do you mean, gone? Gone where?"

"I wish I knew. Look, I don't have much time. Babies don't wait."

He cleared his throat. "She wasn't home when I called from the office this morning, and she hasn't been to see Kimmie all day. She's not answering her cell. I checked with everyone I could think of, but no one has seen her. The housekeeper said she left a note asking if she could stay over with Christopher tonight in case Joline didn't get home."

I looked up to see Red staring at me quizzically, but I didn't want to interrupt the doctor's narrative to fill him in.

"Maybe she just decided to take a day off. Maybe she just needs a break from the stress and—"

"No!" The force of his denial stunned me. "Joline is not a flighty woman. She has responsibilities—to both our children. She wouldn't just take off like this on a whim. Something . . . something's happened to her. I can feel it."

I could hear the panic in his rising voice. He took a moment to calm himself before he spoke again.

"I have to go. I'll call you this evening, Mrs. Tanner, but consider yourself on retainer. From me." He was barely able to conceal the tremor of emotion in his voice. "Find my wife."

CHAPTER TWENTY-SIX

HAT DOESN'T MAKE ANY SENSE." RED HAD RISEN AND begun pacing the small area between my office and Erik's desk while I related the conversation to him. "Why would she leave like that, without telling her husband?"

"I don't know." It seemed to be my stock answer for every one of the questions Red had been firing at me. "And neither does he."

"Maybe they had some kind of row, and he doesn't want to admit it."

"Then why call me at all?"

"Good point. If he thought she'd just come back after she cooled off, he wouldn't want the embarrassment of involving a virtual stranger."

"Especially me. I don't think I'm exactly at the top of the good doctor's hit parade. And you had to hear his voice. He's seriously worried."

Somehow Tracy Dumars's face had planted itself in my mind and refused to be dislodged. She, too, had left home without her husband's knowledge, and Billy had been frantic to get her back. That ended in the worst possible outcome. I shook my head. This wasn't the same, I told myself. Not even close.

"What does he want you to do?" Red's question banished my useless memories.

"I have no idea. He said he'll call me tonight. Until then, I guess we just wait. Maybe Joline will have come back by then, and the whole thing will be moot."

I finished straightening up my desk, my eyes straying to the telephone as I returned all Joline Eastman's family letters to the big envelope in which I kept them.

Red watched for a few moments before he spoke. "So what do you want me to do? I'm feeling kind of useless just sitting here watching you work."

I pulled a scratch pad toward me, wrote, then tore off the top sheet. "This is Erik's cell number. Call him and see what he's up to. Tell him about Joline's disappearance and that I said to get back here as soon as he can."

I thought he might balk at playing secretary, but he turned immediately for the phone on the reception desk. I re-filed the Mitchell papers and leaned back in my chair. I tuned out Red's voice and juggled scenarios in which it made sense for Joline to abandon her dying daughter. It would have to be something so overwhelmingly important that she'd willingly leave Kimmie's bedside, yet something so personal—and awful—she didn't feel she could share it with her husband.

A lover? A threat? Blackmail? Money? Nothing I could envision would explain her actions, and yet Joline Eastman, as her husband had pointed out, wasn't a flighty woman. She loved her daughter more than her own life. I would have bet everything I had on that. Nonetheless, she was gone.

I sat up straighter. *At least according to her husband.* We had nothing but his word for any of it. What if Red was right? What if they'd had some sort of confrontation after he'd left my house? What if it had turned violent? Was Jerrold Eastman devious enough to embroil me in some phantom search for a wife he already knew was dead?

"Erik wants to talk to you."

Red's words from the doorway of my office made me jump a couple of inches out of the chair. I reached for the phone. "What's up? Where are you?"

"I'm almost to Savannah. Just heading across the bridge."

"What's over there?"

"Well, it's kind of complicated, and maybe you'd be better off—"

I sighed and looked at Red. "Is it illegal?"

"Well, technically, maybe. But it's not going to come back on us, at least not if I can work a couple of angles."

"Does this involve hacking into some database?"

Red's chin snapped up, and I was surprised to see him grinning.

"Yes, but like I said, it won't come back to bite us. I'm heading for a cyber café in Savannah."

It took me just a moment to figure it out. I had obviously been hanging out with my partner way too long.

"So whatever site it is you're hacking into can't trace the intrusion back to you or your computer."

"Dead on."

"Just a sec. Red's here, and I'm going to put you on speaker."

"You think that's a good idea? I mean—"

"He's retired. Hold on."

I fiddled with the buttons. "Sit down," I said, and Red slid into the client chair. "Go ahead, Erik."

His voice with its soft North Carolina accent filled the office. "Okay, I got to thinking about Kimmie Eastman's birth certificate. It was easy enough to access, but there's no father listed. Just Joline Mitchell as the mother."

"I know. We checked that right up front."

"But she goes by Eastman, and I was wondering if the doc had formally adopted her. If so—"

"There'd be a record," I interrupted. "But we're pretty sure we already know who the natural father was. And he's dead."

He held his silence for a moment. "We're assuming that. It makes sense, given the information we have, but we don't know it for a fact."

"True. But adoption records are usually sealed tight, aren't they?"

"Right. But that doesn't mean they can't be accessed. Assuming they've been digitized. I did some checking, and the child's father has to sign off on the adoption if he can be located, just to make sure he can't come back later on and claim his parental rights."

I thought about it for a moment. "But this isn't like Joline was giving her up to some other couple. Are you sure it would be the same if she's just changing her last name? And besides, if Kimmie is the result of a rape, the father would be admitting to a major felony."

"You're right, but it won't hurt to get into the records and find out. Maybe we're way off base with this Deshawn Mitchell thing. The trouble is, like you said, the files are supposed to be sealed, so I thought it would be better to keep our name out of it. Just in case."

I glanced at Red, whose smile had disappeared during the two-way conversation. "Something you want to say?" I asked him.

"No. Just that it makes me uncomfortable to be party to something illegal. Takes a little getting used to."

I grinned at him. "If you intend to hang out with Erik for any length of time, you'd better be prepared to skate really close to the line once in a while. Erik," I said, directing my voice toward the phone, "how long do you think this will take?"

"Not long once I get to the café. I'll pay cash for the computer time."

"Okay, fine, but we've got another issue to deal with here." I gave him the sketchy details of Joline Eastman's disappearance and about her husband's insistence that we find her.

"She left Kimmie in the hospital?" Again, Erik had zeroed in on the crux of the whole matter.

"I know it's strange. That's what has the doctor so concerned. So get back here as quickly as you can, okay?"

"Sure. I'm pulling into the parking lot now. I should be back on the road in half an hour."

"That's all?"

"Hey, what can I say? I'm good."

"We may be out on the trail by the time you get back. I'll let you know where to find us."

"I'll keep in touch," he said and hung up.

Red was shaking his head when I looked up. "Does he do that on any regular basis?"

"Yeah, actually, he does. Sometimes there are more important things at stake than privacy and cyber laws."

I could tell he wasn't convinced, but he let it go. "Where are we off to?"

I reached behind me and lifted my jacket from the back of the chair. "The hospital. I think it's time we met Kimmie Eastman."

The room seemed to be filled with balloons and flowers, and brightly colored cards were scattered everywhere. A huge poster with GET WELL, KIMMIE! in bright red letters had been taped to the wall across from the single bed. It looked as if every kid at Hilton Head High School had signed it.

The girl was asleep, although the TV blared with some of the god-awful screeching that passed for music these days. I smiled, remembering that the Judge had expressed just such opinions about Jimi Hendrix and Janis Joplin back in the day. I located the remote on the bedside table and hit the Mute button. Behind me, Red hovered in the doorway.

A padded straight chair sat to one side, and I pulled it around to face the once pretty teenager surrounded by a frightening array of machinery. Her hair had just begun to grow back in, probably after extensive chemo, and lay in short black curls against her head. In repose, she seemed much younger, that vitality and purpose in the picture missing from her sunken face. She looked sick and vulnerable, and I had to choke back the tears that sprang immediately to my eyes.

I glanced back at Red as I took the chair, and he motioned toward the elevator. "I'll wait downstairs," he whispered, and I nodded.

I settled in to wait, not willing to wake the child who no doubt needed to conserve her energy for her battle with the hideous disease that had invaded her young body. I checked my watch. I'd give it half an hour. I let my eyes roam over the stuffed animals that sat perched on the windowsill along with the flowers and cards. This was obviously a well-liked girl. Sometimes life was so damned unfair, I thought. It must seem to Joline as if her daughter had been cursed. After all she'd been through, holding on to her child in spite of everything, how could Joline just take off and abandon her? What terrible thing could have——?

"Who are you?"

The voice was surprisingly strong, and the deep brown eyes with a hint of green at their edges fixed me with a challenging look.

I smiled. "My name is Bay Tanner. I'm a friend of your mother's."

Her gaze slipped past and around me, toward the door. "Is Mom here?"

"No, I'm sorry, she's not. I just dropped in to say hello and see how you were doing."

The girl hitched herself up a little higher in the bed. "I don't think I know you, do I?"

"No. Your mother and I just met a few days ago. I'm helping her with a . . . a problem."

"Are you the private detective she hired?"

The question shocked me. I'd been prepared to spin the girl a story, certain her mother wouldn't have burdened her with the search for a bone marrow donor. Apparently I had underestimated both of these women.

"Yes, I am. She's talked to you about it?"

It wasn't quite defiance, that look she fixed on me, but it was close. "Why wouldn't she? It's my life we're talking about here."

It took me only a moment to rethink my strategy. "Of course it is. Your mother hired my firm to locate her sisters. Your aunts, Contessa and Maeline."

"To see if they'd be compatible donors."

"Right."

"Did you find them?" Kimmie spoke matter-of-factly, as if we weren't discussing her possibly imminent death.

"Not yet, but we have some leads. Good ones," I added, feeling as if I should reassure this poised young woman even if she didn't appear to need it.

"Good. It's kind of creepy thinking that you've got relatives you've never met." Her voice faltered for the first time. "I mean, even if they're not going to work as donors, I'd like to know them anyway."

Truthfully, I said, "I know exactly what you mean." I paused, wondering if she knew the real story of her conception or if she thought Jerrold Eastman was her biological father. How far had Joline been prepared to go with her policy of leveling with her sick child? As I watched, a spasm shook the girl. "Are you okay? Shall I call someone?"

Kimmie shook her head. "No. It comes and goes. I'm just like tired all the time now. All I do is sleep. And watch TV." She glanced at the muted screen across from the bed, and her full smile lit the room. "You don't like MTV?"

I couldn't help but grin back. "I don't suppose they ever play the Rolling Stones?"

"Gross!" she answered. "They're like a hundred years old." Then she seemed to realize that might have sounded disrespectful and added, "My dad likes them."

"We old fogeys stick together," I said, and she laughed, a delightful ripple that lit her eyes.

A moment later, she sobered. "Is my mom coming soon? I have to go down for some more tests, and she always . . . she comes with me." The sigh held way too much pain for someone so young. "It's easier if I have someone to talk to."

Where the hell was she? How could she desert this poor little girl?

"I don't know," I said, and the truth of it stabbed at my heart. "I haven't talked to her today. But I'll come with you, if you like. I know it's not the same as having your mom, but . . ." I clamped my teeth down on my lower lip and ordered myself to keep it together.

"That's nice of you," Kimmie said. "But maybe she'll be here. It's not for another couple of hours."

I stood. "Do you have a phone you're allowed to use?"

"Sure. I've got my cell. Mom lets my friends call after school, but I'm not supposed to talk too long."

I pulled a business card from my bag. "Here's all my numbers. If your mom gets held up or something, give me a call. I'd be glad to keep you company."

Her smile nearly broke my heart. "Cool! Maybe you can tell me about why you like that old dude, you know, with the Rolling Stones?"

"I'm sure Mick Jagger would love to know someone your age thinks of him as 'that old dude.'"

She giggled. "Sorry."

"You'll call me then, if your mom gets held up?"

"Sure," she mumbled, "thanks."

Her eyes fluttered closed. I turned and tiptoed from the room, glancing back once before I stepped into the empty corridor. The girl's thin chest rose and fell evenly.

"Damn you, Joline," I whispered to myself.

CHAPTER
TWENTY-SEVEN

"WHAT'S THE PLAN?"

Red and I stood outside the hospital, a cool breeze cutting through my thin jacket as the sun slid toward the mainland.

"I don't have a damned plan!" I swallowed my anger and frustration and forced my shoulders to relax. "I don't know the first thing about Joline Eastman except what's in the file and the few things her husband told me. I haven't got a clue where to start looking for her."

Red took my hand and pulled me down beside him onto one of the benches set out along the winding sidewalk. "Look. It's almost five o'clock. The doc should be done with office hours. Let's go track him down."

I shook my head. "He was headed over here to deliver a baby when I talked to him, remember? Who knows how long that could take?"

Red chuckled. "Scotty didn't make his appearance for almost fourteen hours after Sarah went into labor. Elinor popped out almost before we could get to the hospital."

I glanced at his face, burnished by the rays of the setting sun that filtered through the branches of the pines towering over us. No matter how much he loved me, there would never be that same bond he shared with Sarah. Unless . . . I kicked that sweet, frightening thought back into its mental compartment and slammed the door.

"You're right. So maybe he's still here." I rose and turned back toward the building. "Let's go find Maternity and see if we can run him down."

"Why don't I do that?" Red had risen to stand beside me. "If he's already gone home, I'll check at his house. You can stay here in case Kimmie needs you."

It made sense. I looked at my lover—my *fiancé*—and marveled at how easily, in less than a day, he'd adapted to working for the agency. And he was far better trained and experienced than I would ever be. I had fought hard against Ben Wyler's constant attempts to take over, to use his law enforcement background to run roughshod over me. With Red, things seemed to be different, thank God.

"Good plan," I said. "I'll try to track Erik down, too. I'm surprised we haven't heard from him by now."

"What are we doing for food?" Red asked.

"Damn! We were supposed to be at Presqu'isle at six. We'll never make it now." I pulled my cell phone from my bag. "I need to call Lavinia."

"She'll understand," he said. "I'll keep in touch." He planted a brief kiss on my cheek and turned away. I had punched in the first two numbers when his voice made me look up. "Oh, and I love you, Bay Tanner," he hollered across the lawn, and an elderly couple turned to stare. With a wave, he disappeared inside the hospital.

Of course Lavinia understood. I could almost see her brown hand flicking away my apologies.

"We'll do it another day, child. No need to worry." She paused. "But it would be good if you didn't wait too long."

The ever-present fear that lay coiled in the pit of my stomach sprang to life. "What's the matter? Is the Judge sick again?"

"No, not physically. But it seems to me that he's got something eatin' at his mind. I catch him every once in a while talkin' to himself."

I waited.

"And your name is in most of those conversations."

"I'll come tomorrow," I said, meaning it. "I promise."

"Don't fret now, Bay. I didn't tell you that to scare you. I just think he has something he wants to get off his chest."

I waited a beat. "And you don't have any idea what it is he might be troubled about?"

"You just come when you can, child. Come when you can."

She hung up before I could reply.

It didn't take a detective to guess what might be bothering my father's conscience. Maybe I wouldn't have to broach the subject of Julia Simpson. Maybe he was ready to come clean on his own.

I hit the speed-dial button for Erik's cell number and pulled my jacket more tightly around me. It seemed from the rising wind that our brief flirtation with summer might be coming to an end. The call switched over to voice mail, and I had just opened my mouth to leave a terse message when my own phone beeped an incoming call.

Erik sounded breathless. "Bay. Sorry. I was just finishing up on the computer, and I didn't want to stop to answer the phone."

"It took a lot longer than you thought, huh? Did you get the information?"

I heard the slam of a car door and the roar of a powerful engine before he replied.

"They really don't want people accessing those records. I almost gave up a couple of times. I'd like to meet whoever designed their firewall and shake the guy's hand. It's awesome."

"But you cracked it, right?"

He laughed. "Yeah, but it was a battle." His sigh told me the outcome even before he continued. "But it was all for nothing in the end. I couldn't find any record of an adoption in South Carolina involving Joline and Kimmie."

"So maybe they just changed her last name. Does that have to be formalized with a court or something?"

"I don't know. I can check on that when I get home. I didn't want to hang around the cyber café too much longer in case someone got suspicious. Traffic's pretty heavy, but I should be home in an hour or so. Anything else I can do?"

I filled him in on our visit to the hospital. He seemed especially interested in my impressions of Kimmie—her courage and strength of character in the face of her failing condition.

"And Red's gone to hunt up Dr. Eastman. We need some solid information if we expect to locate Joline." Again the phone beeped with an incoming call, a number I didn't recognize. "Gotta go. Talk to you later," I said and switched over. "Bay Tanner."

"Hi. It's Kimmie." Her voice sounded small and maybe a little frightened.

"Hey, Kimmie. I'm right outside the hospital. Are they ready for your test?"

"No. I mean, not yet."

I waited, but she didn't go on. I could hear her breathing in the pause, short hard gasps as if she'd been running. Or crying. I jumped from the bench and jogged back toward the entrance to the hospital.

"What is it, Kimmie? Are you in pain? Ring for one of the nurses. I'm on my way in right now."

"No, I'm okay. My mom just called."

I blew through the sliding doors and fumbled my crumpled visitor's pass out of my pocket for the white-haired woman at the reception desk. Two seconds later I was frantically punching the Up button next to the elevators.

"Where is she?" I asked, my own heart pounding.

"I don't know. She said she had some things to take care of. Important things."

The doors finally slid open, and I had to step back to allow several people to exit before I could jump inside.

"Kimmie? Are you still there?"

"Yes, ma'am. I can hear you fine."

"Did you recognize the number your mother was calling from?"

"Her cell phone."

Damn! No help there.

The bell dinged, and the doors slid open. I plastered a smile onto my face and stepped into the room. I waved the phone and punched it off. I stepped up to the bed and forced myself not to smooth the frown lines from her pinched face.

"You didn't have to come back," Kimmie Eastman said. "It's just I told my mom you'd been here, and she got all weird on me."

I pulled up the visitor's chair and sat down. "Weird how?"

Her thin shoulders rose in a shrug. "I don't know. Like she was nervous or something. Or scared." Saying the word out loud made her lip tremble. "The phone woke me up, and I guess maybe I was still out of it. I thought maybe you'd know why she was so upset you'd been to see me."

"I honestly have no idea. What else did she say? Can you remember?"

"We talked for a while about, you know, medical stuff. She said she was really sorry she had to go away, but that Daddy would be here to take me down for the test. If he doesn't have any babies ready to pop out."

For the first time, I heard a note of resentment in her voice and wondered again about Jerrold Eastman's commitment to this child not his own.

"I understand they don't wait on anybody," I said with a smile.

"Do you have kids?"

The abrupt change of subject took me by surprise. "Nope," I said and left it at that. I waited a beat. "Anything else your mother talked about?"

"She said she had to do something, that she just couldn't sit around waiting to hear from you about my aunts." Her thin face scrunched in concentration. "I could hear people talking in the background. Like maybe she was in a store or something. And I heard a bell once or twice." She slumped back against the pillows stacked behind her. "I'm sorry. That's all. She said she loved me and that she'd see me soon. And she told me to be strong."

Without thinking, I reached for her hand, careful of the IV needle taped to it, and gently squeezed her fingers. "You're about as strong as it's possible to be," I said softly. "I'm completely blown away by how brave you are."

Her mocha cheeks darkened in a blush, and she shrugged. "I don't really have much choice, do I?"

We sat like that for a long time, the bustle in the corridor as meal trays were delivered seeming to fade into the distance. After a full minute, Kimmie said, "Do you know what my mom's doing? This is the first time she hasn't been here for a whole day, and I'm a little worried."

Again I squeezed the slim hand. "I think I understand, and I'm positive it's important to getting you well again. You know there isn't another reason that would keep her away."

Her nearly translucent eyelids fluttered closed, and I felt her fingers relax. My brain raced as I sat with this remarkable girl's hand resting in mine. Joline had gone to *do something*. Voices in the background, and a bell tinkling. Just like at the store the Brawleys owned. Joline had taken the information I'd given her and gone to Jacksonboro to find her own answers. And I intended to be right behind her.

CHAPTER
TWENTY-EIGHT

I HAD JUST SLID MY HAND FROM BENEATH KIMMIE'S
when I felt the presence in the doorway. I turned slowly to
find Dr. Jerrold Eastman filling the space, the light from the hallway
and the deep lines of anger on his face making him appear like an
avenging angel.

"What are you doing here?" He spoke softly, but it was enough to
jerk Kimmie awake.

"Daddy!" Her whole demeanor changed with that one word, from
stoic young woman to delighted little girl. "You made it!"

I stood and moved the chair out of the way as the doctor brushed
past me. He leaned over and planted a loud kiss on Kimmie's forehead. "Hello, sweetheart. How's it going today?"

"I'm okay. I just get really tired of lying here. Mrs. Tanner has
been keeping me company."

"Have you heard from your mom?"

Kimmie's gaze shot over her father's shoulder to where I stood just
behind him. I read the message clearly in her startled brown eyes. I
wondered if her father did.

"Unh-uh," she said and turned her head away.

The lie shocked me, but it took only a moment for me to realize
that she was following orders. Her mother's. I composed my face barely

a moment before Jerrold Eastman swiveled his head in my direction. I could see the questions he was bursting to ask—and something else, too. Fear? Before I could put a name to it, he returned his attention to his daughter.

"I'm sure she'll be in soon, honey. Don't worry. Now, what did you order for dinner?"

Ignored, I edged backwards in the direction of the door, but Dr. Eastman's voice stopped me. "Would you wait for me outside? I'll just be a moment."

"Certainly. Take care, Kimmie," I said, feeling as if I was defying the doctor in some unspoken way. "I'll come back and visit, if that's okay."

"Sure," the girl said. "Bye."

"Goodnight," I said and slipped out into the corridor. I glanced to my left and saw Red striding in my direction.

"Is he up here?" he asked when he'd closed the gap between us. "They said down in delivery that he was on his way to see his daughter."

"Inside. He wasn't happy to find me there for some reason." I didn't give him a chance to comment. "Listen, Joline just called Kimmie." I gave him the gist of it along with my interpretation. "And she didn't want her husband to know about it. I think we should head up there. To Jacksonboro."

"Tonight? Why? What do you think we can accomplish?"

I moved to a vacant slab of counter along the nurses' station and set my bag on the ledge. Red followed.

"If she's gone to confront Patience Brawley, I'm concerned about what kind of reception she'll get. Mrs. Brawley is a nice woman, except when it comes to Joline's side of the family. I'm betting she blames them for her nephew's murder. Who knows what could happen if the two of them really get into it? You've always told me that domestics were the most unpredictable calls you had to handle."

"Okay, I see your point. But reason this through. Joline's supposedly been gone all day. It's only an hour-and-a-half drive up there. If she was going to get into trouble, it would have happened before now, don't you think? The fact that she called her daughter should tell you that she's fine."

I had to concede the logic of his argument. It aggravated me a lot less than I would have thought possible just a couple of days before. Perhaps we *could* work together without doing lasting damage to our personal relationship.

"You make a good case," I said. Then another thought struck. "But it sounded from what Kimmie said as if she was calling from the store. Maybe she hasn't actually confronted Patience yet. And why would she ask Kimmie not to tell Jerry about the call?"

"Point taken. There's definitely something else going on." He looked past me down the corridor. "Is this him?"

I turned to watch Jerrold Eastman stop one of the duty nurses. He spoke softly, and the petite woman nodded her head several times.

"What am I going to say to him? He wants us to find Joline."

"Let's just hear him out first."

The doctor finished his conversation and patted the nurse on the shoulder before turning in our direction. The smile vanished from his face as he approached us.

"Bay. Thanks for waiting."

"Dr. Jerry Eastman, Red Tanner. He's working with me on Kimmie's problem."

He frowned. "Tanner? You're related?"

Red held out his hand, and Eastman took it. "Bay was married to my late brother."

"Red's just retired from the sheriff's office," I added, "so he has a lot of valuable experience."

"Fine. Good to meet you." He directed his gaze to me. "What can you do about finding my wife? Something terrible must have happened to keep her away from Kimmie."

"Is there somewhere private we can talk?" I asked.

He motioned us to follow him through the maze of hallways. Three or four turns later he pushed through an unmarked door into what looked to be a consultation room and flipped on the lights. It was furnished with comfortable seating in muted browns and golds, and a series of Lowcountry marsh landscapes hung on the beige walls. Glossy magazines were arranged neatly on a low coffee table. The doctor indicated an overstuffed sofa beneath the room's only window, and Red and I sank into it. He took the single wing chair facing us, which gave him not only the "power" position, but the advantage of height as well.

I found it hard to believe the arrangement had been unintentional. Doctors, especially those who had been in practice as long as Jerrold Eastman, were used to being in control. Nothing for it but to take the offensive right away.

"I'm not sure I can accept a retainer from you, Dr. Eastman," I said calmly. "At this point, we're still employed by your wife. I'm concerned that working for you, too, would constitute a conflict of interest."

I could feel Red's eyes boring into the side of my face, but I forced myself not to look at him. I hoped he'd let me take the lead since we hadn't had time to discuss strategy.

Eastman waited a moment before he spoke. "You're aware, I think, that my wife has no income of her own. Whatever monies she's paid you come from my practice. So technically I've been your client from the beginning."

The statement, delivered in a calm, reasonable voice, told me a lot about the good doctor and his relationship with his wife. There was only one person in charge of the Eastman household, and it wasn't Joline.

I matched his tone and added a reassuring smile. "Be that as it may, Doctor, your wife's name is on the contract. Where she obtains the funds to pay us, unless it's from some illegal enterprise, is immaterial to our agreement with her." I held up a hand to forestall his interruption. "Why do you think you need us to locate your wife? Did something happen that would lead you to believe she's in trouble?"

He'd been about to put me back in my place, but my question stopped him. "No, nothing happened. She seemed fine on Sunday. As

I told you, she must have gone sometime this morning. She left a note asking our housekeeper to stay on and take care of Christopher in case she didn't get back tonight. He's been fussing for his mother, and I'm running out of excuses." He ran a large, well-manicured hand over his face. "Look, I don't want to go to the sheriff with this. Joline is a very private woman, and filing a missing person's report is bound to result in publicity. She's very active in local charities on the island, and her name is well known. It would be impossible to keep it out of the paper."

I wondered if the embarrassment and possible notoriety worried him more than his wife's whereabouts. Whatever his motives, it was clear he wasn't going to be any more forthcoming. I was convinced there had been some sort of confrontation between husband and wife, if not on Sunday then perhaps after Joline and I talked on Saturday. A woman as devoted to the welfare of her children as Kimmie's mother would not leave them alone except for a damn good reason.

I rose. "I think you should wait, Dr. Eastman. Give it until tomorrow and see if you hear from your wife. Maybe she just needed a break."

Red levered himself out of the soft cushions to stand beside me.

"Is that what you think, Mr. Tanner?"

It was the first time I'd heard Red addressed as anything other than "Sergeant" in so long, I felt my heart jump in my chest. Rob had been *Mr.* Tanner. It would take some getting used to.

"Yes, sir, I do. In my experience, stress sometimes causes folks to do things that seem totally out of character, but it doesn't mean they're in trouble. Your wife has borne the majority of your daughter's care, I would guess. Only natural. She may just have needed some time to catch her breath. Marshal her resources, so to speak." He anticipated an argument from Jerrold Eastman and plunged ahead before he could interrupt. "The authorities will tell you that forty-eight hours is the time frame before an adult would be considered missing. Give it until tomorrow. If you still haven't heard from her, you can contact us then."

Hearing it from a man apparently carried weight with the doctor. "Thank you. Perhaps you're right. I appreciate your time."

He spun on his heel and jerked the door open, then paused. "And Mrs. Tanner?"

I had obviously fallen from grace. I was no longer *Bay*.

"Yes?"

"I'd appreciate it if you didn't make it a habit of dropping in on my daughter. Kimmie's health is very fragile at this point. I'm sure you understand."

Without another word, he was gone.

Red followed me out into the corridor. "That went well," he said with a smile.

"Dr. Jekyll and Mr. Hyde," I mumbled, turning both ways to try and get my bearings. "Any idea how to get out of here?"

Red took my hand. "Rob and I used to be Boy Scouts, remember? Come on."

He led us unerringly back through the turns to the elevator.

"So what do you think?" I asked while we waited. "I had to keep myself from belting him one in there."

"Definitely a control freak," Red answered. "That doesn't mean he slapped his wife around or anything. What is that thing Erik always says?"

"Insufficient data," I said as we stepped into the elevator. "Now what?"

"Food. I'm about to pass out here."

"And then what? Still think a trip to Jacksonboro is a waste of time?"

Red checked his watch. "It's only a little after six. Let's grab some burgers and head north. It's a nice night for a ride in the country."

CHAPTER
TWENTY-NINE

MY CELL RANG JUST AS I STUFFED THE LAST FRY into my mouth. We were off the island and headed west on 278, Red driving the Jaguar while I ate. I wiped grease and salt from my fingers onto a wad of paper napkins and picked up the phone.

"Bay Tanner."

"Bay, it's Loretta Healey. I just got your message."

For a moment I couldn't think of a coherent thing to say. I had placed the call—when? I couldn't remember if it had been a day or a week ago. At the time, pumping the daughter of one of my late mother's oldest friends had seemed of paramount importance. Intervening crises involving Joline and Kimmie Eastman had pushed the whole thing to the back of my mind.

"Thanks for calling me back," I stalled. "Were you out of town?"

This time it was Loretta's turn to pause. I should have recalled that her work as a special advisor to the president on immigration and Homeland Security issues would make information about her travels off-limits except for those who needed to know. And I didn't.

"Overseas," she said. "I don't carry my personal cell with me. How's the Judge doing?"

I gave her an abridged version of his recent health problems, which allowed me a perfect segue into the reason I'd called her in the first place. I glanced across the dim interior, but Red stared through the windshield, doing his best to pretend he couldn't hear every word I was saying. It didn't matter. I glanced at the ring on my left hand. He had a right to know.

"I want to ask you about something from the past," I began. I could almost see her perfect eyebrows rise. In our most recent meeting—the first after more than twenty-plus years—we'd clashed on just about everything, from her stern warnings for me to stay out of the trouble Dolores and her family had found themselves embroiled in, to snide remarks about our Lowcountry society and mores. According to her version of things, Loretta had escaped the strictures of our upbringing not a moment too soon.

I hadn't liked her that night she'd flirted shamelessly with my father in the front parlor at Presqu'isle. Her high-handed pressure to try and scare me off the case of Dolores and her son Bobby had done nothing to endear her to me, either. But she was quite a bit older than I. And she'd been around my house a lot back in those days. If there were secrets being kept—especially ones that reflected badly on my family—I was betting Loretta would be only too eager to spill them.

I inhaled and let the breath out slowly. "Do you know anything about a woman named Julia Simpson?"

"Doesn't ring a bell. Some relative of yours?"

I debated whether or not to press the issue. If the name didn't register, chances were she didn't know anything. Still, I hated to pass up the opportunity.

"Maybe," I hedged. "I ran across the name in some old papers. I've never heard her mentioned before, and I thought . . . maybe she was a black sheep or something. Piqued my curiosity." My hand shook with the effort of walking such a conversational tightrope. "I just thought you might have heard her mentioned back in the days when you were at Presqu'isle so often."

Her silence made me grip the phone more tightly.

"And you haven't asked Tally about it." She didn't wait for me to reply. "So it's something that might upset him to talk about." Again she paused. "I wonder . . ."

"What?"

I heard the snap of a lighter and the slow exhalation of smoke. It made me itchy for a cigarette of my own.

"Well," she said, "did you ever know what the big blowup between our dear sainted mamas was all about?"

"No. Do you?"

"I was around the day it happened, but it didn't really register. I was a teenager and pretty oblivious to what the grown-ups were doing. But I remember my mother did a lot of ranting and raving, mostly about how money and position didn't guarantee character, no matter how good your pedigree. It was one of the few times I ever saw the sainted Mary Grace Beaumont lose her temper. Ladies didn't, you know, back in those days. I don't think I was at your house much after that. Until last Christmas."

The nature of our clash on that previous meeting hung in the air between us.

"Well, thanks anyway. It's no big deal," I lied. Some of my mother's constant drilling on the social niceties drifted up from my subconscious. "How have you been, Loretta? I hope everything's going well."

Her laugh, a short bark, almost made me smile in return. "I can't believe you actually give a damn, Bay. But since you ask, the job is keeping me hopping. Literally. I'm only home for about thirty-six hours before I have to head out again." Her cynical tone sobered. "There's always a crisis somewhere these days."

I couldn't argue with that. "Thanks again for returning my call."

"Let me know if you find this mysterious Julia. I'm always up for a good Lowcountry society scandal. About the only thing that interests me about the place these days."

"Thanks again," I repeated and hung up.

I stuffed the soggy remains of my fast-food dinner into the bag and tossed it onto the floor in the back. I could feel Red bursting to ask me about the call.

"She didn't know anything," I said. "Just that our mothers had some big fight and basically never spoke again. The name didn't do anything for her."

"You okay being a passenger?" he asked, completely ignoring my feeble explanation.

"Fine." I slid down into the seat and eased it back a few inches so I could stretch out my legs.

Mary Grace Beaumont. The name conjured up all the memories of my childhood: Presqu'isle decked out in its finest, flowers and gowned ladies filling every room, their tuxedoed husbands flowing out onto the verandah with highball glasses in one hand and glowing cigars in the other. The constant din of conversation, occasionally punctuated by a lilting laugh. The *clink* of crystal and the rattle of the heavy Georgian silver on paper-thin china.

My mother had always been the center of attention, always the most beautiful and beautifully dressed of the company. The Judge had been upright then, tall and imposing in his black and white. They had seemed to me to be the most dazzling couple in the world. I could feel myself smiling as the pictures whirled and dipped in my mind in tune to the small quartet that always accompanied the galas at our home.

Then everyone would be gone. And from my room at the top of the stairs I would hear the arguments, my mother's shrill voice, slurred by too much bourbon, cutting through the thick walls of the old mansion. I shifted in my seat, trying to remember when that had begun, because it hadn't always been that way. Sometime back in my early childhood, the drinking became chronic. Emmaline's temper exploded, usually at me, and I learned to avoid her. Lavinia offered comfort and a steady presence, and I became over the years more her child than my mother's.

I wondered if the split with Mary Grace had come around that same time. Maybe something had happened, some awful occurrence that had turned my mother from an aristocratic member of Beaufort society into a screaming, ranting shrew. I picked up the phone and re-called the last incoming number.

Loretta picked up immediately. "Bay?"

"Yes. Sorry to bother you again, but I wonder if you remember when it was that our mothers had that big blowup. How old was I?"

"Let me see. You were pretty young. I'm not exactly certain. Why?"

Right around the time the drinking got really bad? So maybe that was what had sparked the argument. Perhaps Emmaline had embarrassed Mary Grace in some way. Or flirted with her husband. I heard a lot about that in those after-party shouting matches between my parents.

"Bay? You still there?"

"Yes, sorry. No particular reason. Your call just got me thinking about those days."

"They threw some great parties. I used to come along once in a while. We watched some of them from the landing on the stairs, you and I, remember?"

It was uncanny how she'd read my mind. "Yes, I do. Well, thanks again, Loretta. Goodnight."

I hung up before she had a chance to stroll any farther down memory lane. It was too unsettling, too . . . painful. No sense in dredging all that up. I'd made my peace with my mother's alcoholism a long time ago. Rob always told me to remember the good times and let the rest go. The Judge and I tucked up on the sofa watching a baseball game on TV . . . digging alongside a sober Emmaline in the garden on a hot spring day . . . the fragrance of Lavinia's baking powder biscuits rising in the oven . . .

I jerked at Red's tug on my sleeve.

"Honey?" he said. "Wake up. We're here."

I didn't remember drifting off to sleep, but I sat up with that foggy feeling you get sometimes after an unplanned catnap. I stretched and looked around me.

Red had navigated to the center of the little town of Jacksonboro, pulling in at the Stop 'n Save run by Duke Brawley. The lights were on in the store, and a couple of pickup trucks occupied the small parking area.

"Where to?"

I turned at Red's voice. It had grown dark as I slept, and the lights from the dash cast a soft glow on the planes of his face.

"We have to backtrack a little," I said, running my fingers through my tangled hair. "We need to take the road toward Walterboro." I glanced again at the lighted store windows. "Hang on a second, though. Let me check something first."

Before he could respond, I pushed open the door and stepped out into the chilly night. A stiff wind blew onshore from the ocean just a few miles to the east. The trees behind the parking lot bent and swayed, and I pulled my jacket more tightly around me. It smelled like rain.

Inside, a young woman lounged behind the counter, a magazine spread out in front of her. She looked up at the jangle of the bells over the door.

"Hey," she said in a pleasant drawl. "Help you with something?"

I approached with a smile. "Is either Ellis or Duke around tonight?"

"No, ma'am," she said. "Mr. Brawley was here earlier, but I usually take the evening shift. He'll be back in at eleven to close up."

"I see. Has anyone else been in tonight asking for them?"

She shook her head. "No, ma'am. Not since I came on at six."

Joline would have been here earlier than that, if my guess that she'd called Kimmie from the store was on track. "I see. Okay, thanks anyway."

I walked back to the cooler and extracted a cold Diet Coke and a ginger ale. I carried them to the counter and fished out my wallet.

"That's three-twelve, with tax." She handed me back my change. "Thank you."

"Do you live around here?" I asked, the question out of my mouth before I realized I'd formed the intent to ask it.

The smile wavered a little. "Yes, ma'am. All my life."

Now that I'd started this interrogation, I wasn't certain where I was going with it. I cleared my throat to give myself a moment to think. "Uh, that house out on Holly Hill Road. The old McDowell place. Do you know anything about its history? Or the people who live there now?"

For some reason, the image of Ellis's Miss Lizzie, standing at the end of the dirt road staring after the Jaguar's taillights on Saturday afternoon, had popped into my head.

"Well, it used to be a rice plantation, back before the War. I think one of them was killed at Gettysburg, and then some other family took it over. But it's always been known around here as the McDowell place." She paused. "My pop says they used to let the school take kids through it when he was little, but they don't do that anymore."

"How about who lives there now? I met an older woman the other day out near there. And Ellis talked to me before about a Miss Lizzie. Would that be her?"

I saw the girl look past me, over my shoulder, and I realized someone was standing behind me. I turned to find a woman shifting impatiently from one foot to the other, a series of lottery tickets clutched in her hand.

"I'm sorry," I said and stepped aside.

"No problem." She handed two strips of brightly colored tickets to the girl behind the counter. "Got me a coupla winners here, Becca. Not much, but it'll help."

I moved to the glass door and peered outside. Red had gotten out of the Jaguar and stood leaning against the side of the car. I knew he would be getting antsy. I moved away to allow the lottery winner to get by and turned back toward the register.

The girl had dropped her head back over her magazine, hoping, I was certain, that I was done trying to pick her brain.

"Do you know this Miss Lizzie? And why Ellis and Duke refer to the place as the 'Hall'?"

"Most everyone knows Miss Lizzie Shelly. I heard she came here a long time ago. And some people call the McDowell place Covenant

Hall because they held secessionist meetings there back in the old days. We studied it in school. They signed some kind of paper agreeing to support the Confederacy."

"How about the other people who live out there? Isn't there another woman, younger than Miss Lizzie?"

"You'll have to excuse me, ma'am," she said stiffly. "I have to straighten out the stock before Mr. Brawley comes in."

I conceded defeat. "Is there a motel anywhere close by?" I asked, one hand on the door to signal the inquisition was almost over.

"The little place here in town is closed during the winter. Won't open up again until April or May. Most folks go over to Walterboro. Lots of motels out there by the interstate."

"Thanks for your help," I said, and her shoulders visibly relaxed.

"You're welcome, ma'am. You come back now."

I nodded and pushed open the door. I felt a couple of splatters of rain on my face as I moved back toward the car. We both slid inside, and I handed him the ginger ale.

"Thanks. What took you so long? Bathroom break?"

I laughed. "Sleuthing," I said. Then, sobering, I added, "I think we need to get out to the Brawleys'. Now."

Red nodded and wheeled the Jaguar around and back onto the highway.

The drizzle and the constant slap of the wipers across the windshield made locating Patience Brawley's house difficult. Add to that the fact that there were no streetlights on Holly Hill Road, and it took us the better part of twenty minutes before I finally recognized the place. I told Red to go all the way to the end of the road and turn around.

"This is that plantation I was telling you about," I said when he'd executed two-thirds of his three-point turn. The headlights pointed straight down the dirt driveway, and a hint of the red paint on the STAY OUT sign glistened through the rain.

"Not some place I'd be happy making a call on in the middle of the night," he said a moment before he headed us back up Holly Hill. "Even without being able to see the house it looks kind of creepy."

"So is Lizzie Shelly," I said, remembering again those strange eyes watching me drive off. "I'm wondering if that girl—or woman—I saw running away is mentally ill or something."

"You mean like a batty old aunt they keep locked in the attic?" I could hear the smile in his voice.

"Something like that," I said, unsure myself why the memory of the fleeing figure should have conjured up that particular notion. Or maybe it had been something I'd heard from someone.

We drifted over to the side of the road in front of the Brawleys' house. Red cut the headlamps, and I rolled down my window. There were lights blazing through the rain, and two pickup trucks and a small sedan sat in the driveway.

"Do you know what kind of car Joline Eastman drives?" Red asked.

"No. We should have thought to ask her husband."

Red nodded. "I'm slipping. Only a couple of days off the job, and I'm already acting like a civilian."

I ordered myself not to take offense. "I can call him."

"Hang on. Who lives here?"

I raised my eyebrows. "I told you. Patience Brawley."

"I know that. Who else?"

"Her husband, Carl, and her son, Ellis."

"And they all work. So three vehicles makes sense. Right?"

"Right. So Joline probably isn't sitting in the living room chatting about old times. Or tied to a tree in the backyard."

Red returned my stare. "You really think these people would harm her? Did they strike you like that?"

"No. But Patience was barely controlling her anger at the mere mention of the Mitchell sisters. If all our speculating is anywhere near the truth, she has good reason to despise them, I guess. If she really believes Joline's family killed her nephew."

"That's still the longest of long shots. It makes a nice theory, but there isn't a shred of evidence to support it."

"You were pretty gung ho about the idea this afternoon, after you found that cold case in the files. What changed your mind?"

"Experience. It's way too convoluted. There's no saying whether or not the body in the swamp even was this Deshawn guy. Or if it was anything other than a grudge killing or a drug deal gone bad. Usually the simplest explanation turns out to be the right one."

I bit my tongue, and Red pulled the car into gear.

"What are you doing?"

"There's nothing to be gained here," he said. "Even if we knocked on the door and asked if they'd seen her, we wouldn't be any farther ahead. Whether she paid them a visit or not, she's obviously gone now."

I grabbed his shoulder. "You don't know that!"

"Bay, listen to me. How many times have we had this discussion about going off half-cocked? You can't come up with a scenario and then interpret the evidence to fit your theory. It doesn't work that way."

"Maybe not for the cops. But this isn't about evidence and probable cause and all those restrictions you had with the sheriff. What we do is get answers for our clients. Whether or not it's enough to put someone away isn't our job." I forced my rising voice down to a more noncon frontational level. "It's about doing what we're getting paid for."

Red sighed and pushed the gearshift back into Park. "I understand, sweetheart. And that's what I'm saying. You—*we*—are supposed to find a bone marrow donor for that little girl. All the rest of it is immaterial."

I felt all the tension drain out of my shoulders. He was absolutely right. Nothing else mattered, and my chasing off after old crimes and family vendettas was just getting in the way.

"Okay," I said. "I get it. But can we just find out from the doctor what kind of car Joline drives?"

"Why?"

"So we can swing by Walterboro and check out some of the motel parking lots. I'm still worried about her, even though we wouldn't take her husband on as a client. There had to be something that made her run off and leave both her children."

Red smiled. "Point taken. Call him."

I reached for my bag to retrieve my cell phone just as the figure appeared at my open window. I jerked upright to find myself staring into the eyes of Lizzie Shelly. And the business end of the pistol she held in her right hand.

CHAPTER
THIRTY

ESIDE ME, I HEARD RED'S SHARP INTAKE OF BREATH. I
sensed his hand groping at his side for the firearm that was no
longer there. I straightened slowly and leaned back into the seat. A
moment later, the gaping hole that seemed to fill the open window
disappeared as the woman lowered the gun.

"I thought I recognized the car," she said. "That's twice I've found
you where you don't belong." She slid the hood of the yellow rain
slicker back off her face, and the fury in her eyes made me flinch.

Red had instantly slipped into cop mode. "I hope you have a per-
mit for that weapon, ma'am," he said through clenched teeth.

I could hear the frustration in his voice, and I knew he wished he
could leap from the car and slap a set of cuffs on her. His now being
just regular folks was going to take some getting used to for both of
us, but especially for Red.

"Pointing a loaded firearm at a person is a misdemeanor," he
added in his cop voice.

"No doubt," Lizzie Shelly said. "But so is trespassing."

"Is this your land, too?" I asked, turning so that I blocked her
from Red's line of sight. I still wasn't certain what he might do.

"Technically, no. But out here neighbors look out for each other."
She waited for a response, but I kept silent. "Patience told me you'd

crashed her party. What are you doing back again? And why are you sitting out here in the dark?"

I had no intention of telling this odd woman anything about our mission.

"My fiancé and I were just out riding. I wanted to show him the area, but the rain and the dark got here before us. We were just leaving."

Her eyes studied my face as if they could see through the feeble lie. "Seems to me you have a habit of showing up where you're not wanted. Must run in the family."

The venom in her voice startled me. "What do you know about my family? You don't even know my name."

And then it occurred to me that Patience Brawley knew it. And had probably divulged it to this strange woman.

"I know all I need to know," she said, stepping back. "I suggest you be on your way."

She turned then and walked back toward the old plantation house. I stuck my head out the window; the squelching of her rubber boots was just discernible above the dripping of the trees. In a moment she disappeared in the gloom, her enigmatic words about my family still ringing in my ears.

"I take it that was the mysterious Miss Lizzie. You didn't tell me the old bat was dangerous." Red spoke as he once again pulled the car into gear. "We should report her."

I raised my window and shrugged. "She has a point. We must have looked pretty suspicious sitting here in the dark in an idling car. You really can't blame her in a way."

"If she was worried, she should have called the sheriff. That's what sane people do, not go traipsing through the rain waving a loaded gun around."

I reached again for my cell phone as we moved slowly back onto the macadam road. "We don't know for sure it *was* loaded," I pointed out, scanning for Joline's home phone number, which I'd programmed into the memory. "You just assumed that."

I glanced toward the Brawleys' house as we eased past.

"Stop!" I yelled, and Red slammed on the brakes.

"Jesus, Bay, what's the matter?" His eyes scanned the road in front of us, assuming I'd been warning him about some animal that had wandered into our path.

"Look."

I pointed to the side of the house around which I'd walked just two days before in order to confront Patience Brawley.

Red followed my arm to where a dark-colored SUV sat pulled up onto the grass, nearly lost from sight in the rainy gloom.

We looked at each other for a moment before I bent my head back to the cell phone. "Hold on."

It rang just once. The sound of a woman's voice on the other end of the line made me jump. I jerked my head in Red's direction. "Joline?" I blurted out.

"No, this is their housekeeper. Can I take a message for Miz Eastman?"

"Is the doctor at home?" I felt my heart rate returning to normal.

"No, he got called out for a baby." Wariness crept into her voice. "Who's this?"

I made the decision quickly. "This is Bay Tanner. Mrs. Eastman hired me to help find a donor for Kimmie."

"I see. I'm sorry, but I'm the only one to home right now. Looking after Christopher."

"I wonder if you know what kind of car Mrs. Eastman drives?"

"Oh, Lord, there ain't been an accident or something!"

I rushed to reassure her. "No, nothing like that. I just need it for my records."

If she doubted me, she kept it to herself. "Well, I don't know much about cars. All look alike to me. It's one of them big things with all the seats, but not a van. And hers is dark green. Looks real pretty when it's all clean and shinin'."

"Thank you, ma'am. You have a good night."

"You have any idea when Miz Eastman's comin' home? I got my own family to see to, and I can't be staying here all night too many more times."

"No, ma'am, I don't. I'm sorry. Thanks again."

I hung up before she could ask me any more questions I didn't know the answers to.

"Green SUV," I said, and Red nodded.

He backed up a few yards, almost to the spot we'd occupied when Lizzie Shelly had accosted us, and cut the lights, then the engine.

"I think you better stay here," I said and pushed open the door. "Less threatening this time of night if it's just one woman."

He didn't argue. I skirted the vehicles, found the front walk, and stepped onto the narrow stoop. I couldn't find a doorbell in the dark, so I used the knocker. In the deep silence of the rain-soaked night it sounded unnaturally loud. A moment later, a light clicked on overhead.

"Mrs. Tanner?"

Ellis wore a USC Gamecocks T-shirt, stained sweatpants, and white socks. A bottle of beer sweated in his right hand.

"Hey, Ellis. I'm really sorry to bother you so late at night, but it's important. I need to talk to your mother."

"I'm sorry, but she's already gone to bed. She gets up real early." He glanced back over his shoulder, and I could hear faint voices.

"May I come in for a moment? It's a little chilly out here."

He stepped back reluctantly but didn't move out of the small entryway. We stood very close together, and I knew he was protecting something—or someone.

"Joline's here, isn't she?" I asked.

He began to shake his head at the same moment I stepped around him.

I heard her voice before I actually saw her. "Yes, Mrs. Tanner. I should have known you'd figure it out. Kimmie told you I called, didn't she?"

When I didn't answer, she stepped up behind Ellis and laid a hand on his shoulder. "It's all right. Let her come in."

He stood aside, and I could see down the short hallway into the living room. A man who resembled Duke Brawley in size and features sat on an overstuffed sofa, his arm around the shoulders of Patience, who was fully dressed and regarding me with a stare I couldn't interpret.

I thought about Red and wondered how long he'd be content to sit passively in the car before he decided I needed rescuing. "Hang on a second. My associate is outside. He needs to be in on this, too."

Before anyone could object, I opened the door and called his name. I saw the light come on as he climbed out of the Jaguar, and a moment later he stepped inside.

"What's going on?" he asked as he wiped his feet on the throw rug in the entryway.

"We'll find out soon enough."

We walked into the living area, and four pair of eyes, some more hostile than others, studied us. It seemed as if no one was going to make the first move. I held out my hand and approached Carl Brawley.

"Sir, I'm Bay Tanner, the private investigator Joline hired to help find her family." Behind my back I motioned Red forward. "And this is my associate—and brother-in-law—Red Tanner."

Carl stood and shook our hands, and I completed the introductions. We were invited to take chairs opposite the sofa. I cursed myself for leaving my bag in the car. No way to take notes, so I'd have to rely on Red's experience with interrogation and hope that between us we wouldn't forget anything important.

"May I offer you some coffee?" Patience spoke reluctantly, but her innate hospitality had apparently overridden her animosity, the cause of which I hadn't yet figured out.

Red and I both declined, and she sat back against her husband's protective arm. The silence in the crowded room, which was neatly furnished and spotlessly clean, felt charged, as if we'd walked into the middle of a heated argument or some other exchange heavy with emotion. No one seemed prepared to take the lead.

"I'm surprised to find you all sitting here," I said softly, scrubbing any hint of accusation or condemnation from my voice. I fixed my gaze on Patience. "You seemed pretty adamant on Saturday that you wanted nothing to do with Joline or her sisters."

"No disrespect," the woman mumbled, "but I don't see how it's any concern of yours."

I glanced at Joline, who was twisting her large diamond engagement ring around on her finger. I'd noticed it in my office, the day she first came to lay out her fears for her dying child. I remembered thinking that it must have cost a small fortune, along with her stylish gray suit and Kate Spade bag. She looked up to find me studying her and tried on a small smile.

"I have complete confidence in Bay. She's doing her best to help . . . to save—"

She stopped herself abruptly, and tears suddenly poured down her face. It was the first time I had ever seen her lose control, and it shocked me. Patience leaned forward as if she might push herself upright and offer comfort to the weeping woman. But the moment passed, and she leaned back against her husband's arm.

Red and I exchanged a look, and no one else spoke. In a few moments, Joline mastered herself, snuffling into a handkerchief she pulled from the pocket of her sweater. She blew her nose and drew in a long, shuddering breath.

"I'm sorry. I thought I was all through with tears. They don't solve anything, and I need to keep my head on straight." She looked at Red and me. "Please forgive me."

"It's perfectly understandable." Red's smile brought an answering one to Joline's face. "How can we help?"

It was exactly the right thing to say. Joline straightened her shoulders and glanced briefly at Patience.

"You do what you have to do. You know how I feel about it," the older woman said. "I think it's best if we leave you alone now. Ellis, you wait in your room 'til these folks are ready to leave, and make sure we're locked up tight."

"Okay, Ma," her son answered.

Both he and his father mumbled goodnights and followed the family matriarch from the room. Joline stood and perched herself on the edge of the sofa.

I did my best to keep any accusation out of my voice. "Why didn't you just leave this to me, Joline? We're making good progress." I glanced over my shoulder to where the Brawley family had made their exit. "Why take a chance on alienating our best lead by showing up here?" Again that twisting of her rings as she avoided my eyes. "Joline? What the hell did you think you'd accomplish here? Your husband is just about frantic. He tried to hire us to track you down."

Her head snapped up. "You didn't tell him, did you? About where I am?" Her voice held an edge of panic, and her eyes darted from one to the other of us.

Beside me, I felt Red stiffen to attention. "We didn't know for sure ourselves until just a few minutes ago. Why are you afraid of your husband, Mrs. Eastman?" When she didn't respond, he pushed harder. "Why, Joline? Does he beat you? Abuse your son? We can have him arrested in a heartbeat. All you have to do is say the word."

"No! No! You don't understand!"

"Then tell us," I said softly. "Why did you run away?"

"It's Kimmie," she said, the sodden handkerchief now pressed against her mouth so that we had to strain to understand her.

"What about Kimmie?" I whispered.

She dropped her hands into her lap and stared past us out the window into the blackness. "He doesn't want me to find a donor. He wants her dead."

CHAPTER
THIRTY-ONE

I FELT AS IF SOMEONE HAD KICKED ME IN THE GUT, MY lungs unable to draw breath. I suddenly realized I was squeezing my hands together so tightly I could feel my nails digging into my palms.

Joline's stunning pronouncement had left us all momentarily speechless. I cleared my throat and sucked in air.

"You'd better explain that, Joline. It's an unbelievable accusation. I saw him with her tonight, at the hospital. He seemed genuinely—"

"What did he do? What did he say?"

"You need to calm down," I said softly. I noticed mugs scattered across the top of the low table in front of her. "Do you want some coffee? Or a drink? I'm sure I can find—"

"No." Again she shuddered, and this time she set aside the crumpled handkerchief. "You're right. I'm being hysterical, and that won't help anything." She stared across at me. "Tell me what happened at the hospital."

I gave her a brief synopsis of both my encounters that night with Dr. Jerry Eastman. "I have to admit," I said when I'd finished, "that his abrupt changes of attitude were a little unsettling. It was almost as if—"

"He was two different people?" she said.

"Sort of. Are you aware that he came to my house on Sunday?"

The news didn't seem to affect her one way or the other. "I'm not surprised. He was eavesdropping on our conversation Saturday morning." She sighed deeply and dropped her head. "Eventually he finds out everything."

I glanced at Red, unsure of how to continue. Joline Eastman was unraveling before our eyes. The proud, dignified woman who'd walked into my office just a few days before was slowly dissolving into this strange creature who swung wildly from inconsolable grief and anger to resignation in a matter of seconds.

When the silence had stretched out for nearly a full minute, I said, "Joline. Look at me."

Slowly, she raised her eyes.

"Tell me what you're doing here. Did you find out anything that will help us locate your sisters?"

She seemed to be in a daze. Again I looked at Red.

"Mrs. Eastman!" he said sharply. "We don't have time for this. *Kimmie* doesn't have time for this."

Her daughter's name finally penetrated the fog. "No," she said quietly. "Nothing. I tried to talk to them earlier, but they wouldn't answer the door. I came back, and Ellis finally let me in, but . . ." She let the thought trail away.

I kept my voice low and soothing. "What can you tell us about Kimmie's father? Her real father. Is he still alive?"

Her reaction took me completely off guard. Leaping to her feet, she shouted, "What did that bastard tell you? What did he say?"

I glanced at Red for guidance, and he shrugged. I leaned forward, my elbows resting on my knees, and again spoke softly. "You mean your husband? Pretty much the same thing you have every time I've asked the question. He told me to mind my own business."

I jerked back in shock when she laughed. It was the last response I'd expected.

"Bastard," she said again. "He's only worried about his precious reputation."

"I don't understand."

Joline leaned back against the soft cushions of the sofa and stared at the ceiling. "It doesn't matter anymore. I got pregnant my senior year of high school. At first I was upset, but we were in love and planned on getting married as soon as I graduated. I wanted lots of kids, and I was never college material anyway. We had plans." She drew a ragged breath. "But then he . . . just ran off."

Red and I exchanged a look, and I knew both our minds had conjured up the same horrible image: a skeleton with a hole in its skull, its bones scattered by time and the creatures of the marsh.

"Was it your cousin?" I asked. "I mean, was . . . is Deshawn Kimmie's father?"

She didn't answer my question. Her eyes were fixed on some distant point over my head. "It's the not knowing. All these years I've wondered if he just couldn't handle being a father so young, or if . . . if he didn't really love me." Again she forced herself to speak calmly. "I tried to make a go of it on my own, but it was so hard. And then Jerry came back."

"What do you mean, he came back?"

Joline looked at me as if from a long distance. "Jerry? He used to live near us. He was older, and off to college, but I knew who he was. He was just finishing his residency when he asked me to marry him. Kimmie was just a toddler. It seemed like the perfect solution."

"But it wasn't?" I asked softly.

She sighed. "He resented the time I spent with Kimmie, especially since we were having a hard time getting pregnant. Things got better after Christopher was born, except he seemed almost obsessed with his son. And when Kimmie got sick, he began to show his true colors." The pain on her face hurt my heart. "He wants her to die."

I remembered Jerrold Eastman's words about trying to get Joline to come to terms with Kimmie's imminent death, to give up looking for a donor and just let her go. Still, that seemed a long way from actually *wanting* her dead.

"Then why don't you get her out of there? Move her to another hospital if you're that concerned?"

"Because I can't afford to! Do you have any idea what her treatment and care costs? Without Jerry's medical insurance—" She struggled to control herself. "It's been over two hundred thousand dollars so far. And if we find a donor, she'll have to go to MUSC for the transplant, and—" Joline swallowed. "I need him right now. I'll put up with whatever I have to to make my baby well."

Joline suddenly lost the battle with her pent-up fear, and her sobs echoed through the small, neat house. I hesitated, wondering if she would welcome or rebuff my attempts at comfort, when Patience Brawley stormed back into the room. In robe and bare feet, she marched across the carpet and stopped in front of the weeping woman. Her hand hovered over Joline's heaving back before she dropped it to her side. The look she directed at me froze me in place.

"Why don't you just leave us alone?" When I didn't respond, she said, "I'll thank you to leave my house. Now."

I wasn't ready to retreat, not without some more answers, but I didn't think we'd be getting them in Joline's present condition. "Yes, ma'am," I said, rising. "I'm sorry."

Red joined me, his hand resting lightly on my arm as if for support. I turned as Ellis materialized in the doorway.

"Ma? Is everything okay?" he asked.

"See these folks out," she said without looking around.

There didn't seem to be anything else to say. We followed the young man to the tiny foyer and stepped out onto the porch. The clouds had moved on, I noticed, and the sky had exploded into a canopy of stars. I felt the door edging closed behind us and whirled back.

"Ellis, wait. Were you in on the conversation since Joline got here?"

His mother's strict upbringing kept him from ignoring me, although I could tell from his eyes in the dim light that he wanted to slam the door and be done with us.

"A little," he said, his gaze dropping to his feet. "My mom was seriously pissed off that I let her in. Why?"

"I need to know if your mother can put us in touch with Joline's sisters, Contessa and Maeline. Did they talk about that?"

"Yes, ma'am," he said reluctantly. "But Mama swears she doesn't know." He swallowed hard and met my eyes. "They argued some about how Mama and the rest of the family had to take care of the funeral when Joline's mother got killed, but that's about all." He paused again. "I'm gonna get tested. To see if I might be a match for the little girl. I told Mama I'm going up to Charleston as soon as I can whether she likes it or not."

"That's wonderful." I glanced back inside, but I couldn't make out what was going on in the living room behind him. "Do you know when Joline's going back home?"

"She was just about set to leave when you-all came in. She says she has to get back to her kids."

"Good. Tell her I said to call me as soon as she can, okay?"

"Yes, ma'am, I'll do that." Again he looked at the floor. "I'm sorry if Mama—"

I reached out to pat his arm. "Don't worry about it. She has a lot on her plate right now. Just tell Joline to call me."

He nodded once and closed the door.

Red and I followed the walkway back to the Jaguar. Without asking, I handed him the keys and slid into the passenger side. I had to move my bag, which I'd left on the seat. As I reached to set it on the floor at my feet, I noticed a letter-sized piece of paper, folded as if to fit it into an envelope, sticking out from one corner. I switched on the overhead light and pulled the paper onto my lap.

"What's that?" he asked, maneuvering back onto Holly Hill Road.

"I have no idea."

I unfolded the stiff bond paper. The words COVENANT HALL were engraved in formal lettering across the top. The handwriting was precise and even, the few lines as straight as if whoever had written them had used a ruler. I scanned them quickly, then read aloud:

"'I think you and I have some things to discuss. This is more than an old woman's curiosity, I assure you. I'll expect you on Tuesday at two o'clock. No need to be frightened of the dogs. A meeting will be to our mutual benefit. Don't disappoint me.'"

I glanced across at Red, whose face in the dim light from the dash reflected my own surprise and confusion. "It's signed 'Elizabeth B. Shelly.'"

"I'll be damned," he said. "Miss Lizzie. I wonder what that's all about."

"I don't have a clue," I muttered and slumped down in the seat.

CHAPTER
THIRTY-TWO

AT FIRST I THOUGHT THE CONVERSATION WAS GOING on inside my head, a dream of some kind with vivid audio. It had been nearly midnight when Red urged me off the sofa and into the bedroom, and my head felt as if it weighed a hundred pounds. I forced myself fully awake to find Red swinging his feet onto the floor, the phone against his ear. A glance at the clock made me jerk upright. Calls at 3:27 A.M. always mean trouble.

I laid a hand on his shoulder, and he turned. "Who is it?" I whispered.

He waved me off, his face grave and still droopy with sleep. "I understand," he said into the handset. "Of course."

"Is it Daddy?" I persisted.

"I'll tell her. Yes. I appreciate you letting us know. Right . . . Okay . . . Thanks."

I listened to his staccato responses, which told me absolutely nothing about who might be on the other end of the line, and constrained myself from screaming in frustration. It had to be my father. I threw back the duvet and started for the bathroom when Red's voice halted me.

"It wasn't Lavinia. The Judge is fine. Or at least I assume he is."

I almost collapsed with relief, my knees suddenly feeling wobbly.

I turned and sat down heavily on the bed. "Thank God! Then who the hell was it at three-damn-thirty in the morning? Jesus, I about had a coronary myself!"

Red set the phone back in its cradle. "Come here," he said, sliding back under the covers and pulling me down beside him.

"Just tell me," I said, the trembling working its way from my legs to my shoulders.

Red hugged me tighter. "Joline Eastman was in an accident last night. On her way home from Jacksonboro, probably."

I jerked away from his embrace. "*What?* Where? How is she?"

He answered my last question first. "Not good. She ran off the road and hit a tree on 17 right by where the construction is going on. A trucker came across the accident shortly after it happened."

"But she's going to make it?"

He sighed. "They're not sure. She wasn't wearing a seat belt and got thrown around. She has head and internal injuries." He squeezed me more tightly. "But I guess she's hanging on. Barely."

I felt tears leaking from my eyes and let them fall. So much misery for such a young woman. Why did some people just seem to attract bad things to themselves? I wondered.

Red pulled me closer and let me cry, stroking my back and dropping soft, reassuring kisses on my hair. In a couple of minutes, I snuffled away the last of the tears and sat up straight. I ripped tissues from the box on the nightstand and blew my nose loudly.

"Okay. So who called?"

"Malik Graves at the substation. Joline was just into Beaufort County when she crashed, so the sheriff's office got the call."

"Malik is back to work?" The tall, lanky deputy had been injured during our investigation of Sanctuary Hill, his leg broken in several places.

"Desk duty. He was on dispatch tonight."

"I need caffeine."

I tossed off the bedclothes and belted my old chenille robe around me. I didn't wait to see if Red followed as I padded to the kitchen. I didn't have the patience to wait for the kettle to boil, so I dropped a tea bag into a mug of water and slid it into the microwave. I stood at the counter, mesmerized by the turning carousel, and forced myself to think.

Was it an accident? The nagging question had been the first to occur to me when Red had given me the news. Joline was afraid of her husband. He hadn't been at home when I called. What if he'd figured out where his wife had fled? Had I told him about Patience Brawley on Sunday, or had he figured it out from eavesdropping on Joline's earlier conversation with me? So much had happened since then that it felt as if a month had passed rather than just a couple of days.

The microwave dinged, and I jumped. I'd set the timer wrong, and the tea was boiling. I dumped some of it in the sink and added tap water. I bypassed the sweetener and dumped two spoons of sugar into the cup. I turned to find Red in a pair of sweatpants standing behind me.

"I'm sorry," I said, "you want some?"

"I'll make coffee."

I stepped aside to make room for him at the counter and carried my mug to the glass-topped table in the alcove. I burned my tongue on the first sip and cursed.

"Take it easy." Red poured water into the coffeemaker and joined me.

"Something about this whole thing doesn't make sense," I said.

"Lots of things don't make sense. I can't make heads or tails out of this poor woman. I think she's been lying—a lot—but I'm not sure about which parts."

I blew across the rim of the cup and sipped more slowly. "Okay. First things first. Why did Malik call you? How does the sheriff's office know we have any connection to an accident victim on the other end of the county?"

Red glanced over his shoulder at the slowly dripping coffee. When he turned back, he wouldn't meet my eyes.

"Goddamn it, Red! Did you tell someone up there why you were looking at the old arrest records when you were checking out Maeline and Tessa? One of the most important things we have to offer our clients is confidentiality, and Joline was especially paranoid about it. I thought you understood that!"

He was waving his hand in front of my face before I even finished. "Hold on! I didn't tell anyone anything except that I needed a favor. I'm not an idiot, for God's sake."

"Then how—?"

"I'm trying to tell you if you'll just shut up for a second."

With a hiss, the coffeemaker finished its work, and Red stood and crossed to the counter. I seethed at his bare back, at the muscles in his shoulders that bunched in anger. I ordered myself to calm down, but it took some doing. If Red had compromised the agency on his first day on the job, I'd . . . I couldn't think what I'd do aside from wringing his neck, which seemed like a terrific idea at the moment.

With his head in the refrigerator, searching for milk, he said, "Where's your cell phone?"

"Why?"

"Just answer the question."

I bit back a profanity. "In my bag."

"Get it."

"Red, you are seriously pissing me off. What the hell's going on?"

He dumped the milk into his cup, slopping more on the counter than made it into the coffee. "Just get your phone, Bay. Please?" he added through gritted teeth.

I stomped down the steps and grabbed up my bag, sitting right where I'd left it in the foyer the night before. I flipped the phone open to find a blank gray screen. "It needs to be charged," I said, trying to remember the last time I'd hooked it up.

"Plug it in," he said.

I carried the phone to the built-in desk and jammed the connector into place. "Now will you tell me what this is all about?"

"Sit down and chill out, and I will." When we were once again seated across from each other, he took a deep breath. "Malik was calling you—and me, too, I guess. To give us a heads-up. The deputy who was first on the scene secured everything after the ambulance took Joline away. He bagged her cell phone and took it back to the station. As a matter of routine, they checked to see if it might have had any bearing on the accident. The last call she made, right about the time the crash must have happened—"

"Was to me," I whispered, and Red nodded.

CHAPTER
THIRTY-THREE

IT TOOK NEARLY TEN MINUTES FOR THE PHONE TO gain enough charge so that I could check my voice mail. Red showed me how to put it on speaker, and we sat across from each other, our drinks cooling in front of us, and listened to what might be Joline Eastman's last words.

"*Damn it, I don't want voice mail,*" she said, sounding angry and frustrated. "*Listen, Bay, there's something I—I've made a mess of this whole thing. We have to find my sisters. Forget Jerry. Forget about everything except Kimmie. Nothing matters but getting her well. I'm convinced Patience has something, and I want you to follow it up. She said—What the—? You stupid—*"

Her voice was interrupted by the shriek of brakes, then she yelled, "*Oh, God!*"

Grinding metal and the sound of tree limbs whipping by the car and then . . . nothing.

I felt the tea rising in my throat, and for a moment I thought I might lose it. Red clasped my hands.

"It almost sounds like—"

I heard Joline's shout inside my head. "Like someone else was involved," I finished for him.

"Maybe. If so, whoever it was didn't stick around. Don't be surprised if we get a visit from one of the detectives," he said softly.

"But they can't know what she said. It's only on my phone, right?"

"Of course. But some . . . people might use the simple fact that she was calling you as an excuse to hassle us. Just on general principles."

"People like ace detective Lisa Pedrovsky?"

Red forced a smile. "Anything she could do to make life miserable for one or both of us would be the highlight of her week."

That the combative detective blamed me for the death of my partner, Ben Wyler, she'd made abundantly clear in any number of ways. Whether she had only imagined a relationship with the caustic former New York homicide cop or whether there actually had been something between them, I was never certain. Regardless, the woman had been riding my tail for nearly a year, and her sometimes subtle, sometimes blatant undermining of Red's career had been one of the overriding factors in his decision to quit the department, whether he was willing to admit it or not. The idea of facing her on little more than three hours' sleep made me shudder.

"Let's not borrow trouble," Red added. "Maybe it will be someone else. Or maybe it won't be anybody at all. Joline could have been yelling at a deer that jumped out in front of her." He rose and carried his cup to the sink. "Let's go stretch out on the sofa and see if we can get a little more sleep."

Wired with caffeine and anxiety, I had little hope, but I followed him into the great room. "Sorry about snapping before," I said, determined this time not to let my pride drive him away. "I guess I jumped the gun a little."

He seated himself on the wide white cushions, and I snuggled in beside him. He pulled the afghan over us, and I rested my head on his shoulder.

"This whole case is enough to make a person crazy," he said after planting a kiss on my forehead. "Try to put it out of your mind."

"Fat chance," I said. "Did you notice the time the voice mail was recorded?"

"Not really," he said, his breath soft against my hair.

"Eleven twenty. Which means she stuck around at the Brawleys' for nearly an hour after we left. I wonder what was said that made her think Patience knows something." I yawned. "Hopefully Joline will be able to tell us herself. Either way, I'll make Patience talk to me to-morrow. I'll confront her the moment I get done at Covenant Hall."

"You're not seriously thinking about meeting that Lizzie woman, are you? You don't owe her anything. Besides, I've got a bad feeling about that place. I think you should just let it drop. Seems to me she might be a few bricks short of a full load."

I smiled and yawned again. "I'm curious," I said.

"I see you've conveniently forgotten that she shoved a loaded pis-tol in your face last night."

"I'll take the Seecamp with me," I said. "But I don't think she'd invite me to call in the middle of the afternoon if she had anything ne-farious on her mind."

"You never know," Red mumbled, and I felt his shoulders relax into sleep.

The phone rang at eight fifteen and woke me out of a dreamless void. I rolled over, nearly toppling onto the floor before I remembered I wasn't in my bed. Somehow Red had managed to crawl over me with-out disturbing my sleep. I heard his voice in the kitchen but couldn't make out the words. A moment later he stood in front of me, a mug steaming in his hand.

"Who was that?" I asked, sitting up and accepting the fragrant tea.

"Malik. He's off duty, and he wanted to bring me up to date away from the station."

"Breaking a few rules?" I asked and sipped cautiously.

He smiled. "A couple. He knows we went to bat for him when they tried to claim his injuries weren't work-related. He's got our backs."

Malik and Red had both been officially on their own time when we'd followed the winding, potholed road into Sanctuary Hill. "In fairness, the sheriff stood up for him, too. It was the damn insurance company that wanted to fight it." I sipped again. "What did he say?"

"No one's on our trail just yet, although there's been some discussion. I think we might be okay. A lot depends on whether or not Mrs. Eastman recovers. If there's any evidence it could be vehicular homicide, they'll do a lot more digging. Then we'll have to come clean."

"We don't really know anything."

"True. But if they determine another vehicle was involved, we'll have to give them the voice mail. It's not up to us to decide what might be relevant."

"Did they take Joline to Beaufort?"

"Malik says they life-flighted her to Savannah. To Memorial. They've got the best trauma center around."

I realized that Red was already dressed in a white polo shirt and khakis. "Where are you going?"

"I'm going to fix you breakfast, then I'll head down to the station. Maybe I can pick up some more scuttlebutt. If not there, then I know all the places where the guys hang out for coffee. Somebody will have something to share."

"You go ahead. I have to shower first anyway, then I want to get started on some lists. I need to get this all down on paper so I can wrap my head around it." I paused and set my mug on the floor. "Are you going to tell them about the message Joline left? About the possibility someone else was involved in the accident?"

"I'll play it by ear. Once they examine the crash site in daylight, they may have a better idea of what caused her to go off the road. The voice mail could turn out to be totally immaterial. Maybe she was just going too fast for the wet road conditions while she was talking on the phone. Anyway, I won't lie about it, but I won't offer it up if I don't have to." He sighed and ran a hand through his short brown hair in a gesture that always reminded me of his brother. "I'm beginning to appreciate a little more what kind of bind that confidentiality agreement can put you in."

If the situation had been less serious, I would have laughed. "Welcome to my world." I drew a deep breath and let it out slowly. "Actually, I'm in favor of giving this information up," I said and smiled at the shock on his face. "I know, I know. I'm always the one being accused of holding out on the cops." The smile dissolved. "But if someone is responsible for Joline's injuries, I want them to get the bastard."

"Let me see what I can find out." He reached down to pull me up and into his arms. "You sure about breakfast? You know I flip a mean pancake."

The kiss lasted a long time before I leaned back to smile up into his face. "Go. I'll be fine. Besides, Dolores will be here in a few minutes. But keep me posted," I added as he released me and walked toward the foyer.

"I love you, Bay Tanner," he said.

"You, too," I called as he stepped into the garage and pulled the door closed behind him.

It felt wrong to be so happy on a day filled with the tragedy of Joline Eastman's accident, but I couldn't help it. I hummed in the shower, dressed quickly, and gulped down an English muffin before carrying a fresh cup of tea into the office. I asked Dolores to work around me, and she went happily off to stripping the bed and working on the bathrooms.

My first call was to Erik at his second job at the office supply store. It took a few minutes before he came on the line.

"Sorry to bother you at work," I began, then filled him in on the happenings of Monday night into Tuesday morning.

"God," he said when I'd finished. "Do you think she's going to make it?"

"I have no idea. I won't even bother to call the hospital because they're not going to tell me anything. I'm sure her husband is with her." The second the words were out of my mouth I thought of Kimmie. If Jerry was hovering at his wife's bedside, was the teenager all alone in her own hospital room? "I need to go over there," I said to Erik.

"To Savannah?"

"No, sorry. I was thinking about Kimmie. She must be scared to death, and her father's probably at Memorial."

"Are you sure she knows?"

I hadn't thought about that. "No, not positive. I'll just feel my way around when I get there. She invited me back to visit, so my being there shouldn't alarm her."

"What a mess," Erik said with a sigh.

"Listen. I saved Joline's voice mail, but the sheriff might want a copy of it. Can you do that?"

"Sure, but I think I'll need to have your phone. There might be a way to do it without, by accessing it with your code, but I'd feel better just doing it directly. If it might be evidence, I don't want to take a chance on screwing it up."

"How long?"

"It depends on how busy we are today, but you better plan on leaving it with me."

For years I had resisted everyone's insistence that I carry a cell phone. Now that I'd gotten used to it, I felt naked being unconnected. I said as much to Erik, and he laughed.

"I knew I'd get you hooked. We have prepaid cells here. I'll get you my employee discount. It'll only be for a little while."

I agreed to meet him at the store and turned back to my blank yellow legal pad. I didn't use columns, just jotted down random thoughts and facts as they came to me, but it soon became apparent I'd need some sort of division between what Joline had told me, what I'd learned from my brief conversations with her husband, and what I'd gained from independent investigation.

Lots of contradictions, I realized the moment I began categorizing the conflicting stories. Who, if anyone, was lying? I wanted to believe Joline, but her strange behavior the night before had left me doubtful. I'd asked her directly if her cousin Deshawn had been the man who'd fathered Kimmie, but she'd completely ignored the question. Had she conceived Kimmie during a one-night stand with some unnamed boy as I had assumed after her first visit? Or with this mysterious young man she hoped to marry, who may or may not have been her distant cousin Deshawn? And were his bones now lying unclaimed in a potter's field somewhere? Or had Deshawn suddenly reappeared as his Aunt Patience had told the sheriff? If so, where in the hell was he now?

I rubbed my hand across my forehead where the first stirrings of a headache lurked. *This is getting you nowhere,* I said to myself. I ripped the scribbled pages from the pad and folded them in half. Out in the great room, I stuffed them into my bag along with the Eastman file, unhooked my cell phone from the charger, and tucked it into the pocket of my black trousers. I glanced outside through the French doors to see clouds being driven out over the ocean and the trees bending under the onslaught of a stiff wind. I retrieved my black blazer from the closet and called a hasty goodbye to Dolores on my way out.

It took just a few minutes for me to hand over my phone to Erik and for him to show me how the prepaid cell worked. He'd written the number down for me, and I placed a quick call to Red to pass it along. He reported little progress, but he was heading out to a coffee shop on the north end of the island where many of the deputies ate breakfast when they came off duty. He hadn't encountered Lisa Pedrovsky.

Back in the car, I realized I'd have to give Lavinia my temporary number. I knew I'd promised faithfully to drop in on my father before the day was out, and I fully intended to keep my word. But there seemed to be so many other things to deal with. I turned on the heater against the chilly wind outside and dialed Presqu'isle.

Lavinia sounded pleased to hear from me. "I'm just making a nice broccoli soup. Let me know what time you'll be here, and we'll put lunch back for you."

"I'm sorry. It sounds wonderful, but I have a stop to make on the way. Don't wait for me." I would see Kimmie, swing by Presqu'isle, then head on to Jacksonboro for my two o'clock appointment with Lizzie Shelly. With luck I'd hit the Brawley place about the time Patience would be getting out of school. At least that was the plan. A lot depended on whether or not the Judge was ready to spill the secret of my newly discovered sister, although the urgency I'd felt when I'd first learned of her existence had cooled somewhat. I had time. The Eastmans, mother *and* daughter, didn't.

"We'll be expecting you. I'll save you a bowl," Lavinia said, her tone telling me I had disappointed her once again.

I swung out of the parking lot and pulled up to the Hilton Head hospital a little before eleven. I picked up my visitor's pass at the desk and waited for what seemed like an eternity for the elevator. On the ride up, I ran through the different scenarios I might use depending on whether or not Kimmie knew about her mother's accident. By the time the doors slid open, I knew I didn't have the guts to be the one to tell her.

In the wide corridor I passed the nurse with whom Dr. Eastman had been speaking the night before as he came out of Kimmie's room. I smiled, and she nodded, averting her eyes. I glanced back over my shoulder at her as I approached the room, but she'd disappeared into another hallway.

I pushed open the door and stopped dead. Kimmie's bed was neatly made up. And empty.

CHAPTER
THIRTY-FOUR

I STARED AROUND THE ROOM, MY MIND REFUSING TO process the messages my eyes were sending it. The cards, the stuffed animals, the flowers—all of it had been stripped from the walls and the tops of the furniture. I moved back to check the number, but I was in the right place. A wave of panic washed over me, and I gripped the doorframe for support.

My God! I thought. *Not Kimmie, too! Not on the same day.*

I whirled away toward the elevators, frantically scanning the empty hallways. Where the hell was everybody? Finally I spotted a nurse stepping from a room a few doors down. She looked up as I skidded to a halt in front of her.

"Can I help—?" she began, but I cut her off.

"Kimmie Eastman. Where is she?"

"Oh, the little girl in 416?"

"Yes. What happened to her?"

Her face clouded, and I felt the bottom drop out of my stomach. "Dr. Eastman took her home. Are you a relative?"

"I'm a good friend of her mother," I lied. "You know about Joline's accident?"

She nodded. "So much trouble, and they're just a wonderful family. Dr. Eastman dotes on that girl."

Joline didn't think so, but I let it slide. "Is she that much better?" I asked and got a sad shake of the head from the pudgy nurse.

"No, I think the doctor just wants to make her comfortable. Without a donor . . ."

The trembling inside me felt as if it might shake me apart. "He's taken her home to die?"

"Now, now," the nurse said, patting my arm. "There's always hope. We're all praying for that little girl. She won a lot of hearts while she was with us."

I managed to mumble "Thank you" before I turned away, the tears so close to the surface I wasn't certain I could contain them. The elevator was packed, and I chewed on my lip until I was finally disgorged on the main floor. I walked, unseeing, to the parking lot and slid into the front seat of the Jaguar.

And there I wept. For Kimmie Eastman and for her mother.

When the storm had passed, I blew my nose and started the car. I shook my head. I was being weak and self-indulgent. I told myself it wasn't too late for Kimmie. I would find her aunts, and one of them would be a match. Kimmie would get her transplant, and she'd be fine. If Lavinia was right and there was a merciful God in heaven, that's exactly how things would play out.

I realized I would have sold my soul for a cigarette and tried to swallow down the longing. Out on the highway, I drove recklessly, whipping in and out of the three lanes of 278 clogged with lunchtime traffic. The powerful Jag responded, and I almost wished for a flashing blue light behind me. My sadness had, as usual, hardened into anger, and I wouldn't have minded being pulled over by some rookie deputy on whom I could vent my pent-up anxiety and fear.

By the time I skidded to a halt in the semicircular drive in front of Presqu'isle, I had myself under control. Sort of. I climbed the sixteen steps and paused on the verandah to stare back down the Avenue of Oaks. The ancient, stately trees bowed under the wind off St. Helena

Sound, the Spanish moss swaying in time to the gusts. The few houses scattered along its dirt expanse lay hidden from view by the huge oaks, and I could almost imagine a smart carriage, pulled by high-stepping, matched horses, rolling toward the mansion, neighbors come to call on the ladies of Presqu'isle. I knew my occasional nostalgia for those days was silly romanticism, but sometimes it just seemed as if life must have been a whole lot simpler then. At least for *my* ancestors. I was certain Joline and Jerry Eastman's forebears would have had an entirely different take on things. I forced Kimmie's sweet face and my ridiculous fantasies out of my head as I pushed open the front door.

I could smell the soup from the entryway. "It's me," I called and walked down the hall into the kitchen.

Lavinia stood at the sink, her back to me. She stopped humming, a hymn I couldn't identify, and turned. "Oh, good, honey. I just now set your soup to warm on the stove. You sit right down there, and I'll get it for you. I've got some biscuits, too. Can't have soup without biscuits."

I let her familiar chatter roll over me and dropped into my usual place at the scarred oak table. "Thanks," I said, my mind far away. "Sorry I didn't make it on time."

"Oh, don't fret about that, child. We don't keep to our usual schedule these days. We eat when your father's hungry, regardless of what the clock says."

I shook off my gloom and managed a smile. "How is he?"

Lavinia set the steaming bowl and a basket of her famous sweet potato biscuits in front of me, along with cutlery and a linen napkin. "Kettle's about to come back up to a boil. We'll have tea in just a minute."

I set to work on my lunch, and it took me a moment to realize she had evaded my question. I paused with the spoon halfway to my mouth. "Is something wrong with the Judge?"

Lavinia took the chair opposite me and folded her hands on the table. "I don't exactly know how to answer that, Bay. I think his health is okay. At least, he's takin' his medicine and not grumbling too much about it. His appetite's good." Her face puckered into a frown. "But he's got something preyin' on his mind. I've asked him a dozen times about it, and he just waves me off. You know how he does when he thinks I'm picking at him too hard." She jumped as the kettle whistled. "I'll get the tea."

My spoon scraped against the bottom of the empty bowl. I hadn't realized how hungry I was. I waited until Lavinia had set down the cups and saucers and resumed her seat before I spoke.

"I found something in his papers," I said, the decision to open the subject seeming to have made itself. "When I was looking for the medical power of attorney."

I waited, but she continued to stare into her cup.

"It was his obituary. Apparently he wrote it up himself some time ago. Only his date of death was left blank."

A glimmer of a smile touched her lips. "I remember when he did that. I thought it was morbid and told him so, but he insisted he didn't want a bunch of flowery nonsense written about him by some hack reporter. 'Just the facts,' he said, like that old TV program that they rerun sometimes."

"*Dragnet*," I said without thinking, as if this was part of the Judge's and my quotation contest. "Jack Webb. Sergeant Friday." I mentally gave myself two points.

Lavinia sipped her tea, and finally her eyes met mine. "I'm sorry you had to see it, especially when he was so sick." Her hand reached across to pat mine. "But your father's got some years left in him, don't you fret about that. It'll be a good while before you have to worry about sending that notice to the newspapers."

So she didn't know what was in it. About Julia. About my sister.

I drank my own tea to cover my confusion. Should I tell her? Was it my place to? Before I could make up my mind, Lavinia spoke again.

"No, it's something else. I don't mind saying it has me worried. And he won't tell me the first thing about it. You ask him, child. See if you can help put whatever it is to rest."

"Okay, I'll try." I rose and pushed back my chair. "Is he still awake?"

It lifted my spirits tremendously when she laughed. "Oh, he'll be awake. He's taken to watching soap operas, of all things. He'll likely shut off the TV the minute you step in the room, but don't let him fool you."

I answered her smile. "Soap operas? Good Lord!"

I tried to hold on to the lightened mood as I moved down the hallway, but I could feel the trembling starting up again just below my breastbone. If I thought about it too much, I'd lose my nerve. I pushed open the door to my father's study-turned-bedroom and caught a glimpse of a redheaded woman locked in the embrace of a swarthy guy whose black hair fairly glistened under the stage lights. "Daddy? It's me." A moment later I heard the *click* as the television snapped off.

"*Guiding Light* or *The Young and the Restless*?" I asked and heard his snort. "Don't try to deny it, Your Honor. You're busted."

I moved around to face him and had to smile at the guilty look on his face.

"Nonsense, of course," he said with a slight *harrumph*. "But it passes the time."

"How are you feeling?" I took one of the wing chairs that flanked the empty fireplace.

"I'm eighty-damn years old, and I've been stuck in a wheelchair since God was a teenager. How do you think I feel?"

"That must be where I learned it."

"Learned what?"

"To answer a question with another question," I said, smiling. "It drives Red crazy."

"You and Redmond doing all right now?"

I had no idea where the calm that descended over me had come from, but I silently blessed it. "We're fine. I found your obituary the night you sent me to get your medical power of attorney. It wasn't sealed. Did you mean for me to read it?"

Only his years in the courtroom, both in front of and behind the bench, allowed him to conceal the turmoil my question was causing him. Only a child who had worshipped her father, who had studied every nuance of facial expression and gesture, would have recognized his disquiet. I waited a long time for him to speak.

"I . . . I thought you might. It's been in there for years."

"Didn't you worry that I might stumble on it accidentally? Or that Lavinia would?"

"I considered the possibility." The lawyer was back. I could tell not only by the precision of his answer but by the lifting of his strong chin as well.

"And?"

"It was a calculated risk."

"But you always intended me to know at some point, right?" I could feel the anger creeping into my voice. "Even if it wasn't until after you were dead? When I couldn't ask questions, and you wouldn't be forced to come up with answers?"

I watched my blows land, and the once massive shoulders slumped. He didn't speak. I drew in a deep breath and forced myself to relax.

"So," I said, "I have a sister."

"Half sister," my father said, his eyes fastened on the bay window and the small whitecaps the wind was kicking up on the Sound. "Technically."

At least he hadn't denied it. I tried to catch his gaze, but he stubbornly refused to look at me.

"And what? That's it? For God's sake, Daddy, who is she? *Where* is she?"

"I don't know. Not for certain." He finally focused his clear gray eyes on my face. "In fact, I'd be much obliged if you could find her."

CHAPTER
THIRTY-FIVE

A FEW MINUTES LATER I CALLED GOODBYE TO LAVINIA and hurried out the door. I couldn't handle an interrogation about my conversation with the Judge. He'd asked me to keep it confidential, and I knew I'd be hard pressed to lie to Lavinia. Not that he'd told me all that much. It had been like cross-examining a hostile witness.

I gunned the engine and threw gravel into the rose beds as I spun out onto the dirt road. I forced myself to slow down, but my mind was racing at a hundred miles an hour. I had spent more than half my life under the same roof with a man I had never really known. It amazed me that in a few short minutes my entire world had been turned completely upside down, that what I thought I knew—about my parents, my family, my *life*—had been, in many respects, a lie. A fantasy. A fairy tale, complete with an evil witch and a villain. The princess in the tower had been completely oblivious to the dark waters swirling around the castle.

"Oh, knock it off," I said aloud. "Quit dramatizing."

To distract myself, I switched on the radio, but even the soft strings on the classical station couldn't soothe the waves of anger and indignation that swelled and ebbed in my chest. It was a sordid story, *common,* my mother would have said. An affair. There was a child. My father's efforts to provide had been rebuffed. He had no idea of the whereabouts of either mother or daughter.

He wanted me to find them.

I wondered briefly how much my mother had known.

I drove on autopilot, braking and accelerating when I needed to, without conscious thought or intent. I managed to negotiate the swing bridge and downtown Beaufort all in one piece. As I made the turn at Gardens Corner, I mentally shook myself. The details he'd given me had been scant, and I'd had to drag even those out of him. How could he expect me to conduct a search with so little to go on? Still, he grudgingly agreed that we'd talk later, when the specter of Kimmie Eastman's imminent death didn't rightly occupy my every waking moment. He knew that my primary mission had to be to help save her life. There was time, he assured me. He didn't plan on dying anytime soon.

Unless I strangled him myself, I thought.

I glanced at the clock on the dashboard. I would be late for my meeting with Elizabeth Shelly, but I expected she'd be there whenever I arrived. I had no idea what she wanted of me, and I might have taken Red's advice and blown her off if she hadn't lived next door to Patience Brawley. A quick visit to satisfy my nagging curiosity, and I'd be back on the trail of Joline Eastman's sisters. The doctor had taken his step-daughter home to die. But not if I could help it.

The prepaid cell phone rang, and it took me a moment to grope it out of my bag. I prayed it wasn't Lavinia demanding an explanation for my abrupt departure.

"Hey," Red said when I picked up. "Where are you?"

I tried to keep my voice level. "On my way to see Miss Lizzie. I'm running a little late."

"How come?"

I swallowed the unexpected tears that caught in my throat. "I stopped off to see the Judge and had some lunch. How did you make out?"

"So far it looks like no one's making anything of the fact that Joline called you at the time of the wreck. And there's no preliminary evidence any other vehicle was involved. They found a mangled 'possum right near the site, so that was probably what spooked her. I assured Charlie Carter, who's lead on the accident investigation, that she never spoke to you. When did Erik say he'd have the copy of the voice mail for me?"

I was pleased we were off the subject of the goings-on at Presqu'isle. I still hadn't made up my mind if my father's admonition to keep his secrets extended to Red. It would be my decision, whether the Judge liked it or not.

"He didn't say. Why don't you swing by the store?"

"I'm on my way there now. I'll collect the disk, and we can discuss it over dinner. Why don't I meet you at Jump & Phil's? Think you'll be back by seven?"

"I hope so. I want to get whatever information I can bully or pry out of Patience and get it to Erik right away." Again I felt a sob hovering in my chest. "The doctor discharged Kimmie. The nurse I talked to said he's taken her home."

There was a long silence while Red worked his way to the same conclusion I'd drawn. "So he's given up? He's just going to let her die?"

"That's my take on it, especially after what Joline told us last night. Kimmie must have a nurse with her or more likely the housekeeper. I assume Jerry is spending time in Savannah with his wife. I'm going to try to see her as soon as possible."

"Kimmie or Joline?"

"Both, but definitely Kimmie first."

"One thing at a time, honey," he said, and I felt myself relax a little. He was right.

" 'Sufficient unto the day is the evil thereof,' " I said, quoting St. Matthew.

Screw the points and my father's stupid game.

"Call me when you start back, okay? And be careful."

"See you," I said and hung up.

I turned left at the big intersection, then right onto Holly Hill

Road. A few minutes later I passed the Brawleys'. Patience's small car was not in the driveway, and I kept moving. A hundred yards farther on I swung the Jaguar between two tilted fence posts and slowed to a crawl down the potholed lane that reminded me so much of the Avenue of Oaks leading to Presqu'isle. I passed the warning signs and marveled at how little time had passed since I'd stumbled onto this strange property in my initial search for Maeline Mitchell. Much as I struggled against believing in coincidences, sometimes fate—or an alignment of the stars or whatever—led us down paths where the universe conspired to—

I slammed on the brakes as I came out of a sharp turn and a pack of dogs surrounded the car, their shrill barks and growls sending my heart into my stomach. Without thought, I gripped my injured thigh and felt sweat begin to trickle down between my breasts.

"Alexander! Hoy, you, Rasputin! Nicholas! Heel!"

Miss Lizzie appeared suddenly in front of the car, and the dogs fell away. My fear had magnified their number in my head. Three sturdy, mixed-breed bodies trotted over to sit obediently at her feet. With a snap of her fingers, she sent them slinking off toward an outbuilding that sat beside the road. I rolled down my window as she approached.

"You're late. I had them penned in before, but you can't keep dogs from roaming forever. Pull ahead to the house. I'll put them up."

I felt as if I should salute, so terse had been her command. She strode off, her booted feet kicking up dust from the road, the dogs once again circling around her, jumping and vying for her attention. I moved farther into the property and a moment later spied the weathered plantation house through the inevitable stand of live oaks. I followed the drive to an open area in front of the sagging verandah and shut off the engine.

Covenant Hall had never been grand, although in the period before the War of Northern Aggression it would have been large by most standards. Simple clapboard, once white, covered the outside and was in desperate need of paint. The verandah curved around at least one side of the house, and the short foundation was of tabby, that mixture of oyster shell and lime that had been such an important part of construction a century or more ago in the Lowcountry. The second-story windows stared blankly down, unopened to the breezes swirling around the yard, and I wondered if Covenant's occupants used only the ground floor.

It had been a working rice plantation, if the young woman at the Stop 'n Save was to be believed, and its owners had been more interested in function than form. I tried to imagine the drive and front lawn filled with carriages that had transported the important men of the day to clandestine meetings. Had secession really been discussed and voted on here, had a covenant to support the breakup of the Union taken root inside these unprepossessing walls? I knew there were many such homes scattered throughout South Carolina— Beaufort boasted one—where gentleman planters and politicians had met and plotted their own ultimate destruction.

I shut off the engine and stepped out into a pleasant afternoon. The sun had banished most of the clouds. I gathered my bag and closed the door. It was unearthly quiet. Not even a snippet of birdsong broke the silence. The dogs had calmed down, and I leaned against the fender and waited for Miss Lizzie. A shaft of sunlight pierced the canopy of trees, and I felt its warmth on the back of my head.

"Now that I know, the resemblance is really quite remarkable."

I whirled at the voice that came from off to my right. Elizabeth Shelly stood hidden in shadow, the light on her silvery hair the only hint that she was there.

"It's nice to meet you—formally, that is, Miss Shelly. Or is it Mrs.? I'm Bay Tanner," I added when she didn't reply.

"I know who you are. You're late," she said again.

"I apologize. Family matters."

Her bark of laughter held no amusement. "No doubt," she said. "I'm always being told that family is of vast importance in this part of the world."

For the first time I registered the accent. There'd been a hint of it in our few brief exchanges—at the end of the lane and the night before when she'd stuck a pistol in my face—but now it was more pronounced. British, clipped and formal-sounding, like Helen Mirren, the actress who always seemed to be playing one or the other of the Queen Elizabeths. It made Miss Lizzie sound aristocratic and snobbish.

I waited beside the car. Finally, she pushed away from the huge oak under which she'd been sheltering and walked slowly in my direction. We studied each other without any attempt to disguise the fact. When she was within a couple of yards, I said, "What is it that you find so remarkable? Who is it you think I resemble?"

She stopped in front of me and held me riveted with her intense gaze.

"Your mother, of course," she said.

CHAPTER
THIRTY-SIX

$\mathcal{I}$ STARED INTO THE WOMAN'S COLD EYES, SHOCKED AS much by the malevolence I saw there as by her words. It took me a long time to regain enough composure to speak.

"How did you know my mother?"

Elizabeth Shelly didn't respond. I could feel her assessing me, more than just my appearance, almost as if she could pierce my skin and crawl inside my head—and heart. It was a crazy notion, but I found myself unable to hold her gaze. I brushed imaginary lint from my black trousers and marshaled my forces. When I looked back up, she had turned and moved toward the house.

I gave serious thought to sliding back into the Jaguar, firing it up, and getting the hell out of there. Although the March sun now shone brightly from a nearly cloudless sky, I shivered. But I had come out of curiosity, and Miss Lizzie's reference to my resemblance to my mother had done nothing to dampen it. Quite the contrary. I checked my watch and followed her to the verandah.

She paused on the warped and weathered boards to wait for me. For a moment, I thought she would continue on into the house, but instead she moved to her right. Past a curtain of bougainvillea vines twining around the columns, I spotted two rockers pulled up to a wicker table where a pitcher of iced tea sweated in the slowly warming afternoon. Without a word, the woman sat.

A moment later, I joined her. I set my bag on the floor, crossed my legs at the ankles, and waited. She took her time pouring the tea, never speaking, and finally pushed the tall tumbler in my direction. I was determined not to initiate the conversation, so I busied myself with adding a couple of lemon slices to my glass from the delicate plate on which they'd been artfully arranged. A crystal sugar bowl sat alongside, the silver spoon polished to a brilliant shine. Such contrasts, I thought, as I glanced through lowered lashes at Elizabeth Shelly. Roughly dressed, she still managed to exude British upper-crust disdain for the commoner, to which class I had undoubtedly been consigned.

"I was almost certain when I encountered you last Saturday," she said, her voice making me jump in my chair despite the softness of her tone. "Now that I see you in repose, the family resemblance is quite marked."

I sipped briefly from the glass and set it back on the table. "You chose a strange way to issue an invitation for an afternoon call," I said, remembering the note she had secreted in my bag. "Nonetheless, here I am. It's your meeting. Can we get on with it?"

My brusqueness seemed to rattle her for a moment, but she recovered quickly. "It's not a meeting so much as an interview."

"An interview? For what? Look, Miss or Mrs. Shelly or whatever your title is—"

"You may call me Elizabeth." She might have been one of those queens bestowing favors.

"Fine. Elizabeth. I have another appointment, so could you please come to the point?"

She placed her own glass on the cracked wicker table and leaned back in the rocker. "I want to tell you a story."

"About my mother?"

My interruption annoyed her. "It will go much faster if you allow me to tell it in my own way."

"Fine," I said and used the toe of my black loafer to set the rocker into motion. It was taking every ounce of self-control I could muster to maintain the pretense that I was only marginally interested in what she had to say.

"I came to the Lowcountry as a young girl. My father was a ship's captain. One of his voyages brought him to this area, and he fell in love with the land. Nothing would have it but that he'd settle here. My mother didn't want to leave England, but he could be very persuasive. I grew up on Edisto Island."

She paused, and I thought about all the disconnected threads from the past few days that kept leading back to Edisto. I could feel my heart racing, and I had a million questions, but I forced myself simply to nod at her to continue.

"I had a friend, one of those bosom chum sort of things that begins with simple kindness to a stranger in a small, tightly knit community. We were inseparable all through our school years, until she went away to university. My parents had begun a shrimping business soon after arriving, and I helped them." Her head snapped up as if I'd spoken. "I had the intelligence, but there was no money. I stayed on the island."

I covered my confusion by sipping more tea. Elizabeth Shelly delivered her story in a flat, no-nonsense tone that dared her listener to feel sorry for her. I waited a moment to see if she expected any comment, but she was already moving on.

"She came back after completing her studies, to use her education to help those on the island. She could have made a good living in Charleston, but she came back to us, and we took up our friendship again."

Something was niggling at the back of my mind. If I'd had a few minutes of silence, I felt sure I could tease it out, wrap my head around it. But Elizabeth gave me no opportunity.

"She was quite beautiful. Not like you and your mother. Not striking. Softer, more gentle."

I let the left-handed compliment go.

"She met a young man, a stranger. Charming. Handsome, in an overpowering sort of way. I warned her, but she was besotted."

I almost smiled. I didn't think I'd ever heard the word *besotted* outside of a Jane Austen novel. The overwhelming feeling that somehow I already knew the punch line to this story made my breath catch in my throat.

"Then he left. She was devastated, but eventually she got over it. Over *him*. And life went on as before." I watched her face cloud with anger. "But he came back. And my friend fell once again under his spell."

This time the pause was longer, but she had me now. I waited.

"There was a child," she whispered, and suddenly I knew.

I opened my mouth to tell her, when a sudden shriek pierced the somnolent afternoon. I whirled at the slam of the screen door behind me. A flash of red plaid and denim blue streaked by me. I caught a glimpse of masses of dark hair streaked with gray as she leaped from the verandah. In the distance, the dogs set up an ear-splitting howl, their voices drowning out Elizabeth's shouts as she jumped from her chair and set out in pursuit of the fleeing woman.

CHAPTER
THIRTY-SEVEN

I WAITED NEARLY HALF AN HOUR, BUT THEY NEVER
came back.

Finally, I stumbled down the bowed steps from the verandah and
dropped into the front seat of the Jaguar. I felt as if someone had literally beaten me with a baseball bat. Again I paused, scanning the yard
and the surrounding outbuildings for some sign of the two women. I
rested my head on the steering wheel and forced myself to set aside all
that had just happened. I needed to confront Patience Brawley, dis-
cover what new lead she might have on Joline Eastman's missing relatives, and find them. I made myself picture Kimmie as I'd last seen
her, her mocha skin in sharp contrast to the hospital linen. Her stepfather had taken her home to die. If I had a chance of saving her, nothing else mattered.

I turned the key in the ignition and crept down the rutted lane,
my eyes alert for any sign of Elizabeth Shelly or the wild woman whose
cry had penetrated to the very core of me. I forced my mind away from
the speculation that ran in a continuous loop inside my head . . . was
she the *one*? Had I just spent an hour with my father's mistress? Had all
that talk about her "friend" been just a cover, a way to tell her story
without giving herself away?

I stopped at the end of the drive and turned right onto the blacktop.

Elizabeth would be about the right age, somewhere in her seventies, I guessed, although her body was slim and strong. But how had she recognized me? When had she met my mother, and under what circumstances? What stroke of luck or fate or serendipity had put us together last Saturday afternoon on a dead-end road outside Jacksonboro, South Carolina?

I bit my lip to make myself stop a moment before I registered the small, compact car in the driveway. Patience was home from school. I shook myself, pulled in behind it, and cut the engine. I marched up the Brawleys' front walk while I mentally shoved Elizabeth Shelly and her fantastic story out of my mind.

To my surprise, Ellis opened the door at my knock.

"Mrs. Tanner? What are you doing here?"

"May I come in?" I asked, brushing by him before he had a chance to stop me. "I need to talk to your mother."

"She's not—"

"Her car's in the driveway. I'm sorry, Ellis, but this is important."

He followed me into the living room. It seemed as if it had been weeks since Red and I had sat there with Joline.

"She's really not here. I had her car. She and my dad went to Savannah. To the hospital." He swallowed hard. "You heard about—?"

"Yes. Joline left me a message right before . . . the accident. She said your mother might have a lead on finding her sisters, and she asked me to come here." I scanned the silent rooms. "Damn it! Does Patience have a cell phone?"

I was fumbling for the prepaid, which had sunk to the bottom of my bag, the sense of urgency making my breath come in short bursts.

"My dad does. I'll try it." Ellis turned toward the doorway into the kitchen.

"If you reach him, I need to talk to Patience." I paused. "Unless you know what Joline was talking about?"

I couldn't read his face in the brief moment he glanced over his shoulder at me.

"No, ma'am," he said quickly. Maybe too quickly?

I followed him. "Did you know that Kimmie's stepfather has taken her home to die?"

His whole body jerked, and I instantly regretted trying to guilt him into cooperating. "I'm sorry," I said more softly. "That was cruel."

He lifted the receiver from its place on the wall-mounted phone. "I'd help you if I could," he said.

"I know. I'm just afraid that we'll be too late. And now with the accident . . ."

"Mom stayed with Joline after you and your partner left last night. She told me and Dad to go back to bed. I don't know what they talked about, but it was late when Joline left. It must have happened right after . . ."

"Probably. See if you can get your parents on the phone. I'll wait here."

I couldn't bring myself to sit down, so I wandered around the living room, staring at a jumble of framed photographs, some of them quite old, that decorated the mantel and the tops of several small tables. No one looked familiar, although I thought one was probably Ellis and his sister as children at some amusement park. Both held bright pink mounds of cotton candy stuck to white paper cones. Their grins were infectious, and I found myself smiling back at the simple joy of a childhood outing that shone brightly on their sticky faces.

"I left a voice mail." Ellis's words broke the silence. "Dad checks it pretty often, so they should call back soon." He joined me in the living room. "Can I get you a Coke or anything?"

"Thanks," I said, more to give him something to do than from any real desire for a drink. "That would be great."

I forced myself to sit down on the sofa with its soft, worn slipcover. A brightly patterned quilt lay across the back, and I wondered if Patience had done the needlework. In a moment, Ellis returned with two glasses. I thanked him, and he sat across from me, his concentration bent on his drink, his eyes deliberately avoiding mine.

"Have you had any news about how Joline is doing?" I asked, searching for a coaster on which to set my glass. I found one and glanced across at Ellis.

"Mom called the hospital this morning, after we heard it on the news." His smile was forced. "She told them she was Joline's mother."

I spared a moment to wonder at Patience Brawley's abrupt about-face. What could have transpired between them in the short time after Red and I left to have sent her running to Savannah to offer support to a woman she claimed to despise?

"And what's the verdict?" I asked. "What did the hospital say?"

"It's pretty bad. Mom said they operated, but it's her head they're worried about. She's in like a coma, and they don't know if she'll come out of it."

The phone jerked us both nearly out of our seats. Ellis sprinted to the kitchen. I could hear him responding, but I couldn't make out the words. I had just risen to join him and wrestle the receiver out of his hand if I had to, when he called my name.

In two seconds I stood in the doorway. "Yes?"

"My mom wants to talk to you."

I crossed the room and took the phone from his hand. "Patience? This is Bay Tanner. How's Joline?"

"The same. They have her all fixed up inside, but she's not coming around. They're going to run some more tests." I could hear an unfamiliar quaver in her voice.

"What changed your mind about her?"

For a long moment she didn't reply. Her words, when they came, were softer than any I'd heard from her in our short acquaintance. "I prayed about it. Last night. After I left you alone with Joline. 'Vengeance is mine, sayeth the Lord.'"

I waited, but she obviously felt the scripture verse had said it all. "I'm glad. For both of you." I paused. "Has Dr. Eastman been there?"

She took her time answering. "I believe he was. We didn't meet."

I didn't quite know how to interpret her terse remark, but I had no time to waste on analyzing it. "He's taken Kimmie home from the hospital," I said. "To die. If you know anything at all about Maeline and Tessa, you have to tell me now." I held my breath in the silence. My eyes strayed to the round plastic clock mounted above the sink. The slim second hand swept smoothly around nearly twice before Patience answered.

"Put my son on the phone," she said softly.

The book was old and dusty. It had obviously been unearthed from some box or trunk in the attic or basement. Ellis returned from his parents' bedroom and held it out to me.

"Mom said you could read this, but you can't take it with you. She said you should check out the cards, too. They might help."

For the first time I looked closely at the slender volume and realized it was stuffed with loose papers. Ellis placed it in my hand, and I read the pretentious, scrolled legend on the front: GUESTS. I glanced at the young man who had visibly relaxed now that he'd fulfilled his mother's instructions.

"It's Joline's mother's funeral book," he said. "You know, where people signed. And some sympathy cards and those ones they put with the flowers. That's what Mom said I should look for."

"How did Patience come to have it?" Before he could reply, I answered my own question. "She took care of the funerals when Joline's mother and grandmother were killed. You told me that last night."

Ellis shrugged. "I don't know for sure, but after Joline left I heard Mom rummaging around in the attic until real late."

I opened the book. The signatures had been made with a wide-nibbed fountain pen in blue ink. "Can I use your table?" I didn't wait for his permission but turned back toward the kitchen.

"Sure, I guess." He followed and watched me pull out a chair. "You want some more Coke?"

I took my reading glasses from my bag. "Thanks. Can you turn on the overhead light?"

Ellis complied and a moment later set a fresh glass of ice and a can in front of me. "Anything else I can do? I'd like to help."

"I appreciate that, Ellis, really, but I think I just need to go through everything in here. Your mother didn't give you any hint what I'm looking for?"

"No, ma'am. She just said this was all she had. And that she hoped it would help the little girl."

His voice had already faded into the background as I removed the bulging pile of envelopes and set them aside. The ink had faded a little in the years since Louise Mitchell had died, but most of the names were still legible. I looked at each one individually, forcing myself not to scan for Tessa or Maeline. I didn't expect to find them there. Patience had already told me neither one had come to their mother's and grandmother's services. I thought perhaps bitterness might have colored her memories, but neither name appeared. I retrieved my notebook and listed out the names I recognized from the genealogy along with any other Mitchells I encountered. I would have loved to have a copy of these pages, but—

"You have a scanner, right?"

Ellis jumped at the sound of my voice. I didn't realize he'd sat down across from me at the table.

"Ma'am?"

"You scanned the information from your mother's Bible and sent it to us. Can you do that to these? Only print them out?"

"Sure," he said eagerly. "It'll only take a couple of minutes."

I handed him the book. "Thanks."

By the time he had turned for the doorway I was drawing the stack of cards and notes over in front of me. Most of the formal sympathy cards had been left in their envelopes, probably so the return addresses would be readily available for sending thank-you notes. I separated those out into their own pile and did the same for the florist enclosures. None of the envelopes carried the names I was looking for. The bubble of optimism in which I'd sat down, certain this treasure trove of family names and addresses would finally lead me to the answer, slowly dissolved as I tossed aside the expressions of sadness and condolence. From another part of the house, I heard the whirring of the scanner, but that seemed another dead end. Why had Joline been so certain Patience held the key to finding her sisters?

I took a sip of Coke and pulled a paper napkin from a holder on the table to wipe some of the dust from my hands. Then I opened the first of the florists' cards. Many of the names matched those in the guest book while others were new. About halfway down, I extracted the enclosure from a tiny, square envelope with a legend on the front:

Royalty Florists
Regal Arrangements for Every Occasion
Serving Pickens County Since 1996

The card inside had been penned in large, looping script. The message was simple. The words *I'm sorry* were followed by a single letter *C*.

It was crazy. It was the slimmest of possibilities, but somehow I knew I'd struck gold. I snatched up the card and almost trotted down the hallway.

"I need your computer."

Ellis looked up from the scanner, which sat on a low table next to a desk in what was obviously his own room. The décor was understated and masculine, with lots of dark wood and almost nothing on the beige walls.

I didn't wait for his reply. The laptop lay open, and I pulled out the swivel chair in front of the desk.

"Sure," he said, and confusion was thick in his voice. He probably thought I'd lost my mind. I wasn't certain he was wrong. "I'm almost done here. Just one more page to print."

I clicked on the Internet Explorer icon and was immediately into Google. I typed in the name of the florist and Pickens County and hit Enter. The first result was a map showing the location of the business along with directions for finding it. I opened it and found a phone number as well, but no owner. I scrolled farther down and landed on an article from a local newspaper that appeared to be about some festival. It was long and contained a lot of names, so I backed out and selected the Cached option. I glanced up to find Ellis leaning over my shoulder.

"Did you find something?"

"Maybe." A thought struck. "Can you get my bag for me? It's in the kitchen."

"Okay."

As he moved down the hallway, I called after him. "And your mother's Bible. Can you bring that, too?"

I scanned the highlighted words in the newspaper article and zeroed in on Royalty Florists almost immediately. I began reading, and the name jumped right out: *Proprietor Ann Girard has been a staunch supporter of a number of worthy causes in the area. Her beautiful floral arrangements have graced the tables of both formal and casual affairs from the United Way Kickoff Dinner to the annual Firemen's Rib Burnoff.*

It had to be.

"Ellis!" I yelled a moment before he appeared in the doorway.

I snatched my bag out of his hand and spread out the Eastman file along with the pages from the legal pad I'd been scribbling on that morning.

"Come on, come on," I muttered. A few seconds later I had it. "Yes!" I stabbed my finger at one of the names. "Tessa was married to a man named Roland Girard, and they lived in Greenville. That's right next to Pickens County. But he died. Maybe he left her well off, and she opened her own store."

I looked up to find Ellis staring at me, the well-worn Bible clutched to his chest. "I'm sorry," I said. "I think I found Joline's sister. Look at the page where the family's listed. Do they have middle names?"

I rarely do much praying, but watching Ellis thumb through the Holy Book seemed like a good time to take a stab at it. It was an eternity until he spoke.

"Yes, ma'am. It says here, 'Maeline Louise' and 'Contessa Annalee.'"

"Gotcha!" I hollered and reached for my cell phone.

CHAPTER
THIRTY-EIGHT

ED ANSWERED ON THE FIRST RING. MY WORDS TUM-
bled over each other, and he finally yelled, "Hold it!" into the
phone.

"What?"

"Slow down, honey. I can't understand what you're saying."

"I found Contessa Mitchell."

"I got that part. It's great news. How did you find her?"

I glanced up at Ellis, who had made no move to give me privacy.

I gave Red the expurgated version of my thought process and my
verification of Contessa's shortened middle and married last names.

"How did you get the connection from that particular card? The
C could have stood for a lot of things."

I tucked the cell phone under my chin and began stuffing papers
back in my bag. I didn't ask permission to take the card with me, and
Ellis didn't raise any protest.

"It was the name of the florist. *Royalty*. Contessa. Countess. It just
sort of clicked in my brain, I guess." I stood and edged by Ellis out
into the living room. "Do you think I should go now? I guess I've
spent so much time trying to locate at least one of these women that I
didn't give a lot of thought to what I'd do once I found them."

"Absolutely. Why don't you head out to the interstate? Find a restaurant, and I'll meet you. I can be there in an hour, and we can run straight up 95 to 26. I think that'll be fastest."

I paused at the front door. "Are you sure? Maybe I should just call her."

"You could, but it's a lot for a person to take in. Especially hearing it from a stranger. I think we'll have a better chance of making her believe us if we do it in person."

"I wish Joline was . . . awake. Maybe she'd be able to convince her sister."

"I know, but she's not. I'm leaving now. Call me when you're on the road. And be careful."

He hung up before I had a chance to argue.

I dropped the phone into my bag and turned to Ellis.

"I know this must all be very confusing to you. I'm almost positive Joline's sister is living in Pickens County and owns a florist shop. I'm going to meet my brother-in-law, and we'll drive up and find her. Tell your mother when you talk to her, will you? I hope she'll be pleased to know she had the answers all along."

His sensitive face studied mine for a moment. "My mother's a good person," he said with a touch of defensiveness. "But her family's hurt her real bad, and I guess sometimes a person just can't let go of things like that. She'll be there for Joline now. We all will."

I stepped out onto the stoop. "I want to thank you for all your support in this, Ellis. Going against your mother's wishes can't have been easy, and I know you've done a couple of things that haven't sat well with you. If we save Kimmie, you will have played a major part in making that possible. I hope that makes things a little easier."

Impulsively, I reached out and hugged him, then let go and hurried down the walkway. Behind me, I heard the door close softly. I retrieved the cell phone and punched in Red's number, my concentration so engaged in planning my next steps that I nearly ran into Elizabeth Shelly.

She was leaning against the passenger side of the Jaguar, her hands shoved deep into the pockets of a baggy jacket about three sizes too big for her.

"We never finished our conversation," she said, making me jerk to a halt only a couple of feet from her.

"Elizabeth! God, you scared me. I can't talk right now, but I promise I'll come back soon." I put the phone to my ear and listened to the rings. Where the hell was Red? I'd just spoken to him a few minutes before.

"We'll talk now."

I looked up to find one of the jacket pockets pointing in my direction. I realized it held a gun at the same moment Red picked up.

"Are you on the way?" he asked. "I'm just heading out 278, but the traffic's a bitch. It may take me longer than I thought."

My eyes were riveted to the concealed muzzle of what I assumed to be the same weapon she had been brandishing the night before as she hovered in the drizzle by the window of my car.

"Bay? Honey, are you there?"

"Close the phone. Now." Elizabeth spoke quietly, but there was no mistaking the determination in her voice.

I swallowed hard. "I can't talk now, darling," I said, my eyes never leaving Elizabeth's face. "You go on to the meeting without me."

"Now, Mrs. Tanner," Elizabeth said and took a step toward me.

"You mean with Joline's sister?" Red asked in my ear. "You're not making sense, Bay. And what's with the 'darling' stuff?"

My mind raced, fumbling for some way to tell him. "I know it's important that we discuss the pact, but you and the others can succeed without me. The papers you need are in the hall closet."

Red had no aptitude for word games, and my heart sank as I knew he'd never decipher my message. If only I had been talking to the Judge. . . .

"Bay, what's the matter with you? Is something wrong?"

"The file is marked Genesis fifteen eighteen and—"

Elizabeth took a step closer, and I felt the gun press against my stomach. Her free hand reached for the phone.

"I have to go. Give my love to Daddy."

I slapped the unit closed and dropped it into my bag.

"Ellis is probably watching from the window," I said and saw her eyes flick briefly in that direction.

"No," she said, "he's not. Get in the car and turn it around."

I slid across the front seat as Elizabeth directed me, and a few minutes later I pulled to a stop in front of the old plantation house. The dogs came running full tilt, barking and leaping, and I hesitated.

"Out."

"Make them back off," I said, and she smiled.

"Such a coward you are, Mrs. Tanner."

She stepped out of the car and spoke sharply. In a moment, all three of the beasts slunk away toward the outbuilding, and I slid cautiously onto the dusty driveway. A part of me was certain I could overpower her. I was younger and faster and stronger than this crazy old woman. But another, deeper part of me wanted—*needed*—to know her secrets. Maybe Red would figure out my message, with help from the Judge. In the meantime, I would keep Elizabeth Shelly talking.

"This isn't necessary, you know," I said calmly. "You really don't intend to shoot me, do you? If you want to discuss my father's infidelities, we could do it more civilly, over a cup of tea, perhaps?"

She stared at me a moment, then jerked her head in the direction of the house. I moved ahead of her up the steps and paused in front of the weathered oak door.

"Inside."

I turned the knob and stepped into the nineteenth century.

It was shabby and worn, but spotlessly clean. Much of the furniture had been there since the plantation days—intricately carved wood tables, marred by decades of use, and stiff, formal seating covered in threadbare silk, stuffed, no doubt, with horsehair. It would be scratchy and uncomfortable. Covenant Hall had none of the grace and beauty of my mother's formal rooms where the antiques had been lovingly restored and cared for. The only incongruous touch I noticed as I moved from the hallway into the front parlor was a laptop, its silver cover gleaming on a rickety, spindle-legged table beneath the room's narrow window. The sun had dropped below the level of the oaks in the front yard, and a single shaft of soft evening light arrowed its way through the massive limbs and bounced off the shiny metal case of the computer.

Without invitation, I chose a high-backed, wooden chair and lowered myself into it. If I needed to make a grab for the gun or a run for freedom, I'd be able to propel myself out of it more easily than one of the upholstered pieces. I still found the whole idea of the old woman actually shooting me completely ridiculous, but I'd been wrong about people before.

Elizabeth Shelly stood in front of me and finally removed the pistol from her pocket. She switched it from hand to hand while she worked the jacket off and tossed it carelessly over the back of the love seat behind her. With her eyes locked on mine, she sat.

I waited. If we had been at Presqu'isle, the metronomic ticking of the grandfather clock in the hallway would have measured out the passing seconds. The small woman with the large gun in her hand stared at me in the silence. I had been more startled than afraid, although I had a healthy respect for what damage a firearm could do. I'd taken a bullet in the shoulder on Judas Island, and I had no wish to repeat the experience. I had faith in Red, but more in my own ability to talk myself out of the situation without anyone's getting hurt. Especially me.

"Will your friend be joining us?" I asked when Elizabeth's quiet, malevolent stare had begun to grate on my nerves.

"She isn't my friend," she said, lowering the gun to rest it on her knees. "She's my ward."

Again her choice of words conjured up a Victorian novel, this time peopled with street urchins rescued from a life of crime and poverty by a haughty, pinch-faced aristocrat intent on doing her Christian duty. I smiled at the image and relaxed a little against the back of the chair.

"How long have you lived here?" I asked, forcing my gaze away from the muzzle of the gun and letting my eyes roam over the carved mantel and the heavy oil painting that hung above it. It was a land-scape, with the house I now sat in depicted in a time when it gleamed with fresh whitewash and when ladies in brightly colored gowns wan-dered the expansive front lawn.

"I don't want to talk about the past." Her gaze followed mine to the painting. "At least not that past."

"Then what is the point of this nonsense?" I jerked myself forward, and the gun rose to meet me.

"I don't want to hurt you, Mrs. Tanner, believe me." Her eyes dropped to the pistol. "I'm not an evil person. But you will sit and lis-ten to what I have to say. Wrongs have been done. Perhaps some of them were unintentional, but they exacted a heavy price."

"Were you my father's lover?" I asked.

For a moment there was silence. Then Elizabeth Shelly threw back her head and laughed. If I had been prepared, it would have provided the perfect opportunity to lunge across the narrow space and wrench the gun out of her hand. But her strange reaction froze me in place, and the moment was lost. I felt a shiver pass over my shoulders.

"You find that amusing?" I asked with more calm than I felt. Maybe Red had been right. Perhaps this woman was truly insane, in which case my plan to reason my way out of this absurd situation could prove futile—and deadly.

"I'm sorry. No, I was not your father's lover. I despise him as I have no other man before or since."

A thud over my head drew my startled glance to the ceiling. It sounded as if someone was moving furniture around in an upstairs room. *Ghosts?* I wondered, certain this old house would be entitled to more than its share. More likely this strange woman's *ward,* the elusive sprinter in the red plaid shirt, I thought. Elizabeth seemed uncon-cerned, although her own quick glance upward told me she'd heard it, too. I forced my attention back to my captor.

"And why do you hate my father? No, wait," I added, holding up my hand. "You really did have a friend. I thought for a while after what you said this afternoon that you were the woman who went away to college and came back to take a mysterious stranger for your lover. I apologize for the error."

Again that heavy scraping noise from over my head.

And again she laughed. "No, my dear. Like my namesake, the *first* Queen Elizabeth, I will die a virgin."

"Then why?" I asked, my fear of what this crazy woman might do completely overshadowed by a deep, driving need to know her secrets. "What did my father do to you?"

Anger blazed in her eyes, and she jumped to her feet. The gun swung wildly, but not far enough that I felt confident I could wrestle it from her before she fired. And the blazing fury on her face left no doubt that she was capable of putting a bullet in me.

"He broke her heart! My poor darling loved that bastard, and he left her and ran home to that—that *creature* he married! Left her to raise his child and suffer the scorn and pity of the whole town! It was monstrous!"

I fell back against the chair, my heart racing. She was mad. Hate had turned her mind, hate for my father that could well exact its revenge from me. I forced myself to speak calmly.

"He didn't leave her, Elizabeth. She sent him away. He told me. He tried to do the right thing, to care for their child, but she wanted no part of it. Or him. I know he would have provided for—"

"We didn't need his filthy money!"

With an effort, Elizabeth brought herself under control and sat back down on the love seat. I watched her quiet her breathing by sheer force of will.

"He didn't just abandon her," she said softly, and her eyes now held only a deep, wrenching sadness. "Talbot Simpson is responsible for her death."

CHAPTER
THIRTY-NINE

E STARED AT EACH OTHER FOR A LONG TIME BEFORE I could bring myself to speak.

"That's ridiculous. Unless you mean—" I stumbled over the words. "Did she . . . did she commit suicide?"

"Of course not! She would never take the coward's way out. Even after . . . everything, she simply found the courage to deal with it. Alone, except for me. I would never have abandoned her." The woman's eyes blazed with fury. "Of course she didn't kill herself."

"Then tell me exactly what you mean." I leaned forward in the chair and forced her to look at me. "Quit dancing around. Give me facts. Names. Dates. Who lives upstairs, and why does she scream and run whenever she sees me?" I took a breath and pounded on. "When did you meet my mother? And what has she got to do with any of this?"

My voice had risen on the tide of questions, and Elizabeth Shelly's haughty expression began to crumble. The pistol wavered in her hand, perhaps from the strain of holding its weight, perhaps from a failing conviction that she could still control the situation with a gun. I watched the tears pool in her eyes and finally spill over onto the creases the sun and age had carved into her face.

I eased myself slowly out of the chair. In a few steps I stood in front of the silently weeping woman. When I reached down and slid the gun from her limp fingers, she offered no resistance. My heart rate gradually returned to normal as I turned and dropped the pistol into my bag and resumed my seat. I waited while Elizabeth fumbled in her pocket for a handkerchief, blew her nose, and finally raised her eyes again to mine.

"I've waited so long," she said, and her voice was husky from crying. "And now, I can't . . . Somehow it doesn't matter. It isn't your fault. None of it is your fault." She rose on unsteady legs. "Please forgive me. You should go."

"I'd like to understand, Elizabeth. We can still talk, if you like." I offered a smile.

She didn't smile back. She stood for a long time staring at my face without really seeing me. Eventually she shook herself. "You're really nothing like her at all, are you? She came to Edisto, you know. Asking questions. I saw her a few times in her fancy car, and they told me who she was. I should have done something then. If only I had." Her hands were clasped so tightly together I thought she might crush her own fingers. "Later on, after . . . I went there. To your house. I watched her over time, waiting for her to do something, to admit . . . But she never did." Again that shuddering sigh. "It doesn't matter now. I'll make some tea. It will only take a moment." At the doorway, she paused. "I really am sorry," she mumbled before moving out into the hallway.

I drew a long, deep breath and reached for my phone.

"Bay! Thank God!" Red sounded just this side of frantic. "What the hell is going on? I'm almost there, and—"

"I'm fine. Calm down. It was just a . . . misunderstanding. Where are you?"

"I'm just passing Gardens Corner. I'll be there in twenty minutes. I would have called the local sheriff, but I didn't know what kind of trouble you were in."

"You figured it out!"

There was a brief silence. "Well, not exactly. I got that you wanted me to call the Judge, and when I told him all your crazy talk about pacts and halls, he told me to hang on. In a couple of minutes, he came

back and said you were at Covenant Hall. I think it was the Bible reference that did it. How do you remember all that quotation stuff?"

It felt good to be having a semi-normal conversation without the
muzzle of a gun pointing at my chest. "A misspent youth. Listen, I am
with Miss Lizzie, but everything's fine now."

"She waving that damn pistol around again?"

"Yes, but it's in my bag now. We're going to talk." I made a snap
decision. "She knows about my half sister, and I don't want to spook
her. Can you go home and wait for me? I shouldn't be long."

"You sure? What about Joline's sister?"

It had gone right out of my head. I glanced at my watch. "It's too
late to start out now. We won't get anywhere banging on her door in
the middle of the night. We can get on the road first thing tomorrow
morning."

"If that's what you want. Are you positive you don't want me to
come ahead? I said right from the jump that that old woman was nuts.
I wouldn't trust her as far as I could throw her."

"I'll be fine. She has a lot of anger she's stored up over the years, but
she needs to tell someone her story—tell *me*, I guess. Don't worry."

Red sighed. "Okay. I'll meet you at home." He paused. "You scared
the hell out of me, you know that?"

I smiled. "I know. Sorry. I was already calling you when Miss Lizzie
shanghaied me, and I had to improvise in a hurry. My clues were
pretty lame."

"You be damned careful around that crazy old lady. And be alert
driving home."

I knew both of us were remembering Joline Eastman's last words
before her car slammed into the trees, the same trees that would be
standing sentinel over my drive back down Route 17.

"See you later," I said and snapped the phone closed as Elizabeth
carried the tea tray into the parlor.

I jumped up and cleared space on one of the low tables. She arranged
the tray and seated herself again.

"Thank you. Shall I pour?" I nodded. "Lemon?"

Except for the lingering British accent, her voice could have been my mother's at one of her endless afternoon gatherings in support of historical preservation or some other worthy cause that always drew the cream of Beaufort society to Presqu'isle. I accepted the cup, part of a delicate set of Meissen if I wasn't mistaken, the saucer chipped on one edge. As I raised the cup to my lips, another loud *thud* shook the ceiling.

"My ward is restless tonight," Elizabeth said. "Your presence earlier upset her. It took me nearly an hour to find her and get her calmed down."

"Is it all strangers, or does she have a particular aversion to me?" I asked, recalling how the woman—or girl?—had bounded off down the lane last Saturday afternoon.

"We're very isolated here, not many visitors. Still, I think . . ." She placed her saucer on the table and leaned back. "Perhaps I should start at the beginning."

"Please," I said and settled into the hard chair.

Elizabeth Shelly drew in a breath and let it out slowly. "Your father and Beegie fell in love that summer he opened his law practice here, but I always knew he wouldn't stay. Talbot Simpson was destined for bigger things than a one-room office on an isolated island. I tried to tell her that, and I think she understood, in her mind." She smiled. "Her heart was another matter. But when he left, she seemed to recover. She dated, some nice young men from Charleston she met when she had to go to court or file papers, but none of them lasted."

"She was an attorney?"

"Yes. It was one of the things they had in common. There was even talk of combining their practices, but nothing ever came of it."

Her eyes roamed around the room, and I tried to envision the two friends growing into middle age, sharing this house, perhaps? But no, that couldn't be right, I told myself. They lived on Edisto, didn't they?

I let the silence play out a little, but Elizabeth broke it first.

"Over the years, she carved out a good, quiet life for herself. We were content."

"But he came back." I had a lot of the pieces now, and a pretty good idea of what might have happened, but I wanted to allow Miss Lizzie to reveal things in her own way.

"Yes. And he was married. He never lied about that, I'll have to say. Beegie didn't care. They stole evenings and weekends, and she always came back glowing. 'I'll take whatever part of him I can have,' she'd say. I knew it would end badly again, but I learned to hold my peace." I watched her face harden. "Until she told me she was pregnant. And that she would keep the baby."

I suddenly realized that there was a measured tread of feet going on over my head, as if someone agitated or angry paced the floor, back and forth, back and forth.

"Is it your friend who's upstairs? Did Beegie become—?"

"Insane? Is that what you think?" Her anger lasted only a moment before the same, crushing sadness settled back over her face. "No. Beegie's dead and has been these thirty years or more."

"Then who—?" I stopped myself, the answer so obvious I should have seen it the first time I saw the woman dashing down the driveway toward the house. Too young to be Elizabeth's contemporary, her long dark hair only marginally streaked with gray.

"Beegie wanted her. We *both* wanted her, even after—"

The loud clomping sounded like a gaggle of children in heavy boots racing down the steps. Almost simultaneously we jumped to our feet.

She burst into the room in a rush, her wild hair tangled around her shoulders. For a moment we all stood frozen. What a bizarre tableau we must have made, three women so different and yet so connected.

Elizabeth was the first to move. "Julia," she said, "darling. You shouldn't have—"

I had only a moment to register the shock of having my deductions confirmed before my half sister flew across the room, the blade of the kitchen knife she brandished catching the last rays of the sinking sun. I threw up my hands.

"You hurt my mama!" she screamed a second before I felt the searing pain slice through my left arm.

CHAPTER FORTY

THE ATTACK LASTED ONLY A MOMENT. ALMOST AS SOON as she had struck me, the knife clattered onto the heart pine floor, and Julia crumpled, sobbing, beside it.

I collapsed onto the love seat, my heart threatening to burst from my chest, all sensation gone from my left arm.

Julia lay cradled in Elizabeth's arms. As I watched, the old woman gently smoothed back the mass of hair from the beautiful face—*my* face, only not quite. Even the realization that my sister had just attacked me couldn't keep the wonder from my voice.

"She looks like me," I murmured, unsure if I'd spoken aloud or not.

For the first time, Elizabeth tore her gaze from Julia's face and glanced at me. "Dear God in heaven," she said, leaping to her feet. "Elevate your arm. I'll get bandages."

The cut wasn't deep, but it had bled copiously. I winced when Elizabeth poured antiseptic over it into the basin of reddish-brown water. She seemed to know exactly what she was doing as she secured the thick pad with gauze and wound it several times around my forearm. She forced two aspirin on me, which I swallowed with a gulp of the tepid tea.

On the floor, Julia appeared to have fallen asleep. Sometime during her several trips from the kitchen, Elizabeth had stopped to lay a quilt over my sister and to tuck a small pillow under her head. She was wearing the same red plaid shirt and faded denim jeans as I had glimpsed when she darted away from me, both at the edge of the Covenant Hall property and when she flew from the house earlier in the afternoon.

I still couldn't quite wrap my head around it. Now that I had a chance to study her in repose, the resemblance wasn't nearly as striking, although the general shape of her face and her generous lips certainly pointed at our blood relationship. If I had passed her in the street, and she was dressed normally, I doubt if I would have given her a second glance.

"You look more like your mother," Elizabeth said, and I jumped, aware that she had been watching me study the woman on the floor. "Although there is a hint of your father there. The chin and the way you tilt your head when you're confused."

I felt suddenly cold and reached for my jacket. The left sleeve was stiff with blood, but I managed to work my arm into it. Elizabeth took no notice, her gaze fixed on my sister and the steady rise and fall of her chest. I sank back into the love seat.

"You need to tell me the rest of the story," I said softly.

She didn't turn to look at me. "It doesn't matter now. Patience told me why you'd come to her house last weekend. About the sick child you're trying to help." She sighed. "I told myself it didn't matter, that Julia deserved justice, too. But I can see now I was wrong. The sins of the fathers. They've been visited on this poor girl. There's no reason it has to go any further."

"Miss Lizzie."

That brought her head around.

"*I* need to know," I said. "And not just for myself. My father is old and . . ." I gulped down tears. "He probably doesn't have that long to live. He's been in a wheelchair for years now because of several small strokes, and his heart isn't strong. He wants to see Julia before he dies."

"No!"

I flinched at the shouted word, and Julia stirred briefly before settling back into her strange sleep.

"Why? He's her father. He has a right."

"No Simpson has a right to this child. Beegie put her into *my* care. Mine! In her will. And she passed us this house from her mother's side of the family and her own inheritance so we'd be safe. I've spent the last thirty years caring for Julia as if she were my own. No one's going to take her away from me. No one!"

"Elizabeth, please." I winced as I raised my left arm to lay a hand softly on her trembling shoulder. "My father doesn't want to take her away. He told me he wanted to look for her, for them, but he'd promised her mother that he wouldn't interfere, and he hasn't. He just needs to . . . to know that she'll be all right. And to set his eyes on her just once."

I didn't realize that tears were running down my face until Miss Lizzie's rough fingers reached up to wipe them away.

"I'm sorry, but I just can't," she said. "You don't understand."

I bit the inside of my cheek and willed the tears away. "Then make me understand. Who was Beegie? Tell me about her. Why did Julia think I'd hurt her mother? What happened all those years ago?" I let my gaze fall to the sleeping woman on the floor. "She's my sister. I need to know."

We stared at each other for a long time, and I marked the moment when her resolve softened. Instinctively, I reached for her hand. We sat like that, our fingers entwined, as the sun fell in a blaze of orange and pink. In the soft twilight, Julia's steady breathing marked the passing of the seconds.

Finally, Elizabeth rose and turned on the lamps, low, so that the corners of the large room still lay in darkness. I heard her open a drawer in one of the tables, then the rustle of paper. She sat beside me again, a picture frame and some newspaper clippings clutched to her thin chest. Slowly, she turned the photo and handed it to me.

She wasn't classically beautiful. Her nose was a little too snubbed, and a scattering of freckles marred her creamy skin. Her hair was dark, nearly black, like Julia's, and she wore it pulled back behind her ears, but carelessly, so that several curls escaped to frame her face. But it was the eyes. Deeply blue, sparkling, as if she knew a secret she was dying to tell. In the background, the ocean stretched away. She had one hand raised, as if in greeting. Or farewell.

"She was so alive," Elizabeth said beside me, then laughed softly. "She would have had her desk right out on the beach if she could. Beegie loved the water."

I smiled back. "She was lovely. I can see why my father fell in love with her."

On the floor, Julia whimpered, like a child having a bad dream. Elizabeth reached down and pulled the quilt up over her shoulders.

"Should we take her upstairs?" I asked. "Wouldn't she be more comfortable in her bed?"

"I think it's best to leave her there. She'll sleep for a while longer. She hasn't had one of these . . . spells for quite some time." A frown creased her wrinkled face. "I think you should be gone before she wakes up."

I dropped my gaze back to the photograph. Time was running out, and I still had a million questions.

"How did she die?" I asked. The moment I spoke the words, the answer seemed to materialize in my head. My mind raced, back to the Judge's admission in his bedroom that afternoon. To his obituary, left so carelessly in the hope I might find it. And to the wooden box on Lavinia's dresser. The yellowed newspaper clipping whose duplicate I was convinced now lay clutched in Elizabeth's hand. I should have seen it the moment I heard her nickname. Beegie. B. G.

Brooke Garrett.

"She drowned, didn't she," I said, and Elizabeth's head snapped around to stare at me. "On the Fourth of July. On Edisto."

"She told you?" the old woman gasped. "She admitted it?"

"Admitted what? Who?"

I waited, and the breath caught in my throat at the look of anguish on Elizabeth's face.

"It's why Julia ran from you, why she attacked you tonight. Don't pretend now that you don't know!"

"Know what?" I whispered.

Elizabeth slid onto the floor and lifted Julia's head into her lap. Her spotted fingers smoothed the matted hair.

"Tell me," I said more loudly, my blood racing as if I had run for miles.

Elizabeth's anger was gone, the sadness in her eyes so profound it hurt my heart to look at it.

"Your mother killed my only friend. And drove this poor child insane."

CHAPTER
FORTY-ONE

I DON'T REMEMBER DRIVING HOME.

Night had fallen completely as I'd stared into Elizabeth Shelly's swollen eyes, red from weeping and the reliving of her best friend's death. It had come out as a jumble of disjointed words, partial sentences stammered out between sobs, but eventually I had the story of Brooke Garrett's death. Or at least Miss Lizzie's version.

I'd forced myself to remain calm, to try and reassemble her fragmented account into something that I could investigate and verify, although the drowning had been ruled accidental by both the coroner and the local authorities. There'd been no hint or suspicion of foul play, either in the follow-up articles Elizabeth showed me or in the obituary that had run in the same paper from which Lavinia—or my mother?—had clipped and secreted that first brief account of the body's washing ashore.

The scenario, fantastic and unbelievable as it was, had been supplied by the child. Her hysterical account, however, had been totally believable to Brooke's friend and confidante. My father had already been cast as the vilest of villains in Elizabeth's mind, my mother the usurper who had stolen Brooke's happiness. She was more than prepared—even eager—to accept Julia's wild story of murder on the beach. . . .

I pulled into my driveway a little before ten, the lights blazing inside seeming like a welcoming beacon guiding me back to sanity. In the garage, I let my head fall onto the steering wheel. I could have slept there until morning except that Red's face suddenly appeared at the driver's window. I let him help me from the car.

"My God, honey, you look like you've been in a war."

I winced as his hand brushed against the wound on my arm.

"What's the matter?" His fingers touched the dried crust on the sleeve of my jacket. "Jesus, is that blood? What the hell happened? Are you——?"

"Red, please! I'm fine. Let's just go inside before I fall down."

He guided me up the steps and helped me work myself out of the ruined jacket. I offered no protest when he led me to the sofa in the great room and eased me down beside him. Gently he folded me into his arms.

"Tell me," he whispered against my hair.

I felt the treacherous tears closing my throat and gulped them back down. "I found Julia," I said. "I found my sister."

He leaned back to stare into my face. "Where?" Then, "At Covenant Hall? With the old woman? Why? How on earth——?"

I placed my fingers against his lips. "*Sshh.* Let me just tell it, okay?" My stomach rumbled loudly in the stillness. "But can I have something to eat while we talk? I'm about to collapse from hunger."

We walked hand in hand up the steps into the kitchen. Red made me sit at the table while he fussed with a greasy pizza box and the microwave.

"You sure this is okay? I could cook you some eggs."

"I'll eat the box if you don't hurry up," I said.

A moment later he set a plate in front of me. I wolfed down the first piece and drained half my glass of Diet Coke before I felt strong enough to continue. I looked past Red and fastened my eyes on the calendar hanging over the built-in desk. *Only a week,* I thought. Seven days since I'd raced to the hospital to find out if my father would live or die and set in motion the events that had altered my perception of my own life forever. Would I ever know the truth? Was I, in fact, the product of a heartless philanderer and a cold-blooded murderess?

"Bay?" Red's voice seemed to come from far away. "Can you tell me what happened?"

I wiped my hands on a napkin and leaned back in the chair. "Before my parents were married, the Judge had a relationship with a young attorney on Edisto Island. But he wanted more than what that isolated place could offer, and she wouldn't leave her family and friends. He came back to Beaufort, met and married my mother, and eventually settled into Presqu'isle."

I finished the Coke, and Red brought a fresh can. He poured it over the remaining ice, his eyes never leaving my face, although I couldn't bring myself to look directly at him.

"But he still loved Brooke. Brooke Garrett. That was her name. And my mother had turned cold, more interested in her charities and her friends than in her husband." I laughed, a bitter sound that startled even me. "I can at least believe that part. It formed the basis for my whole damn miserable childhood." I took a deep breath. "Anyway, he started sneaking back to Edisto, and they picked up their affair where they'd left off. I don't know how long he led this double life, but Brooke became pregnant. My father was elated. He wanted children. According to Miss Lizzie, they discussed divorce. My father and Brooke. But in the end she couldn't do it, couldn't be responsible for breaking up his marriage."

This part of Elizabeth Shelly's garbled narrative had struck a false note. It was hard to believe in such altruism, although I desperately wanted to. I would probably never know the complete truth. Only Brooke Garrett could have told me what was truly in her heart. I shook my head. I supposed, in the great scheme of things, it didn't really matter. It was what Elizabeth needed to believe.

"And Julia is their daughter? Your half sister?"

I jerked my mind back to Red. "Brooke banished the Judge. He told me this afternoon that he hadn't heard from her since. And he's never seen Julia. He only knew her name because someone who knew Brooke happened to mention it at some legal conference he attended." I sighed and absently ran my hand over the bandage on my arm. "It's all so pointlessly sad."

"Did you talk to her? To Julia? What's she like? Does she look like you?"

"She's the one who stabbed me," I said, and Red's mouth dropped open.

"Why?"

"Because, according to Lizzie, Julia told a garbled story about a woman who argued with Brooke on an old pier at Edisto on the Fourth of July. The woman hit Brooke. She fell into the water, and the woman ran away. The tide must have been ebbing, and Brooke's body was carried out to sea. They found her the next day, washed up miles from where this all happened. Lizzie said Julia had always been high-strung, prone to fits of anger. She'd even seen a child psychologist. Her mother and mine screaming and fighting put her right over the edge into something resembling catatonia." I forced myself finally to look at Red. "She didn't speak again for nearly two years afterward."

"My God! But why does this Lizzie person think it was your mother who argued with Brooke?"

"Apparently Emmaline had been to Edisto a couple of times before, asking questions. She must have had a hint that the Judge had been screwing around." My laugh held not a trace of humor. "Maybe my mother even hired a private investigator. Wouldn't that be ironic."

Red reached across and took my hand. "But it's still only the word of a disturbed child."

"I think nowadays she'd have been diagnosed with post-traumatic stress disorder, but I guess it wasn't a recognized psychiatric illness back then. Especially in children." I gently touched the bandage on my left arm. "And it's hard to argue with her reaction to me. Even before Elizabeth knew for sure who I was, Julia bolted at the sight of me."

"Do you actually believe all this?"

I let my head fall into my hands. "I don't know." I decided it was time to get it all out. "That night we stayed at Presqu'isle? When the Judge was in the hospital?"

"Sure."

"Well, I did a little snooping that I'm not particularly proud of." I told him then about Lavinia's treasure box and the yellowed newspaper clipping that recounted Brooke Garrett's drowning.

Red squeezed my hand more tightly.

"Lavinia knows something about what happened. Why else would she have that article locked away? My mother may even have confessed to her, although I can't believe a woman of her strict moral principles would have let even Emmaline get away with murder."

"You don't know for certain that's what it was." He forced a smile. "Insufficient data."

We left the dirty dishes on the table and settled again on the sofa. I gave Red the rest of the story: my chance encounter with Elizabeth Shelly on the day I first went to Patience Brawley's house, my glimpse of Julia streaking away down the driveway.

"She thought I was my mother," I said against his shoulder where I lay locked in his strong, comforting embrace. "Elizabeth made the connection, too, after she heard my name from Patience Brawley. She'd stalked my mother for years after Brooke's death."

"Why?"

"I think she had some crazy notion about confronting her, making Emmaline confess or something. I don't know. The two of them shut up in that old house all these years. I'm not sure either one of them is completely rational."

I told him about being taken back to the sagging mansion at gunpoint, about the old woman's grief and my sister's attack. I was proud of how even I kept my voice, how orderly and logical I related the harrowing events of just a few hours before.

"When Julia came around, I helped Miss Lizzie move her onto a daybed in the small parlor, and she went back to sleep. It's funny, but she didn't react to me at all. She actually smiled. Maybe that one act— coming after me with the knife—purged her mind of it or something."

I sighed. "I have no idea what her problems are, but maybe now that she's actually confronted me, she can begin to heal. We're certainly going to do all we can to get her some help."

" 'We'?"

"The Judge and I. It's his responsibility. And maybe my mother's fault. I can't believe Julia's been allowed to stay in such a state for all these years. It's monstrous. Locked up in that old house with a woman who fed her illness."

"There's nothing to be done about it tonight," he said and slid his arm from under my head. "Why don't you take a hot bath and relax? Tomorrow we'll sort it all out." He kissed me softly. "Come on."

"Tomorrow we have to go find Joline's sister."

"Damn! I completely forgot."

I stopped in the bedroom doorway. "What?"

"Dr. Eastman called here. Joline is starting to come around, and she asked for you."

I stared at him. "Is it too late to call the hospital? God, Red, why didn't you tell me right away?" I shoved past him into the office across the hall and snatched up the phone.

"Hey! Take it easy. I told him about your finding the sister in Pickens. He says he'll tell Joline in the morning, and they can decide what to do."

"You trust him? What if he doesn't—?"

His warm hands on my shoulders quieted the trembling there. "He's devastated about both Joline and Kimmie. He's not a good enough actor to fake that kind of anguish. He kept mumbling about losing them both, how he didn't think he could go on. I believed him."

"But what about—?"

"His attitude when he talked to us? Joline's suspicions? Maybe there was some small grain of truth in all that, but I think his wife's near death has jerked him awake. Maybe they both went a little crazy under the strain of Kimmie's illness. It happens."

I wasn't convinced, but I let it go. As I soaked in a nearly overflowing tub, I promised myself that I would be at Kimmie Eastman's door first thing in the morning. I needed to see for myself how she was doing. Then I'd be in Savannah the minute visiting hours opened. In spite of Red's assurances, I wanted to hear it from Joline herself. And then I'd drive to Pickens and put it all in front of Contessa Mitchell Girard. She would be tested for a bone marrow match with Kimmie if I had to force her at gunpoint.

CHAPTER
FORTY-TWO

HE WOMAN WHO OPENED THE DOOR STOOD NEARLY AS tall as I, her erect posture like that of a career Marine. Her white uniform dazzled against her brown skin.

"Yes?" she said, her voice at once crisp with authority and softened by her Lowcountry roots.

"My name is Bay Tanner. I'm a friend of the family. Of Joline's. I came to visit with Kimmie."

I was prepared to shoulder my way past her if necessary, but the woman moved aside. "Please come in. I'm Cady Proffit. Dr. Eastman hired me to look after his little girl while his wife's in the hospital."

"Thank you," I said and stepped into a wide foyer that towered two stories above. The floor was slate, and my hard-soled loafers tapped in rhythm with my gait.

I followed the nurse toward the back of the house to a wide Carolina room, the windows lowered over the screens in deference to its current resident and the cool air that blew in off Port Royal Sound. The bright cushions on the wicker furniture and the potted palms and ferns placed around the pale walls gave the feeling of walking into a garden.

Except for the stark metal hospital bed and its painfully thin occupant.

"Is she asleep?" I whispered. "I don't want—"

"I'm awake. Miss Proffit, could you please lower the blinds? The sun is right in my eyes."

"Of course, honey."

She let the bamboo panels glide down, casting shadows across the colorful quilt that Kimmie Eastman had pulled up under her arms. I noticed the IV pole off to one side and the tubing snaking down to the girl's arm.

"It's time for her medication soon." The nurse made certain I got the message her eyes were sending.

"I won't be long," I said, pulling up a chair set next to the bed. "How are you feeling this morning, Kimmie?"

"I'm worried about my mom. Do you know how she is?"

A cough made me turn my head. Nurse Proffit hovered in the doorway. "Your daddy told you she's doing lots better, don't you remember? They expect she'll wake up all the way very soon, and then she can come home."

Kimmie smiled and ignored her. "Have you talked to her, Mrs. Tanner?"

"No, I haven't. It's just family right now. But your father told my partner the same thing, so I'm betting that's the latest information. How are you feeling?"

"I hate being so tired. I just sleep and sleep. Dad says it's good for me, but I'm bored. They won't let any of my friends come to visit."

Again I turned at the sound of the nurse's voice. "You know why that is, Kimmie. There are a lot of cases of flu going around this spring, especially in the schools. We have to keep you away from any possibility of catching anything."

I wondered what difference it could make now, but I held my peace.

"Please don't tire our little girl out," Nurse Proffit added. "I'll be in the kitchen if you need me."

This time she actually did turn and disappear inside. Before I could draw another breath, Kimmie's hand had clutched my wrist.

"They're lying to me, aren't they? My mom's dead, and they're scared to tell me!"

"No, honey, no. I talked with someone who saw your mom yesterday. They fixed up her injuries just fine. Now all they're waiting on is for her to wake up. She's already showing signs. It won't be long now."

"Swear?"

"I haven't seen her myself, so I can't swear, Kimmie. But I am telling you exactly what I've been told. That I promise you."

She let go of my arm. "Did you find my aunts?"

A lot of her bravado had fled with the near loss of her mother. I wavered, trying to decide between false hope and outright lies.

"Maybe," I said. "We have a good lead on your Aunt Tessa. We may know something for certain later today."

As I feared, her eyes lit up. "Then maybe she'll be a match."

"We're all praying for that," I said, "but there's no guarantee."

"I know. But it's better than nothing."

Hard to argue with that. I looked up as the nurse returned.

"I'm sorry, but this young lady needs to take her meds."

I rose. "I'm going to try to see your mom now. I'll tell her how well you're doing. I'm sure it will ease her mind."

"Tell her I love her, will you, please?"

"Of course. You take care of yourself."

Again she reached for my hand. "And you'll find Aunt Tessa."

"Today," I said. I hoped the promise was one I'd be able to keep. "Don't worry."

"Thank you." Exhaustion and illness pulled her lips back in a grimace disguised as a weak smile.

Cady Proffit set the pitcher of ice water on the bedside table. "You just rest a moment, honey. I'll be right back."

She motioned with her head, and I followed her through the family room toward the front door.

"She doesn't look good," I said when we'd gotten far enough out of earshot. "In fact, she seems a lot worse. Why isn't she still in the hospital?"

"You'll have to ask Dr. Eastman about that, although there really isn't much more they could be doing for her except continue the meds and keep her comfortable. I'm perfectly capable of handling that."

"I didn't mean to criticize. It just seems . . . I'm surprised, that's all. As sick as she obviously is."

"She needs her mother. Especially if . . . It's just tragic."

"I'll report back to Kimmie as soon as I leave the hospital in Savannah. I know she thinks her stepfather isn't leveling with her."

"Thank you. And I couldn't help but overhear something about an aunt. Is she a possible donor?"

"Possible," I said, one hand on the doorknob. "I'm going to find out."

"That poor child needs someone. Soon." She patted my shoulder. "God bless you for trying."

Back in the car, I put in a call to Erik at the office. So much had happened since the last time we'd spoken, and I hadn't had the time or the energy to bring him up to date. It was a few minutes before nine, but he answered on the first ring.

"Good morning," I said.

"Hey, boss. Any news?"

"You could say that. Has Red showed up yet?"

"Just walking in the door. Red, Bay's on the phone."

I heard their muffled exchange as the handset was passed over.

"How'd it go?" Red asked without preamble.

"She's hanging in there, but just barely. She seems a lot worse. I'm heading out to Savannah now."

"How do you plan on getting in? You sure can't pass as a relative."

"I'll think of something." Kimmie's pinched face filled my vision. "I want you to call Contessa. We can't wait to confront her in person."

There was a lengthy pause before he answered. "I'm really not comfortable about that, honey. Dr. Eastman said he'd handle it."

"And I'm not comfortable leaving it up to him. If you'd seen Kimmie this morning, you wouldn't be either."

"Okay. Erik and I will take care of it. If the doc hasn't been in touch with her, you want us to tell her the whole story?"

"Yes. She needs to get tested, preferably down here so we don't waste any time if she's a match."

"What if she doesn't believe us? Or refuses?"

"Then you'll have to go up there and kidnap her. This is getting decided today. If Joline's alert enough, I'll give her Tessa's number, too."

"It's a lot of responsibility you're taking on."

"I'll take the heat. Joline hired us to find her sisters, and that's exactly what we're doing. Either way, let's get this thing rolling."

"We're on it. Call me after you see Joline."

As it turned out, I didn't need a cover story. Jerrold Eastman was standing at the reception desk when I walked in the door of Memorial Hospital. He didn't look surprised to see me.

"Mrs. Tanner. I just spoke to my daughter. She said you were on your way."

"How's Joline?"

"Awake, thank God. As I told your associate, she asked for you. Shall we go up?"

Just like that. I followed him to the elevator. I had braced myself to a certain extent, but the sight of Joline Eastman's head swathed in bandages made me halt in the doorway. Her husband's hand on my back urged me forward, and I did my best to wipe any residual shock from my face. She opened her eyes as I approached the bed.

"Bay?"

"Yes, Joline. It's me."

The hand she reached out was bruised and still swollen, but her grip was strong.

"Have you found my sisters?"

I looked over my shoulder at the figure of her husband hovering behind me.

"No, she hasn't," he said.

I whirled around and faced him. "My partners are working on a good lead right now," I said, daring him to contradict me. "I expect to hear from them any time."

"You shouldn't get your hopes up, Joline," Jerrold said in that smug, ponderous doctor voice that made me want to slap him. "We've had so many disappointments in the past."

"You'd like that, wouldn't you?"

Even though I knew how she felt about her husband's relationship with Kimmie, Joline's venom shocked me.

I heard his sigh. "I want us to face reality. We have to be strong for Kimmie."

"I saw her this morning. She's weak, but hanging in there. She asked me to tell you she loves you," I told Joline.

The tears ran freely, and she made no effort to wipe them away. "We're going to save her, Jerry. Why can't you let me believe that?"

"I want you to tell Mrs. Tanner you no longer have need of her services. I want you to tell her to quit meddling in our lives. That's why I allowed her in here. You said you would, Joline. You promised."

A strange smile, almost feral in its intensity, replaced the tears.

"I lied," she said.

A moment later, I realized we were alone.

"Are you really close to finding them?" Joline asked, not even commenting on her husband's abrupt departure.

I pulled my prepaid cell phone out of my bag. "Am I allowed to use this in here?"

She nodded. "I think the police have mine, and Jerry told the nurses here I wasn't up to having an extension in the room. I need to talk to Kimmie."

"Give me a minute. I'll leave this with you when I go." I dialed the office. "Erik, have you gotten hold of Contessa Girard yet?"

"Red just hung up with her. We had to give her the whole story. She had no idea about Joline or Kimmie. Dr. Eastman never called."

"I'm not surprised." I glanced at Joline's anxious face, still beautiful despite all the bandages and a total lack of makeup. "What did she say?"

I couldn't contain the smile that transmitted itself immediately to the battered woman in the hospital bed. I repeated Erik's exact words: "She's on her way."

CHAPTER
FORTY-THREE

HE WAS WAITING FOR ME JUST OUTSIDE THE MAIN
entrance.

"Joline's sister is on her way to Hilton Head," I said before he had
a chance to speak. "She'll be tested this afternoon. Red is setting it up.
Don't try to interfere, Doctor. Don't go rushing to the hospital and
throw your weight around. This is going to happen if I have to tie you
to a tree."

"You don't understand a damn thing about it," he said, but without rancor, in spite of his words. "I love them both. More than you'll
ever be able to comprehend. I'm doing what's best for my family, and
you've done nothing but make things worse."

The softness of his tone took me aback. I'd been expecting a
knock-down battle, a shouting match we might have to take into the
parking lot. On the ride down in the elevator, after Joline had used
my phone to contact her daughter, I'd even contemplated waving the
Seecamp around if I thought it would keep him from meddling in my
plans.

We stared at each other for a few moments, then were forced to
move aside as a family group tried to edge around us and into the lobby.
I walked a few steps away and sat down on a wooden bench. Seconds
later, he joined me.

"Why?" I asked when he'd reluctantly taken the seat next to me. "Can you just explain to me why you're so dead set against trying to save Kimmie's life?"

"How far does your confidentiality extend?" More visitors streamed past us, and he leaned closer. "If you have information about a crime . . . If one of your clients tells you something incriminating . . ."

I had no idea where this was going, but I knew the answer to the question he was trying to avoid asking directly. "If I have reliable information that one of my clients has committed a crime—or intends to—I'm required by law to inform the authorities."

"But you need proof, right? I mean, just because you hear something . . . What's it called, hearsay? That's not enough. You'd have to be certain before you reported it, right?"

"What are you trying to say, Doctor?"

I watched him struggle for words, saw the war going on behind his eyes. Whatever it was, he desperately wanted to tell me, but something held him back. And I desperately wanted to believe that there was some logical explanation for his strange behavior with his wife and stepdaughter. Over the years, I've become pretty cynical about the human race, rarely surprised at the depths to which some people can sink. Jerrold Eastman seemed like a decent man. He'd dedicated his life to caring for mothers and their babies. What terrible thing could have caused him to reject the last hope of saving Kimmie's life? What— or who—could be more precious to him than she was? His reputation? His son? His wife?

A glimmering of an answer flickered. I fanned the tiny spark, breathing life into an explanation I wanted to run screaming from. Joline was my client. *She* was entitled to my confidentiality. Why had Jerry asked about that? What could she have done that would scare her husband so much he was willing to sacrifice Kimmie in order to protect her?

"Let's walk," I said, jumping to my feet. I could think better on the move, and the idea that had taken root in my mind needed space.

Jerry Eastman fell into step beside me without a word. We followed the walkway around the huge building, and gradually we found ourselves alone. I slowed my pace. I spoke softly, without looking at my companion.

"What's this really about, Doctor?"

"You have to answer my question first. I have to know you won't go to the police."

I shook my head. "I can't guarantee that." I stopped and laid a hand on his arm. "Your wife hired me to help save Kimmie. I've grown to admire your stepdaughter, and Joline is my client. If what you have to say could hurt them, and I can prevent that, I'll do my best to keep your secrets. That's as much as I can promise. You'll just have to trust me. Or not."

He began walking again, and I hurried to catch up. My mind was racing with all the possibilities. Was it about Joline's accident? Kimmie's illness? How far off base had I been with my wild speculation about the girl's conception? Was Joline telling the truth about her vanished lover? There was something there, just out of reach . . . some twist that I hadn't seen, some buried piece of—

I stopped dead on the sidewalk, and it took the doctor a moment to notice I wasn't beside him. He turned and started back toward me, the realization suddenly on his face.

"You know," he said.

"Not for certain, but it makes sense." I looked him squarely in the eye. "Joline killed Deshawn Mitchell."

He opened his mouth to speak, and I held up my hand.

"Wait! Don't say anything."

We began walking again. My mind sifted through all the bits and pieces I knew about Joline Mitchell Eastman. And the partial skeleton with evidence of gunshot wounds, the cold case that Red had run across in his search for Joline's sisters, and the story of Joline's runaway lover. Patience Brawley had lied to the sheriff. Her missing nephew had never come home. The family knew what had happened. Or guessed. They'd kept the secret, but it had split them in two. *Who else knew?* I asked myself. Contessa and Maeline, who had distanced themselves

from their family and never looked back? Their father who had disappeared around the same time? Maybe he'd helped her. So who was
Jerry afraid of? Everyone had kept silent all these years. Even Deshawn's mother, wherever she might be. Why would Jerry think they
might hurt Joline now? Still, he obviously knew as well as I did that
there was no statute of limitations on murder.

"Such a thing could have been a crime of passion," I said, testing
the waters. "Or self-defense."

I glanced up, but Jerrold Eastman's face remained passive.

A moment later, he cleared his throat. "That would be a very believable scenario. And a young girl, driven to desperation by love and
fear, might suppress all memory of what she'd done." He stopped and
looked down at me. "Except in her nightmares."

"Which her husband would be privy to."

"Yes. He would urge her to seek help, even if she continually denied any involvement in the . . . incident. And when she refused, he
would then do everything in his power to protect her. No matter what
the cost."

I turned away from the naked pain in his eyes. He'd been faced
with a terrible choice, one that might well have destroyed a weaker
man. I spoke without looking at him.

"You were terrified that those of Joline's family members who
knew what she'd done might inadvertently or even intentionally ex-
pose her. You couldn't take that chance. You had to choose."

He made no move to wipe the tears away. I resisted the urge to offer comfort, an intimacy I knew he'd reject. Instead, I turned around
and led him back toward the parking lot.

"I'm sorry," I said softly. "I truly am. But even if Joline has re-
pressed her memory of killing Deshawn, I'm as certain as I can be that
she'd be willing to face the consequences if it would save Kimmie."
When he didn't reply, I said, "In your heart, you know that's true."

I heard the anguish in his voice. "But I'm not willing. Don't you
see? She won't survive it. And the chances of any of them being a compatible donor are so small, it isn't worth the risk."

"It is to her," I said. "And, in the last analysis, it's not our decision to make."

We stopped at the entrance to the hospital. "What are you going to do?" he asked, all the bravado and assurance gone from his voice.

"I don't know." I found I could no longer look him squarely in the eye. "Joline's sister will be here in the early afternoon. What are *you* going to do?"

He looked broken, his shoulders slumped in resignation. "You haven't left me much choice. I'll do whatever I can to expedite the bone marrow test. And pray Joline won't live to regret my decision. Or yours."

The earlier sunshine had been displaced by lowering clouds when I pulled into the parking lot of the agency a little before noon. Erik's Expedition was nowhere to be seen. I had just pushed open the Jag's door when Red suddenly appeared beside the car.

I smiled. "Since when do I rate a welcoming comm—"

"Why didn't you call? Why aren't you answering your damn cell phone?"

I winced as he grabbed my left arm. "What's the matter with you? I gave the prepaid to Joline so she could talk to Kimmie. Erik said he'd bring mine—"

"Get in the other side. I'll drive."

I had to jerk my arm out of his grasp to keep him from dragging me bodily out of the seat.

"Red, stop it!" For the first time I noticed the panic on his face. "What the hell is going on?"

"It's the Judge," he said, his voice dropping almost to a whisper. "Lavinia said to hurry."

CHAPTER
FORTY-FOUR

*I*T SEEMED AS IF I HAD SPENT THE ENTIRE LAST WEEK in hospitals.

Lavinia looked up as we walked out of the elevator. Her creased brown face was splotchy from crying, and in a few steps she was in my arms.

"How is he?" I asked, my gaze locked on the glassed-in area of the ICU.

A shudder passed through her body, and I could feel her struggling for control.

"Not good. It's his heart again."

"I need to see him."

Lavinia took my hand and led me toward the nurses' station. As we neared, Harley Coffin stepped out of the room.

"Bay. I'm glad you're here, honey." His somber look and sad eyes made my knees weak. Beside me, I felt Red's arm encircling my shoulders.

"How bad?" I whispered.

Harley took both my hands in his. "It's not good, I'm afraid."

"Are they going to operate?"

"Let's sit down."

Harley guided us back to the empty waiting area. Lavinia and I sat side by side on the sofa, our hands clasped together. Red perched on the arm.

"He's awake most of the time, but very weak. Even Dr. Utley doesn't think he'd stand up to the surgery. We're doing what we can. He's on oxygen, and I've increased his medication. But I don't want to give you any false hope. There's a chance he's not going to make it this time."

I felt numb. The little girl inside was screaming for her daddy, but the woman I'd become couldn't muster even a tear.

"How long?" I asked, and Lavinia put a fist to her mouth, only partially suppressing a sob.

"I can't say for certain. He's still a tough old buzzard, you know. He could pull out of this just like he did last time. But his body has been through a lot. It's just wearing out, and there isn't much we can do about that. I won't tell you not to hope for the best. But . . ."

I forced a weak smile. "Thanks for leveling with us, Harley. Can I see him?"

"They're changing his IV. Give them a few minutes. I'll be here if you need me."

Again I nodded, and he moved back toward the nurses' station.

"What can I do, sweetheart?" Red's voice seemed to come from far away.

I ignored him and turned to Lavinia. "I have to ask you something, and I want you to tell me the truth."

I hadn't intended to sound so harsh, but the time for lies and evasions was over. Perhaps we had a long time to deal with the secrets and half-truths, the illusions I'd grown up with. But perhaps we didn't.

Lavinia reached for her purse sitting beside her on the floor and pulled out a clean handkerchief. She blew her nose and straightened her shoulders.

"I don't make it a practice of lying to you, Lydia. I never did."

Her use of my real first name told me I had angered her, but it couldn't be helped. I glanced back at Red. His face held sadness, but his hand on my shoulder gave me courage.

And so I told my story, the edited version, about finding the news-paper clipping in her keepsake box, my several encounters with Eliza-beth Shelly, and her hatred for my family. About Brooke Garrett's death. And about Julia. Lavinia sat with her head bowed, as if in prayer. She asked not one question, made not a single comment until I'd finished. I slumped against the back of the sofa, all the adrenaline drained out of me. I felt as if I could have slept for a week. I reached for Red's hand, and his strong fingers clasped mine. I expelled a long breath and waited.

"It was an accident. Emmaline never meant to hurt that woman." Lavinia spoke so softly I could barely make out the words. "She only wanted to talk to her, to make her leave him alone. She was afraid she was losing your father. You were just a child, and she couldn't even think about raising you on her own."

"How did she find out?"

Lavinia's sad face hardened. "A 'friend' told her."

I remembered my conversation with Loretta Healey. Had that been what had caused the split between our mothers? Had Mary Grace Beau-mont and her need to carry gossip been the catalyst for all this misery? Had her condemnations been directed at my *father* rather than at Em-maline?

I tried to work out the timing in my head. "But Daddy told me Brooke had broken it off long before that. There was no need for any confrontation."

"It was an accident," Lavinia said again. "Think what you want to about your mother, Lydia, but she would never have intentionally harmed anyone. And she knew nothing about the child. Neither of us did."

A cloud passed over her eyes, and I wondered if she would be able to forgive my father for keeping Julia's existence from her.

"Why did you keep the article about the drowning? Where did it come from?"

Lavinia looked off into the distance, to some other place and time. "It came in the mail. Anonymously. It was a couple of years after it happened, and I thought your mother might go mad when she saw it. She had no idea until then that the woman had died. It nearly broke her. That's when the drinking got so bad. She confessed everything to me." Her gaze drifted back to the waiting room, and she clutched my hand. "Emmaline tried to make up for it by doing good. She suffered for it as long as she lived."

"And so did the rest of us. Did the Judge know?"

I heard her sharp intake of breath beside me. "No! Never! And you mustn't tell him, Bay. Promise me!"

"How could you have protected her all this time? You're probably the most moral person I know, Lavinia. How did you reconcile all those Sunday mornings in church with waiting hand and foot on a murderer?"

I opened my eyes to find her dear, familiar face twisted in anger. "It's not your place to judge me, Lydia. I did what I thought was best. For all of us." Her eyes softened into sorrow. "I know who I have to answer to. And so did your mother."

I had no rebuttal to offer. We sat silently for a while, Red's arm draped protectively across my shoulder. Finally, Lavinia spoke again, her voice soft and pleading.

"If Tally's going to die, let it be peacefully, without this on his conscience. I'm begging you to keep your mother's secret for a while longer, honey. Please."

I rose and slung my bag over my shoulder.

"Bay?" Red stood with me. "Where are you going?"

"To get my sister," I said.

I didn't call Elizabeth, although Red had returned my cell phone to me in the car on the way to the hospital. Instead I dialed Erik's number as I sped along Route 17 toward Jacksonboro.

"Where are you?" I asked the moment he picked up.

"I'm at the Hilton Head hospital. Joline's sisters just got here a few minutes ago."

I thought I had misunderstood. "Did you say *sisters*? Plural?"

"Yes. Apparently Contessa—or Ann, as she prefers—found Mae-line with one phone call. They met up in Columbia and came down together. They're both going to be tested."

"Is Dr. Eastman there?"

"He's taking charge. I think I can go back to the office now. How's the Judge? I was there when Lavinia called."

"Not too good." I couldn't talk about it. "How long before they know if either one of the women is a match?"

"It usually takes a week or more, they told me, but Dr. Eastman's expediting everything. It could be as early as tomorrow."

"Well, we've done everything we can for Kimmie and Joline. It's out of our hands now." I sent up one of my infrequent prayers and hoped someone was listening on the other end.

"I'll be at the office for a few hours. You'll let me know how the Judge is doing?"

"Of course. Talk to you later."

I snapped the phone closed, and immediately Lavinia's voice filled my head. Would I ever understand how she had rationalized protecting my mother for all those years? It was a logical leap from there to Jerry Eastman. Hadn't he done the same for Joline? How could I be so certain my mother should have been made to pay and still be willing to let my client get away with murder? Lavinia had been right about one thing. No one had appointed me judge and jury in either case. Emmaline Bay-nard Simpson was beyond the reach of temporal justice. Joline Eastman was not. As painful as it might be for all of us, she had to answer for what she'd done. Red would know how to handle it. What the sheriff did once he had all the information was out of my hands. The mere act of making the decision shifted a fraction of the weight off my chest.

A while later I made the turn toward Walterboro, then again onto Holly Hill Road. There were no cars in the driveway at the Brawleys' house, and I wondered if they had gone to Savannah to visit Joline or perhaps to Hilton Head to be tested along with Contessa and Maeline. So many tragedies and lost years. Reconnecting with her family might just give Joline the courage to face what she'd done. Justice for Deshawn Mitchell could be the catalyst that allowed them all to begin to heal.

Families belong together, I told myself as I bounced down the rough drive up to Covenant Hall. I braced myself for the onslaught of the dogs, but the place was strangely quiet. I stopped in front of the sagging verandah and cut the engine. A moment later, Elizabeth Shelly stepped out of the door. She folded her arms across her chest and waited. I braced myself and got out of the car.

"I need to see Julia," I said before she could challenge me.

"Why?" There was no hostility in her voice, but she didn't move as I climbed the steps to stand before her.

I drew in a deep breath, and the rightness of it settled over me like a blessing.

"Because she's my sister. And she needs to meet our father before it's too late."

I waited in the front parlor, seated in the same chair I'd occupied the night before. There was a faint patch on the love seat where Elizabeth had attempted to wash away the blood that had dripped from my arm, but she'd been only partially successful.

I stood as the two of them walked into the room. Julia's wild mane of hair had been restrained in a thick ponytail, but wisps had escaped to flutter around her unlined face. She looked about twelve years old. She wore the same red plaid shirt and blue jeans she'd had on every time I'd seen her. Elizabeth had changed into a pale yellow pantsuit that looked to be at least two decades out of date, but she'd made an effort with her hair and even wore a thin coat of lipstick.

I tensed as Julia registered my presence, prepared to fend off another attack, but she smiled and stuck out her arm awkwardly, as if she wasn't used to shaking hands.

"Hello! I'm Julia Elizabeth Garrett. I'm pleased to meet you."

It sounded rehearsed, but she seemed perfectly calm and rational. Beside her, Miss Lizzie relaxed her guarded stance.

I smiled back. "Hello, Julia. I'm Bay Tanner. I'm very pleased to meet you, too."

"Are we going on a trip?" she asked, turning to her namesake.

"Yes, my dear. We're going to meet some other friends. Will you be okay with that?"

"I don't like leaving," she said, her eyes roaming around the room. "It's safe here."

Miss Lizzie linked her arm in Julia's and guided her toward the door. "We won't let anything bad happen to you, will we, Bay?"

"Of course not," I said and followed them down the steps.

Elizabeth let out a long breath and met my gaze. "Are you sure about this?"

"It's the right thing to do. It may not mean anything to Julia, but it will to my father."

"I'm not doing it for him," she snapped.

Julia curled up in the backseat almost the moment we turned out of the driveway.

"That's what she always does," Elizabeth said with a sad smile. "I've tried to take her places, broaden her world a little, but she almost always falls asleep as soon as the car begins moving. I don't know why."

"What exactly is her condition?" I asked, my eyes firmly on the road.

Elizabeth was a long time answering. "They could never really tell me. For years after Beegie died, I dragged her from one doctor to another—psychologists, psychiatrists, neurologists." She broke off. I glanced over to find her staring out the window. "Witnessing her mother's death sent her over the edge. As I told you, she didn't talk for almost two years after. That's when I learned about . . . about the argument with the woman on the pier that night. I wanted to rush out and make someone pay, but I didn't have any proof beyond Julia's wild story. Who would believe her? Especially after all that time." She sighed and turned back toward me. "You know it was your mother.

She'd already been snooping around before . . . And then Julia's reaction to you . . . There isn't any other explanation."

I didn't answer. She was right, but there was no going back. Lavinia believed it had been an accident. Elizabeth would be forever certain that my mother had committed cold-blooded murder. Either way, all of us had paid the consequences. The only thing left now was to try and repair some of the damage.

"Bay?"

I glanced at Elizabeth. "Yes," I said. "I know my mother was probably responsible for your friend's death, although I don't believe she went to Edisto intending that." I looked over at her. "It doesn't make your suffering any less. Or Julia's." When she didn't reply, I asked, "How long has it been since she's seen a doctor? About her mental state, I mean."

"Why?"

"I was thinking last night that her symptoms sound like post-traumatic stress disorder. It probably wasn't even on the radar screen when she was a child. There's been a lot of research done since then. Maybe she can be helped now."

I could sense Elizabeth's anger. "We get along just fine. Most of the time she's perfectly happy. Perhaps a little childish sometimes. She won't hear of wearing anything but that same sort of plaid shirt and jeans. It's what she had on the night Beegie died."

Her lower lip quivered, and I waited for her to go on. "But she loves animals. We have a horse, and she's learned to ride. She's fond of music. She's usually painfully shy, which is why we keep to ourselves, but she's not dangerous. You're the only person I've ever seen her react to like that." I waited for her to continue. "And now she seems to have forgotten all about it. Perhaps confronting you has allowed her to get past that trauma."

"I'd like to help," I said.

"We don't need your help. Don't misunderstand what this is about, Bay. I haven't changed my feelings about your parents. But I don't believe you should be punished for their sins. And if a quick visit will make up to you for what happened yesterday, I'm willing to do it. But after we see your father, we're going straight back home. And that's where we'll stay." She paused. "I guess it would be all right if you came to visit once in a while."

"Thank you."

I'd settle for that, I decided. For the time being.

We rode in silence for a long time then, both of us lost in our own thoughts. As we neared the hospital, I could feel my hands trembling on the steering wheel. I parked illegally, and the three of us walked through into the lobby.

"We should take the stairs," Elizabeth said. "Julia doesn't like elevators."

We climbed without speaking and stepped through the door of the stairwell to find Lavinia and Red sitting quietly on the sofa. Both of them jumped to their feet when they saw me. My heart plummeted at the look on both their faces, and Julia hid behind Elizabeth.

"He's not—?" I couldn't bring myself to say the word.

"No, but you need to hurry." Red gathered me into his arms, and Lavinia wept quietly.

I went to her.

"I've said my goodbyes. He's in the Lord's hands now. Go to him, Bay."

I swallowed down the tears and nodded. "Give me a minute," I said to Elizabeth and moved slowly down the hallway.

CHAPTER
FORTY-FIVE

*M*Y FATHER LAY PEACEFULLY, HIS BODY ALREADY looking shrunken in the big bed. The IV had been removed. Only the thin tubing providing him with oxygen was still attached through his nose.

I slipped into the chair next to the bed and took his hand. He stirred but didn't waken. I sat like that for a long time, the silence almost a third presence in the room. I tried to pray, but no words would come. If Lavinia's pleas had fallen on deaf ears, surely mine wouldn't stand a chance. I glanced around, my mind a blank, until my eyes lighted on an envelope tilted up against the water pitcher on the stand next to the bed.

I recognized it immediately. The last time I'd seen it had been in Lavinia's treasure box the night after I'd first sat like this, my father's hand in mine. Carefully, I slid my fingers out from under his and picked it up.

TO BE OPENED IN THE EVENT OF MY DEATH.

Lavinia must have brought it with her from Presqu'isle. I looked again at my father, his chest barely moving with his shallow breaths, and ripped open the sealed envelope. It was a single sheet of paper written long before his strokes had made his handwriting shaky and uneven.

There was no date. My eyes blurred at the simple salutation: *Princess*—I gulped down tears and read my father's confession.

> *I've decided that, with Emmaline's passing, it's time for me to set down in writing the events that have transpired, to share with you some of the things that have unfortunately impacted your life although you've been unaware of them. If I should die tomorrow, I have confidence that you'll be able to handle what I'm about to tell you and that you'll do the right thing.*
>
> *As a young man, I fell in love with a wonderful woman named Brooke Garrett. We both lived and worked on Edisto Island. But I was ambitious and full of myself as only the young can be, and Brooke was tied to that place by generations of family. I left her and came to Beaufort. I met and married your mother. And I loved her, Princess. Please believe that. She was difficult, I'll admit it, and headstrong. We argued, especially about having children. Emmaline was afraid, and she covered it up by growing a hard exterior. It wasn't entirely her fault, and you mustn't blame her.*
>
> *But I was drawn back to Edisto. And Brooke. We took up our relationship again, and she became pregnant. I was both appalled and elated. I thought about leaving your mother, but I couldn't seem to decide. Brooke finally made the decision for both of us. She refused to let me help her or our child. She begged me to stay out of their lives, not to try to find them or contact them ever again. I had caused her so much pain. I owed her that much, although it grieved me to know I'd never see my child. I agreed, and I've kept my word.*
>
> *Among my papers, you'll find all the information I have about Brooke and our daughter. Julia is your half sister. You should know each other. But this is my burden, Princess, not yours. If you'd rather not make contact, that's your call to make.*
>
> *Try not to judge us too harshly. Your mother's drinking sprang from the unhappiness I brought on her. You were a won-*

derful and blessed surprise, and once you arrived, she loved you as much as she was capable.

As do I. Please forgive us both.

The tears ran unchecked down my face, and I felt as if I couldn't breathe. I dropped the letter into my lap and dashed my hands across my face. When I looked up, my father was staring at me, his eyes dull but aware.

"You weren't supposed to open that yet," he said. "Since you're sitting here, I assume I'm not dead."

A smile twitched at the corners of his mouth, and I reached for his hand.

"Sorry," I said, my voice as steady as I could make it. "You know I never could resist a sealed envelope."

"Just plain nosy. One of your less endearing qualities."

"I come by it naturally." I didn't want to waste this precious time in our usual banter, but I had to follow his lead. Most of all, he'd hate anything maudlin.

"I don't mind, you know," he said matter-of-factly. "I'm worn out. Besides, Vinnie's just about convinced me we'll see each other again. Wouldn't that be nice?"

His eyes were fluttering closed, and panic gripped me. I squeezed his hand, hard.

"Daddy? Don't go to sleep yet."

"I'm still here," he said, and again his gaze fastened on my face. "No tears, though, do you hear me, Princess? Get on with your life. Marry that boy who's been waiting so long for you. Promise me."

I bit down hard on my lip. "I promise, Daddy."

I let go of his hand and stood.

"Where are you going?" His words were whispers now, as if every one were an effort.

"Stay awake, Daddy. I'll be right back."

I rushed out into the hallway. Lavinia's head snapped up, and she half rose.

"It's okay," I said and held out my hand to Julia. "Will you come with me for a minute?"

My sister looked at Elizabeth, who nodded. "It's okay, honey. You can go with Bay. She has another friend she wants you to meet. I'll be right out here waiting for you."

Julia rose and gingerly took my hand. Together we walked into the room where our father lay struggling for breath.

"Daddy?" I said, and he forced open his eyes. "This is Julia."

I watched his confusion turn to wonder.

"Hello, Julia," he said. "You look very much like your mother."

"I know," she said and smiled gently down on her father.

CHAPTER
FORTY-SIX

THE PETITE WOMAN WITH THE COPPERY-COLORED HAIR lifted her arms, palms up, and turned her face to the sky. The blazing midsummer sun, filtering through the twisted branches of the live oak, dappled her white robe with shifting shadows.

"Amen," she murmured and opened her eyes. "Go with God."

Red's hand tightened around mine, and I nearly choked on the lump of tears in my throat. Beside me, I heard Lavinia sniffle. Out of the corner of my eye I saw her take the lace-edged handkerchief from the pocket of her soft lavender suit and dab at her eyes.

The silence, uninterrupted by even the lilt of birdsong, seemed to stretch away forever, rolling down the lush carpet of grass behind Presqu'isle and out across the placid water. It was as if the whole world held its breath.

Scotty's voice cracked a little. "Hey, Dad? Aren't you guys supposed to kiss now or something?"

My sister Julia laughed, a light ripple like sun dancing on water, and the spell was broken.

CHAPTER
FORTY-SEVEN

HE BEDSIDE CLOCK READ 3:17 WHEN I CAREFULLY
laid aside the sheet and swung my feet to the floor. Red mumbled something and rolled onto his side. I sat for a full minute until his breathing evened out.

I crouched beside the bed and groped beneath it for the clothes I'd stashed there early the morning before. I dressed quickly. Outside in the hallway I carried my old sneakers in one hand and felt along the wall with the other as I avoided the creaky boards on the staircase.

From the closet underneath the steps I pulled out the Judge's old hunting coat and slipped it on. In the formal parlor, the scent of the wedding flowers lingered. I especially treasured the bouquet from the Eastman family. Thanks to her aunt Tessa, Kimmie had been in remission for nearly four months. The death of Deshawn Mitchell was under investigation, but so far as I knew, no decision had been made about whether or not Joline would be brought to trial.

At least for now, the circle of life went on.

I retrieved the box from its place of honor on the mantel and tiptoed through the kitchen out onto the back verandah.

The moon had nearly set, but I stood a while, inhaling the smell of damp grass, my ears tuned to the endless sound of moving water that had formed the backdrop of my entire life at Presqu'isle. Somewhere, far off, a dog barked once, then fell silent. When my eyes had adjusted to the darkness, I took the steps slowly, feeling like a procession of one, and walked straight toward the short dock that jutted out into the Sound.

The paper had called for high tide at 2:33, and I could tell by the tops of the reeds poking out along the shoreline that the water had begun to ebb. I set the box on the weathered boards and shoved my hands into the pockets of the old canvas coat. I let my mind wander back over the months and years, the pain and joy, truths and lies, secrets and revelations. Surely more triumphs than failures.

No tears, I'd promised us both.

Some time later, I stooped and retrieved the box, its bronze finish cold in my hands in the pre-dawn chill. I removed the lid and held it out over the water. My voice carried out across the wide expanse:

O'er all the hilltops
Is quiet now,
In all the treetops
Hearest thou
Hardly a breath;
The birds are asleep in the trees:
Wait; soon like these,
Thou too shalt rest.

A wafting, offshore breeze ruffled the damp hair on the nape of my neck as I tilted the box and let its contents drift out onto the water.

"Johann von Goethe," I said and watched the invisible current carry its passenger toward the sea. " 'Wanderer's Nightsong.' Two points."

A solitary tear rolled down my cheek as I turned back toward the house.

I had kept all my promises to my father save one.